The Doomsday Bomb

Book Three
of the
The Zradian Chronicles

The Reluctant Hero
The Professor And His Son
The Doomsday Bomb

James Apps

Published in the United Kingdom
TAUP UK
Sheerness
Kent

Contents:

"They wanted me for a living god - dead or alive."

Glord - NMF Warrior.

Prologue

Varney Haggard, a little known pimply faced lad of less than twenty summers staggered from his bed at the unhealthy early hour of afternoon tea needing to take a leak. He used the toilet and went into the main room and listened to the household panicking about the latest from the war zone.

"The Moral Few are threatening to use a Doomsday Bomb on us!" yelled his father, "What sort of morality is that?"

Varney was not in the mood for arguing with his father; what he wanted was some sympathy from his friends and some relief from the almighty headache and hangover that needed the hair of the Lupe to cure, and that he would rather do with his drinking mates

The whole bloody war cheesed him off more than a full bladder and a hangover ever would. In fact the whole war was a total disaster as far as he was concerned and as soon as it was over the better. The war was boring. The food was rotten. His mates were always getting on the lists of the dead and to make things worse there was no TV worth watching and even the telephone didn't work properly.

The cheap booze that was sold in the shops gave him a rotten headache and that cheesed him off too. He slammed out of the house and walked down the street to the Zradcom phone box to call his mate. He reached the shabby booth that was devoid of glass in the windows, no door and a dish that looked as if all the birds in the neighbourhood had crapped on it. He lifted the receiver and tapped in the number.

"Hi Colly, how...."

The rest was lost to history.

In that moment Varney Haggard suddenly occupied the same space, or vice versa, as the Doomsday Bomb. In his mind he managed a short and surprised sentence that was carried away in the sound of the exploding planet.

"Nong's teeth! Wrong bloody telephone!"

And like the planet Zrad, his essence, the telephone booth and his planned conversation disappeared into a messy planetary conflagration.

It also cured his hangover.

The Doomsday Bomb

The citizens of the republic of Zradia stoically accepted that their harsh way of life was normal. Their President was a despot; the Polisocs were a pack of unthinking lunatics; the Dog Squads were a bunch of homicidal maniacs, and that trying to escape to the Wastelands was worth it if you survived. Many of them knew of the New Moral Few and that there was a Rebel Army that occasionally bombed Republican property, such as its army depots, the army itself and sometimes attacked its troops.

The average Pair knew the story of Glord the Glorious, the great partisan hero of ages past who formed the First Republic. The average citizen Pair had heard of the Children of Glord the Glorious, but knew little about the movement.

The modern Zradian, fed up with the oppressive regime, scared of the despotic president longed for something else to dream of. They thrilled at the tales of the Rebel Army, stories of the Women's Rebel Army and many of them were tempted to desert the towns and cities to join the rebels.

They heard of the organisation called the New Moral Few and wondered at its origin. And that wonder revealed the age old religion of Glord the Glorious and for many that was something they could follow without actually doing anything. The cult of the Children of Glord the Glorious sprung up and appealed to many downtrodden Pairs. The religion offered a spiritual refuge from the horrors of their existence. To show their devotions many groups of worshippers built small shrines to their ancestor and gathered to worship in lovingly erected temples.

Naturally the President didn't like it.

When the Polisocs found a shrine or small temple their retribution was swift and violent. Many innocent people died or ended their existence in the slave labour camps.

But however much the Polisocs tried to destroy the movement more and more Zradians began to follow Glord's teachings and like all oppressed movements it went underground.

One of the most devout Pairs, Nert and Tern, of the western section of Sector Blue, was renowned for his inspiring speeches. He was great loss to the movement when in one vicious sweep he and his followers were transported to a quarry to dig stone.

Although the ordinary Zradian can not be blamed for the state of their homeland that much of their planet was destroyed, many of them followed one despotic leader or another. It so happens that Zrad is the second home for the people who called themselves Zradians. It happened that the war which tore into the idyllic beauty of the planet of their origin and devastated its landscapes produced a group of idealistic dissidents who used the unfortunate invention of the Doomsday Bomb to try and end the fighting.

The Doomsday Bomb was discovered by accident. The Zradians were trying to subdue a particularly well advanced civilisation on a verdant planet in a nearby system and they were having trouble. They surrounded the planet with the latest heavy space borne computer controlled artillery, wafer bombs, space to surface missiles, lasers and plasma cannons and guided heat seeking missiles that could sniff a match strike in a trench from hundred kilometres above the target. The inhabitants protected their planet with an electronic shield that would let light from their sun in but immediately detect and destroy anything else. Now and then windows would open up to allow the inhabitants to attack the Zradian forces.

A weapons operator sitting at his station watching for a window to open up missed it and out of sheer frustration turned the power up high and sent a laser to the coordinates where the window briefly was. That too failed to make an impression on the shield and with a long string of oaths he threw his ballpoint pen at the screen, that being the only missile handy, and at the same time stuck his hand out to catch it when it bounced back off the screen.

Nothing. The pen disappeared.

"Shit," he said. "Where the Nong did that go?"

His jaw dropped when he saw the message on his screen. with a reflex action he froze the data and called for a print out. The type on the flimsy confirmed the message, and for a long time with the screen back into operation he sat thinking about it. He missed three more windows but did not care, his thoughts were on what had just happened.

"So, if I crank up the power and throw an object at the screen it hits the planet," he reasoned and picked up a paperweight, took careful aim and threw it at the screen.

It too disappeared.

"Right, and so what next?"

What he did was to scrabble around in a spare weapons store and with a prayer, turned up the screen to full power and wearing protective clothing, he threw a wafer bomb at the screen. The bomb disappeared, and with a shout of joy he read the strike count, and just to make sure he was right he threw another one, and when that disappeared he sat staring at the screen trying figure out the physics and failed. While he contemplated the implications of what he had discovered his supervisor entered the weapon station.

"You have recorded four strikes, how come?"

The operator showed the supervisor and explained what he had done. He was not surprised when the supervisor called for some technicians to investigate, who in turn called on the engineers. What surprised him was that when he attempted to tell others about his discovery the Military Police arrested him, threw him in a cold cell and eventually without a trial strangled him in the execution yard. When he demanded to know why they had decided to kill him he was told it was in the interests of military security.

"Bastards," he said, and although he did his best to stop his killers from putting the rope around his neck he died as all malefactors died, painfully and slowly gasping for breath and struggling as the oxygen was cut off from his lungs.

What he had discovered was a small magnetic field that if synchronised with the frequency of the weapons system created a neutral field of matter and anti-matter. The effect was to send any object to the target point. They had produced the ideal matrix for the long sought after matter transfer. As a result of their investigations they built a large screen, increased the power and tried it out with a small cluster of missiles. The initial success was short lived because the inhabitants of the target planet increased the power of the shield, gathered their forces under its cover, and suddenly launched an all out attack that drove the Zradians back to their home planet.

Angry and humiliated by their defeat, the Zradians set out to get revenge. Their efforts were concentrated on developing the new Matter Transfer technology. It happened when a bright young engineer invented a bomb that acted, once it was exploded, like a miniature black hole and took a planet with it before vanishing through its own event horizon. Nobody believed that the bomb would work so the young engineer begged to try it out on the planet that had so far resisted their attacks. He dropped the receiver/ locator onto the planet through the matter transfer port and then followed it up with the bomb. The planet, the electronic shield and half the Zradian fleet disappeared into a pinpoint of darkness that itself vanished.

The young engineer presented his findings to the Military tribunal and was surprised to discover that he too was on the end of the executioner's rope as a punishment for destroying Government property, vis-à-vis, one planet designated as a future colony.

Unfairly, so he thought, he was also charged with losing the ball point pen his predecessor had thrown at the screen.

The Doomsday Bomb enabled the Zradian Empire to use it as a threat to subdue whole civilisations to the Zradian way. The method was simple. Drop a receiver on the target planet, inform the inhabitants of the situation, including the mathematics that went with the Bomb along with a declaration that there was a receiver already on the planet, and rudely demand their surrender. Usually the target civilisation decided in favour of slavery.

But that was well in the past and any off-world Zradian Empire had long been consigned to the history books. In fact the Doomsday Bomb was only ever used once more and that was a disaster for the Zradians who had invented it.

The second Doomsday Bomb explosion happened by accident. It ended the war of the Five Factions on the original planet of Zrad. It was the work of the group that called themselves The Moral Few – a ginger group that had niggled at the Zradian problems for years and had gotten nowhere. They built a satellite station in orbit around the fourth planet in their system, Zrad was the third, and planned to blackmail the warring factions into behaving nicely to each other. On the day the receiver was activated and the Bomb placed in the correct orbit the leader of the Moral Few announced to each of the five fighting factions that they were prepared to destroy the planet if the fighting did not stop.

"Prove it," said each of the leaders in turn.

The leader of the Moral Few, a pedantic philosopher named Gorn Trasker, obliged.

The Five leaders reluctantly met but bickered and argued so much over who should answer the rebels that nothing happened. The Moral Few analysts waited in vain for a reply and came to the conclusion a stronger message was needed. It read.

"To the leaders of all fighting factions. War will cease forthwith. All weapons will be placed in designated dumps (See attached plan) and transported to satellite Agra One. The War Councils will meet in Sector Red and will agree to put in place the machinery for devolution of the hostilities. Failure to do so will result in detonation of the Doomsday Bomb. You have Two complete orbits from receipt of this message. Gorn Trasker – Leader of the Moral Few"

The answer came in the form of a concerted nuclear attack on the Moral Few's space station. The star station defences destroyed the missiles and Gorn Trasker grimly said: "I propose we carry out our threat after one more warning."

The committee agreed to talk about it.

Thus began the debate that ended with an electronic vote which rested on the chairman's casting vote. But what the committee had forgotten that the system was set up to return fire unless the committee voted to override the order.

Gorn Trasker, in an agony of indecision finally cast his vote.

But it was too late.

The defence system timed out and the over-ride portal was passed. The Doomsday Bomb was automatically set off. The members of the Moral Few watched the projection with mounting horror. They saw the lines converge; the numbers synchronise and the words 'Operation Complete' come up on the screen.

The committee watched in surprise when the screen displayed and image of a porcelain toilet bowl under which scrolled the last words of Varney Haggard. Such was their horror at what they had done the image of the toilet bowl was etched on their minds but what the young man was trying to say to his mate was lost.

Oops!

A second oops was uttered when a large lump of rock smacked into their Star Station and killed about half their number. More died in the attempt to seal the Star Station against the rock; some from accidents as they worked to drill bolt holes in the solid matter and some died when the seal failed and the space tight compartments closed them off before they could escape. From a personnel of some thirteen and a half thousand their numbers were reduced to fifteen hundred and seventy two.

It was those survivors who landed on the new planet with as much equipment as they could manage to carry in the landing pods. Wisely they had planned the move in the event of what Gorn Trasker described as 'a negative result' but it was a shipwrecked group who made planet fall and attempted to establish a colony.

At one point in their development it was obvious that their race was beginning to die out. The Lupies, the dog-like creatures they brought with them bred prolifically and so, when a genetic engineer suggested that if the DNA of the survivors could be spliced properly with genetic material from the surviving Lupies, the Zradians liked as pets, there was a chance of survival as a race. The result was disgusting but in subsequent generations and weeding out the worst aberrations the people survived and grew. They survived the first generation and thrived for the next.

As with all primitive first colonies the tales of the old ways became obscured by time, and in turn they became myths, and as the centuries passed they also became distorted. Naturally, as with all myths, there was an element of truth in the tale, and the most endearing part of the story of how the Doomsday Bomb was directed at a telephone booth became mixed up with the practice of young men, such as Varney Haggard and his friends, to use the toilet pans to get rid of the results of the previous night's drinking. And so the legend of the Great White Telephone was born and many's the time the tale was told and retold of how it destroyed their civilisation. How the story of Varney Haggard became part of the myth is a mystery. Some say it is evidence of God (Nong), and others say that the computer, feeling guilty for its cock-up created it to salve its conscience.

The myth was so strongly embedded in the Zradian psyche that it gave rise to a worship that involved a fairly accurate sculpture of a lavatory pan that looked almost like a telephone handset, and the noises of simulated vomiting. It was this religion that survived the colony's first period and was replaced by the worship of an all powerful God the Zradians called Nong and as they grew from childhood to adult completely ignored except for use as a mild expletive. The peculiar name of the supreme being was cobbled from the initials of a popular saying that was in fact lost during the transfer to the New Zrad. The full saying was: "In Nothing One is Nothing and that is Good" and the truncated saying was misinterpreted as the name of the Supreme being.

Very few Zradians actually believe in a Supreme Being.

It was not until after the disastrous War of the Four Colours and the dreadful effects of Nuclear fall out that the Zradians evolved into what they are today. The first mutants were destroyed, but when it became obvious that being born in pairs with two pupils, and minds that needed a passive or assertive half in a separate body, were to be the new normality, the Zradians accepted the change and developed their peculiar Twinship society.

Once established, the Pairs swept all others off the face of the planet, and during a time when Earth itself was barely beginning to create a crude history and start emerging from caves, the Zradians spawned their first peace-maker. His name was Glord and he was called the Glorious. His twin was killed in the last battle of the Great War of Freedom, yet he was able to rise above the loss and create the First Republic from the ruins of a vicious feudal system that had bled the Zradian people of all they possessed. It was also the re-emergence of the cult of the Great White Telephone which Glord himself tried to crush.

Glord ruled Zrad for over forty orbits and brought peace and prosperity to the people. Upon his death the squabbling began again and although another hero attempted, and for a while succeeded, to rule a Second Republic the centuries rolled by with constant warring. The present President was born of utter corruption and near destruction of Zrad. The war devastated almost nine tenths of Zrad and forced the survivors to drive the occupants of the northern reaches from the plains into the inhospitable western mountains. These people were persecuted until it was realised that their agricultural skills made them useful and at this time in the development of the republic were almost forgotten.

Unfortunately for Earth, which was by now well into its own Nuclear age, the Zradians needed some more living room and chose the Earth as their new home. It was into this maelstrom that Julian Renfrew and Angela Breen were dropped. Julian, forced to become a hostage in the President's Palace in spite of trying his best to stay out of any fighting whatsoever, is a hero to those who wish to join the Rebel forces. Angela is lost in the wilds of the South West of the Zradian living zone, and mostly this is her story and the story of The Children of Glord the Glorious, a smelly fanatical sect, who have revived the doctrine of The Great White Telephone.

The peace Glord brought to his people was not the peace of rational thought but the peace of might. He unified the four sectors by force of arms and kept the peace in the same manner. He was not a cruel Half Pair but if he made a law he enforced it. Under his rule Zradia prospered, its people were well fed and there was no great wars devastating the land. Glord built many cities and gave the planet its first tourist industry creating resorts in areas that were beautiful and healthy where citizens could disport themselves without fear of being bombed out of existence, raped by marauding troops, were seldom robbed by bandits and hardly ever pillaged. The peace lasted well beyond Glord's reign and Zradians became used to being polite to each other. Apart from some more or less local wars Zradia settled down to enjoy its First Republic.

As predictable as bad weather on the first day of the annual holiday the rot set in as each successive leader became more despotic and the public service grew ever more bureaucratic and increasingly more cruel. Inevitably the rotten regime was overthrown. The wars for domination lasted for centuries of four hundreds until the second republic was formed.

Before that could happen there was the devastating second war of the Four Factions that left the Zradians with no place to live on their planet but the small northern sector. The people of the northern sector tried to remain neutral, but when the survivors of the war poured over the hills to escape the nuclear fall out from the last big thrust they too became belligerents. The invaders considered the Northerners a different race and practiced Genocide on them but fortunately failed to complete their pogrom leaving a persecuted nucleus to live in the West.

These western peoples became the despised but tolerated, some would say forgotten, land workers and peasants that the urban

Zradians relied on to grow their food, husband their beasts and generally do most of the work.

It was as a result of this invasion that the Second Republic was formed and successive Presidents became more harsh and despotic as the orbits passed. The current President is by far the worst. Apart from reviving the dread Polisocs, the Political and Social Police force, he introduced the Elite Stormtroopers, the devastating Dog Squad and public executions. These last were particularly nasty and were devised by one of the former President's Polisoc High Leader Pair as a social deterrent. The Dog Squads became the President's personal hit Pairs and the public executions his personal expression of ultimate power.

The method of execution was slow and nasty. The victim was chained naked by his or her neck to a stout post set in the cobbles of the city square. The executioner, masked and dressed to look like a black cat, assisted by two acolytes, donned a set of steel claws that were strapped to his hands and feet. At the President's signal the executioner would attack the victim with his clawed hands and feet the way a cat will play with a mouse. A skilled executioner could make the performance last for as many as three long periods until the victim finally bled to death or the President got bored and ordered a total disembowelment.

Unbeknown to him that was the fate the President had in mind for Julian, but first he had to bring the filthy scum who had nurtured his destructive skills to book. Unaware of his fate Julian lay in his cell whimpering and sobbing at every noise or footfall and thought only of how life was so unfair to him. Especially he directed his anger first at the President, then on his father and on Glorida for 'persuading' him to go with Arthur Renfrew and then on Angela, who he blamed for going off on her own and leaving him to the mercy of these, as he saw them, raving homicidal maniacs bent on killing him.

He was, as they say on Earth, not a happy bunny.

Angela's Children

On the day of the First City attack Angela was on the outer rim of the fight.

"Enemy sneaking up," she said and directed her troop to attack.

Her three wagons dived into the fray and soon they were swirling around attacking and counter attacking until at last the enemy were sorted. But even although the two other wagons had managed to break through to the main body her own wagon was isolated and she was now running from a force she couldn't fight.

There was no hope of joining up with the main force as the rest of the troop dashed off south. Her wagon was badly damaged but carried them eventually to a grinding halt some thirty kilometres from the site of the battle.

"We must get away from the wagon," she said and led the small group carefully north and west skirting the outskirts of First City and arriving in the early light at a point south but too far west. The small group of Pairs and Half Pairs included the driver Pair, four other complete Pairs and five Half Pairs. All were armed but she noticed the Half Pairs were showing the stress of loss.

"We find shelter and rest up for a while and eat some rations," she said, and after a little more walking they found the ruins of what looked like a temple. She chose a position with exits and a look out post, a pile of rocks stacked behind a wall, and organised the Pairs into a proper shift. She took the first watch and promised that she would take the last. She chose one of the Half Pairs as a companion and suggested the other Half Pairs do the same. She slept but woke looking and feeling as weary as the rest of the troop but with a few words of encouragement she led them on the next stage of the march.

Their tiredness let them down when, at the end of a weary and cautious march they ran smack into a patrol. Two Pairs fell wounded before her troop could even fire a gun and the Half Pairs panicked. The women tried their best to run but the enemy shot them down before they had gone more than a few metres. Angela and the remaining two Pairs took cover and shot back slowing the enemy advance but not stopping them. The small group were soon driven out of their cover and dodged fire from the enemy in an attempt to get away. The enemy group were far too large for a stand up fight and as they dropped behind yet another piece of cover the Pairs suggested they try and sneak away into the nearby forest.

"We will run out of capsules soon and then we will be killed," one Pair, the driver, said. "Every woman and Pair for themselves once we get in or shall we try and stick together?"

"Stick together if we can," said Angela. "We can give each other support."

The Driver Pair suggested that they choose a spot and go for it while the enemy were still looking for them. Angela led the way and with a rush they disappeared into the forest that seemed to spread well to the west and broadened out south. Angela knew that the forest was made up of mainly scrub and cacti, carnibushes and carnitrees but she did not worry too much. If they kept moving and found open spaces in which to rest then they stood a chance of getting through. Certainly the troopers would not want to follow them through the forest. They kept moving all day avoiding bushes that snapped at them as well as having to constantly cut tendrils that latched onto their limbs. It was a matter of using knives and keeping a look out for a clear space to stop. They found a bare rock outcrop that offered a respite and from its top Angela could see where bare hills slid like fingers into the trees and suggested that they head in their direction. Beyond the lower hills above the desert line the trees and bushes changed to what Angela termed as proper trees; the sort that didn't try to eat you.

"At least there will be sand and scrub and although we may meet up with some Carnibeasts at least we can stop," she said, and the others nodded their heads too weary to speak. She made them eat and drink and then with food inside their bellies they set off again. They reached the hills late that day and as it was getting dark they climbed to the top of a hillock and camped for the night. In the distance the fire Julian had set still burned and cast a dark pall of smoke over First City.

"Pairs, I think we should camp down and keep watch and decide what to do in the morning. Take heart girls at least we have escaped from the enemy," Angela said, and to encourage them she took the first watch and the last.

The morning dawned and for the first time since she had been on Zrad there was fine rain. It wasn't much but it dampened the grass and the scrub and as more fell so small plants began to appear in the barren soil around the rocks where they slept. She woke the others and they looked around with surprise and pleasure.

"See what the rain can do," said one Pair pointing to the plants.

Angela nodded and then took a longer more detailed look at the landscape. The whole plain was alive with diving, squawking birds and everywhere lizards ran hither and thither trying to escape the darting twin bills. Plants grew as she watched them and small fungi expanded to large ones. She had seen the rains of the seventh tenth when nobody could move anywhere without getting bogged down, and she was told about the rains on the Western Hills, and of course the rains in the south during the third tenth. In between times, except close to the sea, and to the south and northern poles there was very little rainfall. She had experienced light rain at times when the suns crossed, but that, she found out could happen at any odd time. Other than that fires could bring rain. It had something to do with forcing warm moist air into the stratosphere. She would have liked clouds. Still, the effect over First City was nice.

In the distance the circles of First City glowed with artificial light distorted by the misty rain and Angela was pleased to see the fires still burning. The Pairs stared at the city too and one pointed and excitedly called out to her.

"Angela, look! The city is burning! Julian's fire is much bigger now. We think that is why it is raining. You see, at this time of the orbit we never get rain unless there is a scrub fire. Julian's fire must be strong and I bet that the President is wetting his drunken pants and tearing out what hair he has left. What shall we do now?"

"I think we need to find some transport and get back to base," Angela said. "We should eat first and then go. Is there likely to be any vehicles in this area?"

The two Pairs scanned the surrounding hills and quietly conferred and the Driver Pair explained. "There may be some small townships on the other side of the hills. Whatever is there will have garrisons and vehicles. We can steal one perhaps."

They ate and drank sharing their rations and although the rain was still falling there was no place to replenish their water bottles. They found some cacti and filled up all their water cans and the Pairs said that some of the fungi were good to eat raw. They ate some before they set off and with the Driver Pair leading they trudged across the plain's undulating hills and by sunsset they were on the edge of a cluster of homes. In the failing light the Driver Pair pointed out a vehicle and said that was the one they wanted.

"It has power and is a Pongo truck so we will look like soldiers and it will have at least one weapon on board as well as capsules. We go now and get it before it gets dark?"

"Wait until after dark and I will lead you to it," said Angela and the two Pairs agreed.

They kept watch in turns until it was fully dark and Angela led them down the hill to the truck and while they sat in the shadows she carefully slipped across the road to look at it. Zradians never lock their vehicles having no need to because they were either military or controlled by the administration. All public transport and freight transport was controlled by computer and mostly ran on strip roads at incredible speeds. Military vehicles were designed to be instantly activated. All parked vehicles were supposed to be guarded and laagered up and secured by locking out the computer system. But, like all security systems there is always a way to circumvent them. The on the ball Rebel soldiers carried a code breaker with them and, as D.G often said, 'there's always a way to break a code' and although he had no show of breaking anything other than somebody else's bones, he was right. Angela slipped back across the road and spoke to the Driver Pair.

"Can you break the code?"

"If you give me enough time. My twin and I are game."

The small group followed Angela to the truck and the two Pairs climbed on board. The Driver Pair started working on the code breaker and the other Pair passed some capsules to Angela who slipped them onto her belt and changed the one in her gun. She stood by the rear of the truck keeping guard trying to keep calm as the Pairs worked on the vehicle. She didn't have to wait long for with a little squeal of triumph the Driver Pair fired up the wagon and she jumped aboard.

"Southward ho!" the Pairs cried and as the wagon moved off soldiers rushed out of a nearby building and fired at them. Angela fired back and the shooting stopped. She gave them a burst of fire at long range and with its lights on the wagon raced southward.

Angela could never remember quite what happened to upset the vehicle but it was early in the morning sometime before the twin suns were rising. The light was bright enough to see where they were going without lights and the birds were already squawking when suddenly there was a grinding crash, and if Angela had not been alert she was sure she would have been killed. She heard the Driver pair scream and the other Pair gasp as the truck toppled to the left and then started to tumble. Angela clutched the seat belts and hung on as the truck crashed from side to side and came to a crunching stop that stunned her into unconsciousness.

Dimly, to the sound of screaming Carnibirds Angela woke, shook her head and raised her body from the seat. She unclipped the belts and staggered out of the vehicle. The soldier Pair were dead and outside where the Driver Pair had tumbled from the stricken vehicle there was a mass of Carnibirds and as she emerged from the truck they flew off complaining. Both Pairs were dead and so with sadness she found their tags and gathered them up into her top pouch pocket. The rain had stopped and there was a mist rising from the warming soil that made the carnage look eerie. It seemed, from the marks on the rocks on the track behind them the vehicle had slewed off the way and smashed into some jagged rocks. Possibly, she thought, the Driver Pair had lost concentration or maybe had dozed off, however the vehicle was wrecked and so with resignation she gathered what rations she could find, added more capsules to her store and slung another gun across her shoulder and started to walk south. She walked all that day stopping only for a natural break and some food putting as much distance between herself and the crash as possible. Late in the evening she saw a ruined building, and approaching it carefully she hid in some bushes to watch. There was no activity but to make sure she threw some rocks. Nothing happened and with some relief she walked into the clearing and before entering circled the building. It was a temple or a shrine of some sort and she searched her memory for the information but could not place it. She found a sheltered room inside and with vegetation gathered from outside she made a bed and settled down to sleep.

It was still dark when she woke to the sound of a stumbled footstep and with one smooth movement she had one of the guns in her hands ready to fire. The soft footsteps were almost too soft to hear and if it were not for the slight clink of stones and metal she would not know that somebody was creeping into the building. She controlled her breathing to feign sleep and waited in the gloom determined that whatever happened next more of them would die before they caught her. She slipped the safety button off as the faint footfalls hesitated at the door. She sat for a long time waiting in the dark and as she waited she became aware that the suns were rising and soon the room would be flooded with dawn light. And as she thought about daylight and the intruder figures suddenly appeared at the door.

She raised her weapon and aimed at the gap.

Angela eased the gun to ready and waited for the Pair to move closer. She slowly moved her legs and her bottom so that she could immediately deal with any attack and was glad that she had left her sword belt on when she lay down to sleep. The men moved forward and she became aware of two things. One that the light was beginning to brighten and the other was the smell. The light told her it was getting near morning and that was normal, but the smell? Either her nose was working again or something smelled so bad that even her damaged olfactory senses could detect it.

The two men leapt forward and Angela dived sideways. She fired a stream of plasma at the wall above them and shifted to the door trapping them inside the ruined room. She took a quick glance over her shoulder and saw four more men waiting outside looking anxious.

"Drop your weapons or die," she said, and shot another stream of plasma and shifted position. The two men dropped their weapons and cowered against the wall. "Get up and walk in front of me."

The men stood up slowly and clutching each other in terror walked across the room and unsteadily walked through the doorway. Angela followed with the gun pointing at them and when they reached the main doorway she ordered them to halt.

"Tell your friends that I will kill you if anybody so much as raises an eyebrow. Tell them to drop their weapons and move away from the building and stand against the wall. Do it!"

One of the two ordered the others to do as she had said and she shooed them over to the pathetic group that huddled nervously against the low perimeter wall. She kept the weapon trained on them and as the light from the twin suns bathed them in early morning warmth she saw a scruffy group of Half Pairs huddling nervously against the low perimeter wall. What was more they were dirty beyond belief and the stench of unwashed bodies and something more sinister than that was almost enough to make her complain.

"All right, who speaks for you?"

"I do Great Warrior," said one of the men who had attempted to attack her. "I am Nert."

"Nert the Nervous," she said and added. "I suppose your twin was named Tern?"

"Yes, yes he was, we are all Half Pairs here."

"Lost are you?" she said, and looked at the motley crew drawing nearer intimidating them a little and wanting to stop them getting brave and attacking her.

"No, we are not lost. This is our territory. Our sector if you please, we conquered it," said Nert showing a little confidence.

"You conquered it, what with?"

"Our army, the Children of Glord the Glorious," Nert said with a little pride. "We are few yet but our numbers are growing every twentieth. We have arms and determination and we have the right of history on our side. Together we will fight the President and his despotic regime."

Fortunately Angela was sensitive enough to realise that laughing out loud at their pretentious ambitions was likely to upset them, so instead she smiled warmly.

"Then my smelly compatriots we are on the same side. I too wish to see the fall of the President and his cohorts," she said, and grinned broadly. "Can we be friends?"

"You wish to join our army?" said Nert.

"No," said Angela, "I wish to command it."

For a while the small group of Half Pairs conferred quietly glancing at her at intervals and back again within the group looking alternatively worried and almost, sadly, enthusiastic. Angela waited for them to finish, enjoying the dawn chorus and the world as it woke up. Eventually Nert asked her what she would do as commander and she smiled, and asked him if there was any chance of breakfast.

Surprisingly within a short time there was a cooking fire and food and with a firm apology for her absence Angela found a place to complete her morning ablutions and fetched her pack and her spare gun from her sleeping place. She strolled into the camp and took a proffered seat, a block of wood, and sat down waiting for food. The meal was not good but it was edible and as they ate she explained what she would do. The first thing she demanded was that they find a place to wash. She told them that she would help them recruit more people, steal weapons and organise the army.

"I will help you build a strong army but first you will have to tell me what The Children of Glord the Glorious stand for."

While she ate the rest of her food and took draughts of water mixed with cactus juice Nert explained.

"We will bring the spirit of our glorious ancestor back to Zrad and rouse the people against the despot. We will worship the Great White Telephone as did our ancestors in the distant past and bring peace to the people. It is this peace and equality of all within the spirit of Glord that we believe in and will bring to the people."

"Whether they want it or not?" said Angela.

"They will welcome the truth," said Nert.

"And I can help you with the practical side of all this," she said, and thought, I wish you were Christians, instead we would have a fanatical if somewhat small army to fight against Satan and his hordes. In the meantime this scruffy mob will have to do. At least she had company and separated from the women's rebel army she had a force to continue the fight. Her ideas differed from theirs, she thought, inasmuch they wanted a religious and political revival to bring down the despotic President, she wanted a social upheaval to change the inequality in Zradian society that placed women as second to men. Oh yes, there will be some changes, and if she had anything to do with it they will be big ones that will shock these men out of their complacent ways. See if I don't.

"Firstly after we have eaten you will wash and then we will plan what to do next. Each one of you will command a cohort and each cohort will consist of one hundred Pairs or mixture of Half Pairs and Pairs and for each person there will be a portion of rations and weapons as we need them. Take me to meet your soldiers," she said grandly taking command from the beginning as befits a great leader.

Nert stood with his head bowed a little and twiddled his toes in the dust looking sheepish and spoke so quietly she almost missed what he said.

"This is the army?"

"All of us," Nert said and grinned broadly. "We have only just begun."

Angela stood with her legs apart and her arms folded across her chest with her weapons hanging over her back and looked from one pathetic but eager face to the other and shrugged her shoulders.

"Oh well, I suppose we have to start somewhere," she said, and sighed. "Come on then, washing and then we will get something sorted."

Angela found a place for them to wash and when that chore was over she marched her cohort leaders off to find their soldiers. She was a good organiser, and at the first township the party came upon she found the Leader Pair and set up a meeting. There were no Polisocs or regular soldiers in the township and when she asked why she was told that nobody bothered with the lower classes in sector Blue. The ignominy of their plight did not seem to occur to them, but when Nert spoke at the meeting and explained what he and his group were trying to do they seemed to understand.

"You people, my people, have been ignored, used as cheap workers, enslaved at times, given the worst of the benefits of Zradian technology and treated like second class citizens. In place of this my friends and I offer our services to you to lead you to a new freedom. The freedom to do as you want with your lives; the freedom to worship as we once did freely and openly. We have with us a great warrior – a woman who comes from a different place – who has become a trusted warrior within the Zradian Rebel army. To her we have pledged our special support; we have agreed to follow her where she leads, and she has agreed to help us spread the word and raise an army to defend our freedoms. An army to lead us out of bondage, out of poverty and to take what is rightfully ours," said Nert, and stood down from the platform looking apologetic.

Angela spoke next telling the people what she intended to do if they decided to join with the Children Of Glord The Glorious.

"I will form an army made up of the free citizens of Sector Blue, and of those who wish to join us and become Children," she said. "I will teach you how to fight against the President's soldiers, and show you how to defeat them. I will help your women and men to become equal and free citizens of the New Zradia. Your children will grow up in a world that does not terrify them or teach them that war is the only way of living. I promise to guide you and lead you until you are ready to take control for yourselves. This I have spoken."

She gazed steadily across the room and saw women pairs looking at her with admiration. She realised that to them she must seem like a figure from the past, a heroic warrior, and understood that what she had taken for granted with the Women's Rebel Army was alien to the women here.

"And remember, pairs," she said, "I come from the Women's Rebel Army, and I am here because I was cut off from them in a great battle in First City. It is an act of God, or fortune, that I came here and met up with Nert. I am a woman, and as a woman I am also a warrior. In my own land I was a person who cared for others; a woman who wants children of her own, to care for and raise a family; to love somebody who also loves me – and for that I am willing to fight and wage war if I am called upon to do so. Do you call on me to wage war?"

There was a huge cheer from the pairs and, she noted, happy and excited cheering from the women.

In the morning the Leader Pair sent messengers out to other townships in the area, and as if by magic produced a collection of weapons both ancient and modern. The Leader Pair offered the weapons to the newly formed army and suggested that they stay for at least seven turns before moving on.

"Why so long?"

"We can gather the Leaders of the other townships together in this sector of the sector and plan a march from here to speak to more Pairs," said the Leader Pair.

"In that case I want sentries posted and a watch kept for the enemy. I want defences placed around the highest point in the township, and it will be from there we will meet the delegates. I will need the Half Pairs I came with as helpers and together with your help we will speak to all the volunteers. I will need to know what they can do, if they have any weapons, do they know of any and have they had experience in the armed forces, savvy?" Angela said and smiled to reassure them.

The Leader Pair were extremely helpful and supplied her with all she asked for. She was given an apartment block with four escape routes, an irregular force of militia armed with a motley collection of weapons and a string of clerks ready to interview prospective volunteers. She was worried about the Leader Pair's enthusiasm and the sudden influx of untutored and unarmed Pairs, but as the days went by she changed her mind. On day three several delegations of Leader Pairs from many of the townships arrived and they too waxed enthusiastic for the formation of a people's army. Angela learned of a valley in the low hills where the army could train and from where they could begin to march and when she asked for details she was pleasantly surprised when one Pair produced a map and pledged to supply produce and other foodstuffs. Most of the Leader Pairs promised weapons and Pairs, and those that could only promise supplies and some Pairs she thanked them and let them go back to their townships to organise what they could. She marked the townships on the map and promised that she would visit them on her journey to the valley. The remaining Leader Pairs she asked to stay for a further day and explained how she wanted the cohorts drawn up.

"The original group will at first be in charge of the cohorts in groups of ten. Each group of ten cohorts will be called Tens, and each group of ten Tens will be known as Hundreds. The officers in charge will be known as Hundred Leaders, Ten Leaders and Cohort Leaders. Each group of Ten Hundreds will be commanded by a General Leader, and each General Leader will have a section in charge of Spiritual matters who will work alongside the military leaders. Their task will be to teach the volunteers the doctrine of The Children of Glord the Glorious and to take care of the spiritual welfare of the troops and the camp followers and helpers," she said, and turned toward Nert. "The Half Pair Nert and his followers will form that core once they have chosen the Pairs who will be the officers and helped to teach them in the way I have already explained."

Nert visibly swelled with pride and smiled gratefully at her and all eyes were upon him as he cleared his throat to reply.

"Pairs, Half Pairs and Angela, I am honoured to be chosen for my task and will serve the Children to the utmost of my humble ability," Nert said with so much sincerity that his words sounded like an absolute truth.

Angela glanced at him sideways and frowned a little recognising a disturbing fanaticism in his manner that she knew from the born again Christians she saw so often on the streets of London. She filed her reaction away for later determined to talk with him quietly when she had an opportunity. She liked the idea that the core group of worshippers were led by Nert and his Half Pairs but she didn't like the underlying tone of righteousness that Nert managed to convey in his simple acceptance. At least when a vote was taken everybody agreed that she should lead and organise the army and for the moment that was fine by her. Nevertheless she grasped the thought that she could be expendable after the victory and decided she should plan for that event.

On the eighth day the small army set off on foot with as much provender as they could carry, and a promise from each of the Leader Pairs to give them a welcome when they reached their respective townships.

At the end of the first day's march Angela ordered a regular camp to be set with pickets and a proper rostered guard. She organized camp cooks and made sure they understood the need to replenish water supplies and place their latrines in a safe place. She put latrine digging on a roster as well and although the first camp was a little chaotic at least they were willing to follow her orders. On the third day they reached the first township, and by this time they were reasonably well disciplined, and when they marched into the central square many Pairs and Half Pairs, both men and women, came to meet them and for the first time Angela saw children who stood with their parents looking on, some of them even cheering.

The rally that night was full and somebody had rigged a public address system for her and Nert to speak. Her speech was stirring enough, covering all the reasons for throwing down the President's regime and urging them to rise against the oppressors and take the land back for the people but Nert's inspired them. He spoke quietly and almost deferentially but, as she had learned during the journey, he was one of the displaced who were driven from the cities by the invaders. The invasion was several Presidents in the past but the insult was still fresh in their minds. All they needed was a reason to revive their flagging resistance and they would rise up to take back what was theirs. Nert told them in simple terms how they would become the army of The Children of Glord the Glorious and bring meaning into their lives.

Again Angela felt the chill of fanaticism and shivered.

The next morning the whole township, men, women, children and their animals declared that they would march with them. The citizens took two turns to gather their goods and load them onto wagons. Those with weapons declared themselves to be soldiers and those without took over the tasks of cooking, digging, gathering fuel and water. The men and women marched and the children and the old folks rode and so, as the dawn broke on the third turn the column started out.

So it went. At each township the whole population abandoned their homes and set off for the valley and by the time the guides and scouts led them down into it after a long and weary climb there was well over a hundred thousand Pairs and Half Pairs wending their way along the twisting track that led into the wide grasslands. In the centre, looking a little like a fairy story castle, was a fortress that Nert said was once the home of a High Leader Pair and their family who commanded the sector.

"What happened to them?"

"The Polisocs took them away and tortured them to death," said Nert, and looked wistfully at the tall building. "My grandpair escaped from them."

"How did he escape?" Angela asked suspecting a heroic tale.

"They were in the toilet at the time and hid in the tank. Not even Polisocs are willing to look in a cesspit," said Nert.

"Ooh yuk," said Angela.

When the great column reached the building Angela claimed it for her headquarters, and with the aid of many willing workers she had it cleaned out and repaired well enough to live in. She gathered the officers together in one large room and explained her training regime. She was surprised and pleased when the whole mob cheered her and went out enthusiastically to organise their troops. In fact when she looked out over the valley she was pleased to see the camp set out as she wanted it and the pockets of guards and outposts that she had ordered set up to control who came into and who left the valley.

"I think we got ourselves a nice little revolution here," she said quietly realising she had spoken to herself and liking the solitude.

And as darkness fell she was impressed by the number of fires that burned in the camp, and smelled the cooking. She was glad when a voice called out to her to come for a meal and with a sigh of contentment she walked down the stairs from the roof to the dining room. Tonight she would eat in comfort with her officers. Tomorrow she had to supervise the training regime and take inventory of the weapons. She also had to make provision for a place of worship, and for that she needed to consult with Nert. One of the questions she needed to answer was how she stood with their religion. As a good Christian she was unwilling to embrace another religion even if by doing so she would free these people from the yoke of tyranny. Not even, she realised for the sake of the women on this dangerous planet. Late that night as she lay on the camp bed they had found for her she tried to give her problem to her God, and although she tried to pray nothing came.

"Oh to Hell with it," she muttered, and turned over on her side to sleep.

The Storm Gathers

Tzu contemplated the toilet in his back yard with some trepidation. He had sat for a long time in his room thinking about the problem and during that time he had reached several conclusions. To help sort out his thoughts he had telephoned the University to ask about Arthur but nobody knew anything. He took a punt and called Julia.

"Whadafuck ya want?" she said at high volume.

"Ah, Julia, it is Tzu Wu, have you heard anything about Arthur?" he said, and waited for her to reply. She seemed to be taking her time answering and Tzu suspected she was drunk.

"He's gone off with that fucking slut from his stinking bloody varsity. Fuck him. Who the fuck are you?"

"I am the Chinese gentleman from the emporium, Arthur's friend, you remember the fireworks party? We met there once; Mrs Renfrew. Are you all right?" he said, and discovered he really did feel concerned.

"Go ask that fucking black haired tart he's shagging if I'm all right you dozy gook. He tole me he was going to shack up with her. At least he's not dipping his wick in me any more the rotten, stinking, four-eyed, shit faced arsehole. Bastard!" she said with a sound like a rasping saw.

"Julia, have you been drinking?"

"Of course I've been fucking drinking you slant eyed old git. What else is there to do? I got no Julian, me fucking husband's fucked off and there's bills to pay!" she said, and Tzu could hear the desperation in her voice. "It isn't fair!"

Tzu listened to Julia wailing for a few moments and then firmly but with gentleness in his tone he quieted her, and when he spoke it was with patience and he chose his words carefully.

"Julia listen to me," he said once he had her attention, "I need to know if you have seen Arthur or heard anything about him. I will send somebody to help you, all you have to do is tell me."

Through her sobs Julia explained that she thought Arthur and Julian were lost or dead and that if Sue, as she called him, read the papers then she would know what was going on. Tzu didn't correct her but listened and let her ramble on until she was exhausted and cried again.

"I will send somebody to be with you soon, today," he said, and wished her a soft goodbye. The next telephone call he made was to Byrde's number and waited as the connection clicked over to Emily's number. He asked for her and recognised the Ferret's Younger Brother and approved.

"Emily, have you heard anything of Arthur or Richard?"

"No Venerable Father I have not. I did not think that you would be able to telephone us what with the invaders cutting the West Country off from London."

"I have my own satellite communications system. I am worried that there was something I missed. Did Richard say anything about going away? Did he ever find Sherman Holmes?" Tzu said.

"No to both but he was worried about personal attacks. Tzu, I am worried myself as you can imagine," she said, and Tzu detected the break in her voice as she tried to remain calm.

"I am doing my best to find them both. Do you know Julia Renfrew's favourite drink?

"It is gin and she can shove a lot of it down her throat I am afraid," Emily said, "Why do you ask?"

"I think we need to help her, so, if you hear some strange things regarding Julia please do not worry. Not only that but will you pass on a message to Richard if you do see him that I and some of my people are about to exit through a toilet cubicle,"

Emily gasped, giggled and then asked why.

"As I said to my people, it is a matter of convenience," he replied, and laughed when Emily groaned. Tzu explained as briefly as he could and at the end of the explanation, although Emily was still reasonably mystified, she at least proffered to pass the message on in case Richard should turn up. When Tzu rang off he was sure that she sounded happier and feeling a little easier he made some more telephone calls. His houses, a row of them, were in a street just around the corner from one of the roughest streets in the area. Tzu had discovered the place during the first years of the new century and bought a house there because it was cheap. Abandoned by the developers the area was scruffy then, but today it was a little untidy and next to it was a dingy street where the parking spaces were filled with abandoned cars, and the cats fought with the dogs for the contents of the garbage cans. Tzu liked that recognising that the street itself was a buffer between his operations and that part of the region the police considered normal.

Two days after his party in the late afternoon he unlocked the door of the new toilet and was surprised to see a package laying on the seat and with careful consideration for the glowing LED that signalled the port was active he lifted it out and closed the door. Locking the toilet behind him he took the package into the house choosing a quiet room and examined the bindings. It was a simple plastic box that unlatched at one edge and so with a shrug he opened it. Inside was a DVD and a video cassette. Both were marked with similar symbols that resembled Chinese and although he could not read the language it was obvious that he was intended to watch the contents, and so with a relaxed attitude as if the thing had not taken him by surprise he found a room with a screen and fitted the DVD into the slot. The machine operated immediately and Tzu sat down on a chair to watch.

At first he could barely understand what was happening but as the movie rolled on he began to pick out words and phrases and then with dawning comprehension the story came together. Part way through he saw Julian in action and realised what was happening. He saw the Rebel army and the Women's rebel army, with Angela Breen and Julian and realised that this was a compilation of events. In between the events throughout the story he was treated to a potted history of Zrad and shown a wonderful three dimensional plan of the Presidential palace and the place where Arthur Renfrew was kept, and beneath that the dungeon deep below where Julian was captive. Toward the end twin faces appeared and spoke of a plan to rescue Arthur and Julian but, as the Pair explained, they needed some outside help.

"Mister Tzu Wu, we wish you to use the loo to come through where we will help you to rescue your friend Arthur Renfrew, if it suits you."

The final piece of alliteration amused Tzu and he determined to let whoever was organising the push know he was keen to help. He thought that as a significant number there should be a Thousand fully armed Kung Fu artists. When his Centre leaders and chief instructors asked him why that number he replied that a thousand seemed a nice rounded number and would give everybody a chance to send a decent group without too much training. He told each centre to provide forty five people and choose a leader from each region and nominate a candidate for a group of eight leaders who would work with him and Arthur Renfrew once he was rescued. He left the choice up to the locals and gave them a date by which to arrive at his establishment in London.

At no time did he consider that his people would not want to follow him, and in that he was vindicated when after the Thousand were chosen his leaders told him he could have had another Thousand if he wanted.

"One Thousand is enough," he said.

"We haven't had anything from that ratbag Julian Renfrew have we?" asked Donald Best of his partner and heavy, Denny Block.

"Shall I go and git him for yer boss?" replied Denny rubbing a fist into his hand and grinning. "I'm getting' bored."

"I think we oughter visit our punter. We got a few calls to make first Denny before we can set out to find him. He's into us for over a thousand quid and if he don't pay up by next week it'll be another four 'undred on top of that. Wot wiv this war on and money getting a bit tight I'm getting a bit anxious." Donald Best said and picked up his order book. "We'll pick up the rent first Denny and then we'll call in a few instalments, okay?"

Denny brightened and clambered out of his chair and switched off the television. He looked wistfully at the screen but shrugged his shoulders and followed his boss out of the house. At least he could record his favourite cartoons on the video and usually whenever they went out he programmed the machine to copy the best ones.

They walked to the corner and although the street looked like a dingy street where the parking spaces were filled with abandoned cars and the cats fought with the dogs for the contents of the garbage cans he loved it. This was home.

Glorida's Plan

Glorida and Glorid walked along the main strip toward the Leader Pair's hut. They walked slowly, stopping now and then and clutching at each other. Glorid hugged her twin close at intervals and fussed with a handkerchief to dry the tears that filled Glorida's red rimmed eyes.

"They'll murder him," sobbed Glorida, "He's so vulnerable!"

"Cowardly, a back sliding no-good bum," said Glorid quietly. "He'd betray his own grandpair to save his skin. You had to force him to go."

"It's all my fault!" she wailed.

"No it isn't, the President is a Pig. Julian is just a scared ratbag who is more scared of the immediate threat, you with the knife, than he is of what will happen in the future. He thinks he will wriggle out of anything. So what do you want to do?"

"We have to save him," said Glorida, and looked at her twin pleadingly.

"I have to ask this Glorida, do you love him?"

"Yes, of course I do, I cannot live without him," she answered and sobbed deeply again.

Nong's teeth, thought Glorid, what a waste. She did not like Julian much knowing what he was like and having seen him often in the field running away, or trying to, but Glorida's eyes were closed to his faults. The only reason Julian was so good at his work was because he was frightened of having to go back to the same place twice. Julian always hid when the fighting started and many was the time when she or Glorida or one of the others had to drag him quivering with fear out of a funk hole. They also had to make sure the wagons were immobile or guarded to prevent him from stealing one and scarpering back to camp. She didn't like Julian but at the same time she wanted her twin to be happy, and she was aware that she was also jealous of Glorida's relationship with Julian and felt the pangs of loss. Deep inside her was the fear all Zradians felt, the loss of their twin. If this were an ordinary relationship she and Glorida would both be in love, or attracted to, a Pair, and they would both share the same strong feelings. With Glorida being so besotted with Julian she was finding it difficult to handle her own emotions and harder still not to let her anxiety show. Looking at Glorida sobbing her eyes out against her she realised that Glorida herself had no idea how her twin was feeling. That lack of empathy was hurting Glorid very much and she was torn between promising to help Glorida rescue Julian and persuading her twin to give him up.

"So we have to risk our lives to try and save the useless slob," said Glorid.

"He's not useless, he's my boyfriend!" wailed Glorida.

"So we have to go to First City, find out where he is and grab him. Then when we have done that we have to escape from the city and bring him back here so you can fornicate in your tent and take him out with us to blow up buildings?"

"Yes, yes, what's wrong with that?" Glorida said, and faced her twin. "You don't like him do you?"

"Not exactly don't like him. I think he's a rotten, low down no good, coward, a thief, a cheat, a liar and has the manners of a Polisoc Pig, but I wouldn't say I dislike him," said Glorid viciously.

Glorida bit her lip and with a sniff she cleared her nose and throat and looked long and hard at her twin. She shuffled her feet in the dust and dropped her eyes a little and then with a snort she lifted her head and spoke.

"Come on Twin, it's more than that isn't it? I know he's a ratbag and all those things you said but I can't help it, When he touches me I want to, I do melt, and when he looks at me with his peculiar eyes and gives me that twisted smile I want to flop over on my back and feel him on top of me. You're scared of us splitting up aren't you?"

"Yes I am and I hate the feeling. I feel as if I am dying by bits when you are with him. Where's mine? Where's my Half Pair?" said Glorid, and gripped her twin's hands tightly. "Tell me?"

Glorida hung her head and for many short periods they stood thus each in her thoughts and each wanting the other to begin the empathy wave. It was Glorid who began, admitting deep inside that she was the passive twin, and when it swept over them as they responded to one another's compassion Glorid knew that she would do as her twin asked of her.

"I have a plan," said Glorida. "I think we can convince our Leader Pair to give us the resources."

Glorid shook her head and as Glorida commenced walking she fell in step with her and together they walked to the hut, up the steps and into the inner room. The Leader Pair looked up from their work and glanced significantly at each other and placed the flimsies they were working on in a neat pile on their desk and suggested that Glorid and Glorida sit down.

"I take it," said Dorida, "you have a plan to rescue Julian?"

"Yes but how did you know?" said Glorida.

"It's written all over your emotions," said Dorid and giggled.

"So let us hear what you have to say," said Dorida.

Glorida took a deep breath and outlined her plan, adding details when the Leader Pair questioned her more closely. When she had finished, Dorid and Dorida sat silent for a while and doodled on spare flimsies and finally, after muttering closely together, Dorida turned to them with a grim look.

"It will work but we will have to arrange a back up. You can start as soon as you wish," Dorida said.

Glorida rushed across the room and hugged her.

"There is the problem of the Professor," said Dorid. "We will need to help him too."

"It is through him we can rescue Julian," said Glorid, "It is the contacts he made that we can talk to. They say they will come with him but we have to pretend to capture them."

"You will bring him out too?" said Dorida.

"Of course we will," said Glorida, biting her lip.

"Then we will back you all the way," said Dorida.

Glorida hugged her again and rushed out joyfully eager to get started. Glorid followed her casting a glance over her shoulder to the Leader Pair that told them how she felt. She noticed that all Dorida and Dorid did was smile and shrug their shoulders.

Under cover of darkness the wagons moved slowly and as quietly as they could with no lights guided only by the blue tell tales showing on the rear of the centre two wagons. They eased through the radials of sector yellow and cautiously worked their way to the centre of First City. Inside the lead wagon Glorida watched the screens and let the driver Pair do their job but acted as the spare eyes looking for the gate she wanted. The sector narrowed to a series of warehouses flanked by the blank faces of worker buildings that had no windows, and even if there were any no Pair dared look out in case there was something going on below them they might have to report. The workers knew that if you saw nothing it was safer. Glorida knew this and so she chose that part of sector yellow to approach the Palace. She knew also that gates in sector yellow were closed electronically and as long as you had a coder you could get in quite easily. Getting out again if you were caught was a little more difficult but then, she reasoned, the trick was not to get caught.

She was grimly aware of the burned and broken buildings on the way in that were the result of Julian's bombing and she felt desperate. The President would kill him for that alone.

She saw the gate ahead and spoke into the mike.

"Gate ahead one hundred and twenty metres. Slow and steady and wait for the signal," Glorida said, and watched for the expected contact ready with her fingers on the weapons buttons. The troops were ready for action and she had ordered the rear wagon to guard their rear. With ten fighting Pairs in each wagon not including the driver they had enough room for many more fighting Pairs and those Pongos who wanted to come with them were welcome. Figures appeared at the gate and one of the Pair flashed a signal on their coder. It matched with the code but even so Glorida quietly ordered the Pairs to remain on the alert. The driver Pair slid the wagon to the lone Pair waiting in the gloom and Glorida and Glorid alighted to speak with him.

"Take your wagons into the compound but leave one by the gate. My Pairs will lead you through and with yours will act as guards. Tens and Snet will show you where Julian is kept. You will need at least six Pairs. We will bring Professor Renfrew," the Pair said and grinned as the passive Half finished the sentence. "We are looking forward to some action. Our families are gone to the west."

"Oh, that is good, but how come?" asked Glorida.

But the Pair just smiled.

"We have some wagons of our own waiting for the escape," the Pair said and smiled again. "Just in case."

"Glorida smiled at him and nodded.

"Lead us to our target," she said.

With the wagons set in defence positions in the compound Glorida and Glorid and six Pairs followed Tens and Snet into the Palace. The corridors were dimly lit, and as they moved along them Glorida marked the way with a permanent marker and at every locked door she reset the code for her own coder. They passed deep under the Palace to the dungeons and when the corridors changed from a pleasant but dull décor to grim stone and metal grilles Tens and Snet signalled they should slow down.

"Guards around the next corner."

Glorida peeked and saw two guards at a gate and waved a Pair forward. The Pair crept past them and unslung a crude weapon from their backs, loaded it with a vicious narrow double blade, took aim and released the blades. The two guards fell clutching their throats and gurgling liquidly as their lungs filled with blood and every movement they made to try and ease their pain only drove the barbed blades deeper. Had they lived long enough to remove the blades so they would have cut their own heads off. Glorida's Pairs stepped over the bodies and with her coder she locked the gates wide open.

As they approached Julian's cell Tens and Snet said there was a squad of Polisoc guards on duty.

"Spread out behind Tens and Snet and when they give the signal move in," Glorida said.

The moment the signal came her Pairs swooped past Tens and Snet and fell on the Polisocs with their blades flashing. Instead of engaging Pair to Pair her troops were trained to attack separate Half Pairs, and as expected, this method took the Polisocs by surprise. The enemy were routed almost before they had time to react and the fight was short and sharp. They killed all of the Polisocs except one Half Pair who sat on his haunches against the chamber wall his face showing hatred and fear.

Glorida looked at him and raised her blade.

"No, don't kill him my twin, we will tie him and let him tell the President who has paid him a visit," said Glorid, and stayed her arm.

"Why is he yelling so much?" Glorida asked.

"That is not him yelling. That is your dearly beloved screaming in panic. Listen," said Glorid.

From the cell came a loud panicky voice that blubbered and begged for mercy that, as the battle noise subsided sounded quite plainly. "Don't kill me you fucking bastards! I'll do anything you ask, anything! Go away, please leave me alone, please, please don't hurt me, please! Please!"

The rest was lost to moaning and wailing as Julian cringed at the rear of the cell in the foetal position neither looking out nor actually looking completely away. She opened the door with the coder and crawled inside.

"Julian, it's me, Glorida!"

"Oh fuck, they've got you too!"

"No my love I've come to rescue you!"

Julian unrolled from his position, looked up wide eyed and grasped her hands urgently and levered himself past her and out into the chamber. He squealed when he saw Tens and Snet and backed away leaning against the wall in panic, his eyes flickering from side to side open mouthed at the carnage. "Well don't just stand there gawping you crazy bitches, get me out of here!" he said once he had found his voice.

Glorida took his hand and drew close to him and kissed his face and wrapped her arms around him and for a moment he was quiet, and in honeyed tones she spoke softly. "Be grateful my love. We have come to rescue you from the President and his nasty Polisocs and you, my love, are complaining. Please shut up or we will leave you here. Now keep with us and do as you are told, my love."

Julian stared at her wide eyed and frightened and watched as a Pair tied the lone survivor's hands together and then to his ankles with the leather thongs of a couple of the whips the Polisocs used to flog their prisoners with. Certain that the Half pair could do him no more harm Julian kicked him hard in the ribs and snarled.

"Let that learn you not to mess around with Julian Renfrew."

Glorida glowed with pride.

"That's my hero," she said, and led the way out of the chamber.

"And true to type," said Glorid sarcastically.

The journey from the dungeons was uneventful until they reached the corridors and there it was obvious that somebody had raised the alarm. As they approached the last two corridors to the entrance where it opened out into a wide storage area a group of Polisocs were fighting a strangely clad group of men and women with the support of a mixture of Pongos and women Pairs. Tens and Snet led them past the fight to the outside where there were more men and women and four wagons that were ready to move off.

"Get in the wagon," said Glorida, and opened the door for Julian. Julian needed no prompting and gratefully took a seat and sat down impatient to get going. Somebody gave him a weapon and some capsules and told him to get to one of the slots and get ready to fire.

"Don't shoot until you are told to."

He didn't want to shoot anyway having no desire to fight, only to run, and with much reluctance he stood by the slot and waited. He was confused by what he saw and as his nerves settled down a little he began to see how the battle was unfolding. His rescuers and the strangely clad fighters were falling back to the wagons and it was obvious that the enemy were losing. There was an explosion near the door as the last of the fighters retreated and ran toward the wagons.

He was fascinated by the way the newcomers and the soldiers with them moved in a coordinated fashion using only hand gestures and by leading people in lines and directing them to points in the yard.

Eight more wagons joined them driven and Paired by Pongos and into these the newcomers were led.

Quickly the Pongos organised the fighters into groups and as the wagons moved off slowly so four figures detached themselves from the main group and headed for his own wagon. He gasped when he recognised his father and saw that Tzu was with him.

"Bugger me! What on Zrad is he doing here?"

The Thousand

Three days after his telephone calls the first of the Kung Fu Thousand arrived and Tzu's household began the complex exercise of accommodating them. With the help of his numerous nieces, cousins and more distant relatives he fed and housed them. As they arrived he met each leader and give them a schedule and some instructions confirmed that each artist was a volunteer and that all who needed weapons had them. In blocks of ten he let them view the DVD and by the time he was ready to go everybody knew what they had to do.

It was a bright day when in neat rows that snaked around the back yard to the door of the toilet the Kung Fu artists waited in line to be shot into the unknown. Tzu stood by the open door and greeted every fighter with a smile and wished them 'hard work' as they stepped into the booth in groups of five. Each group went equipped and immediately ready to fight, but as Tzu had told them they must also be ready to move off as a troop. The transfer took most of the day and with a bow and a flourish to the women who were left behind to clean up after the guests Tzu pressed the button and waited ready to act as soon as he arrived. He had a sickening sense of being mildly out of control, and then, with an almost instant reaction he slipped to one side moving fast and fluidly to avoid something that threatened him.

There was a chuckle and one of his eight chosen, Silas, held his elbow loosely but strongly and spoke as Tzu glanced around the chamber.

"Steady Master, we are all here safely. The guides are waiting for you. It seems we have work to do,"

Tzu felt a little disorientated but soon recovered when Silas introduced him to a diffident Zradian Pair who spoke in halting English addressing him as Master.

"We am takings you when you need going be. Is all yours ready?"

"Please, we are ready," said Tzu in their language surprised at how easily he dropped into it. "I learned your speech from the DVD. I am Tzu, and so who are you?"

"I am Craz and this is my twin Zrac. Your warrior, Marion, explained to us your system. She has gone to find the Professor and his group. We will lead you."

"Craz and Zrac, I am honoured," Tzu said liking the idea of calling his people Warriors and, with Silas behind him, he followed the Pair through the gathered Warriors who were formed up into their tens and hundreds. Tzu was already impressed by the organisation when small groups of armed Zradian Pairs formed a vanguard to protect them as they marched through the seemingly endless corridors. At intervals there were more armed Zradians who grinned as they passed and Craz and Zrac explained that they were guards and would act as a rearguard once the Warriors were past. The levels rose steadily and they became aware of the sound of clashing blades and yells of agony mixed with the Chi shouts of his people. They turned a corner and there in the centre of a large mixed group of his Warriors and Zradians was his old friend Arthur looking frustrated as he dodged around trying to get into the fight. Tzu chuckled because he had given specific orders that Arthur was to be protected until after the escape. Craz barked an order and with a pad of soft shod feet his pairs rushed between the Warriors and the group of red and black clad guards and began to engage them Pair to Pair. Tzu immediately saw the problem. The Zradians were used to fighting like that, and with a quick word to Silas and Marion as she came to greet him he told them to attack Half Pairs instead.

"One on one but split their Pairs," he said.

Within a few minutes the red and blacks began to fall in confusion and panic and although Tzu had stressed that his people should kill the enemy he was sickened by the carnage. The Zradian Pairs showed no mercy and killed wounded and active alike. Leaving their dead behind, the Zradians led the thousand out of the building to a compound where four strange wagons stood. At the moment the group emerged from the doorway a fresh group of red and blacks descended on them and this time Arthur insisted on joining in. He had a knife but he did not use it preferring to use his Aikido to throw his attackers and let others finish them off. By the time the fight was over Arthur was carrying a number of knives and swords in their scabbards like bandoliers and he rattled with metal as they climbed into one of the wagons.

"Fucking arseholes," said a thin, frightened and astonished voice, "It's Tzu and me old man!"

"Ah, Julian, so good to see you my young friend," said Tzu, "I do hope you are keeping well."

Professor Renfrew snorted, was about to make a sarcastic remark but changed his mind and grinned at Julian.

"Son," he said, and didn't choke over the word, "I too am glad to see you. I believe we have Glorida and Glorid to thank for our rescue. I am proud of you my boy and if Tzu is your friend then I have misjudged you."

"Yeah, right so it's Daddy now is it," Julian said loading all the sarcasm he could manage into his voice and cringing when Tzu gave him a withering look.

"We have to get going," said Glorida cutting through the tension. "Julian you are on watch so stand by your post."

Julian turned immediately and moved to the side slot with his weapon at the ready. The wagons moved off slowly and formed protection for the marching Warriors and Pongos. Progress was slow and although Glorida was sure they would make it out of the city she was anxious that instead of driving out at speed they would have to march. It was not yet light but the alarm must have been raised and soon there would be Polisocs and Stormtroopers to deal with and that worried her. With her own troops and the Pongos she was sure she could cope, but with the Warriors in tow armed only with wooden weapons, captured blades and a few odd looking swords and cutting instruments that looked more like farming tools, she was bothered.

The two Pongo wagons were a great help but there was not enough room to carry all of Tzu's people as well.

The column reached the outer limits of circle three before they met any opposition and when the enemy hit, although she had expected the attack, when it came she had to think quickly. Glorid patched in the call system while she spat orders to her Leaders and within a few small periods the column was sheltering behind low buildings protected by the six wagons and the guns of the Pongos.

"Let them come in!" Glorida said and ordered the wagons to retreat while the Leaders pulled back the troops and the Warriors.

The enemy fell for the ruse and rushed in for the kill. The hand to hand fighting was vicious and although the warriors exacted a heavy toll they too lost men and women but out of the Thousand only five died. There were several wounded but none who needed more than standard dressings. Glorida was amazed at the Warrior's ability.

That they won the battle was almost a foregone conclusion and when the last enemy was stabbed to death or shot, Glorida ordered their own casualties collected and loaded onto one of the wagons. The column moved on through circle four to six without incident and then when they were in position to make contact with their back up, the enemy struck again. This time there was a small burned out fortress close by and with the wagons giving covering fire the column retreated to within its boundaries. Glorida was glad that she had ordered the Pongos and Warriors to collect guns and capsules from the dead and now everyone was armed with a gun and enough capsules for a lengthy battle. She put Craz and Zrac in charge of the Pongos, the Leader Pair having been wounded, and asked them to help coordinate the efforts of Tzu and his warriors.

"Make sure that you go for Half Pairs and not try and fight twin to twin," she said, "You saw how that worked last time."

Eagerly they trotted off and started to disperse the force around the shattered defences while Glorida with Julian reluctantly in tow set off to take command at one of the towers. The wagons acted as roving fire platforms and she left the control of them in the hands of the Leader Pair of wagon two, Salida and Salid. She led her foot soldiers into the tower prodding Julian ahead of her whenever he tried to dive into a side room.

"Cripes Glorida do you have to be so nasty?"

"No my love I enjoy watching you cringe."

They reached the top of the tower and took up positions with Julian next to Glorida, and with a look of glee Glorida ordered them to start shooting.

"Shoot the nasty Polliwogs my love," Glorida said to Julian and showed him her knife.

"All right, all right," said Julian. "What's got into you?"

"We set up a mission to rescue you and all you can do is complain. Why can't you show me you're glad or give me a kiss, a hug and a smile instead of whinging and moaning and trying to rush off to hide from the fighting? I know you are a coward and a backslider, a scumbag and a nasty piece of work but I happen to love you, you shitfaced Bulger's arsehole and don't you forget it! Now fight or so help me I will hand you over to the Polisocs and watch them kill you unless I slit your scrawny neck myself," Glorida said, and glared at him.

"Attagirl," said Glorid, and grinned broadly when Glorida glowered at her. "You're a real inspiration my twin."

Julian's face went deathly pale and he trembled but when Glorida told him to shoot at the enemy he did and perversely but understandably when his target fell dead on the ground he rejoiced.

"Got the bastard," he said and flinched when plasma hit the fortress wall close to his head. "Christ, the shitheads are shooting back!"

"Yes my love they do that. The trick is to shoot better than they do until they can no longer shoot at you. Do what I do and remember to go for Half Pairs, take time to aim and always be ready to move," Glorida said and smiled at him.

Julian smiled back and when she began shooting again he took his cue from her and as he worked he found a rhythm, and soon he was concentrating on the task instead of wishing he were somewhere else. He was almost disappointed when a column of battle wagons appeared bearing the Rebel Army logo. Glorida gave the order to keep up a covering fire and then when the wagons started to engage the enemy the troop moved from the tower down to join the rest of the forces. With a new capsule in his gun and a determination not to earn a slit throat Julian became part of the skirmishers and ducked from cover to cover firing at targets as they arose. As a result he was there with Glorida and Glorid to greet the Leader of the wagon column when it broke through and routed the enemy troops.

The Leader Pair climbed out of the lead wagon and strolled casually toward them. Julian raised his gun and pointed it at the figure on the left.

"Put the catch on and lower the weapon," Glorida said, and he felt the prick of twin blades against his neck. "Do it."

He did as he was told and the Pair ambled closer.

"Hi hero," said D.G, "Still with us then?"

"No thanks to you," said Julian relieved that Glorida put her knife back in its sheath as soon as he lowered his gun and made it safe.

"Maybe not but we all have our part to play hero and right now we have to take your people back with us. Is Angela with you?"

"Nah, she was lost way back after we bombed the city warehouses. Good riddance too," Julian said.

Julian didn't see the blow that knocked him backwards. He felt the effects afterwards when he recovered in Glorida's wagon. Nor did he see Glord grab D.G and stop him killing Julian with his bare hands. Nor did he see Glorida leap at D.G to be held back by her twin who quickly disarmed her. Both angry Half Pairs were kept separated while Julian was carried to the wagon and when they were calmer Glorid explained what had happened.

"I'm sorry," said D.G. "I like Angela and Julian's attitude annoyed me."

"But there was no need to try and kill him," said Glorida still dangerously angry.

D.G hung his head but as he looked at Glorida he realised that as much as she loved the no good, useless Julian for whatever reason he knew that he felt more than a liking for Angela. He felt Glord's hand on his shoulder and reached out with an empathy wave and was reassured.

Later with the Warriors loaded on their wagons and the extra Pongos settled into troops D.G sat next to his twin and thought about Angela. He determined to find her but for the while he would concentrate on the next phase and channel all his energies to getting their charges back safely to the Headquarters.

"Bulgers to it," he cried out, "I love the woman!"

The Children Gather

Angela climbed onto the rough platform and stood beside Nert who stepped back and smiled at her. She took the vacant place behind the double lectern and gazed down on the sea of faces caught in the artificial light of fires and the myriad flares that lit the rim of the small natural amphitheatre. Formed by the low hill on which the tower stood and the valley floor the hollow was sheltered from the night wind. Nert had told the waiting Pairs and Half Pairs about the structure of the religion and who would hold the posts of Guide. He had not liked the word priest that Angela suggested, and said that the title guide was a better one because it meant to lead and not preach. He apologised to her and explained that the early form of the religion was administered by men and that according to the myths it was men who would carry it on. She argued that women should be allowed to minister but when it came to the vote even the women voted in favour of male ministry. Standing facing the group of mostly males she was astonished that they had accepted her leadership, and when she asked Nert about it he said they had all heard about her from the rebels they met and second only to the Pair Glord and Drogl and one step above Julian the Bomber, she was a great hero. Besides, she was an Alien and likely to leave eventually.

"You are all here," she began, "to act as Leaders of the Army of the Children of Glord the Glorious. I divided you all into Cohorts, Tens and Hundreds and as you have seen I propose to make larger collections and these will be called Millens and Groups. A Millen will be one hundred Hundreds and a Group will consist of one hundred Millens. I expect you will divide your duties between Leader Pairs, Senior Leader Pairs and I expect you will add to that, Section Leaders and the usual divisions at the very top. I expect to have at least one representative of each Group close at all times and a chain of command that will give me instant access to you, and I expect scouts to be placed at my disposal. What I shall ask of you is that when I and my staff make a plan that it be carried out. At the same time I expect all Leaders at whatever level to be aware of their troops and to fight sensibly, I do not want any heroics or waste of life. You must learn to withdraw and learn when to attack. The training we will give you will hopefully do that, and as you train new people I expect you to train that feeling of safety into them. I want no stupid, pointless charges but I do want people to go in to the battle willingly. So, we fight for freedom, our land and for the glory of Glord the Glorious!"

The crowd cheered and Angela was amazed at the enthusiasm they showed her and gave the signal for the first Pairs to mount the platform to receive their tags. Nert had wanted an emblem for the arm for the Leaders to wear on the right lapel of their tunics. The main colour was white, and for each rank there was a different colour flash on the tag which Angela was both amused and embarrassed to see was in the shape of a porcelain lavatory bowl. The Group Leader Pairs had red flashes with the colour of their group below, the Millen Leaders had green and their colours, Hundreds with yellow and their colours and Tens with blue. The Cohort Leader's tags carried a colour on the top rim and a flash in their own colour on the bottom. Angela and Nert handed the tags to each Leader Pair and received their vow of allegiance. It was an exhausting process but when it was over she addressed them again.

"Thank you all for your patience. I am proud of you and know that when we are ready you will be willing to give your all for the cause, to beat the President and to bring the love of Glord the Glorious to the Republic!" she said, and paused to smile at them. "Now, let us go and enjoy the good food and ale the Pairs have prepared for us."

She let them cheer for a while and then she and Nert led them along the pathway to the camp site where there were spit roasted beasts garnished with herbs and vegetables ready to eat and large plastic barrels of ale were set up behind benches of salted treats and sweet syrup baked foods. For the first time since she had arrived on Zrad she saw musical instruments and groups of musicians. The songs they sang were haunting and very emotional but also they enjoyed playing music for dancing and already there were men and women dancing to the more lively tunes. And even in the camp there were children which made her feel as if things were normal. Nert explained that during the past in the old Northern Sector there used to be music."

"We wanted to revive the old ways but the President crushed us. The people hid the musical instruments and the music all those four hundreds ago and now because you have come we can bring them out again. Angela, when do we go to war?"

"When the many have been trained in weapons and the way of stealing them, when many know how to fight hand to hand and when we have reached the right moment. We will know the time and then we will strike," Angela said, and took a dish of meat offered to her by a happy Half Pair. "Let us for now enjoy the party."

The time came when, after a Twentieth of hard work, Angela decided that one army group was ready. She led them out of the valley leaving behind the second army group still training; she was not aware that Tzu was about to become involved with Julian's rescue, or that things were moving on in such a momentous way. She marched over the top of the valley ridge and felt a warm feeling of pride that was tinged by the apprehension of going into the unknown, although she knew that whatever they did now she could control.

Their first target was a small city in the lower end of Sector Yellow; Fourteen City Yellow Three Sector Blue. The city was not far from the valley by vehicle but on foot it would be a journey of at least seven complete turns. Logistically the chances of making a raid and getting back to the valley were low and so Angela outlined a plan that would take them to the city and stay there with the land in between declared as captured territory.

"The valley will be our headquarters. There should be enough people there to defend it, and it will be there we will store our supplies and organise the routes. As we conquer new lands we will create connecting depots in the cities we occupy. We will leave strong townships garrisoned by our Pairs and spread out from them until we have captured the area up to the northern Sector Yellow ridge, the one you call hill range four yellow," she said, and gave out orders to each of the Group Leaders and made sure that they were assigned their share of wagons and weapons. It was a motley crew that set out but she knew that with the best will in the world nothing could be perfect and, like the Children, she believed in what she was doing, believed in the Pairs themselves and believed that if you are going to fight a religious war you may as well lead from the front.

As they marched down the slopes from the valley watched by the warriors above Angela hummed the tune Onward Christian Soldiers and was pleased when Nert took up the tune.

"Sing some words please my Leader," he said, and looked at her wistfully, "we need a song to inspire us."

Angela sang *"Onward Christian soldiers, marching as to war, with the Cross of Jesus going on before! Christ the royal master leads against the foe; Forward into battle see His banner go!"* and was not surprised when Nert shook his head and denied they were the words he wanted.

"We can use the tune but we will write words more suited to our needs," Nert said, "I will ask an Acolyte to find some new lyrics."

Angela smiled and strode out feeling comfortable with her pack and her weapons which she had insisted on carrying. Nert and the Group Leaders had said that they wanted her to be protected at all times but she insisted on Leadership from the front and allowed them to have a phalanx of warriors going before, and a number of scout units reporting back regularly. The scout units came back within the first half turn reporting that the township ahead was willing to give itself up to them. Angela made a point of meeting the Leader Pair and thanking them and explained that she would leave a small garrison with them and that they should be prepared to send Pairs back to the valley for training.

"If you have workable weapons and blade weapons then send them too. Even if there are Pairs here who were soldiers send them to the valley for training and indoctrination and feel free to let others know of us. We have come to set you free," she said, and at Nert's suggestion gave them an honorary award. The Pair became the first Township Support Pair in the campaign.

The Group camped overnight and during their stopover Nert and his people wrote words for the song. Angela suggested that every scout unit carry Acolytes to speak with Leader Pairs at each township they approached. Nert agreed, and suggested that the Acolytes and Guides be given plain symbols as their only marks. Angela was a little disturbed by this but agreed anyway knowing that the Guides and Acolytes were their best weapon they had after a well trained army. The people must have a reason to fight but also they must have an ideology to cling to and justify indoctrination. Power may come from the mouth of a gun, she thought and blushed remembering where that statement came from, but there is nothing more important than giving a direction to that power. It was as she sat thinking of the consequences of her actions that she realised how far she had come from picking up drunks and down and outs on the Embankment. She was even more reminded how alien this land was when she gazed across the camp and saw the Children at worship.

Nert stood before a white toilet bowl that rested on a raised dais so that all could see it. He raised his hands high toward the night sky and called out the mantra which was echoed by all more or less in unison.

Hail Glord the Glorious! We, your Children salute you!

The entire camp apart from her knelt on the ground facing the toilet bowl with their hands held together as if in prayer. And with a reverence she had only seen in priests, Nert knelt on the cushion placed beside the bowl and grasped the porcelain edge with both hands. He leaned over the bowl, groaned and then with his chest heaving he threw up.

The crowd did the same and with a feeling of unease Angela turned away and tried to ignore the cries of agony of those who could not manage the action. She was reminded of Julian after his parties and how she had often to clean up after him at the flat. She would have to speak with Nert about the practice or her soldiers were going to starve.

She had her chance when Nert returned from the worship and sat with her watching the Pairs cleaning up their vomit with small spades and scrapers. The oddness of it amused her, and with much constraint she suggested that the practice was likely to wear down the troops and would it not be better to make a token sound.

"Oh no, we have to do it right," said Nert.

"But not every night surely?"

Nert looked confused.

"I mean, if they do it every night they may as well not eat a meal. Why not save it for special occasions?"

Nert sat silent for a long time thinking.

Angela sat and waited equally silent.

"Do you think so?" said Nert.

"I am convinced," Angela replied.

"We will do that then," said Nert.

"And the song?"

"Ah yes, we have yet to finish the lyrics but we have a song and we will sing it in the suns rise."

The army started off not long after the first period, having broken camp and breakfasted led by the phalanx of warriors. In the reverse vee of the phalanx a group of Guides and Acolytes began humming the new tune that swelled from a musical chant so soft as to be almost an echo to a full chorus. The chorus was taken up by the warriors who followed the music and the words as the Acolytes and Guides sang.

> *Forward glorious warriors*
> *Marching off to war!*
> *With our pallid symbol*
> *Going on before!*
> *And Glord our ancient Master,*
> *Shapes our destiny!*
> *Onward glorious soldiers*
> *Glord will set us free!*

Followed by the refrain of the first two lines which on the second singing was slotted in between each pair of lines – to eventually become a point and counterpoint roundelay.

That was all there was but Angela had to admit that the way they sang it; with the lines being alternatively sung by the Guides and Acolytes and the mass of warriors and then back again was delightful. As the march progressed so the chorus passed back along the ranks and forward again and Angela had to admit it was beautiful.

And so they progressed into the enemy area with so much success that Angela began to worry that the movement would be top heavy. She was concerned that instead of a well organised army at her disposal she was likely to end up with a mob. Mob rule. The unruly rising of the masses. Whatever happened next she knew that her guidance was valuable, and she would have to lead them to an organised victory. She thought about the many people's movements on Earth, the Long March, Garibaldi, the Sandinistas, the French Revolution, Ghandi, and the Land March in New Zealand. She wondered how she knew this last item and recalled the photograph of the old woman and the child that was so poignant and remembered where she had seen it. It was one of the girls who worked with her on the Embankment doing her OE with Christian families; she had a book that showed all sorts of pictures from her homeland. The Land march was the most inspiring, the connotations of communism in some of the other events worried her. Ghandi was sort of religious and political and the others were political but they were all good models for her movement, and one of the lessons she had learned from most of them was that as a leader she was likely to attract attention and so she must guard against treachery. Paranoid? No, just practical. After all, she thought, Jesus was betrayed.

They reached the low hills above the city on the tenth orbit with at least a quarter more soldiers than when they had started and many more who were on their way back to the valley for training. She halted the army on the hills and deliberately ordered camp fires to be visible; to let the defenders know they were there.

"We will attack at daybreak," she told Nert and when the Leaders were settled in her circle she explained what the plan was. They marked their roles on their maps and when they had finished the details she asked if they had any questions. One Pair looked at her and cleared their throats before speaking.

"If the plan goes wrong what do we do?"

"If your troops do their part the plan will work. Stick to your part and let us on the high ground guide you. I urge you to hang on if you are in trouble and let your scouts pass the messages and the replies but if you have to then use your initiative to advance the cause. I will ask you to retreat at times and I will want that obeyed. You must understand that there are techniques to fighting the enemy that we can use that are more effective than merely attacking. Your left flank arm will split into three forks and come in from the rear as well as the flank. The timing is crucial as we want to draw the columns into the centre," Angela said.

"Yes Leader," the Pair said and bowed.

"One more thing, and I think a most important one is that you must remember what I told you during training. That is not to attack Pair on Pair but to attack Half Pairs and split Pairs up, remember?" she said, and was pleased when the Leader Pairs nodded in agreement.

"There is open land beyond the hills and although the plan is to sneak around it is possible we may be seen. What happens then?" asked one Leader.

"Simple, you will be in touch anyway. Move on the enemy if they attack and wait for the order to retreat but keep up the communication. You will be a great diversion if you are seen too early and if not you will make the decisive blow and we will win easily," she replied and smiled at them all. She answered a few more questions and as she settled down to sleep she was pleased when during worship the army vomited symbolically; pleased that even the most fanatical were keeping their food in their stomachs and making sounds instead. The noise was revolting but at least they were all fit for action the next day. At one period before Sunsrise Nert woke her, handed her a towel and some soap and led her to a private latrine where she completed her ablutions screened from the rest. The screening was not at her instigation but Nert's insistence that she be separate from the troops as befits a Leader. She went along with the idea and welcomed the privacy happy to wash and tidy up without having to vie for space. She thought of Glorida and Glorid and their Pairs and Julian who lost his embarrassment of communal toilets through a mixture of having to get used to it and lust; and, she thought, amused when she realised that he had seen her naked. Clean, she went to breakfast with Nert and ate whilst the troops marched off to attack the city. They were dressed in scruffy clothes and carried a motley collection of weapons but they were as well trained as they could possibly be. At sunsrise the troops moved off taking several lines down the hillsides in a pattern that looked random and from a distance as moving slowly each group was spread out in a pattern that would lead them to a specific point one, a low ridge and the others the sides of a valley through which ran the road. The army took a full period to reach a flat desert area that rose to the ridge, and right on cue columns of troopers from the city came roaring out in their wagons. Angela gave the signal for the troops to advance on to the ridge and watched as they dropped over the top to meet the oncoming soldiers. She watched and bit her lip as the Pairs engaged and retreated to the ridge in apparent disarray and split up to take refuge in the rocky outcrops along the edge. The second wave was already on the flat and the enemy wagons split their forces to 'mop up' the first wave and decimate the second.

The enemy troops dismounted from the wagons to engage with her soldiers and Angela had to wait until the time was right before the next stage of the attack. She watched anxiously as her troops retreated steadily glad that in spite of the strength of the attack her soldiers gave way as planned.

The enemy lead wagon did what Zradian Troop wagons always did; it led the way firing with wagons on its flanks until all the company had advanced deep into the enemy lines. The Leader Pair barked orders.

"Dismount! Spread out and shoot the bulgers out of these peasants!" he cried and as an example he led his troop out of the wagon leaving the driver Pair to keep it running ready for action. Resistance was steady but they drove the peasants back and through his intercom the Leader Pair gave orders to move. "Mop these creatures up. Troops to pursue on foot and shoot them or if they stop running engage in hand to hand. Is that understood?"

There was a chorus of replies mixed with a few chuckles as his Troop Leaders acknowledged. The City defenders moved steadily out in a circle hunting their quarry who seemed elusive yet attainable. The soldiers were eager to mop up these unskilled rebels and instead of being cautious moved mob handed into the attack. The counter attack came suddenly. First the enemy on foot suddenly ran to a ridge where they turned and started shooting back. As the Leader Pair realised the situation had changed he was aware of a new sound. "Wagons! For Nong's sake back to the wagon lines!" the Leader Pair cried, but it was too late, the peasant enemy were upon them.

The enemy wagons were already between them and their own wagons, and as they were torn between a quick retreat to consolidate and defending against the troop counter attack Angela's wagons fired on their transport.

The Leader Pair did not see the result because they were shot dead before they had a chance to lead their soldiers out of danger.

Angela hoped she had the timing right and gave the signal for the wagons to attack. From their hiding places on the edge of the flat her wagons moved in on the columns and attacked the enemy wagons. Her wagons cut through the defenders and her soldiers mercilessly mowed the Troopers down. Those wagons that were not destroyed were captured leaving the Troopers no choice but to fight on foot. It was time for Angela's soldiers to attack. They poured down from the rocks and the ridges to attack the Troopers with whatever blade weapons they had supported by the gunfire from the wagons and pushed the Troopers back faster than they had advanced.

It was a rout.

The enemy survivors ran back to the city to regroup but when they arrived it was to discover that a smaller, but well armed force was waiting for them. The city had been encircled and they were driven into a deadly trap. Angela's troops triumphantly entered the city and it was their turn to mop up. Only the Polisocs and a small group of fanatical Stormtroopers put up any resistance but they were defeated and mopped up by sunsset. Nert suggested they let the Stormtroopers escape to tell the tale but Angela disagreed and those that survived the fight were captured and handed over to the people. She was not surprised when the Stormtroopers were executed.

"Sorry Nert but it is better that the President find out in other ways. We kill the enemy not alert them. I think the Stormtroopers would tell a more coherent story than rumour will allow. It is better the citizens tell the tale than trained soldiers," she said, and clasped his arm tightly, "but you are right, the President has to know about us. We must issue a declaration. We must announce our presence!"

Nert's face lit up, and with a large grin he spread his arms and looked at the waiting Leader Pair.

"Citizens, would you agree to let us use your city as our headquarters. We would name it as the First City of Glord the Glorious. What say you?"

The Leader Pair gaped and then with an equally large grin nodded their heads.

"Thee are most welcome," they said, and bowed first to Nert and then to Angela. "Welcome to our Liberators!"

Angela smiled and bowed back but inwardly she was worried. The movement was going much faster than she liked. But as she looked across the cityscape to the outskirts, ignoring the dangling bodies of the executed Pairs, she realised that all she saw was hers by right of conquest. She emphasised hers, and with a touch of satisfaction she called the Leader Pair and asked, politely but firmly, to meet with the women of the city. She was pleased when the next turn as the breakfast meal was disposed of and the business of the new turn was begun, the first of the women Pairs arrived at the central building. Happily she greeted an ever growing number of female Pairs. She had especially asked that the women be allowed to gather on their own and that the men be given the tasks that they would normally do for the rest of the turn. That some had brought their young Pairs with them was neither here nor there but their presence was a pleasant change from the grim warrior class she was used to. When the hall was full she began by calling on them to listen to what the women's rebel army were doing.

From that moment on she had a captive audience and when she had finished telling them her thoughts there was a prolonged and satisfying cheer as the female Pairs rose to their feet and cried out for revolution.

"And women, female Pairs! You can take your destiny in your own hands, and instead of being chattels of the male Pairs you too can be Leaders! Glorida and Glorid, Dorida and Dorid and the marvellous ancient Pair Lavia have shown you the way! I call on you to make a change and begin the change here. Let not the men rule you but let them be ruled by you! Show them that you can take a part in the building of the new republic, that is if you want a new republic!" she finished and raised her arms with her palms outward as if she were an evangelical preacher at a Christian rally.

The effect was tremendous and with almost one voice the women changed from cheering to wild and ecstatic chanting.

"Angela! Angela! Angela! We will follow Angela!"

And amazed at the effect she lowered her arms and bowed her head. She looked up after a few short periods and saw Nert standing in the portal gazing at her with a mixture of fear and amazement.

Oh dear, she thought, I think I may have gone too far.

Fireman Weddell Breaks Out

The Bywater allotments Flower Day was in full swing. The plots were bright with displays of cut flowers, well manicured vegetable patches and both judges and participants looked smart.

Except for one of the allotments which stood out like a sore thumb. Although the organisers sympathised with the gardener because of all the activity relating to the tool shed close by his plot they were disturbed by his strange display. The poor gardener in the isolated corner spot, normally a keen and respected grower of vegetables and seasonal flowers, was steadily going off his trolley.

The chairman approached him cautiously supported by the rest of the committee who stood a little way off, and watched by other interested plot owners, spoke quietly about the state of his garden.

"Look Silas, I'm not complaining, but I am worried that something is dreadfully wrong, with your gardening this year," he said, and looked around at the plot which was planted with plastic and paper displays. The scarecrow was still wearing a policeman's uniform but it was now decapitated, and Silas stood with a rake in his hand glowering at them.

"What do you buggers want?" he snarled.

"Er, well, we thought you might like some help," the chairman said.

"What with?"

"Er, with sorting out your plot for the..." but the chairman got no further and backed hurriedly away. Silas roared incomprehensible sounds at him punctuated by the odd reference to 'effing coppers' and 'bloody nosy bastards' and proceeded to attack the chairman and the committee with the rake.

They retreated rapidly stumbling against each other in their haste to escape the swinging garden tool. The chairman was knocked down, and three of the committee were hit by the flat side of the rake before the watchers piled in on top of the demented gardener, disarmed him and sat on his wriggling form whilst one committee member called the police and an ambulance.

Both services arrived. The police arrested the poor gardener and the paramedics treated the chairman for cuts and bruises. Silas, the gardener was taken away in the ambulance subdued and restrained until he was taken to the same ward as the cause of all his troubles. He lay in the bed tranquillised and watched by orderlies and a police officer unaware that he was lying where Julian had once lay. He was assessed and committed and because of his violent nature he was constrained before being transferred to a more secure hospital.

His fellow gardeners postponed the Flower Day until the following week. A couple of volunteers cleared Silas's allotment and tried to explain to his wife what had happened.

"Gorn orf his head has he?" she asked.

"Er, yes, but you know that surely?" said the chairman.

"Well yes, but he always was a bit loopy. I suppose I will have to get used to it," she said, and that was all they could get out of her.

The fact that the Alien invasion forces were only a few miles away, and army units were often seen on the roads as they advanced on the enemy, or that aircraft had blown Heathrow to rubble did not deter the gardeners from their annual event. Life as we know it must go on, they said, and even the gardener's wife would agree.

Sidney Weddell watched the orderlies carefully and just as carefully he took the pills they gave him, ate whatever they fed him and drifted around the institution just like everybody else. He watched the movement of the ones with the keys and the ones who came in with the vans. He was there when they brought the new man in and watched how he was driven to the side door and carried in strapped in his stretcher. He listened to the orderlies talking of him and what he learned was enough to make him want to fight his way out of the building. He heard the name Renfrew repeated and learned that this was a gardener who had an allotment where Renfrew was last seen. He knew the Bywater Road and pictured in his mind the junction with the High Street and the small car park where he and his crew sometimes parked the wagon to show off to the public. A few metres from the junction the gardens began and he knew them because in the summer he used to take Damien there to show him his uncle's plot. He remembered the newspapers making much of Sergeant Orange and his little green men remark and as he sat thinking about the new man and the gardens and Renfrews, he grew steadily more determined. On the day when they shifted the gardener from the recovery room to a room in E-block he was fully dressed and ready to go. Predictably the gardener objected and with much shouting and a lot of violent thrashing around he created the diversion Sidney Weddell needed and unseen he slipped out of the day room into the gardens. The workers, used to seeing patients wandering around in the grounds took very little notice of him. When they were not looking his way he dashed into the shrubbery, across the neat beds and ran for the fence.

He was up and over the first fence ignoring the electric shocks as the power flashed through his body and down on the other side before the workers were aware of what he was doing. He heard the alarm ringing but did not panic and climbed the next fence quickly to land on the grass verge and once on the road he ran and kept on running until he found a crowd before slowing to a walk. He had no idea where he was and did not care that he had no money, or that his clothes were hospital drab and that his shoes were slip-ons that slopped loosely on his bare feet. He looked conspicuous but because he ignored the fact that he was, he passed along the streets unmolested and unnoticed. By nightfall he was far from the institution and with his instinct for self preservation he found a house whose occupants were absent and plundered the owner's wardrobe. He ate food from a well stocked larder and found some Eurodollars and some pounds which he gratefully put in his pocket.

Fireman Weddell slept in the master bed room and in the morning slipped out of the house to look for a bus. He found his transport and although he was told repeatedly that the service depended on whether or not the Alien Invasion was stopped he found what he was looking for and late in the afternoon he was walking down the hill past the West London hospital toward the Bywater Road. In the distance he saw a thick column of smoke. It was a massive fire and he thought bitterly of Renfrew and looked up with renewed interest at the huge fire in the west. He climbed to the top of the hill where he nearly caught the Renfrew and gazed across the houses and commercial buildings. He saw the glint of the river Thames and beyond that the gardens of Kew and was glad the fire wasn't there. It was much further than that and when he looked in the sky and realised there were no aircraft flying he thought of Heathrow. Heathrow was burning and it was all Renfrew's fault! Renfrew was burning the airport!

"I hate that skinny little bastard!" he snarled, and marched forward to the edge of the park gardens and for a few minutes he was lost in the alleyways that backed onto the High Street. As the evening grew darker he sat in a fish and chip shop waiting for a portion of fish and chips which he bought with the last of his money. He sat quietly and calmly thinking of what he was going to do after he had eaten his meal. Renfrew. He was going to follow Renfrew and like the fish he was about to eat he was going to batter him to death.

He took his food to the allotments and sat on the ruined garden shed to eat it and as the night fully took over he thought about the day when Julian disappeared. His memory played him tricks as he thought about the events of that day and somehow he mixed up the fire at Byrde's factory with Heathrow and the look of disappointment on his son's face when he accidentally ran over his Teddy Bear with the fire engine and crushed it. He blamed the fire at Byrde's factory, the Heathrow conflagration, the burned out house, his son's damaged Teddy Bear and the demented state of the gardener on Julian. He threw the paper bag and the few remaining cold chips on the grass and rolled over onto the platform and lay on the dirty floor gently sobbing.

Suddenly he was aware of two people who clambered onto the platform and kicked him aside. He sat up when the two men spoke in a strange language and gazed with uncomprehending amazement at the lights that flashed in the gloom above him. He felt a lurch and a sickening feeling of things coming apart and then he was in a chamber filled with light and somebody was grabbing his elbows.

He struggled, felt the gas wash over him, caught a whiff and the next thing he knew after that was he was lying on a bunk strapped down and staring at an unfamiliar face.

"Who are you?" he said and blinked.

"More to the point my Earthman who the Nong are you?"

Sidney Weddell hissed his name and with a tone that relayed his hatred to the face above him he asked for Julian. "Is that dirty little child molester Julian, firebug Renfrew here. I want him and I want him dead," he said.

The face above disappeared.

"Your Honour, I think we can use this wild creature for our own ends," said Zarb and grinned at his twin. "Braz seems to have a rapport with him; he says the right things and makes him happy. We searched the data for the name Renfrew and we have discovered much."

Braz handed Pour and Roup a flimsy each and the Pair stood politely by and waited for Pour and Roup to absorb the information. Within a few short periods Pour had a grasp of the information and nodded his head. "So, the President wants this Earth man, Julian Renfrew, badly enough to offer a reward of over twenty thousand Tokens dead and thirty thousand alive. This new wild creature is capable of finding him?" said Pour.

"I believe so," said Braz.

"And how will this help us?" said Pour.

"We can set him off after the enemy bomber and when he kills him we can claim the kudos and the Tokens, the President will look on us with great favour and we will be heroes," said Zrab enthusiastically.

"Why did you not do this for yourselves?" said Roup.

"We thought that after our last meeting and what happened we thought that we owed you a favour. We are loyal citizens and wish only to serve our Glorious President and so we must offer your honour, as the official representative of the President, all the favours belonging to your esteemed rank," said Zrab.

"And how do you propose to effect the execution?" said Pour.

"We will let him go but prepare him well before he leaves with images from the learning aids and prime him to do his task. We can't go wrong," said Braz.

"Indeed," said Roup but agreed that the Pair should go ahead.

Braz and Zrab bowed and left the control room pleased with themselves and happy that they were of service to their Leader Pair. They were an excessively loyal Pair and when they were fingered as the Pair who sent the rude message before the Paper War they fearfully took the blame. It was their duty to suffer for their Leader Pair they said and stoically prepared for execution. When the opportunity came to redeem their guilt they took it with great enthusiasm and pride, glad of the chance to honour their Leader Pair.

"Prats," said Roup as Braz and Zrab left, "we must find a way of murdering that Pair."

"Let them do what they plan and if it works we eliminate them and take the credit and if it doesn't then we disown them and let the President kill them," said Pour.

Zrab and Braz led the stunned and mildly tranquillised ex-fireman Sidney Weddell to the learning rooms and with a mixture of coercion and persuasion set him on a course that after the third session he was more than willing to follow. He lay under the machine and learned much about Zrad, the Palace and the Wastelands. He learned about the rebels and saw a short but exciting passage on Julian's bombing work.

"Kill Renfrew," he said and writhed with pleasure when the machine answered back and began to show him how. He lay watching the instructions and gradually as the image shifted from a simple instructive movie to one filled with little gambolling cartoon rodents he saw another, more worthy, target and drooled deliciously as the happy little pink rodent explained what he must do.

When Zrab and Braz took him back to his room after that third session he was happy to be moved around, fed and tutored with mock weapons and measured for a proper outfit. After a sleep period he was given one more session and this time there were no tranquillisers.

"We can trust you now Earthman,' said Braz.

He grinned at them both and marched along between them freely and happily and climbed into the learning bay cheerfully. The little rodent took over as he had hoped and told him more, much more and what he learned excited him. He left the bay and marched back with the Pair not saying anything but allowing his mind to scheme and plot as he walked back to his cabin.

Inside there was a new outfit and real weapons waiting for him. A sharp axe, short sword and a gas gun. Casually he hefted the gas gun, noted that the portal was open and casually shot Zrab and Braz. He left them laying on the floor and headed immediately along the corridor remembering the instructions the rodent voice gave him. He passed Pairs of administrators who looked at his uniform and weapons and did not question him. He found the transfer port and entered it tapping the numbers the rodent voice gave him and braced himself for the sensation as the door hissed shut.

The new door opened and with the cunning of the hunted he dived out sideways and took cover. The group of Pairs sitting around a fire not far from the exit saw the door open and were immediately on guard; some moving with weapons drawn and lamps flashing and others raising their battered weapons to the ready position. The gloom was not quite dark but not light either and Fireman Weddell assumed that this was a Zradian night. Good, he thought, I can travel in the dark and with a quiet chuckle he easily evaded the searching Pairs and headed east and a little north.

He travelled by instinct slowly and carefully obeying the rodent and as the twin suns rose and the squawking birds bellowed their chorus he sought a place to hide up. He was hungry and thirsty but for now his fanatical need to carry out his task bade him find shelter and hide from the inhabitants.

He chose a ruined building that was blackened with fire yet was complete enough to hide him. He settled down in a small room and with plastic rubbish and some charred and nameless material he covered his body and slept the daylight through and as he slept he muttered the name Renfrew and fingered his axe.

Braz and Zrab stood in the control room and explained to Pour and Roup what had happened. They tried to make their report optimistic but failed to convince Pour and Roup that everything had gone according to plan.

"We set him off and he went to the port as we had directed and he is on his way," said Zrab.

"Then why did the code show figures for Sector Blue?" said Pour and waited impatiently tapping his foot on the floor for their answer.

Braz looked at Zrab and Zrab in turn looked at Braz and with a tremble in his voice Zrab answered.

"The code is a disguise," he said.

"A disguise to throw the enemy of the scent, these rebels are clever and, and..." said Braz.

"No," said Pour. "You cocked it up. Polisocs!"

At his dread call Braz and Zrab shifted and ran for the portal pumping their arms and legs hard heading for the nearest transfer port. They ran straight into the waiting arms of the Polisoc troopers who laughed, wrestled them to the floor and kicked them to insensibility.

"Take them and do what you wish with them," said Roup with a tight smile. "They are traitors and deserve a long and lingering death."

"Oh yes, we will, we will," said the Polisoc Leader Pair and fingered his blades.

The troopers dragged Zrab and Braz out of the control room by their ankles and as he left the Polisoc Leader Pair sneered and gave Pour and Roup a long meaningful stare.

"Those Bulgers are after us," said Pour.

"Yes and that frightens me more than that crazy robot," replied Roup.

Byrde and Arthur

Byrde sat in the wagon with Lugs sitting cross legged opposite waiting for D.G and his troop to return. He had offered Lugs a chance to go with the wagons but the big man had said he preferred to stay and look after Byrde. D.G had agreed, and promised Byrde that Lugs would be in the thick of it later if Byrde himself wanted to take part.

"I wanted to meet Arthur," said Byrde wanting to be in the fight but having to agree that he was not fit enough nor trained enough. For now he would settle for being on the outside with the communications wagon and wait for the operation to be over.

Lugs grinned and pointed out across the land to where a dust cloud announced the arrival of the column. A voice crackled in the wagon and Byrde grinned back at Lugs.

"Sounds like he made it," said Byrde.

Lugs grinned, and as the line of wagons curved into the clearing and stopped, Byrde stood up with Lugs beside him and watched as the lead wagon cruised up to stop right beside them and two figures disembarked.

"Arthur! Tzu!" cried Byrde and almost jumped up and down with glee. "I'm so pleased to see you alive and well and Julian? Is he all right?"

Arthur ambled up to the side of the wagon and Tzu walked with great dignity to stand with him and for a few moments they faced each other grinning. Tzu broke the silence.

"Greetings Earthman, your employee is safe and comparatively well and, so it seems, has conducted himself with distinction. I apologise if I sound even more pompous than Arthur but I realise that I am regarded here as a master and must act accordingly," Tzu said, and smiled broadly. "I am overjoyed to discover you both alive and well. And you Lugs, I trust mister Braine and the Ferret are fine?"

"Both all right mister Wu, you gonna play cards with me we get back?" said Lugs eagerly.

"I may just do that my friend," said Tzu his eyes twinkling with amusement when Byrde stared at him with his mouth opening and shutting like a goldfish in a bowl.

"My son is notably not asking after any of us but I am certain that his young lady will explain that he should be doing so, and I daresay that soon he will be making his noxious presence felt," said Arthur and laughed. "Good to see you Richard, very good to see you."

"You will wish to travel with me Arthur?" said Byrde, "and hopefully we will fight together, if they let us that is."

Byrde and Lugs alighted from the truck and stood in the sunslight as the wagons reformed and waited for the rearguard. The last to arrive was Glorida's wagon and that was allowed to enter the circle and slide to a halt close to Byrde's party. A figure got out accompanied by another and together they walked to where Byrde waited expectantly.

"Julian, good to see you, I do hope you have applied for annual leave because you seem to have neglected your duties somewhat, have you an explanation?" Byrde said, "or a note from your probation officer?"

"I got involved in this bloody war didn't I," said Julian defensively and was about to say more when he realised Byrde was grinning. "You're having me on, right?"

"Yes and I am pleased to discover you safe and well and I can assure you that I too am involved in this bloody war. Now you know Tzu and Arthur, and the big bloke is Lugs, now please tell me who the young lady is?" Byrde said and gazed at Glorida with admiration.

"Oh, this is Glorida, she and I are, er, um sort of ..." he began and blushed unable to say any more.

"Lovers?" finished Byrde feeling as if he had just begun a conversation with Bates and Fish. He reached a hand out and took Glorida's in his and smiled at her. "Good luck, Glorida, you can call me Richard. You look as if you can deal with my friend's annoying little foibles."

Glorida grinned and when Byrde let her hand go she fingered her knife and looked meaningfully at Julian and giggled.

"Pleased to meet you Richard. I can handle Julian. He is a scumbag, a coward, sneaky, bad mannered, will betray his own world to save his miserable spotty skin but I love him and he had better not forget it," she said, and fingered her knife again.

"Oh Christ," said Julian and groaned.

Byrde, Tzu and Arthur laughed while Lugs stood by looking puzzled.

Julian travelled part of the way with Byrde and Tzu in the communications wagon and told his tale with corrective interjections from Glorida and Glorid. Whenever Julian exaggerated or missed an essential detail Glorida quietly reminded him by fingering her knife while Glorid interrupted now and then to correct her Twin's version. Eventually, before the columns were due to split up Julian admitted that he was grateful for their concern for his safety and thanked his father for his help.

Byrde noted that for this he did not need a threat from Glorida's knife, and when he finished thanking them he lowered his head and muttered a few words that sounded like an apology.

"Speak up my friend," said Tzu.

"That's what I don't get," he said, "you all call me your friend and I dunno what to say. I got into trouble with D.G for slagging off at Angela, and even she called me her friend. I ain't got no friends."

"That's cos you don't try to make any. All you do is take, and you don't wanna give nuffink," said Lugs, and shook his head sadly. "If you was more like mister Byrde or my mate Ferret, you'd do all right."

Everybody turned to face Lugs and all gazed at him with varying degrees of amazement. Lugs looked embarrassed and gave them all a silly grin and shrugged his shoulders.

"Well spoken Lugs," said Byrde.

And before Julian could reply the wagons hissed to a stop and it was time for them to part.

Byrde watched Glorida's troop move off and waved at the lonely figure who stood on the back platform of her wagon and reflected on Julian's attitude. The young man was his own worst enemy, he thought, but then nobody had really given him much of a chance. The chances he had been offered were fine as far as the authorities were concerned but he needed more than that, and Byrde determined that when all the fighting was over, if ever it was, he would help him.

"I'll sort out Denny Block for Julian," said Lugs, "he owes me and if he don't wanna know I kin bash 'is lights out and that'll sort it out."

"Paying his debts off won't help?" said Byrde.

"Nah, better to wipe them clean by wiping out them two ratbags," said Lugs with some conviction.

Arthur sat drinking a tall glass of best Outland Brew and listened as D.G, Glord and Braine, with the occasional remark from the Ferret brought him up to date with the current situation. The Ferret rattled off the figures and as Glord and Braine talked of the latest movements of the rebels and the President's forces. Lugs, Tzu and Byrde were at another table playing snap and if it were not for the fact that D.G was getting ready for his and Glord's next military outing he too would be playing.

"We have to go out on another battle soon. It's going to be another quick fight that takes us in and out, and it will be up to you and your friends here to give the Pres a flea in his ear," D.G said and grinned. "I like fighting and these Bulgers in charge seem to think they are punishing us."

"Oh why is that?" asked Byrde.

D.G looked at Glord and bit his lip.

"That's all right my Twin, tell them. The bar is not wired," said Glord. "I think somebody needs to know."

D.G told his story and when he had finished there was a silence while Byrde, Braine, the Ferret and Arthur sat thinking.

"So in fact you tried to help him and somebody here tried to kill him," said Byrde and added, "or Angela."

D.G stared at Byrde and for a few small periods he held Byrde's gaze as the two men realised what they had just understood. D.G's mind raced and with a snarl of anger, not directed at Byrde, he spoke softly.

"Now I understand," he said, "they wanted to kill Angela. The filthy Bulgers wanted to kill Angela! I will get them for that."

The others stared at D.G, and Glord for the first time in their company gripped his twin's hand and held it in both of his. Byrde felt the empathy wave although it was the Ferret who picked up on the real emotion.

"You love the woman?" he said softly.

"Yes and she is missing," D.G said and smiled at the Ferret. "Stupid eh?"

"Nah, you're jest a bloke and blokes fall in love wiv birds don't they. How can we help yer?" said the Ferret, and looked at the others. "If we kin help him we will won't we?"

"We can use the system to find out who wanted to kill her and maybe we can find out what has happened to her. I reckon she is a survivor and she is out there somewhere doing her bit or on her way to the women's camp," said Braine, and touched D.G's arm.

"I may be able to help if I can use the system myself," said Arthur.

"Right, and I will coordinate the operation. If we find out who wanted Angela killed and where she is then we must plan what to do," said Braine.

"And then we can go on a spree ourselves," said D.G.

"I think I can say who set the killers on to Angela but I would like to know how many were involved," said Glord.

"Then it is agreed, we do our jobs and in the meantime we search the data for files and build a case," said the Ferret. "More ale? The Leaders are here."

And with the Ferret's warning the group talked of the past events excitedly with D.G leading the gory descriptions avoiding any mention of Angela but talking of Julian and his prowess with bombs and fire setting. In effect as far as the Leader Pairs were concerned the group of Earthmen and the Pair Glord and Drogl were doing what any fighting Pair and Half Pair were likely to do in the headquarters bar. Bragging about their part in the war against the

President and that, as far as they were concerned, was as it should be.

Julian rested for several turns. Dorida and Dorid suggested that he be given a few turns to get back to fitness and some more training. In the meantime Glorida and Glorid went out as back up to a fighting patrol happy to act in a supporting role for a change. Glorida said that she and her twin could do with some rest herself but all the same the troop went out fully armed and ready to wage war. Lavia ran Julian through his techniques and with an unprecedented departure gave him some bomber Pairs to train. It was a task he took to with enthusiasm because it gave him a chance to leer at the women in his charge. At the end of the turn Lavia called him into their office and gave him some mulled ale and a portion of their home made bread with butter, and the nearest thing the Zradians had to honey, a syrup gathered from the Carnibush.

"A warning for you Julian," said Lavia.

"Why, what have I done," said Julian feeling a knot of fear.

"I suggest you stop leering at your charges and forget any ideas of having it off with the bombers. I have promised to tell Glorida all you get up to. As a Pair I love that woman and her twin and I love you too Julian, but if it comes to looking after her interests or yours then she comes first, understand?"

Julian knew that by the way both Lavias were speaking at once, she was serious and would do exactly as she promised. Normally they spoke as Half Pairs teaching him different things and there was no difference between the passive and dominant half. Their determination rattled him, and for the first time since his rescue he examined his actions and found himself wanting. On the tower when Glorida had told him to shoot he had realised that he was an integral part of the troop and although the idea of fighting still scared him spitless he saw his place. He also realised why D.G had flattened him, and the word he came up with was loyalty. You had to be loyal to your friends, and mister Byrde and Tzu had called him friend. As he thought of their warm greetings he felt tears well up and roll down his cheeks.

One of the Lavias wiped the tears and tut-tutted.

"No need to cry," she said.

"There is. There is. I been a rotten bastard and I promise you Lavia that I will stop leering at the girls. I reckon that I got a lot of things to sort out in me head and I oughter start with being true to me girlfriend," he said, and when both Lavias smiled at him and offered another jug of mulled ale he told them about Tzu and Byrde and how he had slagged off at Angela. What surprised him was that when he had finished instead of telling him that he was an idiot they hugged him in turn and laughed.

"You have started to see life as it is not as others tell you it is. Julian, you are beginning to get some self esteem and that is a plus. Drop the bullshit and you might even turn out to be a nice bloke. We love you and it is obvious that your friends do too. I think that by the time this is over you and your father might even get on better."

"Nah, never," he said and laughed. "Never."

But he had an uncomfortable feeling that he was wrong. The feeling puzzled him because for the first time in his life he was caught between an idea of family and his defensive reaction to anything that threatened him and his desire to look after number one. He was unsure of the new, to him, idea that people actually liked him.

"Nobody likes me," he said and pouted his lower lip.

"We like you," said Lavia, "and so does Glorida."

"Yeah, maybe but I don't really like me and that don't help much does it?" Julian said and looked at them both defiantly.

"No it doesn't, and as soon as you start liking yourself the better it will be for you. You could start by looking at the things you do that annoy others and that you feel ashamed of, and after that you can find out how to put it right. Remember that you are you and you have to live with you," said one of the Lavias while the other looked on.

"Oh," said Julian and could find nothing to say.

Lavia laughed and one of them gave him another jar of mulled ale. He staggered back to his hut that night and dreamed of friendly rodents who told him where he was going wrong. He woke with a headache but during the training he was more attentive to his method of teaching and making certain the Pairs got things right rather than staring at their bodies. He still felt uncomfortable but he was much happier at the end of the orbit.

While Julian was coming to terms with his relationship with himself Arthur Renfrew was searching the data systems for a reference to Angela. He searched a whole raft of media releases but found nothing except for a reference to an unusual activity in the south western area of sector blue. He made some notes and copied the current messages and set a search for all references within the parameters he devised to cover the range he thought might give useful information. Glord and D.G were out on another patrol and as both Byrde and Braine were working on a separate project he took the flimsies to the Ferret.

"I reckon they is something we oughter ask the old farts about later. Sort of find out a bit more and get some idear what's happening," the Ferret said. The two men sat side by side examining the flimsies and with a sudden insight Arthur tapped a code onto the Ferret's work station.

Rodent #4

The screen filled with a rodents, faded and then with a quick flash of colour changed to blank blue with a small cheerful rodent bouncing happily in one corner. Arthur tapped the code numbers into the keyboard, flipped the flimsies into the copy slot and tapped the icon for read and waited. The answer was quick to come and bounced across the screen like a Karaoke song chart, the marker a small chirpy chipmunk.

Try looking for the Children of Glord the Glorious
May the President sail into an iceberg
Beware the Ides of Tatania!

"I think my source is getting a little more demented as time marches on," said Arthur and blushed when he realised that he had spoken to the Ferret whose education he had thought would lack any Shakespeare.

"Doesn't he mean Titanic; I thought Tatania was Midsummer Night's Dream?" said the Ferret, genuinely puzzled.

"Yes it is but I think whatever my source is he, it has some personality problems and it has a tendency to mix things up a bit. I'm sorry but I didn't realise you knew any Shakespeare," Arthur said, ashamed.

"I had a teacher what used to make us do bits when we was at Intermediate. We did Macbeth, Midsummer Night, Twelfth Night, Julius Caesar and Henry Fifth and it wasn't half bad either, and fer a bunch of kids what could hardly read or write we did all right. I learned me letters more proper when I was working as a janitor. I wished I'd learned more when I was a kid," said the Ferret and this time he looked ashamed.

"You made up for it then if the Zradians picked you for this job," said Arthur. "How come you were not recognised back home?"

"Oh that, I was sort of passed over by the system and by the time I was given the tests I was ready to leave and couldn't be bothered. Apart from that me Mum and Dad was split up and then me Mum got sick and I ended up looking after me brother. Then when we was almost on the bones of our arses Lugs Mum took us in and me and Lugs has been mates ever since. Poor old Lugs is a bit simple, and when his Mum popped her clogs I took him out of the fight game and sort of kept him with me. I promised her I would see him right. And I did too," the Ferret said and grinned.

64

"I take it Lugs can be hard work?" said Arthur.

"Yeah but he's sort of nice as well and if nobody takes any trouble over him he would be doing bird. I sorta try and keep us both out of chokey. Sometimes Bates and Fish tips us off when some occifer gets it in his head to clean up crime. Them two has got a lot of bottle and they use it proper."

Arthur laughed and was glad that the Ferret had confided in him.

"Yes, I have the impression that there is a whole world I do not know anything about. I live for my work and I suppose I have forgotten the rest," said Arthur.

"That's all right prof, people like me and Lugs get along all right. You could say we helps make the world go round, at least we keep the fuzz busy," replied the Ferret and added his laughter to Arthur's.

The President Upset

The High Consuls marched down the aisle and stood nervously at the entrance to the arena. He dropped to his knees and then with the scrolls clutched to his chests with one arm he[1] crawled along to the centre at the President's feet.

"We have news your Honour," they said together making sure that their voices followed each other in perfect double time.

"Speak to Us."

"You are not going to like it your High Honour."

"We will listen to your news and make Our mind up," said the President petulantly.

The High Consuls cringed and read from the flimsy.

"His Honourable Highness, know that we, Leader Pair, First City sector Green have learned from your servants in 15 City sector Green that traitors have taken command of 14 Yellow Sector Blue. In your Honourable name we have dispatched a strong force to re-take the City and execute the traitors. It is expected the insurrection will be crushed instantly."

The President glared at them with a face as black as thunder and sat thinking about the message trying to work out how on Zrad the rebels had managed a force so large it could take a city.

"There is more?"

"Yes your Honour. We have discovered who the leader is," the High Consuls said and cringed even deeper on the flagstones.

"Tell Us."

"It is the woman who came with Julian the Bomber. Her name is Angela."

The shocked silence that fell over the assembly was deep as all Pairs, Dog Squad, Polisocs, Troopers, Guards and Courtiers all held their breath to wait for the President's reaction. It came in the form of a howl of anguish that echoed around the large hall that confused even the Dog Squad and the Guards. The howl emerged from the President's throat beginning as a scream of sheer frustration and developing into a cry of anger that forced the President to his feet where he stood on the dais with his fist clenched and his mouth open. "Aaaaaaaaaaaargh!" he finished and faced the High Consuls. "I want that filthy piece of alien pig fodder captured and brought to me alive! Bring Julian and his father to Us!"

---

[1] *It is correct to refer to a Pair as he or she and then to use we and they - even Zradians have difficulty.*

There was another deep and breathless silence.

Two Pairs were suddenly ejected from the mass of terrified courtiers, immediately seized by the Guards and pushed forward. The unfortunate Pairs grovelled on the flagstones and lay with their hands clasped together trembling uncontrollably.

"What have these worms to tell Us?" the President demanded.

"Your Honour, Julian and his father have escaped," the Pairs explained, their voices muffled due to their prostration.

There was another deep silence, breathless but filled with awful anticipation.

"Why has nobody told Us!"

Because we were scared to, thought the High Consuls, scared of being the bearers of bad news and scared that to fail meant death. They backed away from the prostrate Pairs and breathed softly and deeply knowing that the Guards had chosen these two at random to explain their failure. The Guards had made their case even worse by pretending they still held Julian and his father in the dungeons by showing old film of the two aliens suffering torture. True that most of it was fiction but at least they had captured Julian's attitude and his father's stoic resistance. The whole episode was a macabre farce that, the High Consuls had allowed to happen, and managed to shift the blame but even so to leave now was going to be difficult. The trick was to survive the next few short periods and disappear as soon as they could find an opportunity.

"Your Glorious Army are chasing them your magnificence," said the Pairs. "They will have the traitors back soon, your Greatness!"

"Polisocs! Take them away and torture the truth from them!" the President roared and glared around the hall. "We wish to know all things! Polisocs! The entire Guard is under arrest until we find the traitors that let the captives go!"

The Polisoc Troopers surrounded the Guards, and in the corridors there was confusion and fear as the Polisoc Troopers swept along the corridor and disarmed the Guards herding them into the lower halls. In the main hall the President gazed at the two Pairs as they were lifted by their elbows and dragged out to the Polisoc torture rooms. He faced the High Consuls and ordered them to stand.

"You will make a full report and deliver it to Us directly."

"Yes your Honour, we will concur, immediately. We will retire to our workroom and concentrate on all aspects of the event," said the High Consuls.

They backed out of the main hall and walked unsteadily to their workroom, where in the uncanny quiet created by the absence of the Guards they wrote their report, searched for the latest data and sent copies to all offices.

"My twin, we must take the opportunity to escape and I suggest we name ourselves Zrid and Driz and head for Sector yellow and hence off to the Wastelands."

As a result of their defection the President received a double flimsy that explained to him in great detail all that the High Consuls knew about Angela and her army. It also raised the long dead spectre of the First Republic and the great myths of Glord the Glorious. And as an even more disturbing turn to the events the President remembered that the most wanted Pair in the rebel army was the fourball player Glord and Drogl. The thought occurred to him that the so called Children of Glord the Glorious had for their leader none other than Glord the rebel.

"Bring the High Consuls to Us!" he demanded, and when he learned that the High Consuls had deserted his rage was beyond any that he had so far shown. He had the dungeon duty Guards flogged, the messengers murdered and ordered the Dog Squads to execute every tenth Guard Pair, and then he called for his scribes.

With a cold and vicious edge to his voice he gave them his orders and asked them to read them back.

"To Our Glorious Army – with all expedience your task will be to seek out and capture Angela from Earth, the Leader Glord of the filthy Children of Glord the Glorious, Julian the Bomber and His dirty Father who will be brought to Us for public execution. All and any members of the Children of Glord the Glorious are to be slaughtered and all insurrection will be put down. Your plans will be made known to me for approval. And to Pour and Roup – all relatives and significant friends of Arthur Renfrew and Julian Renfrew on Earth are to be sought out and killed.

Your Glorious President."

The scribes read the message with tremulous voices and waited ready to obey further orders. They were in the habit of re-writing the President's orders and this was the first time they had actually written down any coherent words directly from their master since the war with Earth began. They sighed with relief when the President dismissed them and called for his drinks Pair, another poor unfortunate servant Pair employed to serve his concoctions. He drank three straightway and wandered back into his chamber and swallowed six more. The scribes watched through the small windows set in their room as the President reverted to his latest habit of drinking directly from the bottles. First a large draught of gin and then a smaller one of tonic until both bottles were empty. With a groan and much muttering the President dropped onto his futon and lay snoring and twitching.

In the halls the carnage sliced to a bloody halt as the Dog Squad followed their orders to the letter. The surviving Guards still had to contend with the Polisocs and their capricious ways but at least things were more or less back to normal. The Courtiers were subdued and the surviving Guards with replacements for the dead or imprisoned took up their positions and the Dog Squad slowly returned from their task. Troopers took their places and servants washed the arena and all the places where blood was spilled.

Angela's name or the Children of Glord the Glorious was not mentioned by any of the Courtiers unless they happened to be working on the plans to subdue them. Those who were forced to speak of them did so softly or found the use of initials were valuable life savers. The rest quietly dealt with the requests of the petitioners and thanked Nong they were not chosen to work on the plans.

In all, the spirit of the Children of Glord the Glorious permeated the minds of the Pairs in the Palace, giving the common Pair some hope that at last things might be different. And if the President made it his business to inquire about such things as his image and what the people thought about him he might have been aware of the increasing numbers of citizens who were becoming brave enough to leave the city. Like all regimes that oppressed the people permits and ID cards were required for any movement other than in pursuit of their duties. Yet people moved steadily and carefully at night if they could or risked slipping out of the suburbs in small groups. Of those dissenting citizens who remained behind to continue working and living their protest was passive – a matter of keeping out of the way of the authorities and hoping for change.

When Arthur learned that it was Angela who led the Children's Army he cheered and ran out of the computer room into the communications room to send a message to his son and Glorida.

"Tell D.G as well," he said to the amused Pairs who dealt with the communications to the troops. "Let him know that Angela is alive and well and fighting with the peasants!"

He rushed out of the building to find Tzu and his people, and when he saw the old man with his Kung Fu artists and the Trainer Pairs he ran calling out the news and stopped before the old man, who smiled toothily at him surrounded by his leaders.

"Tzu, Angela is leading an army in the west. She is alive and has aroused the countryside against the President. Look! Read this!" he said so excited he almost crushed the flimsy before Tzu could read it.

Tzu took it, read it and handed it to Marion and Silas.

"So, good, now we can find a place to help. My people are getting restless. Richard has agreed to come with us. If you wish you can too. We intend to join up with the women's army. My people are getting tired of being treated like second class citizens. Angela offers a reason for going. The women in my group are angry. The Leader

Pairs here are no good. Help us move Arthur. Help us move and come too. We have our part to play and it is not here eating dog sausage and boiled vegetables. Eh?," Tzu said, and smiled broadly.

"I will be only too willing and I am sure that we could persuade the Ferret and Oliver to come too."

"So sorry, they already decide to come. And Lugs. And D.G and Glord and many others. We have a small army, okay?"

"What will we do?"

"Go find the women and then go find Angela."

And so it was that the news of Angela and the Children of Glord the Glorious came to the ken of the Rebel Leaders.

The High Leader Pair of the Rebel Army sat in their office and took a deep breath. They were reading the latest propaganda message, and although it carried a mocking message for the President, it disturbed them. It was written by the Earthman Braine and approved by Glord.

Let it be known that your President's forces are again beaten by the people. The New People's Army is already Victorious!

Already Cities have fallen – the President's finest troops beaten and sent packing – Pairs are flocking to the banner – Pairs are welcomed in peace to the New People's Army. No more Polisocs! No more Dog Squad! No more Slavery! The People take control of the land with the People's Army.

And who is the leader of this new People's Army?

A woman! An Earth woman.

Who is this woman?

She is the friend of the Great Hero Julian the Bomber.

What is this new People's Army?

The New People's Army are the followers of The Children of Glord the Glorious - the Great Hero of our Glorious Past has risen in spirit from which Angela – the Great Warrior – has taken her inspiration. Long live the Power of Glord the Glorious and the Great Warrior Angela Breen!

The other Elder Pairs looked at the screen and sighed looking at each of the other members of the Leader's committee in turn and shaking their heads. The High Leader Pair gazed at the rest of the team and said with a tinge of real sadness. "We should have killed her ourselves that first day."

"Let us bring in the hit squad and let us do it secretly. I have a plan, a long term plan that will serve us well."

"Let us discuss this and put it in action."

The second Half Pair explained in detail what he had in mind, and when he had finished his twin gripped his hands in both of his and thanked him. Together they took a drink from their ale jars and touched them with a small clunk and grinned.

"To us and to our mission."

"To our mission."

And both pairs drank.

Julia

The little green elephants Julia Renfrew saw climbing the wall chased the blue ones that raced across it. The yellow snakes and the red butterflies seemed to want to fill the room, one to writhe uncontrollably on the floor and the other to fill the room with soft flapping wings. The small Chinese women that kept popping in and out of her vision disturbed her, and when she tried to sort out how she felt about them she calculated the impact in elephants and snakes. The elephants won.

Julia groaned and sank deep into the sea of snakes and tried to bat the butterflies away from her face so that she could watch the elephants. She liked the elephants. The other animals were too busy but the elephants had a gracefulness that belied their size. Besides, she had often watched fantasia and always thought that the elephants and the hippos were the best. Or was that the bust? Bust, breasts, her breasts were elephants. Her legs were snakes. Her arms were hippos and there were butterflies crawling over the Chinese women who were feeding the snakes.

"Julia! Missy Julia Renfrew!"

A voice. Kind and gentle. A woman's voice and a soft touch. The Chinese women grew larger and the animals began to crawl away. Seconds passed. No, it was hours or days, and the Chinese women were all that was left. A bottle. No, a plastic cup. Water. Water and something to eat. The animals, banished behind the walls, and a headache, a big, big headache. Her mouth dry and her body weak and thin, clean but thin.

"How long?"

"Long time missy Julia. We look after you all right. We have friend here to see you. You like her verra much?"

"Tell her to fuck off."

"No, you like"

"I said tell her to fuck off."

"So sorry but mama says you must speak with her. She tell you about Julian. She verra sorry you have trouble."

Julia thought about Julian and let a little sob escape from her lips. She wondered who the woman was, and with a little nod and a soft yes she agreed. The woman who walked in was not too tall, dark and warmly attractive. Julia liked her immediately and gave her a weak smile.

"Who the fuck are you?" she said forgetting to be polite but aware that the Chinese women winced.

"I am Marjorie Watts, I am your husband's friend," she said, and stood by the door as if waiting for Julia to bid her come further.

"Who?"

"Marjorie Watts, I am at the University with Arthur and ..."

She got no further because Julia, realising who she was, screamed and rushed forward with her mouth open wide and her hands raised like talons ready to tear and slash and bite.

"You fucking bitch! You slut! You're his piece of University trash! You filthy slag," Julia yelled as she rushed at Marjorie.

Marjorie stood her ground and waited for the onslaught but it never came. The two girls, both young and alert, stopped Julia gently and firmly before she reached the door. They placed her onto the settee that made up part of a three sided seating arrangement in a lounge lost deep in Tzu's complex home. Behind Marjorie, Colin's man growled, but relaxed when he saw that Julia was under control.

"So sorry miss Marjorie," said Beth, the younger girl.

"That's all right, it must be uncomfortable for her to see me so suddenly. I will go if you wish?" said Marjorie, and gazed sadly at Julia as she sat held between the two girls her face a picture of anguish.

"Come in and sit down with us. Miss Julia will be verra good now," said Beth.

"Bitch," spat Julia.

"I have news of Julian," said Marjorie, "do you want to hear what I have to tell you?"

Julia looked up at her so Marjorie sat down opposite and waited for the other woman to answer. She wanted to tell her that so far Arthur was all right but she instinctively knew that any information regarding Arthur was bound to be unacceptable. Besides, when Tzu's sister had called on her to speak with Julia she had explained that Julia herself was being dried out and was bound to be difficult. She had expected a clinic but instead she was confronted with a confusing labyrinth of rooms that were filled with cheerful Chinese people doing a variety of tasks, and tucked at the end was a haven of quiet where Julia was being looked after.

"We give her acupuncture and acupressure and keep her off drink, give her food and water until she is clear and then you come. We know she is unhappy. My brother give me job to care for her," said Tzu's sister and smiled.

She was glad that Julia took a while to clear, as Tzu's sister put it, and glad too that she had asked Dart and Drat to help her. The Pair told her about Arthur and Julian, and afterwards, although she was anxious that he would be safe with the Rebels, she was glad he was out of the President's clutches. She watched the DVD Tzu had of

Zrad showing Julian's part in the fighting and was glad that she could tell Julia some good news.

"All right, tell me and then fuck off," Julia said, and squirmed in her seat unable to move far, restricted by her arms where the two Chinese girls held her tightly.

"I have seen a DVD of Julian and I suggest when you feel like it you can have a look too. Two people from the land that is currently trying to invade Earth told me that Julian is safe and back with the people he was with. They say that he is a hero and has done some grand work with bombs and fires to help fight the enemy. You should be proud of him. May I call you Julia? You can call me Marjorie," she said, and held up her hand to still the other woman's tongue. "I may be a bitch in your eyes but believe me I do not wish to be your enemy. I have Arthur and you have your son Julian. With Arthur gone you can have Julian back with you and I think he may be different. My friends from Zradia asked me to invite you to visit them. Please do so."

Julia glared and with a mean look she spoke.

"I should hate you. I should scratch your eyes out and kick the shit out of you. I should sue you, I should do as many nasties to you as I can but, but you, oh I don't know what to think," Julia said and stared at Marjorie. "What do you think?"

"I think you are probably right but then I would have to hurt you and I haven't come here for that. I came to help you, woman to woman. If you like I will go, and let somebody else tell you the details. You see, I was desperately worried about Arthur and I knew you would want to hear about Julian," she said, and made to go. She reached the door before Julia replied.

"Please stay Marjorie, I'm sorry. You love Arthur don't you?" she said and, this time her voice was softer with no trace of anger. "I did once but somehow things went wrong and I don't know what I thought I wanted."

Marjorie resumed her seat and smiled at Julia.

"I think we ought to have good chat and clear the air between us. I think we should be alone."

The two Chinese girls smiled broadly and let Julia go, and with dainty movements and some giggling they pushed Marjorie's bodyguard outside and closed the door behind them.

Alone the two women looked at each other and saw similarities and wondered how great the differences were. Neither wanted to be the first to speak but when Julia began to look around the room nervously with some agitation Marjorie realised that it would be up to her to speak.

"I take it you are looking for a drink?"

"Yes, a real one not water or cordial, God I need a drink!" Julia cried out. "I'm so, so unhappy." Julia burst into tears and with an instinct Marjorie found extremely uncomfortable she gathered Julia in her arms and cradled her, cooing soothing words to her and patting her gently like a child.

"Sister, I will stay with you as long as you need," she said and thought of Arthur.

The small group of Pairs moved quietly keeping to the shadows as much as they could. The dark Earth night made things extremely difficult, and in spite of the street lights they had trouble finding their way along the pavement. They split up at the junction of the alleyway and the street and two Pairs slipped into the darkness using as much of the light from the lamps as they could before switching on their torches. The remaining two Pairs moved carefully along the pavement to the front gate and slipped into the front yard. One Pair tried the door while the other stood in the dark waiting. Out back the other two Pairs negotiated the alleyway and the back gate, tromped across Julia's untidy back yard and closed on a lower floor window. Quietly they broke the glass and reached in to open the window. One Pair used a lever to break the security stays and quickly they climbed inside and spread throughout the house searching all the rooms upstairs and down. One Pair opened the street door and let their companions in. Within moments they discovered the house was empty.

"Nobody here!" said the Leader Pair and led the way out of the house and walked straight into a group of Chinese men who proceeded to beat them up.

What confused the Pairs was the strange noises the little men made in a language that was similar to their own as they delivered their painful blows. Within a few minutes the Pairs were subdued, tied hand and foot, bundled into the backs of scruffy brown vans, and laid on tightly packed boxes. The van doors were closed and with a crunch of gears, a revving engine, the click of a radio switch and the tune A Whiter Shade of Pale playing to them as they lay on the boxes the captives were kicked and trodden on by numerous feet. They had no idea where they were going, who the men were or that they were lying trussed up on a fortune in Tokens.

A few minutes after the vans left another van arrived, stopped, disgorged a group of workers carrying tools and window parts who descended on the Renfrew home. They fitted a new window pane, two more security stays and, leaving two of their number behind, dashed off again.

McCord trips up

McCord was aware that something was wrong when he slipped through the rear gate of his flat. The silent alarm indicator was open and although the hydraulic fire escape was still in place he knew that somebody was inside. He operated the fire escape and waited for it to stop, settle and stepped on to it walking soft shoed up the steps. He reached the top and from the side of the small balcony he peered through the window into the room. There was a shadow in the lounge but the kitchen was empty. He tried the door which opened quietly, and although he knew there would be little noise he was careful to hold the fittings and ease the door open shutting it quietly behind him as he stepped into the kitchen. He slipped into the main room and an instinct made him duck. He slipped sideways, turned and struck with the edge of his hand at soft flesh connecting with a crack. There was a gasp and in one continuous movement McCord turned and forced his assailant to the floor.

The young punk lay on his back his throat a purple mess, his eyes staring wide at nothing. He was dead.

"Shit, now I gotta get rid of the body."

He left the corpse where it was and checked the flat. It was obvious how the kid had got in. From the fire escape and through the window. But why? He searched the flat thoroughly and when he saw the mess in the kitchen he knew why.

"Bollocks, all the kid wanted was some grub."

He started the monitors and with a sigh he tapped in the number and tapped in a code.

"What do want McCord?"

"I have a stiff in my working flat. Can I have some cleaners."

"On their way but this had better be good."

"Oh it was, it was."

Again the connection was broken and methodically McCord shut down the monitors and returned them to record. He took pictures of the mess in the kitchen, the position of the body in the lounge the entry point plus some of the wound that had killed the punk and loaded them into his computer. He clicked onto 'send' and was satisfied that copies would now be in his control office. He cleaned up the kitchen, made coffee and sat beside his table reading a book ignoring the body in the lounge as if it were so much trash. Later when it was getting dark he cooked his meal and was partway through when the doorbell buzzed. He tapped the button.

"Who is it?"

"Dry cleaning."

He operated the camera and saw two men and behind them more or less parked in the street was the van marked as they all were with the legend 'Metropolitan Cleaning Services – Est. 1946' The date was a joke but the services they carried out were complete and thorough.

The man answered McCord's unspoken question.

"Mister Ponsonby at your service."

McCord let them up and watched as they slipped the corpse into a body bag, wrapped it in a long cardboard box and after a cheerful chat about the Zradian invasion, football, and some amusing anecdotes about the company, they left carrying the box down the stairs and into the van. McCord watched them go courtesy of the cameras and settled back into his routine. He switched the monitors back on and looked at the screens idly listening rather than watching and now and then bringing to the surface the window that showed him Dart and Drat's movements. Tight as a drum and no way in with Hicks' mob of animals guarding them.

And as he was almost ready to give up he saw the small item he was waiting for. There on the list was a function in a public place and that was what he needed. Dart and Drat were booked for a civil function after the next Presidential program on ETV. And what was better the jazz band, Con's Dixieland Stompers, were providing the musical entertainment. McCord played trombone and cornet under the name Harry Roy.

He called Con immediately.

"Do you want me for the ETV gig Con?"

"I was about to ask if you were available," Con replied. "As smart as and we will be doing a mix of trad and dance."

"Suits me Con. I will be there," he said cheerfully.

"Good man. The times and other info is on its way." Con said and with a cheerio he hung up.

McCord smiled to himself.

"Good, now I've got them."

He printed out the information and set up a plan on his white board and tacked sheets of paper to his cork board until he was satisfied.

"In and out and off like a robber's dog."

He calculated the expenses and set them against his earnings. He made a list of his needs and sent them through the system. Mostly he needed cash to pay for items and a list of codes for payments to his operatives. They were the group he was least likely to cheat knowing that if he did they would be after him and then it would be curtains. He had no illusions about his ability to beat people as mean as he was. The boss he could handle. Too soft.

He packed the gear away, and took his pistols from a drawer under the computer and carried them and the cleaning gear into the lounge. He switched on the television and while he watched the programs he laid out his weapons on the table and began to carefully dismantle first one and then the other making sure he had a loaded pistol resting beside him. He liked carrying guns. He liked the smack of a bullet into a body.

The television screen, showing a news program replete with its dancing rodents, showed a scene at Heathrow where the Zradians were held up and switched to the north where another army was marching into obscurity chased by the Scottish Highland regiment. All over the world the Zradians were fighting battles with mixed fortunes. In China there was a full scale war with the invaders trapped between the main Chinese armies and the forces of India and Pakistan who had agreed to bury their differences, not in each other, but spend the energy fighting the new invader. In America the Zradians were again attacking but this time there was no sudden rush to use Nukes. In Africa the Zradian forces were winning hands down and threatened to squeeze the Israelis and the Arab nations in a tight wad between the Sahara and India. In Europe the Germans and the Austrians were fighting small pockets that somehow seemed to be less able to make any headway. Australia suffered from an invasion that spread as far east as Melbourne and west to edge of the Nullabor racing to Perth and the River Swan. McCord didn't care much that there was a Japanese high command network trying to sort it out, nor did he care that he was ordered to eliminate the Aliens Dart and Drat or that his action would damage the war effort. He was getting paid a lot of money to carry out the task and left the political problems for his superiors to worry about. He did not even ask why Dart and Drat had to be eliminated. Somebody wanted them dead. It was up to him to make sure it was done.

"Bollocks to the bloody war effort." He said, leaving the television going and finished cleaning his weapons and with a ritual he enjoyed he cleaned the leather straps he used to carry his Browning and the body strap he used for the short nosed Smith and Wesson. He polished the leather and oiled the clips making sure that he could slip the weapons out quickly and smoothly without even thinking about where they were. He practiced the familiar routines until he could do it without even a noise that would alert anyone to what he was at.

On the umpteenth evolution he stopped and gasped as a face appeared on the screen and there was the punk he had killed. The face, the story and the sobbing father appealing for his son to come home. The grieving father appealing to the nation to find his boy. The little wanker was a rich man's son and he, McCord the great unsung hero of the nefarious side of UK intelligence, had done the bugger in.

"Shit, now that is something for the cleaners to think about."

The problem, he thought, was if somebody saw the punk hanging around his place. He thought, sod it, and carried on with his work. If anybody did see the kid there was no need for them to connect him with the brat but it would be best if he kept a watch on the locals.

The locals; that was his immediate neighbours, were hardly likely to bother about the dead boy but they were concerned about what their neighbour was doing. In fact they were aware that from him they could trace Dart and Drat's movements, and although they had not planned it that way they were glad of the data; glad too of the organisation McCord was putting into his arrangements.

"Neat," said the Leader Pair and smiled a sick smile that was picked up by the others to mean they too should be pleased.

"We monitor this Earthman and join in at the time. Do we waste the Bulger's breath or not?"

"When we have slaughtered Dart and Drat's party, yes," said the Leader Pair.

There was no laughter only the rustling of blades in sheaths and the slight cracking of joints as the Pairs rubbed their hands together in gleeful expectation. They settled down to sleep leaving a Pair on watch in rotation. They were on alien territory and therefore on active service so all precautions must be taken and yet they should be ready to spring in to action at a small period's notice. Their highly trained and finely tuned senses told them that this was the greatest adventure short of a civil massacre that a Dog Squad could undertake. They were keyed up and ready to take on the world, the rebels, the Polisocs, the Stormtroopers and any Nong dammed, Bulger smelling, mothers of Carnibeasts the enemy could hand them. Yes Sir!

Their only problem was that they couldn't see a bloody thing in the dark. However, in ten Earth days from now they were to go into action and the Earthman in the flat below them was going to show them the way. In the meantime there was the problem of J Renfrew (female) to solve.

"And by Nong we will solve it," said the Leader Pair softly and ground his teeth in the best Dog Squad fashion. The small group of highly trained and dangerous Pairs ground their teeth too, and Pair by Pair enjoyed the feeling of acting as one; angry as one; finely tuned as one, and totally lost.

Although the flat had been chosen for them by Pour and Roup and all their equipment had so lovingly been transferred to Earth the one item each Pair needed was a strong electric torch but that was the one item none could afford to use.

Luckily the function for Dart and Drat was scheduled for early evening and as long as they could be in place in time then all would be well. The next turn would reveal whether the spies would find Renfrew J (female) for them soon.

What they were unaware of was that not far from where they were hidden Julia was safely ensconced in a warm room with Tzu's household watching over her. Nor were they aware that Tzu's people were searching the airwaves for their transmissions assisted by a crazed robot wandering slowly through the jungles of Brazil searching for the Pair Clard and Dracl, its father/mother/brother/sister/ruler/maker/friend/enemy. Nor did they know that sitting in Star Station One the private detective Sherman Holmes was linked into the network the robot had created and, confused and convoluted as it was, had discovered the President's plot. In addition to being trained for his part in Blard the Barmy's immanent attack on Star Station Two, he was also passing on information to the New Moral few on Zrad. In fact Sherman Holmes was getting the hang of being off the bottle and enjoying his part in what he called the Invasion festivities. He looked forward to the coming action and welcomed the chance to help screw up the President's plans.

The Dog Squad Pairs knew nothing of all this but even if they had their concentration was such that they would dismiss it with a toss of their arrogant heads and utter a scoffing guffaw with the calculated intention of scaring their victims witless. That they were coming up against Colin Hicks and his men meant little to them accustomed as they were to their name being enough to frighten any Pair.

In his turn Colin himself, unaware of the impending doom prepared for him was alert for other reasons.

Denny Block had told him about the strange bloke who had moved into the flat further along the street.

"The geezer needs watching Colin," said Denny.

"Has he got any mates?"

"I don't fink so."

"Right then mate, keep me posted and there's a wad innit for you."

"But I ain't gonna go against what mister Best says,"

"That's all right Denny mate. I ain't gonna ask you to."

And at the moment when the Dog Squad were getting ready and McCord was making his own plans, Denny Block used the telephone in his room to let Colin know that McCord had used a cleaning service and was practising his music again. "Shall I go and duff him up Colin."

"Nah. McCord is a killing machine Denny. Blokes like you and Lugs don't stand a chance against him. Even me and my blokes wouldn't take him on without shooters. Leave him mate and keep that shit bag Best out of it too or your mister Best will find himself filling a wooden overcoat." Colin told Denny, and laughed when he heard the involuntary gasp of Donald Best who was listening in on the other telephone.

After he hung up Colin Hicks knew that whatever he did he had to be prepared for the after program function. As sure as eggs is eggs McCord was bound to have a go. Funny, he thought, how easy it is to trip up when you live sleazy the way McCord does.

And that beggared the question. Who was paying McCord?

The Gentleman who approved McCord's expenses and monitored his activities leaned back in his plush chair and tut-tutted. He held the flimsy paper in his left hand letting his right hover over the red button a few moments before pressing it. He gave it one press and waited for the security process to complete knowing that the delay was necessary and looked once more at the sheet. The voice when it spoke was quiet emanating not from the instrument on the desk but from the speaker in the right wing of his chair.

"Cleaners, how can we help?"

"I have a job for you. Listen. You made a collection, code 7431BLIntruder. I want a burn job done. Details on their way. Inform me when completed."

"Yes sir. What level?"

"Oh, high grade two."

"Yes sir."

"Oh, and a grade one termination. Again, details on their way."

"When sir?"

"Termination details will explain. The burn can be done anytime, but soon."

"Do I have a name for the grade one sir?"

"Yes, McCord. He made a mistake."

"Yes sir. It will be a pleasure sir."

"Thank you."

The conversation ended, the Gentleman placed the sheet in the shredder, watched the fragments swirl around before being sucked into the tube. The paper evidence at least was gone.

The Australian Connection

Brigadier Harry Chin gave the order to attack in the early hours of Thursday morning and watched the troops move off, and thought that the timing was perfect. Perfect because today was his birthday. He was thirty three and had reached a position his parents could have never expected of him. He had paid them a visit during his short leave and showed them his commission.

"I will be working with Japanese officers but I am in charge," he explained, embarrassed when their faces registered confusion and shock. It took most of the leave to explain to them what was happening. They seemed to understand. His mother smiled when he talked of Colonel Troy and cut in with a question.

"You marry this girl? She seems nice," she said.

His face glowed red with embarrassment.

"Maybe, how do I know? We have a war to fight," he replied, a little angrily and even more embarrassed when his mother smiled knowingly. To cover his confusion he explained again realising that their small world in the town of Nowra couldn't cope with interstellar invasions. He told them to watch the telly and look out for him.

"I will be leading the first assault but do not worry we have good weapons and this is our land. We are to be a free nation, a free world and no invader, from outer space, is going to take it away from us!" he said, and stood in his uniform blinking at them.

"You are Chinese," his father said.

"Australian first, then Chinese."

"For all that you are Chinese; a Chink, a Gook, a Rice Arse, Yellow Peril, Chinee, even a Wog to some. You don't belong here any more than the aliens or my father and his family. We are new people and this land you claim as your own is not yours."

"I am an Australian whether the Australians like it or not," Chin said, and left his father laughing as he went out. His mother hugged him and pressed a small charm gift into his hand, and as usual told him he was getting too thin. He hugged her and reassured her he would eat more and smiled to himself. He ate more than enough; army rations were designed for energy, and as he exercised regularly during training sessions he was never worried about his weight.

"And don't forget to ask that girl to marry you," his mother said.

His ears were still burning when he climbed into the car that arrived to collect him. He waved to them as they stood watching the car disappear. Beside him Helen smiled and said: "Welcome back sir."

He looked at her and laughed.

"What's that for?" she said.

"Something my mother said that I have to do," he said, and grinned broadly.

But here in the early morning gloom before the sun was due to rise the action he had been waiting for began. The assault on Melbourne began with a simple command.

"Go for it," he said.

The noise of the advance although comparatively quiet could be heard all around him as vehicles hummed along the road behind his and on his flanks. Chin imagined the vehicles in a fan using every track they could find to converge on the western and northern outskirts of Melbourne. In his command entourage there were his own officers and a Japanese General Officer who kept his rank insignia out of sight as much as he could and spoke excellent English but let his own small staff work through interpreters to Chin's staff. It looked like a complicated arrangement but in fact it left Chin and the Japanese Officer free space to make proper fighting decisions. The arrangement meant that they had flexible control over the troops without having to clear their orders through Sydney, the current headquarters of the Australian High Command.

In that first dark hour the armed forces attacked the invading Zradian forces with a demonstration of accurate fire that set them buzzing like a swarm of wasps. The wasps buzzed back, unable at first to see their enemy but by the time daylight had arrived and the sun began burning the live and the dead alike the Zradians realised that the Australian forces were too strong. The Zradian Leader Pair ordered a withdrawal and immediately regretted their decision. The Australians attacked with aircraft and backed that up with fire from their land wagons. As soon as the air strike was over the troops moved in on foot and attacked using the new Kamaguchi weapon that matched the Zradian gun, and in better hands drove the invaders back even further.

Chin's forces clattered through the streets pushing the bewildered invaders to the dockside. Zrat and Traz led the remnants of their army to the waterside and immediately ordered a carapace to be erected.

"Take defensive positions on the perimeter. I want all Leader Pairs to report their status," said Zrat while Traz quietly gathered a group of trusted Troopers around what was to be their temporary command post. They had hatched a plan to leave the Polisocs and the Stormtroopers holding the Bulger pup and intended to slip off to sea. Traz had suggested they opt out of the war.

"Why so my twin?"

"According to my Atlas projection we are going to lose and I think it is better to die with the planet than fighting against it. You never know, but we might survive if we disappear and hide," said Zrat and added that as far as he knew some Zradian troops had already done so.

Traz looked at the figures and he had to agree.

"What's the plan?"

"We select friendly Pairs, plenty of food and weapons and we take off across the ocean. My Atlas tells me there is a land across the water where we can hide in the forest. But we need some loyal Pairs to arrange it for us while we pretend to fight the locals, my twin," Zrat said and grinned.

"And with a bit of luck we can get out of here until the war is over?" said Zrat.

Dutifully they fought their enemy and directed that the outer rim Pairs lay out an ambush for the flying machines. They ordered the outer wagons to divide into two task forces. The first to fight the ground forces and the second to attack the enemy vehicles and instantly fight the flying machines. The Leader Pairs of task force two were to keep a watch on the air and send out electronic signals to intercept them as they flew in. The ploy worked and the very next attack they destroyed several and cut their own losses. Their success encouraged the Polisoc Leader Pair to call on Zrat and Traz with a plan.

"We are of the opinion that it is time to break out. We will call base for reinforcements?"

"Why not? If you wish to, please be our guest, but remember that so far we have no means of connecting up with them unless they can form up quickly and head this way with a massive relief column. This crowd have weapons as good as ours," said Zrat ignoring the Polisoc Leader Pair's disapproving look.

"Have you a plan?" persisted the Polisoc Leader Pair.

Zrat looked at their eager faces and as calmly as he could he gave them a verbal plan making it up as he went and added that he and his twin would immediately confirm it in writing.

"So we simply break out north and west and leave the eastern perimeter to be defended by the troops already in place." Zrat said and waited for them to leave.

"Is that it?" said the Polisoc Leader Pair looking somewhat miffed.

"Yes, that's all, now shove off and attack the enemy while we arrange for reinforcements," said Zrat and shooed them off with his hands. And so bemused were they that they turned, stomped their feet and with due obedience to protocol marched off to execute their orders.

To give them their due Zrat and Traz called up Star Station Two and asked for help. They arranged for the transfer drop and explained exactly what they needed to continue with. Pour and Roup's team dutifully took their request and processed it correctly and within a period they received a reply. Zrat and Traz read it and shook their heads.

"One Troop, two squads of wagons, supplies for same and a message of encouragement and that's it," said Traz.

"So our plan of escape is on then?" said Zrat.

"It sure is and I have arranged for our amphibious wagon to be Paired by trusted Pairs. We leave at dark."

"We have only one wagon?"

"For us yes with a group of Pairs loyal to us and three other wagons with Pairs who support us. All Pongos."

"Good, that will mean one hundred and fifty Pairs all told?"

"Yes and supplies to match."

"In that case we had better send this plan to the Polisoc Leader Pair and make it look good. We should tell them there will be reinforcements on their way. Perhaps they can send a guide patrol to meet up with them. We will also give them the extra fire power they need and that will keep them happy for at least a turn."

Zrat laughed and quietly tapped the data into the Comsec and watched it disappear into the system.

The moon was high when the four wagons eased off from the Melbourne Ferry wharf and slipped out across the Bass Straight heading for the Tasman sea. They passed Tasmania in the early hours of the morning and wobbled into the cold ocean amazed at the vast empty water that glistened brightly in the early morning sun. The wagons sped across the ocean skimming the waves as easily as they skimmed the rocks and stones on their home planet. That was until a storm blew up sometime after mid day and they were subjected to the onslaught of huge breakers that rolled onto each other and tossed their vessels around like tubs. Those Pairs who were the least affected by the seas managed to keep the wagons on the surface but that was all. Most Pairs wallowed in the scuppers and vomited, begging Nong to take them to their deaths. Some managed to remain more or less upright and with great difficulty succeeded in securing most of their supplies and equipment.

The storm lasted only a short time but the following high seas created a problem for Zrat and Traz. Not only did they not know where they were, having to guess as much as Abel Tasman himself where the land lay, they lost sight of the rest of the vessels.

"We have lost our friends," said Zrat, greenly.

"Should we set beacons?" asked Traz and nearly vomited as he spoke.

"If we want to find them. Shall we go below and set them up?"

Zrat nodded and with great trepidation they dropped through the hatch and alighted on the driving deck. The Driver Pair looked at them with a cheerful grin but wisely did not offer them any of their refreshments.

"You are wishing us to set beacons for the rest of our wagons?" the Pair said and shifted position to allow one to guide and the other to tap the data into the system. Traz nodded.

The main screen flashed and showed first a series of dancing rodents and then a pretty display of bouncing kittens that vanished to give way to a clear screen with a central point and three moving points heading in three different directions.

"Activating beacon now."

They watched the screen for many short periods and noted that all three points slowly turned to converge on their projected course. Zrat was the first to remark on the obvious.

"How far are they away from us?"

The Half Pair on the console tapped some keys and a series of figures highlighted by a dancing mouse rolled down the screen. A lolloping Rabbit carried three final figures to each point and with soft white paws expanded each one in turn. In a cartoon voice that was unfamiliar to either of the Pairs but one that many Earth people would recognise the rabbit explained the details.

Wagon one is six hundred and fifty kilometres north, wagon two is seven hundred and eighty kilometres south and wagon three is nine hundred kilometres south and a little west, oh boy! Convergence point at eleven hundred kilometres east and north so watch out you dummies! Oh boy!

The rabbit disappeared to be replaced with a diagram that showed where the three wagons were likely to meet up.

"What was that?" asked the driver pair.

"It's a cartoon character much liked by the Americans and the Australians called Wodger Wabbit," explained Zrat shrugging his shoulders, "They seem to like it."

"Oh, strange."

Zrat managed a weak laugh.

"Keep the beacon running. We will have contact after dark so I want all Pairs to remain alert," said Zrat and helped Traz to a vacant seat where the Pair sat until the cook Pair announced there was a meal ready. By that time the screen was projecting that in less than three periods the four wagons should meet up. The sea was calmer and Zrat and Traz found that food was welcome and ate the simple meal. As they sat the communications Pair turned and said together.

"Your Honour, there is news from Star Station Two."

"Tell us, tell us," snapped Zrat.

"Pour and Roup have just welcomed the arrival of Star Station Three and the President has announced that within ten turns the battle for Earth will be over."

Zrat and Traz visibly paled and while his twin leaned against him in despair Zrat gazed at the Communications Pair who also looked frightened, and gathered his thoughts. This was a new and horrible development. Deserting when the battle was lost was fine but when your own people suddenly came up with a new and bold plan for success defection would mean certain death. But Zrat was made of stone not plastic and once set on a logical course he was hardly likely to give up.

"Do not despair my twin. The projection still holds. The battle here is doomed. We are committed and while we are on the water we are out of harms way. We keep going. We can hide in the bush for many four hundreds disguised as natives if we have to. We need details before we react." Zrat said, and was pleased when the communications Pair turned back to their task and tapped in a query. Within a few small periods Zrat and Traz held a small sheaf of flimsies in their hands and were busy reading.

The information was comprehensive and with a look of concentration on their faces they huddled over their Atlas and tapped in calculations and waited for the message to appear. Zrat sighed with relief when he read it and for the benefit of his twin he scrolled it again.

"So we still lose," said Traz.

"Yeah and now all we have to do is let the rest know and carry on," said Zrat happily. "I will send a message immediately."

The message he sent to the other three vehicles was worded with optimism, laced with threats and larded with flattery.

To all Pairs –

In spite of recent developments our estimation of the expected outcome of the invasion remains the same. It may take a little longer but as you are aware the President cannot afford to destroy planet Earth and with the advent of a great rebel movement beginning at home there is little chance the situation will change overmuch. We have to remind you that as we are already earmarked for execution, we are non-persons. Any rebellion or attempt to return to the invading army will be foolish and fatal. You are brave and heroic for realising that we are fighting a lost cause and that you are all doubly heroic for taking such a positive stand against the corruption of the Polisocs and the President's forces. We salute you for your courage and we are happy to have such a well trained, well balanced and supportive group of Pairs as our friends and supporters. We humbly request that we be allowed to lead you onward and eventually to victory over the oppressor.

Zrat and Traz High Leader Pair 23rd Pongos.

The response to their message was predictable but at least it was positive and the three Leader Pairs on the other wagons, knowing where their dead Bulger was likely to lie, pledged their loyalty. And so the four wagons, with their load of fighting Pairs raced across the Tasman Sea toward the wild western coast of New Zealand's South Island.

Sometime during that night a slight miscalculation turned the wagons a little further north and as the second morning broke bright and fresh land loomed ahead and to the south east. It was a long low land of glittering sand and flax covered dunes. It curved from a rocky cape where two oceans met to an equally rocky cliff a distance of eighty kilometres. Along the length of the shining sands the sun glinted on the polished painted metal and glass of hundreds of vehicles and warmed the eager lines of fishermen who waded into the surf with long rods and bait trying to catch the largest fish. The prize was worth more than the proffered four-wheel drive vehicle, rods, clothing and cash to the winner. It was not the cash, the vehicle, or the other goodies but the prestige of catching the biggest Snapper of the contest.

The Zradians, unaware of the competition or indeed that they were not about to approach the remote Fiordland coast but the famous Ninety Mile beach on the west coast of the North Island, headed for the beach. They hit it at slow speed and switched to land mode as the water disappeared under their hulls and swerved to avoid the panicking fishermen and women who rushed hither and thither not knowing whether to save their vehicles, their fishing lines or themselves. The result was chaotic, and with the instinct of many Ninety Mile Beach users the Zradians found the slip road from the beach and went looking for a place to stop and regroup. They found Kaitaia where the lead wagon slid to a halt.

"The power is down," said the Driver Pair. "The sea journey sucked most of it. We need to repose."

A short time later the other three wagons rumbled to a halt, and like the leading wagon they too were exposing their charging panels.

"It will take at least a full turn to re-charge, so we will have to stop here for a while Pairs," announced Zrat and was about to give orders when from all directions vehicles filled with angry residents and fishers came racing into the town. At all points the vehicles came to a halt and men piled out, some with powder weapons and others with sharp blades or sticks and others with jack handles, spades and axes. All were ready to do battle and for the first time in their lives as Zradian Pongos Zrat and Traz were unwilling to fight.

The locals gathered in a circle and one man in a uniform stepped out from the rest and nervously walked toward Zrat and Traz. He came to a slow stop about two metres from them and with a muttered order to the other Leader Pairs to put up their weapons Zrat and Traz advanced a pace and bowed politely.

"Zrat and Traz of the twenty third Zradian Pongos, er, how can we help you?" said Zrat feeling slightly silly.

The uniformed local looked startled and nervously adjusted his pants in his belt with his thumbs and fingers and looked from one to the other and then at the troops standing in Pair formation behind them before he spoke.

"Yeah, well, er, youse jokers created a bit of strife back there. I dunno but I reckon I'm gonna have a hard time stopping this mob from wringing yer bloody necks. Your blokes hadn't oughter cruised up the beach like that and buggered off without stopping ter sort out the bloody mess," the man said, and squinted at them adjusting his hat against the glare of the sun. "Whaddya reckon?"

Zrat and Traz were at a loss to answer the man having no idea what he wanted and both spread their hands and looked puzzled.

"I'm sorry but we had no idea," said Zrat trailing off and feeling inadequate. He knew that his troops could fry the locals with their weapons but he had the idea that it might be better for his Pairs if he tried to work with them.

"We come in peace," said Zrat feeling even more silly than he did before.

"Yeah?"

"Yes. We escaped from the land you call Australia," said Traz.

"Illegal immigrants," the uniformed man said.

"No, we want to surrender to somebody but the Australians don't seem to want to know. We're fed up with fighting," said Zrat.

"Is that right?"

"Yes."

"Then Whaddya mean by stuffing up our fishing contest then eh?"

"Your what?"

"Fishing contest. We have a bloody fishing contest every bloody year and there ain't nothing gonna stop it, that is until youse jokers come flying outer the Tasman and buggered up about a quarter of our lines. That mob behind me are bloody furious."

"We didn't know anything about it," said Zrat feeling confused as well as silly.

"Jeez mate, it's been advertised all over. Typical bloody Aussies, no idea?"

"We're not Aussies, we are Zradians and we want to surrender," said Zrat desperately.

"Yeah, right, well you had better shift yer wagons then. You block the streets too long and ain't nobody gonna get past."

"For Nong's sake all we want to do is give up!" shouted Traz.

"Yeah but you gotta shift them wagons first and if them weapons ain't licensed you gotta give them up."

Zrat looked at Traz and Traz looked at Zrat and their eyes glazed over. Slowly they moved to the side of their wagon and with a low howl of anguish they lifted their legs and began to urinate.

The uniformed man followed them and with a face as grim as a Dog Squad soldier he grabbed them with one hand each and shook them free of the wagon.

"Hey you can't do that in public! I gotta take you in," he said, and with a deft movement he handcuffed them both and led them toward a low wooden building set on the corner of a side road and the main street. The building was marked with the legend 'New Zealand Police' and as the Pair were led toward it another uniformed man addressed the mob telling them to keep back. Zrat and Traz heard yet another uniformed man order his Leader Pairs to shift the wagons as they were led into the watch house charge room. They heard the wagons start up winding slowly out of the road as they used up the residue of their power.

It took Zrat and Traz nearly a whole period to convince the Police officer that they really did want to surrender. At last when the officer allowed them to leave the building the Pair crossed the silent street and explained to their Pairs what was required.

"We have agreed to surrender to the New Zealand Government forces but first we have to put right the damage we've done. It's all very confusing," said Zrat but as he spoke he realised that he felt relieved.

Somebody else was responsible for them now.

Brigadier Chin gazed on the destruction the Zradians had wreaked on Melbourne as calmly as he could manage. It was only a city; it could be rebuilt. Whether the trams could be replaced, or the residents would come to terms with growing new gardens, and losing the bridge that had cost lives to build and the damage to the waterfront, both residential and commercial remained to be seen.

He looked at the ruined buildings, blackened and burnt by the plasma fire that belied the image of a city that was as thriving as Melbourne was before the invasion. Houses in the suburbs were burning and although the troops were waging a fire fighting war on the flames there was little they could do other than contain the damage and let most of the homes die under the fires. Their major concern was mopping up the Zradians and cutting a track around the city to stop a massive bush fire.

The first attack ground to a halt but they had driven the Zradian forces onto the wharves and forced them to battle it out. Amazingly the first day and a half of fighting had resulted in an almost complete encirclement of the Zradians but on the fourth day of the battle the Zradians broke out and forced a corridor for a retreat west to Ballarat. General Chin's forces cut the retreat off before they got to Ballarat and simultaneously attacked both enemy forces. Chin ordered air strikes and listened as the Japanese officers happily coordinated them and reported the effect with great glee.

"Boom, boom! Airplanes give them heaps!"

Chin laughed and ordered his troops to follow up. He listened to the individual commanders calling up air support and watched the battle unfold on the screen as the situation reports were evaluated and entered into the system.

"Colonel Troy what is the state of play? What do you think we should do?" he said.

"I think we should stonk them once more and then we can go in and mop them up. Their western forces seem to be stopped in their tracks. We can move in on them as soon as Melbourne is secured. Does that sound right?" she said and grinned. "Sir."

The Japanese advisors looked at them, puzzled..

"Do you advise a further air attack," Chin said, to the advisor.

"Oh yes, give them bloody rice," the grinning Japanese officer said. "And then crush them between two jaws. We win battle for Melbourne."

Brigadier Chin and Colonel Troy watched the battle develop on the screen and as the Japanese advisor had predicted the Zradians were crushed and whatever reinforcements they had ordered up were destroyed and Chin was able to hold a line west of Ballarat.

In the air above Melbourne as they headed west to find the enemy, the pilots of the Australian airforce were coming to terms with fighting alongside their Japanese counterparts. In the two rushed weeks they had before engaging with the Zradians they were ordered to make way for a few flights of Japanese aircraft. The Nipponese craft flew in from aircraft carriers and landed in Canberra. Above the capital city the two forces practised communications and formation flying. Some Australians flew the Japanese aircraft and some Japanese pilots flew the Australian craft and in the two brief weeks forged a strange bond that went beyond historical memory. Both nationalities were aware that the history of their aircraft, the one American made and the other Japanese, took them back to the Pacific war of nineteen forty one. Both sides appreciated that Grumman and Mitsubishi were equally good fighting craft and settled down to win the war against the Zradians, and to do so they solved some language problems and ignored others.

In the last attack, the final stonk on the enemy outside Melbourne, an Australian pilot called his Japanese counterpart.

"Ichiban fifteen degrees left Nippon ichisan."

The Japanese answer came immediately.

"Aussie ichisan a-okay."

The flight dropped to the target at a shallow angle to their left and fired the Kamaguchi cannons at the enemy wagons and troops and overflew at a rapidly increasing angle to turn and make another attack.

"Got the bastards!"

"Bruddy oaf."

And so on as the day progressed the Zradian troops were battered from the air and the ground; there was no mercy until the Zradians themselves ceased firing back and resorted to hand to hand fighting. Their soldiers were good but their swords were no match for the foot soldiers' guns and machines. The Zradian wagons failed and their weapons ran out of pods and so the skirmishes were reduced to chasing the enemy from the buildings and out to the ever decreasing circle on the outskirts of Melbourne. Those Zradian supplies that did manage to appear were immediately confiscated by the Australians and put to their own use. The few troops to arrive were either captured or killed according to their reactions.

Captain Stapalopolous marched his men through the western suburbs cleaning out pockets of resistance and driving the enemy inexorably on toward Ballarat. He stopped for a break at mid day to allow the prisoners to be sent back and for the men and women of his company to have some lunch. He stopped in a clear street where most of the dwellings were either intact or only lightly damaged and set up the kitchens. With a plate of food and some hot coffee resting on somebody's garden table he sat back and relaxed in the warm sunshine. In the distance he could see the smoke from fires rising in dark columns and now and then the rush of plasma fire or the crack of a rifle.

Crack of a rifle?

Bullets whistled past his head.

He ducked and caught the flash of fire from a large garden shed two houses down the slope. He saw the old man peer out the window and called out to his troops.

"Hold your fire!"

Bullets whistled past them but everyone was under cover with their plasma guns aimed at the shed.

"Somebody give me a horn!"

One was handed to him almost immediately and from the corner of his command wagon he faced the shed and put the horn to his mouth.

"You in the shed! Hold your fire! This is Captain Stapalopolous of the Australian Army. Come out with your hands on your head or we will roast you alive! Throw your rifle down at the door and come out slowly!"

"Fuck off you four eyed bastards!" came the answer backed up by a bullet that ricocheted off the top of the wagon.

Captain Stapalopolous lowered the horn and spoke to his first lieutenant.

"Set the shed alight."

"Yes sir!"

A sergeant fired a thin line of plasma at the shed stopping when the shed itself was burning. From within came shouting and clattering and the old man came out, dropped his rifle to the ground and stood outside the door with his hands on his head.

"Move away from the weapon!" called out Stapalopolous through the horn, and while his men grabbed the old man and frog marched him out of the garden others doused the flames using the company fire unit.

The old man was presented to Stapalopolous as he continued with his interrupted lunch and made to stand between his two escorts while the Captain finished his nearly cold coffee.

"Why did you shoot at us?"

"I thought you was them aliens. Youse got the same guns as them."

"We could have killed you."

"I would have gorn down fighting mate, bloody oath yes." The old man licked his lips and eyed the remains of Stapalopolous' lunch and groaned. "Reckon youse kin git me a bit o' tucker, me guts is as empty as the Nullabor. I ain't had a proper bite fer days."

Captain Stapalopolous grinned and called for some food and drink and let the old boy sit in the sun to eat. "Somebody find his rifle and the ammunition and let the old joker enjoy his tucker." A few minutes later a wagon pulled up in the street to disgorge a Brigadier and some of his staff.

"Attention!" barked the sergeant major and all but the old man immediately obeyed.

Where do they learn to do that, thought the Captain, rigid to attention himself.

"As you were," said Chin and approached the table where the old man was staring at the officers, with a piece of bread and cheese partway to his open mouth.

"Bugger me! Fucking Nips!" he said and dropped the bread and cheese.

Chin glared at him and turned to Stapalopolous for an explanation and waited for the Captain to speak.

"I met the gentleman when we were trying to evacuate the citizens before the invasion sir. When we stopped here he was shooting at us. It seems he has a long memory of his grandfather in world war two, sir. I shall arrest him," he said and looked wistfully at the old man as if he were claiming the first chance to interrogate him.

"Leave him and find us some lunch Captain. The headquarters cook house is up ahead somewhere. The old man can finish his dinner and then somebody had better take him out of here," said Chin, and he and the Japanese advisors took the proffered places at the table where the old man sat.

"The Japanese officers are on our side," said Chin puzzled by the old man's reaction.

"You mean you lot are fighting for us red blooded Australians. They ain't invaded good old Oz?"

"Nope, they are here to help. I'm Brigadier Chin in charge of the relief of Melbourne. Brigadier Chin of the Australian Army," Chin said and glanced at Helen Troy as she approached with a sheaf of messages.

"So we're not all going into concentration camps then," the old man said and glanced sideways at the Japanese officers.

"Never crossed our minds," said one Japanese officer, "we are here to defeat the invaders and leave."

"Jeez mate, then what are all them compounds doing over there then?" the old man said and pointed to the north and east over the houses.

General Chin stared at the mess and his face showed unaccustomed emotion. He was angry, very angry and when he gave the order that all Polisoc Zradians found alive were to be brought to the compound it was obeyed. He showed them the small but angry mob of citizens who stood nearby and explained to them that their task was to clean up the dead and lay them out and do anything that the soldiers asked or he would let the mob have them, one by one.

The red and black clad Stormtroopers did as they were told and when he and his headquarters wagon set off to chase the Zradians west of Ballarat he was determined to show no mercy unless the enemy begged for it. The exception he was prepared to make was to the Pongos; the confused ordinary soldiers who were brow beaten by the more fanatical Zradian troops. He had learned of the defection of the High Leader Pair out to sea and had accepted the surrender on their behalf of the Pongos by the Pair named Draz and Darz whose command of English had saved their soldiers from complete destruction.

From the Pair he had learned of the divisions in the Zradian army and with this knowledge he had quickly brought the enemy to their knees. He drove a wedge between the Polisocs, Stormtroopers and the Pongos and leaving the Pongos alone he had concentrated on the others. As a result all the Pongos in the region surrendered immediately Australian troops arrived. As for the Polisocs and Stormtroopers whenever they attempted to surrender the Australians said a collective 'no bloody way' and mowed them down with their new and powerful plasma weapons.

As one Lieutenant explained to his Captain.

"They's just like rabbits sir. Too many of the bastards."

And it was true of the troops they still had to fight that had retreated beyond Victoria to South Australia. It seemed that the forces heading for Perth had come up against determined local opposition and now that the main thrust east had failed, the Zradian army leaders had decided to consolidate. Chin's assessment was correct, but the reason was because the transfer system worked in the area around Port Augusta and Port Pirie forcing the Zradians to concentrate on the western section of South Australia.

It also meant that Adelaide bore the brunt of the invasion.

Star Station One

Sherman Holmes sat comfortably in his floating chair and dangled the flimsy in front of Blard the Barmy rubbing it between his thumb and forefinger enjoying the low level squeak the plastic made against his skin.

"That's what I found in my slot. My source seems to think that we need to know the new location. The Bomb is armed and ready and the Rodent Robot has either lost the plot or lost control over the bomb," he said and grinned. "Read the flimsy. Oh, and I've got some news for you two buggers from my source," added Holmes."

"Oh, and what..." Fish

"... can that be?" Bates.

Holmes grinned showed them the screen reading out the message: "Tell your two friends, Bates... rodent free... rodent friendly... and Fish, they are now Detectives. Beware the ides of incompetence ... we are not afraid of the buckets ... best Wishes, Inspector C."

"Oh good..." Fish

"...we always wanted to be..." Bates

"Detectives...?" Holmes finished for them.

Bates and Fish looked at Holmes and pointedly read the flimsies whilst he gazed at them from the food bar watching them mutter as they read.

Sergeant Orange, still struggling to control his chair, spun twice, turned sideways and crashed into the wall and swore profusely. "I'll never get the hang of these damn things." He jumped off the chair and crashed to the floor as the chair, bereft of its burden, pushed into him and tried to get under his butt to help carry him to his destination however short the journey. Everybody stared at him as he lay sprawled on the floor with the chair hovering dutifully above him.

"Pride and fall courtesy of C&D enterprises, we aim to serve you at every opportunity," said Bradl and giggled uncontrollably as Sergeant Orange attempted to stand. The chair nudged him each time he managed to raise his heavy body on all fours and knocked him back down again.

On the fourth attempt Bates and Fish moved as a Pair and with deft touches on the outside controls lowered the chair so that Sergeant Orange could sit in it from the all fours position and shoved him in it.

"Try walking with your feet..." began Fish

"... flat on the floor and ..." said Bates

"...and sort of wobble your..." continued Fish

"...fat arse and lean back..." explained Bates

"...as if you are riding a..." said Fish

"...Harley Fat Bob," finished Bates.

As they explained what to do the two detectives arranged Sergeant Orange in the chair and shoved him off watching with great amusement as he headed directly for a wall and came to a halt.

"Okay, if you don't want to ..." started Fish

"...join us," said Bates joining his partner in a shrug.

Blard and Bradl almost fell off their own chairs laughing and with a sense of duty Holmes rolled over to the trapped Sergeant and gently eased his chair across the room to join them.

"We missed you," said Holmes.

"Stuff it Holmes," said Sergeant Orange and glowered at everybody.

"I think that now our mister Plod has joined us at last we should get on with the planning. You all know the layout of the Star Stations now, and as we have discovered from mister Holmes' crazy contact there is a new Star Station in place and the Bomb itself is locked in position. We have received two sets of locators and all we have to do is place them on the Star Stations. That is the plan and to do it we will have Bradl with Bates and Fish who for many reasons do not wish to be separated, placing a locator on Star station Three. Holmes, Sergeant Orange and myself will do the deed on Star Station Two. All I ask is that in addition to setting the receivers both teams create mayhem wherever they go, and mostly on the Polisocs. We will be armed with everything and you have our permission to use it," said Blard with a grin.

"The transfer port codes will get us out of trouble will they?" asked Sergeant Orange.

"Yep, providing you get to one," replied Blard.

"When do we go?" asked Fish.

Blard, Bradl, Holmes and Sergeant Orange waited for Bates to speak. Bates merely began a shrug and Fish finished it off. Bradl quietly laid out a set of weapons on a low floating bench and when he had them arranged neatly he named them. He spoke quietly with a relish for his task that was obvious.

"Knife for slitting throats and slashing at close quarters; sword for killing as you have been shown; gas gun for stunning; short cosh; marble grenades and incendiary grenades for effect. You will find these useful to slow down your enemy. Throwing blades for terror attacks; short plasma gun with a rack of capsules for maximum damage. Electronic decoder for Blard and myself and a pack of rations plus a water bottle. You find what you can until you need the rations. As far as we know there will be patrols on the look out for us when we flip out of the Star Stations so we should not need to dive into the rations," Bradl said and added. "There's one kit each and you all know how to use them."

"Yeah, great," said Holmes and laughed when Bates and Fish rubbed their hands together in glee. "When do we start?"

"We flip off as soon as we have gotten all of us kitted up. The Pairs in the lab have tested the receivers and they are ready for us to use. Note also that when we set them if they are found and removed from their locations they will self destruct, and that is useful to us because when our forces win and defeat the President we may not have to neutralise them, which will save a lot on Star Stations," said Blard. "In the meantime the avengers will have a last meal and then we are off."

Bradl led them into an ante-room where there was a meal and a long low table with four sets of weapons laid out. They all moved on foot leaving their chairs hovering dutifully by the console, much to the relief of Sergeant Orange, and at the portal they changed into fighting dress. They ate and then began the solemn task of kitting up each helping the other until they were all satisfied that everything was as it should be.

Nervous but excited the Earthmen lined up outside the transfer ports and waited as Blard and Bradl conferred briefly with the Pairs on duty and then they walked into ports opposite each other in their groups and waved as the doors slid shut.

"Here we..." said Fish

"...go," said Bates and with a feeling of momentary disorientation that lasted only until the doors opened they were flipped across space and, so Fish assumed, time. But then Bates could not be sure. All they knew was that as soon as they arrived Bradl was urging them out into the pristine corridors. The corridors were empty and Bradl was pleased to see they had landed in sector yellow which was mostly served by robots designed to handle goods. Zradians had never devised fighting robots; not because of any ethical reasons but simply because they liked to do the fighting themselves.

"We look for a telephone booth," he said and grinned. "It is a joke."

Bates and Fish giggled.

Blard, Holmes and Sergeant Orange slipped out of the port and into the bay. It was dark and messy and had a smell of burnt plastic and a faint odour of rodents. Something glowed faintly in a side bay and with curiosity born of wanting to know what was likely to hurt him, Blard signalled Holmes to guard the bay and Sergeant Orange to stand by while he investigated. He moved to the bay quietly and peered around the shattered edge where the wall was split and burned. Inside, on the floor with booby trap lines leading to some rather nasty looking anti-personnel mines was a large impact bomb. It was one of those that when triggered shot along a central rail driven by a small linear motor powered by induction that crashed into the nearest obstruction. This was the bulkhead of the next cargo bay and Blard guessed that inside that there was a store of plasma capsules.

"Holmes? Will you come here a moment," he said, and when Holmes arrived he said. "What was that you said about the mad robot?"

"I said all sorts of things. The creature was crazy," said Holmes.

"It was obsessed with rodents right?"

"Right."

"And I smell rodents."

"So do I".

"And it did not want Pour and Roup to follow it, right?"

"True."

"And right there in that bay is a bomb, right?"

"What are you getting at?"

"That there bomb is meant to destroy the Star Station."

"And so we are redundant?"

"No, because judging by the plastic smell and the burnt trigger system it seems that something has gone wrong. There are booby traps but with my decoder I can disconnect them for a while. I would like to have a look at the bomb. Can you warn the good sergeant to keep alert. You stay here and back him up while I have a look," said Blard.

Blard released his decoder from its pouch and aimed it in turn at the mines, and then with hardly a break in his stride he approached the bomb. He brushed the top and with a grin pulled something black and thin out of the mess of burnt plastic and carried it out to Holmes.

"A dead rat."

"Oh, what is it doing?"

"Not a lot but it has totally buggered the trigger. It seemed to have created an involuntary organic bridge between two sets of terminals and neutralised the system. The bomb is inoperable.

"What do you mean?"

"It got fried when it tried to eat the cables."

"And melted the system?"

"Precisely, and with a little jiggling around I can create a back up and link it to the Doomsday bomb," said Blard. "Keep watch and let the good Sergeant know what's happening."

Blard casually wandered to the bomb and gently laid the body of the rat on the plastic cover and immediately started to work on the mess of burned out cables. Holmes slipped back behind the wall to where Sergeant Orange was standing with his gun at the ready.

"All right Sarge?"

"Yes, nothing happening so far. This place is a bit manky isn't it?"

"I think it is an abandoned cargo hold."

"What's Blard doing?"

Holmes told him and Sergeant Orange grinned.

"Quite a scrapper that one. I like the bloke, him and his twin are raving ratbags but they have a sense of purpose that I like. When I get back to Earth I'm going to give up coppering and go in for creating mayhem. I might become a private dick like you. My boss is an arsehole and most of my squad haven't a bleedin' clue. I've learned more in these few weeks that I ever did in the force," said Sergeant Orange with a hint of wistfulness.

"And end up drunk and disorderly like me?"

"Nah, I'll start a proper agency and get some of the thugs on my side; run a bouncer service and a private army if I have to; get lawyers in as well. Even do escort duty," Sergeant Orange said and looked at Holmes who stared at him open mouthed.

"You thought all this through?"

"Sure, I saw a business I wouldn't mind taking over just off the Bywater Road close to the river. General and Services it was called. I would buy that if it were for sale."

"I might be able to help you there," said Holmes, and thought about Hermoine and her lad Oliver. Young Norman Oliver Braine could well do with a buyer for his business, and that might set him up as an artist like he wants to be, thought Holmes and grinned. Might even go into it meself, he added.

Sergeant Orange was about to ask more questions but Blard returned and they were off again.

"We fix the receiver in the next bay and with a bit of luck I may be able to link it up with the bomb next door," Blard said.

The next bay was a small one but on one wall it had a telephone booth, and while Blard carefully bridged the cables to keep it operative Sergeant Orange and Holmes remained on guard. Blard opened the box cover and with deft movements inserted the receiver, connected it and took his decoder from its pouch. He took a pace or two back and as if he were channel chopping aimed the end of the instrument at the receiver. An LED on one end flashed red, green, red and then remained steady at green and almost imperceptibly the tune A Whiter Shade of Pale tinkled gently in the bay. Blard closed the cover, sealed it and turned to his companions with a grin.

"We are now ready to create some strife."

"Do we have to?" said Sergeant Orange.

"For propaganda purposes. To give the President a poke in the eye," said Blard. "And tie up some troops, as well as make the bulger nervous."

"Okay," said Sergeant Orange.

Holmes simply grinned and fingered the buttons on his gun.

In Star Station Three Bradl stood back from the telephone booth and activated the receiver. He closed the cover and with a look of satisfaction he turned to Bates and Fish who were standing on guard like book ends, and nodded.

"We can now go and find a port to leave by or we can do some fighting on the way. I would prefer to do some fighting," he said and raised an eyebrow.

"I think that..." said Fish

"...would be a good idea," said Bates.

"Then follow me gentlemen to at least a few levels up. We will take the elevator. "

He led them to a portal and dabbed the pad. The portal opaqued, cleared and they stepped in. Three Pairs of Polisoc troopers gaped at them, and with a whoop of delight Bradl leapt at them with his knife followed by Bates and Fish with theirs. The fight was sharp and short; sharp because it was done with blades and short because Bates and Fish worked like whirlwinds as if they were in a local pub brawl, and because Bradl was simply aching to kill something.

"One and half is better than one!" he shouted as they dispatched the startled Pairs. The elevator lurched to a halt and they piled out arriving armed and ready in a busy corridor.

"Polisocs are Bulgers' arseholes!" yelled Bradl and laughed loudly when the Pongos and workers dropped to the floor or dived into rooms leaving the Polisoc and Stormtroopers standing reaching for their swords. Bradl shot all he could see and behind him Bates and Fish fired their guns. He was pleased to hear the pulses complementing each other as Bates and Fish timed their shots to make a tune. He almost lost his concentration when he listened to the song they sang as they murdered his fellow, albeit enemies, citizens.

"Polisocs have only ..." sang Bates

"...got one ball, Stormtroopers have two,..." sang Fish

"...but very small, and the President,..." sang Bates

"...has got no balls,..." sang Fish

"...at all!" warbled Bates.

From that moment on all was confusion and Bradl, with whoops of joy, led them from corridor to corridor, sometimes in the elevators and at others along wide open areas, and at all times attacking the Polisocs and Stormtroopers and leaving the other Pairs alone. Inevitably the forces against them became organised and when a group of Polisocs pushed toward them using workers as a shield Bradl decided it was time to go. He threw two gas grenades along the corridor and under cover of the smoke and confusion they shot into a transfer port and closed the door. He quickly tapped in a code and there was a sickening lurch and they were gone.

"I hate..." began Fish

"...this feeling," said Bates.

Fish, surprised that he started the sentence before transfer, and Bates, amused that he had finished it at their destination.

The door opened and the three men stepped out onto a carpeted corridor that suggested luxury. As they stood watching and waiting they became aware of voices, and with a finger to his lips Bradl led them along the corridor to a portal and with caution pressed his body against the wall close to the edge and peered around the corner. Bates and Fish flattened themselves against the wall. Bradl turned back and whispered to them.

"Bates, you cross the portal when I give the signal and Fish stay this side. When I go in follow and be ready to shoot. Be ready also to hold your fire, okay?"

They nodded and with their guns ready, new capsules dropped into place Bradl gave a nod. Bates dashed across the gap and Bradl burst into the room with Bates and Fish behind him ready to kill everybody.

The panic was complete and Pairs either froze in terror where they sat or jumped up and dashed to the walls, some running willy nilly and others yelling in fear. One old Half Pair stood his ground and although visibly shaken gazed at Bradl's sudden appearance, and said: "Who are you?"

"Bradl the Barmy and two friends working for the NMF," he said. "Who the Nong are you?"

"I am the Half Pair Crad and I too work for the NMF. We are the NMF."

"Oh," said Bradl, "then we don't have to kill you."[2]

"Hopefully not," said Crad.

"Pity, I was beginning to enjoy murder and mayhem," said Bradl.

Bates and Fish looked significantly at each other and flicked their guns on to safe. They thought it was a pity too.

---

[2] *Bradl's mild disappointment aside the location they arrived at was planned rather than random although the building was similar to Byrde's destination. The buildings were intended as holiday resorts.*

Holmes giggled. They were in a remote corner of Star Station Two with four terrified captive Stormtroopers who were repeating the message Blard was teaching them. The Pairs were linked together by their Polisoc compatriots' chains with their hands behind their backs and their feet linked one to the other the way cut out paper men are strung out when they are opened out. Why Holmes giggled was because every time one Half Pair missed his lines Sergeant Orange gently tapped them on the head with his cosh and chanted a silly rhyme.

"Remember what the nice man said – or I will hit you on the head."

As he chanted the rhyme he hit each one in turn with a wrist action that looked limp but was in fact relaxed and, from experience, for the recipient of the blow, quite painful. It was not enough to knock them out but enough to hurt and hurt often. The kidney punch Holmes called it. Holmes giggled because it looked like Sergeant Orange was trying to play a tune on their heads as if they were part of a toy xylophone.

Eventually the men got it right, and satisfied that they could recite the message exactly Blard suggested they get going. They had left the cargo hold in sector yellow and with a glee that Holmes never thought he would feel they had followed Blard's lead and slaughtered as many of the red and black uniforms as they could find. They took out some Stormtroopers too and Holmes was glad that he and Sergeant Orange had guns. When Blard engaged the enemy with the vicious double bladed sword there were too many limbs and heads falling off for his liking. Blard was a whirlwind of violent movement with a sword in his hands and used the two handed blades as if they were welded to his body. He was so quick that whenever a Pair engaged with him he took them both sometimes with the same cut and immediately seemed to know who was dead or harmless and who wasn't. Holmes and Sergeant Orange shot those Blard didn't get with his blade. Several times Blard decoded a room portal and threw a grenade inside laughing when the explosion was followed by agonising screams.

Not far from where they decided to flip off the Star Station they came across a terrified group of four Stormtrooper Pairs who immediately dropped their weapons and surrendered. Behind them a small group of Polisocs raced up to fight and Holmes and Sergeant Orange shot them down while Blard calmly ordered the Stormtroopers to get down on the floor.

A few moments later he was teaching them to recite a rude and insulting message to Pour and Roup.

"What if we don't tell him?" asked one frightened Half Pair.

"He will want to know because before we go we are going to tell him where you are and that you have something to say, enjoy," Blard said, and closed the portal behind him. He walked to a telephone booth close to a transfer port and with the port open and ready to go he calmly picked up the telephone and called Pour and Roup. "Hey you Bulger's vomit, there are a group of slimy Pairs in 40518, sector red level 11889 just waiting to talk to you. I hope I've spoiled your turn," Blard said, and made an obscene gesture as Pour and Roup gazed out at him from the screen. "Up yours!"

In the transfer port with the door closed Holmes was laughing but before he could say "I like your style" they were somewhere else. In fact they emerged from a concrete bunker in the middle of a shattered desert town and it seemed they had also arrived in the thick of a battle.

"Oops," said Blard, "this is not quite what I expected but if we sort out who is fighting who we could possibly join in."

It was Sergeant Orange who saw her first and gripped Holmes shoulder as he pointed to their left.

"Cripes, look there on that wagon! It's that Angela, that scumbag Renfrew's girlfriend!"

"Is that good?" asked Blard.

"Yes, at least we know which side to fight for," said Holmes.

"Cor she can't half lay it on," said Sergeant Orange.

"Yeah," said Holmes and rolled his eyes. "Look at them tits!"

Bates and Fish at Your Service – Cor!

"You are running a radio station?" said Bradl

"Yes and we are beamed directly at the citizens of sector Red. There are others who are attacking sectors Green and Yellow and I believe there was one group in sector Blue. You do not approve?" the old Half Pair said, and smiled gently, worldly wise and patient.

"And you transmit propaganda sent to you from the rebel headquarters? Any chance of doing some for us?" Bradl asked and smiled benignly back. "We have just caused a little mayhem in Star Station Three and we would simply love to let the President know what a Bulger's bum he is."

"Write the transcript and we will send it, as long as you allow my Pairs to edit the text, I will be delighted," the old Half Pair said.

Bradl nodded and took over a workstation and busily wrote with Bates and Fish watching as the text developed.

"I think that might not be..." Fish

"...quite strong enough..." Bates

"...to piss him off but..." Fish

"...then I quite like the subtle..." Bates

"...mockery of his prowess as a..." Fish

"...piss artist," finished Bates.

The message as finished read: - *To the soon to be ex-President of the Zradian Republic -*

On behalf of the inhabitants of the lost Star Station One, and a host of raving rodents, We, the wild and woolly harbingers of your downfall wish to tell you that the End Is Nigh. Your disgustingness would do well to go back to drinking cactus water as it is obvious that your stupidness is too drunk to realise that your arse is too remote from your elbow to tell the difference. We have a little surprise for you, and we know you like surprises, but there is a catch. If you can get your scrawny nose out of your gin and tonics then you might find out what the surprise is. Be assured that because we too love rodents we will be coming to get you and if we had lamp posts we would love to see your shredded, near dead carcass hanging by its feet in First City. May the Carnibirds feed on your intestines. In the meantime, may your earholes turn into arseholes and shit all over your shoulders, at least we will know you are on the level.

As the Earth people say, lots of love, Blard and Bradl the Barmy, and friends.

"Yeah, I think it is subtle and witty," said Bradl, well pleased with himself.

Bates and Fish laughed.

"You wish to send this to the President?" asked the old Half Pair.

"I do."

"It is a bit crude?"

"Crude is what I want."

"Then with a few modifications I will send it."

"As long as you say it the way I want it I do not mind but no toning down please, I want the President to get good and mad at my twin and I," said Bradl, and bowed. "Crude will do the trick."

The Half Pair bowed and with no further objections added the flimsy to his pile and carried on with his work. He tapped happily at the board and ignored them. Bradl turned to Bates and Fish and shrugged.

"May as well get cleaned up and find out where we are," he said and led them across the room to gaze out the window.

The scene outside was a surprise for Bates and Fish and they stood for a long time staring out of the window at the landscape. Bates drew in a breath and Fish whistled softly. Both men stood with their hands in their pockets rocking to and fro heel and toe feeling stereotypical and took a few minutes to sort out what they saw.

"I like the colours..." Fish

"...of the plants and the two..." Bates

"...suns dangling in the pink ..." Fish

"...sky but I think the birds with the double..." Bates

"...bills are a bit over the top and the hills..." Fish

"...look a little barren..." Bates

"...and dusty," said Fish.

"Yeah, and rocky..." said Bates.

Fish was silent and Bates looked at him oddly.

"We are on my home planet somewhere south of Sector Red and from the location we are not far from a rebel base. The Pairs behind me say that there is one but they are a little bit coy about who it is and exactly where. We will go and find them simply by walking out into the scrub and making ourselves obvious," said Bradl.

"What if they don't like the ..." Fish

"...look of us?" said Bates.

"Then we will probably get slaughtered," replied Bradl, "but that is unlikely because this lot will let them know we are on our way."

Outside in the precincts it was obvious that the Pairs in the centre were well guarded by soldiers. There was at least four troops supported by wagons. The soldiers patrolled the perimeter steadily both on foot and with wagons.

Bates and Fish remained at the window watching the action below while Bradl went to where the old Half Pair was working on his statement. They watched birds flitting from bush to bush, swooping close and then diving up again with a flash of purple and green and others who sat on the smooth tops of huge cacti just watching and then suddenly to swoop on a lizard. There were large dark red birds wheeling in the air and instinctively the two detectives knew they were carrion birds. Bates had seen enough western movies to recognise vultures, and Fish, who liked wildlife documentaries, knew his vultures and buzzards. Both men were amazed at the bright colours and the wild landscape that, as far as they were concerned, was a change from the city.

"Looks a bit like South Australia," said Fish.

"Er, yeah, you bin there then?" said Bates.

"No but I got a cousin there what ..." Said Fish

"...sends you some postcards?" said Bates

"...photos actually..." said Fish

"...of course, sorry," said Bates.

"Are we gonna get going then?" said Fish.

"As soon as you like," said Bradl, "that is after this lot have sorted my message and we have confirmation that the bomb is in place."

The old Half Pair called out and handed Bradl a flimsy and with glee he read it out to Bates and Fish.

"Mission completed – weapon orbit under control – both receivers operating and protected – message applied – delay mockery to confirmation of final setting – proceed with operatives nearest rebel forces," said Bradl, "and that comes from the high command of the NMF. We get going in a few short periods. Like right now. We grab some food on the way and take a walk in the bush. Do you two fancy that?"

"I like a stroll in the countryside," said Fish

"So do I," said Bates.

Bradl looked surprised, and with a gesture that suggested he was also puzzled he turned from them and picked up a pack. He stood at the portal and pointed at two more packs and then at Bates and Fish.

"I take it that..." said Fish

"...you want us to get going," Bates.

They did not wait for his answer but moved quickly from the window, and watched by the remaining Pairs, slipped the packs over their shoulders, picked up their weapons and followed Bradl out of the room. They did not look back but walked confidently after Bradl who, they assumed, knew where he was going.

Two levels down they were out onto a forecourt that led to a fine garden of red, green, blue and yellow plantings in equal proportions that for all the world looked like a Disney version of Alice in Wonderland.

"The troops will let us through and I am sure they have already passed on the information that we are on our way," Bradl said.

"They could give..." Bates

"...us a lift," said Fish.

"Nice to take a stroll," countered Bradl.

They walked through a gap between two low walls and crossed a dusty road, walked at least two hundred metres and Bradl led them along a path and on up into the hills past cultivated fields that cascaded down the slopes from the rough hills. The plants were tall and fleshy with developing red and purple heads on each stem that rattled in the slight breeze as green and mauve leaves swished gently to and fro. Bates thought that the plants seemed to be watching them and instinctively drew away if the path got too near the crude fence of tangled thorn bush. Fish eyed them carefully and as if they had asked the question Bradl answered with a grin.

"Food plants genetically modified from the Carnibush that likes to eat people. It has the same tendency but no tendrils. The plants in the field on the right are another Carnibush plant. We use that for oil the way you use butter. They're quite safe."

Nevertheless all the time they were walking the path Bates and Fish kept a wary eye on the vegetation. Like dogs, you can never tell.

"Is that what we have been..." Fish

"...eating?" Bates.

"Some."

"Good," Bates and Fish.

Bradl giggled.

The going was easier once they reached the hill top and for many long periods they marched steadily along a ridge that meandered in the general direction of west and south. Now and then Bradl consulted his Atlas and other than a few stops when he gazed at the horizon they kept going until the twin suns were high and the heat unbearable and he led them into some shade where they rested sheltered by rocks and took some food and water.

"Sleep if you can and when the suns go down a bit we will walk on and find a place to camp. I can watch and doze at the same time so you guys get some rest," Bradl said, and with some relief Bates and Fish settled down on the ground, rested their heads on the their packs and went to sleep.

Bradl drew his Atlas from his pack and tapped in a query. The screen displayed a series of changing coordinates and with a little adjustment he managed to figure out where they were and made the query again with new data. He examined the terrain and with some satisfaction he located a feature that seemed to be right and gazed at it for a long time. What he wanted was a set of quadocculars but there was none to be had in the kit on Star Station One and so he had to do what Angela had done when she looked over the deserts of Zrad for the first time. He shaded his eyes from the suns and concentrated his gaze on the landscape. He sat watching as the suns reached their zenith and dropped to the horizon and anxiously searched the slopes and the steaming desert that created mirages as if it were deliberately mocking him. In the distance he saw movement but could not make out whether it was a vehicle or an animal. He adjusted the Atlas and set a pulse going and watched the movement. It changed and headed directly for him. Vehicle. Time to wake the Earthmen. He shook Bates' shoulder and was amazed to see Fish wake as well.

"Okay guys, get ready with the weapons, we got company," Bradl said.

Bates and Fish said nothing and swiftly put the packs on and eased the safety catch off to set their guns at ready.

"This sounds like a ..." said Fish

"...John Wayne movie..." said Bates.

"...without the horses and Indians," said Bradl.

Bates and Fish glared at him but did nothing more as at that moment the vehicle hurtled over the edge of the ridge and skidded to halt.

A soft voice that carried well across the still air called out and figures appeared from the vehicle carrying weapons pointed directly at them. Bradl relaxed and lowered his own gun as the figures approached fanned out covering them completely.

"Place your weapons on the ground and step back two paces. Do nothing else or we will kill you."

The figure who spoke was a woman and it was obvious she was capable of carrying out her threat by the way she and her companions aimed their guns and covered each other's line of fire. They did as they were told and the women surrounded them to be joined a by a nervous and scrawny Earthman that Bates and Fish instantly recognised.

"Cripes it's that rat..." Fish

"...bag Renfrew,..." Bates

"...and with a crowd of right little..." Fish

"...ravers, how does he do..." Bates

"...it, a scrawny scumball like..." Fish

"...him..." finished Bates.

"You know this Earthman?" asked Bradl.

"Only because we have been ..." Fish

"...trying to arrest him for murder, arson and escaping custody," said Bates.

"I know who you are, you are Bradl the Barmy without your twin but who are these two?" said Glorida, waving her gun in the direction of Bates and Fish.

"Detective Fish and," said Bates

"And Detective Bates," said Fish and both men pointed at each other and said together, "at your service, ...cor!"

Glorida bit her lip gently and glanced at her twin.

"Lechers," said Glorid, "they must be to be associated with your darling Julian."

"Yeah, right but leave off will you. Shall we kill them or take them with us?"

"Ask Julian, they're his mates," said Glorid and grinned.

"No way, that idiot hasn't got any mates," said Glorida, "we take them with us because Bradl and Blard is on our side."

And if there was one thing that was guaranteed to get Bates and Fish excited and enthusiastic it was the sight of their quarry and a bevy of beautiful women, even if they were armed, dangerous and alien. On board the wagon they wasted no time in informing Julian that he was under arrest, and even less time in speaking with the women.

"Julian Arthur Renfrew you are under arrest..." Fish

"...on the charges of Arson, Murder, escaping custody..." Bates

"...and anything you say may be taken down in ..." Fish

"...writing and used as evidence..." Bates

"...and all that legal crap. In other words..." Fish

"...scumbag, you are nicked," finished Bates.

"You ain't got no right to arrest me here. I'm a bleedin' hero I am and I ain't goin' back with you to do bird when I can have me own bloody life here after this poxy war is over. So you two can stuff your nicking up your bleedin' jacksy as far as it will bloody go and if you don't like it you can bloody well go suck a dead Bulger's bum!" Julian said, and cringed as Bates glared at him and Fish snarled.

The pair didn't get further than that because as quickly as they moved Glorida and Glorid had their blades out ready. Bates and Fish backed off and as they sat back in their seats both of them muttered.

"You'll keep."

Bradl grinned and Julian flashed him a haughty look that Bradl returned with a cold smile that chilled Julian to the bone with fear.

"Yeah, right but don't push it see?" he said, and knew he sounded lame.

We are what we are

"Why mister Holmes and Sergeant Orange, it is so nice to see you," said Angela sweetly, "As you can see we have a little war going on here which I am sure you will appreciate is taking up most of my time. I suggest you attach yourself to whatever Hundred mister Blard will join and have some fun."

Sherman Holmes goggled at Angela who looked truly magnificent, and relaxed surrounded by a group of grim looking women who sported the logo of what was known as the Glorious 14th and consisted of the number 14 on a white and red background.

"You have captured the city?" asked Blard "You took prisoners?"

"No. Those who were captured were given the option of either joining us as slaves or getting the chop. Some ran away and others decided to fight to the last Pair. They did. The Pairs expect execution and it satisfies their blood lust, saves on food and supplies and keeps troops free to fight," she said and looked sad.

"You mean that you murder people?" asked Sergeant Orange.

"Yes," Angela said and smiled sweetly. "It used to happen all the time in the Crusades."

"This is a crusade?" Asked Holmes.

"I will explain," Angela said and gave them both a potted history of how she met Next and how the movement grew to become a religious campaign.

"So you are in charge of a crowd of fanatics?" Holmes asked and looked at her anxiously. "And you, what part do you play?"

"I just direct the fighting," she said.

"Okay, so what do we do now?" asked Blard.

"We are about to head into Sector Green proper and soon to attack First City Green in the centre of their Sector Red. Nert will conduct a service this night and after the thousands have recovered from their religious efforts we will spend most of the turn moving off into position. You will join a Hundred but whatever you do stay in touch with me please" Angela said, and so they found themselves assigned to a special unit that was used to cut out what the Leader Pair called 'stay behinds'. Blard licked his lips and grinned at Holmes and Sergeant Orange and rubbed his hands together.

"Looks like we got some dirty work to do lads," he said and laughed.

They listened to their instructors and were given a troop to work with and as the suns lowered in the east took their place at the fires drawing rations like any ordinary soldier. They sat chatting with the other Pairs and Half Pairs and ate and drank as keenly as the Children themselves. They learned of the battles and how Angela had led the army into the fight with a style that they all admired. But one sad Half Pair caught Holmes curiosity.

"But what, old friend?" said Holmes.

The Half Pair lowered his head to hide his expression but Holmes was intrigued and pressed for an answer.

"Come, tell me."

"It is Angela, she does not follow the true religion. She does not worship with the people yet she leads us. We can accept that she is a great warrior and Nert has chosen her to lead us but what happens when the war is over and the Children take their rightful place? Will she worship with us or will she stay with her own God. Glord the Glorious is mighty and through him we can find peace in the Great White Telephone," the Half Pair said, and looked up at Holmes with the fire of fanaticism in his eyes.

"Right," said Holmes and shuddered. He had seen holy rollers before and they worried him. He never knew what to say that didn't upset them and hated the thought of making enemies with all these millions of Pairs and Half Pairs with their dander up. But at least he knew now why Angela had a guard. She must have talked to the women about women's lib or something and that thought made him shudder too. Holmes was never sure of women and he always seemed to get them wrong. He hoped his mouth and his luck would keep him from making mistakes here.

"Tonight you will see," said the Half Pair.

The Half Pair looked worn out and Holmes realised he was quite old. In fact there were quite a number of the troop who were old and somewhat tired looking. A geriatric army? Holmes gazed around at the rest of the soldiers and saw that almost without exception they were older men and with a shock he recalled that few of them were described as Pairs.

"Excuse me but how come nearly all of you apart from the Leader Pair are, well sort of elderly?" Holmes asked.

The old Half Pair grinned.

"This is a people's army and when you have a people's army you get everybody," he said and grinned. "We are fighters with a purpose; to defeat the President's loyalist forces and take the republic back where it belongs. With the true founder of our people, Glord the Glorious."

"Ah yes, the great leader syndrome," said Holmes.

Blard shook his head but Holmes was determined to make his point and waited for the old Half Pair to retort. Which he did.

"The unbeliever shall be eliminated!"

"Of course and to do that you will wipe out half the populace in the name of the great leader instead of torturing them to death in the name of a despotic President?" said Holmes, and glanced around ready to act.

There was a silence over which the chatter and noise of the camp could be heard like a poetic musack in an elevator. The silence was accentuated by the sound of metal on leather as the old Half Pair slipped his knife from its sheath. His movement was matched by Blard's blade that touched his throat pushing the twin points into the skin enough to create a small sharp pain and Holmes own blade as he drew it ready to cut anybody that moved.

"Stow it Holmes," said Blard.

Holmes put his blade away and behind him Sergeant Orange sheathed his and growled softly.

"Knock it off Holmes, we are totally outnumbered," Sergeant Orange said in English and shook his head. "Leave it and concentrate on making friends with them."

Holmes grinned and with a gesture that was obvious to all the watchers that he had given in he faced the old Half Pair with his hands open and wisely explained.

"Listen, on my home planet we have had so many leaders and people who think they can lead turning bad, that we find it hard to believe in anybody. Sadly if anybody good starts to do something worthwhile they are either murdered by jealous rivals or attacked by the bad ones. I'm sorry but I am cynical when I hear such idealism and I tend to get insulting. I apologise for my rudeness. Your people are entitled to bring peace to your land in any way you wish. I am here to help you so I am on your side and will do my best to help you win. In fact we are here because we are trying to help you win. Blard and his twin have a scheme for the President that will upset him as much as your own glorious army," Holmes said, and glanced at Blard.

"And what is that?" asked the old Half Pair.

"We will tell you later when the time comes," interjected Blard, "just believe that Sergeant Orange and mister Holmes are here because of a great task we have begun. For now we are honoured to serve with your Leader and honoured to be part of the people's army."

It was obvious to Holmes that the old Half Pair was still unconvinced and he cursed himself inwardly for letting his mouth run away with him. Why should he care if the Children of Glord the Glorious would eventually fall apart and the new religion destroy itself by factionalising as it inevitably would. Or would it? Were the Zradians that much different from Earth people? Aliens but not quite as alien as he thought or maybe he hardly knew them enough to judge. That thought was a shock, something he would not have thought of before Blard took him off the drink. He could do with an ale but he had promised, and not only that but the medics on Star Station One had given him something that suppressed the urge to drink. What it was he had no idea, but since then he had drunk only water or tea brewed from aromatic dried herbs. Hermoine will be proud, he thought, and almost giggled.

"Tell me about the religion?" he asked, and sat more comfortably on his little hummock of coarse turf to listen while the old Half Pair explained how the Children began and told him about the coming of the Great White Telephone.

Holmes listened not interrupting but only encouraging the old Half Pair with grunts and nods. Surprisingly enough he was actually interested in what the Zradian was saying, and as the story unfolded he understood how he felt. The fanaticism was no more strange than that of his own people, Muslims, Israeli's, Capitalists, Marxists and all the isms that pop up to annoy you when all you want to do is eat breakfast and do the crossword. Holmes hated crosswords almost as much as he hated the people who did them, and with that thought he realised how easy it was to be intolerant.

"And so when you worship you, er sort of throw up?"

"Yes, its all part of the ritual," replied the old Half Pair.

"And we have to dedicate ourselves to the Children before we can worship?" said Holmes.

"I understand that you and any person from your planet need not join with us to fight for us but Blard here may do so."

"You mean he has to," said Sergeant Orange.

The old Half Pair was silent but his look suggested that he expected no less.

"Don't be put off by old Trev," said a Half Pair equally as old, "he's an enthusiastic convert. Mostly it is up to you. That you are willing to fight against the President is enough. First you have to learn about the Children and then you can make up your mind. That's as I see it anyway."

Trev was about to reply but there was a call from the centre where a low tower was set up and all eyes turned to face it. On the upper platform stood Nert with his arms spread wide. For a few small periods he stood like a cross as the people spread out and formed rows to face him. Below his platform Angela and the Leaders of her women's elite stood legs apart and their arms folded. They looked exactly what they were; warriors, alert and wary, ready for anything and they stood rock steady as Nert began to chant. Slowly as voices took up the chant it turned into a song that Sergeant Orange recognised but with different words and an arrangement that was amazingly complex. It began as a roundelay close to the tower, spread outwards and changed tempo as it rolled back to emerge again as a slow haunting melody swelling to a full voice rendition as it returned.

"Blimey," said Sergeant Orange. "I've never heard the Sally Ann's sing Onward Christian Soldiers like that!"

Holmes grinned at him and then looked to where Angela was standing and realised that it was she who had given them the song.

"What a woman!" he exclaimed.

The song wound down slowly to a beautifully melodic finish and Nert raised his hands Mullah style and began to speak. He was a quiet speaker, neither ranting nor haranguing the people but calmly explaining how their campaign, led by the great hero Angela, was a campaign of righteousness. He told them how humble they should be and said they should be merciful.

"All those who wish to join us must take the vow and become our slaves until they are properly converted. We must treat slaves with care. Those who oppose us are to be sent to Nong where they can explain to Glord the Glorious why they are against His Children."

He paused long enough to allow them to cheer and then raised and lowered his hands again. The crowd quieted to a low buzz as an acolyte climbed the platform carrying a porcelain toilet bowl which he placed before Nert with a reverence that was an act of worship in itself. The acolyte stood back a pace and knelt on the platform.

Nert knelt before the bowl and raised his arms spreading them out to the crowd.

"Let us pray!" he cried.

From his mouth came a low sound that grew and was taken up in unison by the crowd. Holmes heard it way back in the mob, and it was all one unified sound as the Pairs and Half Pairs knelt on the ground and supported themselves by their arms with their heads hanging down. He glanced at Sergeant Orange and Blard and when he realised what it was Holmes stared at Sergeant Orange and uttered the word as a question.

"Ralph?"

"Yeah, you know, after too much sherbet you cry Ralph! You savvy?" said Sergeant Orange. "They are about to throw up."

He was right for as a Pair the whole army apart from Angela and her women vomited on the grass as Nert himself spewed into the toilet bowl. It was also a reward for the acolyte to vomit in the bowl afterward, and as the heaving Zradians worshipped their idol Holmes did his best to stop laughing. Instead, like Angela, he and Sergeant Orange remained poker faced and sat by the cooking fire ignoring the spectacle. Blard stood watching impassively; eventually when it was all over joining them at the fireside. "Silly Bulgers," he said. "Glord the Glorious was a raving arsehole."

Holmes stared at him.

Blard shrugged his shoulders.

"Although it seems silly it is a religion and I guess like your people on Earth, we are what we are," he said, and flexed his biceps. "Or was that supposed to be I yam what I yam?"

Sergeant Orange and Holmes looked blankly at him.

"Pop Eye the sailor man?" he said.

The pair shook their heads.

Cartoon character? Olive Oyle, cans of spinach and all that?"

"Whatever turns you on," said Holmes.

"Ah well, thems the breaks. I suppose we should get some sleep and prepare ourselves for the battle ahead. "

Two days passed in marching, training and eating until on the third day Angela called the Leader Pairs in and for a whole afternoon there was a conference that lasted to the night meal. Ahead just over the next ridge sat First City Green Sector Red and the biggest target the Children had aimed for. The city was the first of the model cities built on the plains and from their position they could see its towers and circles cut by the radials where it sat in between two finger-like arms of the mountains. Farm lands spread around it in a circle and except where the cultivation met the slopes it extended into the valleys. The radials joined the circles in the city but there was only two main roads leading out; one east and the other north. This was a major target but Angela had planned that whatever happened the city should be taken.

Their troop did the dirty work of cleaning up pockets of resistance. Blard liked the idea of that and so, apparently, did Holmes. The whole army settled down to wait for daybreak and as the camp hushed into silence that gave way to the noises of pickets, sentries and the quiet movements of those engaged in last minute tasks a messenger came to Blard.

"Quiet friend. Bring the two aliens with you. We have a task," said the messenger, a ratty looking Half Pair. Blard woke Holmes and Sergeant Orange and explained that they were to follow the messenger. "Bring your gear."

The two men followed the Zradians led by a lamp that shone enough to light their way although Holmes and Sergeant Orange didn't need the light. The messenger led them through the sleeping throng and with admonitions to remain silent stopped at the edge of Angela's guarded sleeping quarters. A woman warrior emerged from the gloom and dismissed the messenger and beckoned them to follow her. She showed them into Angela's tent, a rude cover made of plastic, and asked them to sit on the hassocks that formed a semi-circle under the cover. Angela sat on a wider hassock and either side of her sat warriors mostly Pairs, all women.

"Hello mister Holmes, Sergeant Orange and Blard the Barmy. I am pleased to meet up with you at last. You were allocated to a specialist group but my spies tell me that there are some fanatics after your lives," Angela said and smiled. "It seems, mister Holmes, that you cannot keep your mouth shut and Blard himself is not a sympathiser."

"I have never been a Glordist," said Blard.

The women warriors sighed with relief.

"That is good because neither are we," she said. "The women came to me after we conquered our first town and complained about their treatment. I offered them a better life and we foreswore the religion."

"But how come you are the Leader?" said Blard.

"Because Nert realises that I am the best one for the task and so do his followers. I promised him that I would allow him to spread his religion. I offered the women a chance to become warriors in their own right and this I have done. Like all religions that I have ever come across including my own, this one excludes women from holding leadership posts. No woman can become the High Priest. I explained to Nert that I cannot accept that and he got stroppy so I threatened to destroy him and his followers. He said 'you and whose army?' and I explained, mine, and showed him the women. He backed down and agreed to reconsider."

Angela grinned.

"Now the silly creatures are plotting to kill me, hence the warriors."

Angela grinned widely.

"And also you."

"Its nice to be wanted," said Blard.

"I don't know about that," said Holmes.

Sergeant Orange looked around at the warriors, worried now, and thought about Blard and Holmes who didn't seem to care about danger. He shuddered, admitting that Angela frightened him. He had to admit she looked magnificent and for a moment or two he forgot his fears and gazed at her.

"Of course, you two will not be too worried about that as long as you can gaze now and then at my breasts," Angela said.

Holmes looked embarrassed and shrugged his shoulders.

"Sorry."

Angela grinned even wider.

"So you will you will join us here and fight with me and my girls," she said.

"Suits me," said Holmes licking his lips. He glanced at Sergeant Orange who grinned broadly.

That night they waited with Angela for the day to break and before the suns rose they were up and busy. Angela calmly carried out her ablutions, took breakfast and quietly mounted her wagon making places for Blard and his companions. Already troops were in position on the ridges beyond the city and as the suns rose they launched attacks on the left and right with a weaker thrust to the centre. The Loyalist troops raged out of the city and engaged the invaders who fought, backed away and fought again until they were pushed back along the road fighting what looked like a desperate rear guard action encouraging the enemy to attack. On the left and right flanks the thin line bunched up, stretched and thinned out to group up again, each time fighting and backing off until the loyalist troops were stretched and unsure how to push their advantage. They finally made their attack in force when the Children's rearguard turned and ran. The Loyalists raced after them going for an easy kill but too late, the trap was sprung. Angela's army poured down the valley slopes cutting them off to attack from behind and with the precision of a surgeon's knife more troops dropped down from the ridges to cut the attackers into isolated pockets. Angela's elite warriors rode through the retreating troops and bore down on the enemy vanguard raking it with devastating firepower.

Blard, Sergeant Orange and Holmes fought alongside Angela and her warriors obeying the directive to kill all Polisoc troops and Stormtroopers and with blades and guns they created more than their share of the havoc among the enemy.

Holmes dived into a wagon with two warrior Pairs behind him and Blard and came face to face with a group of Polisoc Pairs who begged for mercy.

"Bollocks," he said and sprayed them with plasma.

"Nice one killer," said Blard and helped the warriors drag the steaming bodies outside ready for the driver Pair to remove the wagon.

Holmes noted that although Angela took part in the fighting the warriors protected her sometimes taking wounds in her stead. He thought that leaders were supposed to lead from behind and not actually get stuck in with the gun and sword, but he could see that Angela liked to be in the fighting. He wondered how she controlled the battle, puzzled by the lack of messengers, but accepted her ability and somehow he trusted her to win.

They fought all that day and by nightfall they camped on the outskirts of the city and prepared to march in the next turn at a full period after sunsrise to claim it from the High Leader Pair.

Everything had gone according to plan and Holmes found out that for the two turns they were camped in the hills Angela's troops had surrounded the city and remained hidden until the main enemy force was drawn out by the overt attack. He found out too that Angela used the electronics in her wagon to keep in touch with her commanders. The plan itself was always simple but had room for flexibility. As she explained.

"If something goes wrong we stay with it, wait for the order to retreat and then try again. Mostly we get it right. This is a zero defect army," she said and laughed.

Holmes looked puzzled.

"In other words we do it right first time or work it so that it looks as if we did it right first time. Not only that but the President's army only knows one way to fight and it ain't the same as ours. Ergo, we win," she said.

Holmes thought that was a fair enough comment.

As the city settled for the coming surrender so a dark figure crept from the ruins of Sector Green. Ex-Fireman Sidney Weddell, near naked, dirty and carrying an axe found a wagon and slipped inside. He had moved across the country in part on foot but by sneaking into wagons that criss-crossed the land wherever they were wanted. He had no idea where he was at any one time but the guide leading him on in his mind seemed to be driving steadily toward First City. IIe saw the army approaching and decided that the fighting was not for him.

He watched as a group of men gathered goods and rations and put them inside the wagon and decided that if they were leaving he would hitch a ride. He had watched the crazy horde descend from the hills to kill everybody who wore a uniform and stripped his clothing off leaving only his underwear on for warmth. Confused and hungry he huddled into a corner and sat munching on a tasty sausage he had fished out of a pack. When the group of men saw him he showed them his axe and glowered at them muttering oaths and growling the name Renfrew making it obvious that he was staying put.

The Zradians left him alone, none wishing to be the first to taste the edge of his axe and perversely tolerant of crazy Half Pairs ignored the staring eyes, the spittle running down his chin, his semi-nakedness and his mumbling. And so ex-Fireman Weddell travelled to First City and when the wagons stopped in Sector Yellow ran off and crawled gratefully into a low tunnel that was cool if somewhat smelly. Above him rose the turrets of the Presidential Palace but ex-Fireman Weddell cared little for it as long as he was left alone to search for his enemy, Julian Renfrew. He climbed onto a low stone bench and lay down to sleep. A small animal shuffled by and instinctively he reached down to pat it. The creature swelled up and rubbed against him. The stench the creature exuded was revolting but he was too tired to worry about it and although he recognised the animal as Zradian Bulger he continued to caress it and when its glands burst spraying him with its vile effluent he welcomed the cool fluid and slept soundly. The Bulger crawled off to recover puzzled by the sudden explosion which in spite of it experiencing the same sensation many times before was still unable to cope with the effects. It was soothed by the tune ex-Fireman Weddell was humming, and as it lay recovering it moved gently to the tuneful sound that was ex-Fireman Weddell's version of A Whiter Shade of Pale.

In the jungles of the Amazon a crazed robot stood in a valley and waited for the small army to approach. Its father/mother/brother was with that army and it wanted comfort. The disturbed parts of its personality were deteriorating as Didi, Gogo, Godot, Murphy, Plato and a ragged character that kept complaining about someone called Hezoos and the need for an endless supply of shoes, entered the equation and promised to upset them all by telling the truth about Christianity. The robot raced through all of its contacts and caught the sleeping thoughts of ex-Fireman Weddell and added some strong subliminal images of its own to his crazed dreams. It found a willing receptor, and when it finished with the small disturbed mind it turned back to the problem of Clard and Dracl.

It seemed that the Pairs they were with had decided to make a weapon of destruction which they intended to aim its way. This, it thought, was very confusing and it was with a multiplicity of mixed emotions it prepared to face the new threat.

As it waited it played from its Octophonic sound system the tune A Whiter Shade of Pale and filled the jungle with the melody of the original song tumbling the sounds one upon another and was well pleased with the effect.

Life, if that was the word, was almost exciting.

Well, perhaps.

Like rats deserting a sinking ship.

Glord stood before the High Leader Pair attempting to explain how it was that Angela could command so vast an army and do what the Rebels had failed to do. He had deliberately chosen the Half Pair approach to create a truce of respect. Protocol demanded that all of him be present so with D.G absent the interview was informal and anything he said would be only on the records until he and D.G presented the story together. That, he thought, was the problem. The rebels were failing because they were too much like the regime they were fighting. He knew of many Pairs and Half Pairs who would willingly follow a leader like Angela and many who did not even know the name of their High Leader Pair. D.G was helping to organise their defection from the rebel army.

"And you say this...this...female has already taken most of Sector Blue and much of Sector Green and is now attacking Sector Red?"

"Yes your honour, she has a large army and her methods are based on a way of fighting in the wars on her home planet."

"And what are you suggesting we do?"

"I submit that we give our support to her effort by opening up another front and committing our forces to the battle and recruit as we go. That is what Angela is doing and it works. The High Priest Nert inducts the newcomers into the religion and they fight for him and Glord the Glorious. I suggest that if we ignore the message we will become an also ran and the Children of Glord the Glorious will take over." Glord said, aware that the High Leader Pair was not listening to what he was saying. The two old Half Pairs were out of touch and like their colleagues they were happy to replace the present corrupt regime with a cleaned up version. What Glord and his soldiers wanted was an elected government involving men and women.

"You suggest that we attack and allow females to be part of the fighting force?"

"Yes and give them a place at all levels of our society. To fail to do so will cause a rift that will never be healed," Glord said and watched them as they tried to find an answer to his message.

"Let us have a few short periods of discussion with our advisers and we will let you know what we decide. We will call you back."

Glord left the room walking past the guards who nodded affably to him and instead of sitting in a rest room biting his nails he found a seat outside and watched the training. He realised that the seat was the one Julian used to use to get away from everybody and reflected on the scrawny Earthman's twisted philosophy.

"If something needs to be done, leave it because eventually somebody else will come along and do it," he said quoting his twin's summing up of Julian's thoughts on life.

"He also used to say "if a thing is worth doing then it is worth getting paid for doing it" said a voice close to him.

He turned and saw Arthur Renfrew grinning, and he moved along the seat to make space for him.

"I was thinking of your son," said Glord.

"Yes and I think that you were also worrying about what the High Leader Pair are going to do. I gather the Children are bothering you?" Arthur said.

"Sure, we have enough people to do some real damage and the High Leader Pair are procrastinating. The sooner the rebel force gets going the better."

"I believe Oliver is doing something about that. You may see something in the flimsies soon. He and Ferret have cooked up a piece of propaganda that will leave this mob with no alternative. I will say it is about due now and by tonight we should have a result. Tzu and his people are ready to go, and we are too, so whenever you and D.G want, we can start. That is what I came over to tell you," Arthur said and smiled at Glord who looked relieved.

Glord told Arthur about the meeting with the High Leader Pair and how he felt about their reaction."The problem is that if they ignore the needs of the ordinary Pairs and the women then they will lose their cause to the religious crazies, and we will have a repressive regime as bad as the present one. I think we have to break up the Children," Glord said and his face showed a grim determination. "If not all our efforts will be as nothing."

Arthur was saved from any reply by a messenger who came to collect Glord. He watched Glord go and shook his head. He hoped that Oliver and the Ferret were successful.

Oliver Braine read the reply and grinned.

"Ferret, we have it. Rodent #4 has responded and the NMF have taken the bait. We have a confirmed report of the President's forces being committed to fighting Angela. Read this," he said and handed the Ferret a flimsy.

Re - current situation:
All resources required to attack President's forces from South and East. Rebel presence to be felt Sector Yellow and into Sector Red. Women's Army to cut south and penetrate Sector Green and

assist Western forces. Imperative all forces begin immediate action.

High Leader Pair NMF.

"I like that but it seems a little subdued," said the Ferret.

"True but when the rebels see the plans and find out what has actually happened they will do what they are told. Remember the Doomsday Bomb. I have it from Rodent #4 that the bomb itself is being taken care of. The next series will deliver the plans and...ah here they are," he said as the machine spat out more plastic sheets.

Braine picked them up and sorted them out slipping them into folders and handed one to the Ferret.

"One copy for you and the one for me to take with us."

The Ferret read swiftly through the sheets and whistled.

"The complete plans. All of 'em and kosher?" he said.

"As kosher as they can be."

"So whatever they do we will know?"

"Right on mate."

"And the other project?"

"In hand and as far as I know there should be a result soon. Rodent #4 says that all is in hand but there is something he has to deal with, a personal problem. His last message was a bit odd. He or it said that he has to get in touch with his feminine side and could he/it/she have a new set of aprons, beware the ides of March, and that there is nothing to be done. Apart from that the creature sounded almost rational. Oh, yes, it says that Herb Alpert should have played A Whiter Shade of Pale and that they don't make tunes like that anymore. Odd," Braine said.

"Odd," agreed the Ferret.

D.G waited for Glord as patiently as he could and eventually gave up and walked outside in the gathering gloom of the Zradian night. He had organised the exodus and all he wanted was for his twin to give him the nod to go. He had two hundred and fifty loyal Pairs ready to help escort the Thousand and the other Earth people and enough wagons to carry them. The Pairs were on alert waiting for his signal. D.G had sorted some of the Thousand to act as drivers for night driving and he was proud of that. His own Pairs having a marked reluctance to drive in the dark without lights. He said they could use glasses but gave in when they explained that they were 'not much Bulging good' which he had to admit was a fair observation. He was still smarting from his debacle with Professor Renfrew. When he explained to the Professor what he was doing in the street near the Drunken Clown Arthur had replied that he was sorry but he had to defend himself from attacks, and as far as he was concerned D.G was an attacker. The embarrassment he felt was not because of the sudden beating he took at the time but the fact that the Professor had no idea what the hell he was talking about. He blamed the glasses for the problem and when the Pairs said they were loath to use them he let the matter be. Much better to use people who could see in the dark.

In a mood bordering on frustration at being inactive he walked the grounds and almost cheered when Glord called out to him and caught him up.

"My twin, we are on our way. The High Leader Pair has agreed to fight the President's troops and ordered a move out tomorrow!" Glord said.

"We go this night?"

"No, we stay and go with the rest and then we move out. I suggest we slide off as we leave the outer ring. Can you hang on for that long my twin?" said Glord, and grinned broadly knowing that D.G was itching to go.

"Let me eat," said D.G.

"We must also pretend to get ready with the rest. I have spoken with the High Leader Pair and they have reluctantly agreed to let us take the Ferret and Oliver Braine with us. Lugs will go with you and Richard Byrde will slip out with Arthur and join up with Tzu and his Thousand."

"Meanwhile we drink and be merry," said D.G.

"Not too merry, there are spies around and I think we should watch our backs," said Glord.

"That, my twin is in hand. I have Pairs watching out for us," said D.G.

"Good man," said Glord.

In the darkened corridors in the early periods of the turn a half dozen Pairs moved in the gloom and split up. Two Pairs headed for one cabin and others chose targets separately and crept off to do their deeds. The two Pairs overrode the portal gate and slipped inside the cabin. There was a double gasp, a flurry of soft, wet slicing sounds followed by grunts and the soft, heavy sound of bodies falling. Small periods later another group of Pairs appeared from an elevator and swiftly removed four bodies. Glord and D.G closed the portal and went back to sleep. In other parts of the sleeping quarters the clandestine activities of the remaining ten Pairs were noted, plotted and acted upon. As each Pair reached their target others reached them and with quiet violence snatched and dispatched them. The bodies were removed by the watchers who were replaced by fresh and alert newcomers to continue the vigil. Those who were snatched met a messy end outside in the yard. Of the intended victims only Glord and D.G were aware of the danger, the rest, Arthur, Oliver, Richard, Lugs and the Ferret slept on. In his chambers, Tzu forewarned of likely activity, kept watch and let his people practice their killing style on any transgressors.

In all an eventful but pleasant night passed to be broken by the early call to breakfast and the bustle as troops prepared for the big push north.

Glord smiled at the High Leader Pair as he and his twin sat on the edge of the command step of their lead wagon. It gave him great satisfaction to see their faces trying to mask their anger and disappointment as the cavalcade prepared to pull out. Getting Byrde and Arthur on board Tzu's lead wagon was easy. Directly after breakfast Byrde had simply walked up to Tzu as the latter was loading his gear onto the wagon and asked if he and Arthur could help. Tzu had agreed and gave them tasks to carry out which meant that they could go back and get their gear and boldly bring it to the wagon and load up. Several times they returned with stores and weapons and when the Thousand were milling around ready to embark they stayed on board hiding behind the packages in the storage section.

When it came time to move off nobody seemed to notice they were not in the crowd left behind. Glord had kept the High Leader Pair talking while Tzu and his Thousand had driven out, and when they were well clear of the gates he ordered his driver to start the engines ready to move off.

"Long live the Revolution!" he said as they moved off and grinned when the High Leader Pair's expression changed from subdued anger to open fury.

The revolution was supposed to end in peace.

They chose their time to leave having deliberately selected the rearguard position. It was when the Leader Pair of the first echelon called for a camp late that turn Glord took the lead of his sections. He waited until the rear of the tenth echelon was out of sight and turned left off the track onto a rougher road that led west. As darkness fell he ordered Tzu's people to take over the driving, and while some slept the troop moved across the landscape like a dusty lizard putting a great distance between them and the rest of the rebel army. As day broke and the birds began to call he called a halt and allowed the troops to relieve themselves and cook a meal. He was wise enough to post lookouts, and to make certain all would be well he put D.G in charge.

D.G took Richard Byrde with him and together they sat on top of the wagon listening to the sound of the birds and watching the activity on the ground below. Pairs were spread out in the rocks and scrub watching in all directions using the peculiar quad-ocular glasses that gave split images that to Byrde's eyes were half an image upside down and the other half the right way up.

"Funny place this," said Byrde.

"My home, I am used to it," said D.G.

"Pity it is so polluted by radiation. It is really beautiful and although the climate is hot and dry I like it. I like the colours and the myriad animals and the odd plants. I even like the idea of a large carnivorous cat and hungry trees," Byrde said and gazed at the horizon hungrily.

"The radiation is mostly myth," said D.G.

Byrde stared at him.

"What do you mean?"

"Just that. We have monitored the radiation levels for several generations, that is the NMF have done so, and the figures show that the levels are fine. There are a few hot spots but we have the means to deal with them. We use the technology that produced matter transfer and the Doomsday Bomb to accelerate the radioactive breakdown and it disappears. We let the figures show high radiation to keep people out of the area where we operate. As soon as the President falls we will open out the lands and show that there is no need for any extra planetary expansion," said D.G.

"You mean that there is no need for Earth to be colonised?" said Byrde.

"No but the President has made up his mind and so it goes," said D.G sadly. "Even if we wanted to stop him we could not once he had made up his mind."

"So, why are we here, diving off and not with the rest of the rebels? I have a feeling there's more to the reason than a mere threat to our lives D.G?"

D.G looked at Byrde and bit his lip.

"Come on, tell me."

"Okay, Glord and I suspect that the Rebel leaders want to replace the President with their own Pair. We believe that they want all the power to themselves and want to keep the system going as it is but without the violence."

"What about the NMF?"

"The NMF are the leaders."

Byrde stared at him for a long time aware of the bright surroundings but feeling as if time was suspended and he had missed something important. He sifted through all the things that he had noticed since he had arrived. He thought about the animosity toward Angela, the plot against Julian and ploy to keep the Thousand separate from the rest of the troops. He recalled Tzu's concern that his women Kung Fu fighters were being isolated from the men and the feeling Tzu had that he was not safe.

"I have a guard all the time Richard," had said. "I have my own guard to guard against them and I suggest you ask D.G and Glord to protect you."

He had done that and he knew about the attempt on their lives that last night in the headquarters. He did the political sum in his head and came to a conclusion.

"So, it is in the Rebels best interests to have Earth conquered and Angela and Julian and the women's army destroy all that. And I expect the Children are a big threat too. Is the NMF in control of the rebels?"

"Not all of them. The leadership is but there are a large number of true revolutionaries who are opposed to the recidivist attitude of the old school. The reactionary nature of the leaders is unacceptable to most of us. We want men and women to take an equal part and anything that does not achieve this is not wanted and that includes misogynist religions. We want equality and a form of republicanism that is fair for all people. We intend to establish elections but first we have to enforce our will on the Loyalists. And that will include giving votes to all Pairs, male and female alike. The Rebel Army as it is now is on its way to the main battle as we have hoped it would. If those of us who are in support of the new NMF regime are successful we can do what we set out to do."

"So maybe we can get down to the truth then. We are fighting an enemy within as well as the President. Earth people are fighting against a corrupt regime that may well be replaced by an equally corrupt system disguised as a revolutionary army?"

"Yep and it looks as if our Pairs have seen something.

Two Pairs were running from different directions calling out and from what they were saying there was a patrol heading their way. D.G raised his glasses in the direction they were pointing. He moved his head following the patrol and then with a grin he lowered them and called out for the Pairs to climb aboard the wagon.

"Let us go and meet them," he said and with Byrde sitting beside him he showed his happiness as the wagon approached the patrol.

The two groups met part way stopping a few metres apart. Two women descended from the lead wagon and covered by the guns of the others and followed by a scrawny soldier nervously carrying a gun walked to where D.G and Byrde stood in the shade cast by their own vehicle.

"Hello Glorida and Glorid and Julian," said D.G. "We've come to join you. Glord and the rest of the force are just over the hill and await you. The rebel army has decided to break out."

"Yeah, saw the writing on the wall did they," said Julian with a sneer. "Like rats deserting a sinking ship are you?"

"Can it Julian," said Glorida.

"Well they are. The rebel army is shagged now that bloody Angela is on the rampage. Christ that ..." he changed his tone when he saw D.G fingering his knife. "crowd she's with is getting all the kudos and bloody good luck to her, makes it easier for us don't it?"

D.G eased his knife back in his belt and Glorida giggled while Glorid gave Julian a mocking glance. "That maybe so mister Renfrew but that is not why we are here. Glord will explain when we go see him," he said and glowered at Julian.

Richard Byrde shook his head and smiled. He liked to watch Julian suffer for his own mistakes and although he realised that Julian would never be any other way he could see some personal growth and he was pleased about that.

"Are we to have a council of war," asked Glorida.

"I think so. We have Tzu Wu's people with us and two hundred and fifty loyal Pairs plus the Earthmen, Richard Byrde who is with me, Julian's father, Lugs, the Ferret and Oliver Braine. Come with us and Glord will explain," said D.G.

Glorida listened quietly as Glord explained what had happened at the rebel headquarters. Now and then she glared at Julian when he tried to interrupt and slapped her knife into her hand angrily as she listened to the tale of treachery unfold. She learned of the duplicity of the High Leader Pairs and how the plot against Julian and Angela was not about being useless mouths but as a threat to the Pairs' own hold over the rebels and the cause they supposedly represented. She learned that there were measures by the radical elements to overthrow the old hands although Glord refused to give any details or names saying that the least known about the plot at this stage the better.

"I understand that you and D.G were in fact duped into believing in the loyalty of the Elders?" she said.

"For a time and when we worked on the plot to let you and Glorid get Julian and Angela off their hands we thought that it was all above board but now we know better. You were meant to be killed. If it hadn't been for Angela diving off on her own we would have lost all of you," said Glord. "D.G was so angry after we found out that he was all for slaughtering the Elder Pairs on the spot but I managed to hold him back."

"And if it wasn't for that the NMF would have broken down. The loyal Pairs in the higher command were really Bulgered off. There is a warrant out for Julian, unofficially that is, and that really gave me the needle," said D.G.

"The rebels want to kill me?" said Julian much alarmed and looked around wildly as if an assassin was about to pounce on him.

"Well, yes but nobody here. We are your friends," said D.G and grinned. "In spite of your nastiness and your stupidity, we are still your friends, okay hero?"

"Piss off ratbag," said Julian but he did not really mean it.

"So what now?" asked Glorid ignoring Julian.

"We mount up and join forces with you," said Glord.

"Okay, we'll let headquarters know, let's go," said Glorida.

The column, led by Glorida and Glorid's wagon swept into the camp, and with a neatness that did the Earth drivers credit as well as their Zradian counterparts the wagons lined up neatly in a square facing the headquarters hut. The troops and Tzu's people disembarked and with a flamboyance learned from their practice back at the rebel compound they lined up neatly like a well drilled army. Their shadows stretched westward as the suns set in the east and once settled with Tzu's Kung Fu artists, and Lugs standing proudly with them alongside the Ferret, stood in ranks as Glord and D.G with Arthur, Byrde, Oliver Braine and Tzu marched to the steps of the verandah where they stood waiting for the Leader Pair to welcome them. Glorida, Glorid and Julian stood to attention at the foot of the steps and announced their arrival.

"Your Gracious Honours, we present Tzu Wu from Earth and his Thousand Warriors, Arthur Renfrew, Richard Byrde, Oliver Braine also from Earth; Glord and Drogl with a force of two hundred and fifty Pairs and the incomparable Lugs and his mate, the Ferret, at your service.

Dorida and Dorid gazed at the ranks and the wagons and smiled.

"We are glad that they have arrived," Dorid said. "We will take the salute if you please."

Glord's Leader Pairs called out the commands and with no hesitation the soldiers, the Kung Fu artists and the civilians gave the salute. Dorida and Dorid returned it smartly and bowed.

"Please let them dismiss and follow the guides who will show them where to sleep and eat," said Dorida.

"Let all Leader Pairs come to the hall this night for we are on the move. In the next few turns we are waging all out war on the President's armies. The revolution is about to begin in earnest!"

"Thank Nong for that," said Glord.

Julian gasped and true to form fainted.

Our Imperial Highness

The President was furious, in fact it could be said he was beside himself with fury, so furious he ordered the entire High Command to wait on him at the Palace. Trembling with suppressed anger he waited in his ante-chamber for the Polisoc escorts to march them to their seats, He ordered the Dog Squad troopers to sharpen their blades in the halls outside the grand hall and ordered Polisoc Troopers to surround the palace lest any escape. Too angry to speak he walked out into his courtyard and sat in the yellow quarter admiring the flowers and moved to red where he took a bottle from its secret place and drank half the contents in one long satisfying draught.

As he sat drinking and thinking he was unaware of a figure lurking in the dark recess of the cleaner Pair's portal. He did not see the figure touch the edge of a sharp axe with his fingers and lick his lips with a pink and furry tongue nor that the figure was naked and dirty except for a skimpy loin cloth that barely covered his parts. He did not see the figure watching him with a peculiar puzzled expression and mumbling, with the occasional snarl as it realised there was no way to get at the enemy. If the had heard the words that tumbled from the madman's lips he would have been scared spitless.

Ex-fireman Sidney Weddell sat hunched up in the portal unable to pass the electronic field to get at the man who was the root cause of all his trouble. The voice in his head told him that this was the one, that Renfrew was not the real culprit but this man. The President, not Renfrew, President Renfrew. Kill the Renfrew President. But the portal wouldn't open for him and now the man was leaving. The enemy child molester, arsonist and utter, utter, raving ratbag was leaving. Ex-fireman Sidney Weddell cried in frustration as the enemy wandered out of the garden and back into the nice Palace. Ex-fireman Sidney Weddell liked palaces and wanted desperately to show his darling little boy this one. He would love it. Red like a fire engine. Lovely fire engine. Lovely fire axe. Lovely blood. Lovely, lovely, lovely dead Renfrews. Lovely dead President Renfrew.

Suddenly the portal clicked open and with a spurt of energy ex-fireman Sidney Weddell dashed into the garden and into the inner sanctum of the President's palace. Instinctively when he saw people he dashed into hiding and rushed into a darkened corridor becoming hopelessly lost in the labyrinth of service corridors and finally holed up in a clothing store where he made a nest and slept.

The President, unaware of the minor drama played out in his private garden, walked back to his chamber fortified by his intake of strong raw spirit to exact his form of justice on his High Command. He was met by his group of personal scribes who stood nervously fingering their tablets as if plucking up courage to speak.

"Your Honour," said the Leader Pair and waited for his permission to speak.

"What is it?"

"We wish to offer some advice your honour,"

"Well, offer it then."

"We think that executing the entire High Command will be a mistake. We think that you would be well advised to let them live but let them declare you as their Emperor and to let them take command of the cities they take back from the filthy upstart enemy," the frightened Pair said.

The President gazed at the Pair and his look changed from that of indignation to pleasure and with an uncharacteristic display of emotion took a hand of each and squeezed it dancing lightly on his feet smiling broadly.

"Better still we will give them cities to command and order them not to lose them to the enemy," he said and straightened his back letting go the tense hands of the scribe and with a new spring to his step walked into the great hall. As he entered the hall and walked to the throne the Pairs fell silent and prostrated themselves at the base of their seats with the Dog Squads standing at the ready in eager anticipation of the slaughter to come.

"Rise and be seated scum," the President said. "We have an announcement."

There was a rustle of leather and tunics as the High Command rose from their positions and sat in the double benches and tried not to catch the President's eye. With bated breath and trembling limbs they waited for the expected announcement of their immanent deaths. It did not come as the President casually explained the terms under which he would become Emperor.

It was the scribe Pair that began the spontaneous acclamation by simply calling out over the public address system.

"Long Live His Imperial Majesty!"

The cry was taken up immediately by the relieved High Command Pairs and also by the surprised and pleased Dog Squad Pairs who were disappointed by the lack of bloodletting but ecstatic that their President had chosen to become His Imperial Majesty. They were now the Imperial Dog Squad and that sounded much grander than their previous title. Their acclamation of the President's new title sounded not so much a cry of joy but a demand.

The High Command Pairs shuddered but dare not let their expressions betray their inner misgivings.

The effect on the now Imperial Army of Zradia was immediate. Instead of the Polisocs strutting around arrogantly in the name of the President they strutted around arrogantly in the name of the Emperor. Stormtroopers threw their weight about with the Pongos even more belligerently and in their turn the Pongos had something new to grumble about. In response to their new mode of command the High Command Pairs took up their new posts and built empires of their own. The new Emperor insisted that they meet the threat from the Children with full force and that they fight with all their might against all enemies.

"Not another city or Sector shall fall," the Emperor ordered. "Or you will fall with it."

That edict added an imperative edge to their commission and to a Pair they determined to obey interpreting 'with full force' to mean at the expense of the battle on Earth. With a messy scramble for resources each Command Unit, now split into four sectors, drew on the invasion troops and those that were not already totally committed to the fighting on Earth were thrown into the civil war. And so in almost utter confusion the vast forces of the new Emperor marched to oppose the organised might of the Earth woman Angela Breen and the combined forces of the rebel armies.

The Emperor of Zradia had unleashed the dogs of war to crush the insurgents and by Nong he was going to crush as no other ruler had crushed before! How dare a rag-tag army of religious no-hopers challenge the might of the ruler of Zrad! How dare a band of half baked insurgents presume to oppose him and drag along with them a band of scummy women. And then there was that nasty little bulger's arsehole Renfrew, the dirty little bomber and most of all his stinking girlfriend who by all accounts was running the army of religious fanatics. Glord the Bulging Glorious! Hah! A dirty myth.

But wasn't there a Glord who was with the rebels?

The Emperor clutched his throat, paled at the thought that crossed his mind and with a free hand supported himself against the wall of his chamber not realising that he had actually left the great hall.

"We wish a gin and tonic!" he cried.

A serving Pair came rushing with a tray loaded with gin and tonics that were poured already mixed from bottles made in his own cellar breweries. He had resorted to the expedience of mass production for two reasons. The first was that he could not keep up with the process on his own and the second was that he had hit on a pleasant mixture and wanted it repeated every time. Besides, having them ready saved on servants.

He gulped two down one after the other and with the servant Pair holding the tray close to him he staggered back to his futon. There he drank three more and sank down on the bed to consume two more before laying full length on the bed watching his room spin around. As he fell into a restless drunken sleep he was struck again by the thought that Glord was somehow more than a myth. Mixed into the dreams of rodents, terrible defeats and an endless supply of gin and tonics suddenly coming to an abrupt halt he had a vision of the second coming of Glord the Glorious.

In his makeshift temple Nert stood before the acolytes. He raised his arms to the heavens and spoke quietly.

"And so it shall come to pass that before the fall of the Evil One there shall come to save us the spirit of our great leader. He shall be known by his likeness and by his name. He shall further be known as a great warrior and be recognised by his humble mien. This has come to me in a vision from meditation on the Great White Telephone."

Nert genuflected placing his fingers in his mouth and bowed to the worshippers.

"And so be the word of the prophet," they replied in dull unison.

Angela watched the acolytes emerge from the temple and line up before the platform and she sighed. This religion was getting too strong, too complex and there was too much mysticism being created around it. She had used the fervour of the priests and acolytes and Nert's strange personality to her own advantage but now the whole thing was getting out of hand. Her own elite force of women was in itself creating a charismatic branch of the religion that fed upon the stories told about her origins and exploits and that worried her. The story currently being mangled was how she destroyed the Polisoc troopers all that time ago when she first arrived. It was said that she could cut down whole armies with her sword and that with the might of Glord behind her their enemies would fall like fodder before them.

She had tried to explain that she was only a woman like them but they wanted to believe in something more powerful than that. They did not accept that it was their own efforts that gave them the power to overcome the enemy as much as it was her leadership. She told them that all she did was guide them on the way and the rest was all theirs and their faith in their strength. That was the trouble. The faith was seen as power from their gods and many added her name to the list of gods. The implications of their worship were horrendous as far as she was concerned. She had to be right all the time or the whole movement would deteriorate into a mob and she recalled the lessons of her own history on Earth too well to want that to happen. These questions of her own omnipotence gave rise to questions of her faith in Jesus and that disturbed her. Did Jesus die like any common felon and was he just a man, a prophet as Mohammed said or was he indeed the son of God? It hurt her to doubt her own faith and she understood how easy it was for the Zradians to find salvation where it was offered.

Nert climbed the platform and started with the usual exhortations to seek salvation in the example of Glord the Glorious and gave them a speech about the virtues of the First Republic. There was nothing new in any of it and Angela was uncomfortably aware that Nert was apt to quote history and mystify it to create a pleasant experience for his followers in a bid to drive them on to greater exertions. This night he was speaking of the prediction that one will come when the time was right who will learn from Glord's experience and lead them to a better life. He stressed that he was only one of many prophets and only paused long enough to allow the crowd to demonstrate their belief that he was the last prophet. Angela pricked up her ears when she heard that and listened carefully. This was new and if it was what she suspected then she despaired of the future.

A few small periods after the pause Nert launched straight into the vision of a second coming and Angela groaned. Beside her Blard swore and for once she didn't automatically correct him. The crowd were now on its feet and calling out for Glord the Glorious. They clashed their weapons together and began to call Nert's name.

Nert the Nervous! Nert the Prophet!

For the first time since she had met the smelly Half Pair and taken control of his small and deferential band she was worried. This was too much. Far too much and now, she thought, the whole thing was out of her hands. Impassively she watched the faithful go through their revolting worship and thought of the coming battle. Her scouts had told her that the President's forces were gathering on the edge of Sector Green in great numbers and rumour had it that they were seeding the area with transfer ports. Angela assumed that the tactic was possible and made plans to meet that threat with special troops and in general trained the Leader Pairs to think in terms of circling movements. She explained that the best way to deal with the threat was to encircle the enemy and attack them as they tried to form up. Other than that then they will have to be isolated and go for the transfer points with fire and strong attacks. She detailed exactly what they had to do and urged them to stay alert.

"We have the numbers but we have raw troops and zealots and they have experienced soldiers. The saving grace is that they do not have the will to fight to the bitter end as we do. The people's faith will overcome the problems because they are willing but that does not mean we are invincible. If I call a retreat then that will be because I am willing to give way to save lives. In all things our lives are important and no amount of useless brave sacrifice will win the war," she said.

She was about to say more but a messenger ran into the camp and spoke animatedly with the guards. The guards trotted with the Pair to where she sat and the excited Pair knelt down before her and gasped out their message.

"The President has just declared himself Emperor and given charge of all his provinces to his Leader Pairs in the High Command!"

Angela absorbed the information and sat for a while thinking and slowly she came to the realisation that what she was doing was actually making a difference. She was the catalyst and knew that the President by declaring himself Emperor was either mad or taking a calculated risk.

"Good, this works in our favour. We have his back against the wall. The new Emperor is setting up against the myth of Glord to try and take the glory from your faith. You must let Nert know," she said, although in spite of what she said she was not so sure. This second coming stuff was dangerous and she imagined the hordes of fanatical faithful looking for a Messiah and being angrily disappointed when the chosen one let them down. Better that they leave it at a prophet. She remade her plans to fit the new idea and explained to Blard what she thought.

"So if the faithful find their messiah we are in deep Bulger shit," said Blard.

"Right, and I have a feeling that we are likely to find that messiah pretty soon," she said and lapsed into silent reflection that Blard did not disturb.

The Emperor watched the screens as his High Doommand Pairs sent in their reports. He chuckled. The frightened Bulgers were crapping themselves and falling over each other to please him and cutting each other's political throats to gain the advantage for their own territory. The stupid Pairs were working their backsides off to outdo each other and their efforts showed on the screens. The pattern was clear and his orders were followed to the letter with each sector creating a structure that would work together to attain one object. The capture of Angela Breen.

The Emperor sucked gin and tonics through a straw and rested on his comfortable private chair attended by his servants. The arrangement was better than sitting on the throne all day dealing with the day to day petitions. As Emperor he had appointed a Pair to deal with the dross and allowed the Twin High Consuls to act as go-between, concentrating instead on the pleasures of issuing royal decree. He took pleasure in ordering the Great Push and looked forward to having Angela Breen in his dungeons. He looked forward even more to the day when he would see her tied to the execution stakes and publicly gutted.

He sipped deeply at the gin and tonic and sighed with extreme happiness. It was wonderful to be the most powerful person in two worlds.

He liked that.

Is there Hope?

Pour and Roup were the first to notice the change. Fewer troops poured through the Transfer ports and the reserves they had put aside in the event of emergencies were already being demanded by the ground troops. Sweeps for serviceable equipment and fit soldiers were turning up less and less and when they sent urgent messages for more troops and supplies they received evasive replies that suggested that troops and supplies were on their way but that they were not to expect consignments in the near future but to have patience and persevere with what they were already allocated.

"In other words we've been abandoned," said Pour.

"Time we left," said Roup.

"But what about that bomb?" said Pour.

"Maybe we can fix it?" said Roup hopefully.

"Perhaps if we forget all this crap about invading the Earth and being loyal to the president and the republic and start concentrating on us for a change we will survive?"

"Fine, fine, let us go and take a look at the bomb shall we and leave the crowd in there to get on with it," said Roup.

Pour gave him a sickly smile and quietly advised the Aide Pair that they were going on a tour of inspection. They had hardly begun their journey down to sector yellow when they were urgently called back by the Aide who ran along to the elevator together waving a flimsy. Roup grasped it and read it through and with a groan showed it to his twin who read it with his mouth wide open unbelieving.

"In a Bulger's arsehole, he must be out of his gin pickled mind," Pour said and turned to the Aide, "read that out to all personnel from our office."

The Aide turned away and walked back to the control centre and as the Pair vanished through the door Pour and Roup entered the elevator and hurtled down to sector yellow. Finding the hold where the bomb was placed was easy. Getting to it was harder but with their coders they defused the booby traps and approached it cautiously.

"I suppose it is better to be right on top of it than trying to get out of the transfer ports and being cooked or sucked out into space," said Pour.

His twin grimaced.

They saw the dead rodent; the fused wire and registered the smell and saw the control box with its LED showing green and red and the tell tale blue light blinking on and off.

And then with a shock they saw Blard's note.

Pour and Roup – stuff around with the controls and the bomb will go off.

All the best – Blard the Barmy.

To say they ran out of the chamber was not quite how they moved but they moved and hopped from point to point avoiding the mechanical triggers of the booby traps and raced out of sector yellow to their cabin where they clutched each other and sat staring at the wall. They sat staring silent and still until the Aide Pair came with the news that there was a group of Pairs who needed to speak with them urgently.

"Where are they?" asked Pour lethargically.

"In the centre under guard."

Pour and Roup followed the Aide and as they were shown into the centre and hence to the small chamber set aside for interviews they straightened up and looked almost confident. The group of frightened Pairs pressed back against the wall nervously as Pour and Roup walked in and glowered at them.

"You have something to say to us?" said Roup.

The Pairs all began at once but when Roup almost smiled they were encouraged to settle down and spoke instead in turn, each Pair chanting their message as if they had learned it by much practice.

"Blard and Bradl, the Barmy wish to leave you with a gift...."

"....and regret they could not deliver it themselves..."

"....but appreciate that you would not wish them to stay..."

"....behind unnecessarily. For your amusement they..."

"....take the unusual step of letting their victims know..."

"....in advance how it is they will die, that is namely, ..."

"....your horrible selves and regret any inconvenience...."

"....you may suffer as a consequence. However, they ..."

"....wish to inform you that device you have no doubt..."

"....by this time discovered in sector yellow, is no longer ..."

"....linked to your filthy persons but to the Doomsday Bomb..."

"....And that we, the Pairs who are delivering this message,..."

"....are to inform your dirtiness's that the countdown to ..."

"....your destruction will begin on the first turn of the fifth tenth.."

"....at the exact time of zero zero. You will know when because.."

"....we have chosen to channel the code from Rodent four into..."

"....communications system and link you with Star Station Three..."

"....that will likewise be destroyed."

Pour and Roup looked up at the time face and watched as the small periods clicked steadily up the scale to zero zero and declare the turn.

00:00:00 − 732:01:05

And as the zeros clicked over so the count began. A cheerful but slightly mocking voice said: "Beginning countdown! You have two tenths minus ten small periods to Zero! Have a good dayeee!"

Pour and Roup stared at the clock but before they could say anything the voice called out again, "You have two tenths minus twenty small periods."

And no matter what they did wherever they went in the Star Station the voice called out the countdown to them, and to add insult to injury it added that this was a recorded message and finished with the tune, A Whiter Shade of Pale.

"Cut that Bulging music!" shouted Roup.

The Pair in charge of communications shook their heads and looked glum. The Pairs in the chamber cringed even more. The Aide looked distressed and apart from the music there was a heavy and frightened silence as the message sank in.

"We are Bulgered," wailed Pour.

The small enclosed room deep in the secret headquarters of the NMF echoed to the faint sound of a recorded voice. The originator of the voice sat in a seat with her twin and grinned. She was pleased that they had been chosen for the project. Her to use her diction and her twin to create the wonderful variation on the tune that they knew would be so annoying to the occupants of Star Stations Two and Three. On the large screen on the far wall of the room an electronic map showing the disposition of all the forces involved in the conflict on both planets changed and rotated from one scene to another and displayed figures that counted as accurately as it was possible the gains and losses on each of the warring sides. In the next room to theirs there was another battle going on to which they were not a party. This was as deadly in its nature as the one they were watching but the outcome was likely to be different. The Pairs involved would either be removed and imprisoned or be confirmed as the Leaders.

Whatever happened in the sealed room would sure to be conducted in a civilised manner and affect only those who were in the wrong. Whoever should win were of course right and whoever lost wrong. That, the Pairs in the operations room understood, was the logical and acceptable outcome.

In the sealed room the upstart Leader Pair who had accused the Elders of gross conservatism calmly made a statement suggesting that the Elders intended to replace the President with one of their own, and accused them of wishing to continue with the oppressive regime.

"We know how the governance of Zrad should work," the Elders replied. "You are upstarts and have no right to accuse us of wishing to continue, as you say, with a corrupt system."

"Yet you resist the call for proper and legal elections?"

"The time has not yet come for such childish ideas," the Pair said. "Now, you will suffer arrest and punishment for daring to oppose us!"

"I do not think so," replied the upstarts and with barely a change in their manner nor a wasted movement, he and his twin drew their swords and slaughtered the Elders, their Aides, two Leader Pairs who had jumped to their assistance and another who had attempted to break the seal and leave the room.

"Is that all of them now?" asked one.

"Yes and now we can take over," said the other.

"Shall we call the cleaners and get this mess removed?"

"I think so my twin and maybe check that the other clean up operations were successful?"

Thus the Pair Snert and Trens took over leadership of the NMF and hence the control of the rebel armies opposing the Emperor. Their action was the result of many tenths[3] of quiet plotting. Their agents had worked quietly and under cover to infiltrate the highest echelons of the rebel army and the NMF. The agents waited for the signal that came in conjunction with the announcement to the rebel forces that the NMF had taken control of the Doomsday Bomb and redirected it to home in on the two government star stations. The struggle for control over the bomb was aided by a mysterious outside source that called itself Rodent #4 who had not only supplied information about the bomb but had located Star Station One. It had also sifted through the records of NMF personnel and named the people it had considered, in its own words, dodgy. Snert and Trens had acted on the information and under the guise of loyal NMF executives had trapped the six treacherous Pairs in the bunker and explained the error of their ways.

"It will all end in tears, I know it," said Trens when the senior Pair argued that their interests and that of the present leadership were one and the same and offered them a huge sum of Tokens to shut up.

---

3 *Always a niggling problem with the Zradian fashion of dividing their year. The tenths are ten turns, and the actual divisions being of twenty turns each are called twentieths. Perversely the Zradians have no concept of fractions as progressively smaller the higher the number of divisions. This is a most puzzling use of nomenclature . Attempts to explain the system in terms of, say, cutting a cake into sixteen pieces the Zradian, on receiving a portion would say only that it is one piece of cake - which is perfectly correct. End of argument.*

Snert and Trens were no longer listening.

In the rebel headquarters some hundreds of kilometres north of the NMF headquarters a group of thirty Pairs tied hand and foot to each other marched slowly and sadly out into the dusty compound. Escorting them were a mixed bunch of male and female Pairs who were once employed by the rebel leaders as cooks, bottle washers, laundry Pairs, cleaners, clerks, janitors and gatekeepers. All the escort Pairs carried full weaponry regardless of sex or age and with hardly a word ushered their charges through the corridors to the execution grounds.

The two Elder Pairs who so opposed Glord and D.G begged for mercy and for their trouble they were the first to be cut free from their companions and lashed to the killing posts.

"You share the same fate as Grul and Lurg," they were told shortly before they were cut to pieces by the executioners' swords.

The group of servant Pairs, for that was what they were, returned to their companions within the building having dispatched all thirty Pairs by the same method and with enthusiasm took up their new tasks as part of the leadership of the rebel war against the Emperor. Their elected High Leader Pair, Danida and Danid, having abandoned their former job as lavatory cleaners in the former women's quarters, informed their counter parts, Snert and Trens, of the completion of their unpleasant but necessary task. That done they got on with the job of directing the efforts of the rebel forces in support of Angela's army and ordered their troops to make plans for the evacuation of the buildings.

"Pairs, we are on our way!" they said.

But it must be noted that they did not neglect their former duties.

The watchers sitting in the command post overlooking Sydney harbour's circular quay noted the drop in activity. They marked the steady decline in the strength of the opposition and saw the line heading toward Perth halt just before the town of Esperance and then retreat. The forces rolling toward Darwin came to a stop and likewise bogged down. The spur that had broken out from north of Melbourne and headed across the plains through Broken Hill halted and abandoned their wagons to retreat on foot. The Japanese Field Marshall whose task it was to oversee the control of the Australian forces deemed it time to roll up the enemy and gave the order. He telephoned his High Command in Tokyo and in that city there was a buzz of polite activity and a flurry of telephone calls. The huge set of screens that hung from the walls of the massive hall taken over by the armed forces to monitor the world wide operations showed in all areas a similar tale. The threatened attack in the middle east that had so upset the Israelis dissipated. In Africa the great advances by the Zradians ground to a halt and dug in behind their wagons in the hope of more supplies to repel the Combined African forces of the southern states. The African armies could not break the Zradian forces but neither could the Zradians do much except stave off attacks with carefully organized defence. It was, as one South African Colonel remarked, much like batsmen defending on a bowling wicket, but with the chance that even scoring singles might be difficult. His 2IC commanding agreed with him but cautioned that even the best bowlers don't have it all their own way.

In China and on the borders of the Indian peninsular and South East Asia Zradian forces were driven into the rain forests and bush to fight fiercely for survival. In northern China and Mongolia the Zradians who had lain waste to the land and the population escaped annihilation by nuclear weapons partly by accident and partly because of political intervention.

The ageing Premier of China when asked by his own Military Advisers to authorise a nuclear strike was at that moment taken by a bout of debilitating diarrheic incontinence and removed by his medical team to a private hospital ward where he was cleaned up and treated. While his would-be successors again resumed the quarrel over who was to take charge the Zradian forces ground to a halt. In the meantime, the Siberians, the Russians and a number of the new Russian states informed the Japanese that the Chinese were about to launch a nuclear strike. The Japanese politely informed the Chinese that if a strike was launched they would order the American nuclear submarines in the area to annihilate Beijing.

The nuclear strike plan was hastily abandoned.

The forces in North America fizzled to a halt bringing with it a sense of disappointment. General Schwarzkopf, whose forces were almost poised on the verge of victory, rushed into the space and found themselves herding demoralised Zradian prisoners into hastily prepared prison compounds. In addition to the task of looking after prisoners of war they had an even more difficult task of trying to persuade American citizens that it was unhealthy to cross the Sierras.

Making much of the coming defeat of the invaders President Horace Revere called a meeting of the world's press to the White House and made an announcement. He spoke confidently, sure of his position and told the press and the nation that the Zradian threat was contained and soon at the invitation of the British Prime Minister he would travel to London and speak with their Alien allies, Dart and Drat.

"While I am there in conference with the European leaders and the two Aliens, Denise will look after the good ole US of A. I am sure the nation will be in capable hands," he said, and expansively beckoned his Vice President forward. He smiled for the press as the two of them posed for the cameras letting everybody see how well Denise Walker and Horace Revere could work together. Inside he was fuming. The Japanese advisors had insisted in their own slimy way that he go to London. He didn't want to, and from the moment he was forced to agree, like when everybody agreed with the Nip, he began making plans to cover his ass. He had to make good in London or he was out. He knew that and the thought of his Vice President taking office made him want to kill something.

Preferably black, female and gay.

In London Prime Minister Smith examined the latest reports and looked up at the row of men and women who made up his war cabinet. He felt very Churchillian and imagined the reception he would get when he addressed the nation later that day. He was a little disturbed that the television people had insisted that he make his number 10 announcement before the program this evening. He wanted to make it during the program and inform the nation then. He had heard members of the cabinet muttering, making rude references to fighting on the beaches, never surrendering and laughing at him behind their fat hands. It was true that he had borrowed parts of the great Winston Churchill's speech but he had thought memories might not be that long and it did sound so grand. It was his speech. He had faced up to the Zradian invasion and bravely remained in London while his heroic soldiers had fought the enemy. The fact that the Royal Family had insisted they stay where the people could see them was neither here nor there, was it? Besides, he thought, there was nowhere to go.

"So the enemy are bogged down on the outskirts and in the north they have come to a halt on Ilkley Moor. In Europe and Russia they are stopped like Napoleon's forces outside Moscow. I would say that we can ask the question, 'Is there Hope' and the people can rejoice in our victory."

The First Admiral snorted. His forces had been used to evacuate people from the stricken areas and so far the navy had not engaged with the enemy except to send aircraft in support of the airforce.

"I don't think our forces can actually claim a victory, it is more likely that this is a temporary respite and we should be ready to resume hostilities soon," he said and glowered at the Army and Airforce contingent who looked overtly smug.

"But there is hope," insisted the Prime Minister.

"There is always hope," retorted the First Admiral.

The two men faced each other glaring angrily, each trying to outstare the other. The Prime Minister broke first but before he could embarrass himself by making another angry outburst a messenger entered the room and coughed to gain attention. Prime Minister Smith turned and snatched the sheet of paper out of the young woman's hand and read it as if it were a bad school report. He grunted and threw the paper down.

"Ladies and gentlemen, this appears to be a summons from Dart and Drat to a meeting prior to tonight's program to brief me on some most important news. It seems that the war on their home planet is taking a turn for the better and the, it says here Emperor's, loyalist forces are facing certain defeat. They mention a small group of people from Earth as responsible. One, a young man, the son of that fusspot Professor who warned us about the invaders, a young woman and an old Chinese bloke. It seems also that the Doomsday Bomb is no longer a threat, thanks so they say, to something called Rodent#4," the Prime Minister said, and grimaced at the cabinet members.

"Which means we will be able to get rid of the Japanese and take the credit for ourselves?" observed the First Admiral.

"Something like that," said the Prime Minister ignoring the sarcasm.

Slippery bastard, thought the First Admiral and smiled benignly at the Prime Minister.

"So there is hope," he said ignoring the angry looks his leader gave him.

Tell it like it is.

Maurice Bannerman fussed around the studio like a mother hen. This was the biggest thing to happen in the history of the media since the last biggest thing to happen happened and he was going to make the best of it. All over the known world there were television sets tuned in to his program and billions of people waiting to hear what Dart and Drat had to say. The Prime Minister and the President of the USA were there as fillers, and linked up with O'Rourke in Australia and the young mister Ghandi in India it looked like being a momentous success. Drat had suggested that the real reason for their presence was to show the world that this was a combined operation and that the Earth was still functioning as a planet unbowed by the Zradian invasion.

"It will be like sticking two fingers up at the President," said Dart, "And shows that whatever he attempts to do he will fail. We show the Zradian troops no mercy unless they surrender. Give the Pongos a chance to escape and surrender, and let the Japanese coordinate the fighting and we will win. We have the will, we have the resources, we have the people behind us, we will never surrender!" And when the Prime Minister's pompous speech was disseminated to the journalists and the press desk it was the words "We will never surrender!" that the press made a feature of reporting ignoring the rest of the speech, which most of them described as dull and uninspiring. Prime Minister Smith was, as they say in Australia, spitting bloody tacks. During the program other leaders would be allowed to have their say but mostly the program would be focussed on the events as Dart and Drat saw them. He was glad of Colin Hicks and his mob and glad too that they were acting as security at the party to be held in the studio's reception hall.

Maurice Bannerman hummed the popular tune A Whiter Shade of Pale turning it into Hava Nagila and put a smile on his face that in turn let him rub his hands together in fiscal delight. Sally Aitcheson was getting ready to front the program and Joseph Green stood by with the techno-crew to feed her the information as it came in. There was a crew of fresh faced telephone people ready to take the calls in the on screen call centre and a bank of operators in the regular call centre ready to monitor the incoming calls and arrange for translators. The team was working hard to make the event the best ever and Maurice had covered every contingency including, on the advice of Dart and Drat, of letting Colin Hicks and his mob to 'get fitted up' with guns.

"Why do you want shooters?"

"Because we do not trust your PM's government," said Dart and grinned. "We have it on good authority the PM is not enamoured by our charms."

"And for this you would carry weapons in my studio?"

"There is also likely to be a plot against us by the President's Dog Squads. We have no doubt that they will be lurking in the background," said Dart, and grinned. "All part of the job."

Maurice shuddered. These aliens were cool, seemingly unafraid of anything. He was sure they were capable of defending themselves and he was equally sure that if there was a fight they would join in. But for now there was the pleasant task of welcoming the guests and at the moment he started to leave the chaos in the studio he saw the indicator over the reception room door light up.

"Ah, guests have arrived," he said and strode through the studio avoiding the cables, operatives, cameras, lights and the crew doing sound and lighting checks. Technicians smiled at him as he passed and he acknowledged their smiles.

Maurice stepped through the door and immediately the noise of the studio was shut out. Rising from his seat the Prime Minister, David Smith, glowered at him and at Dart and Drat and made to speak.

"Good afternoon sir," said Maurice. "I hope you were not too inconvenienced by the sudden call?"

"Inconvenienced! I don't like being summonsed to appear on television!" he said loudly. Dart and Drat, ignoring the agitation of the PM, sat quietly in their chair chatting with Colin Hicks who was dressed in a smart suit open at the front to display leather strapping and a holstered service revolver that dated from the latter half of the twentieth century.

"I think the word is summoned unless of course you think we are about to prosecute an action against you. We have some developments we need to discuss with you here in private and I think to do so I will leave you to talk with Dart and Drat while I go meet President Revere," said Maurice calmly and politely.

He left the reception room and headed for the main door where he expected President Revere and his entourage to arrive from London airport. He also expected to meet General West and confirm that the link with Brigadier Chin in Australia was about to go ahead. He smiled as he walked out of the room knowing that what Smith was about to hear would upset him.

"Get that thug out of here," said the PM.

"Which thug is that?" asked Dart.

"That one, the Hicks fellow."

"He stays," said Dart.

"Not while I am here."

"Then you had better leave," said Dart, and smiled at him. "Someone else can take your place. We can use mister Kisogi to explain what part Britain played. We don't need you for that."

The PM looked stunned and stared open mouthed at Dart and his twin and Colin Hicks who grinned broadly but showed contempt in his eyes.

"What part of fuck off don't you understand?" Colin said and fingered the pistol.

"I didn't come here to be insulted," said the PM.

"And until you demanded that Colin leave we had no intention of doing so," said Dart.

"Yeah, the trouble with you is you react to everything and don't just accept what ain't gonna change, see?" said Colin.

"Not true."

"It is."

"No it isn't."

"Yes it is."

"No!"

"Yes!"

"No!"

"Stop it you two," said Drat and gently pushed the PM back into his chair and waved Colin to the background where the latter sat on a bar stool and grinned. As the PM sat down looking like a fair imitation of the Norse god Thor Colin poked his tongue out at him and giggled.

"Always wanted to do that," he said.

This time the PM ignored him.

"Why we asked you to come early, and it was only a request not a summons, was to brief you on some recent developments on our home planet and we wish to give you an opportunity to be the first to honour some of your own nation's people," said Drat. "We think that you should think about giving them some sort of award as heroes. We would also like your propaganda, sorry, your Party Office, to exploit the situation. All in aid of the war effort you know, the way Sir Winston would have done it."

"You taking the piss?" said the PM.

"No, just trying to be patronising," said Drat, and grinned.

"Cheeky sod. What's in it for me?" said the PM and looked at Colin who turned his face away and gazed at the ceiling polishing his nails on his lapel. "Cheeky sods."

"You will be set up for life if you want to be. We will need a contact here to whom our people can identify and as some of your people are now heroes of the revolution you will be the obvious choice," Drat said.

"And if I do not cooperate, because that is what you want of me isn't it?"

"Then we will choose somebody else and smudge the place they come from or, alternatively we will choose the leader of the opposition, said Drat sweetly.

"Bastards."

"Yeah, ain't they," said Colin.

"I suppose you had better tell me then," said the PM.

Dart took a deep breath and related the story of Angela and Julian to him. He told him about Tzu Wu and Arthur and finally about Blard and Bradl and their assistants.

"We will have some DVD clips of their exploits and we want you to acknowledge them as they are shown to the world," said Dart.

"There is a snag," said Drat.

"And what is that?"

"Julian Renfrew is wanted for the killing of a police officer, escaping custody, arson and breaking probation. It might be a good idea to get one of your spin doctors to sort of make him out to be a victim of circumstances or something," said Drat and smiled glancing at the clock. "You have about an hour or so before the program."

Smith looked stunned and with a resigned look on his face that would have deceived all but his closest associates he took the telephone that Colin offered him and called his office. When he had finished his call Colin looked at him with a mixture of respect and disgust and shook his head.

"You are nasty," he said.

"That's politics."

Dart and Drat laughed.

McCord sat on the coffee table and carefully strapped the knife sheaths to his legs making sure that his socks covered the lower portions of them and that they lay flat against his leg so that when he lifted his pants he could pick either blade quickly and without even thinking about it being there. He put his pants on and tucked his shirt in neatly strapping the shoulder holster on making sure that it was fitted perfectly. He adjusted the straps and slid the pistol inside slipping it up and down satisfied that he could get it quickly. He put his jacket on and tried reaching the pistol again and found that he could snatch it out as quickly with the jacket as without. He felt comfortable with the arrangement and packed the holster, straps and gun in the instrument case. All that remained was to put the broken down pump action shotgun and he was ready.

He had already stripped and cleaned the shotgun and made sure that the action worked smoothly. He liked the heavy gun and the modified magazine that allowed him an extra three shots. The Confederates in the American civil war would have liked one like his. Remington, a great name in guns and one he liked to support.

He checked his make up in the mirror and saw a man who was hard to describe; an ordinary face above an ordinary suit and hopefully someone who would fit in. He hoped so because his plan relied on the idea that nobody notices ordinary people. His method had worked before and was usually much better than hiding and attacking. He remembered the last job and smiled. He had simply walked into the room hardly noticed by anybody and shot the punter, slipped the pistol back into its holster and walked out again before anybody had time to react. Nobody had so far given a description of him that looked anything like his real self.

McCord left the flat, locking the door behind him leaving his gear behind knowing that after the operation the cleaners would come and take everything away. He liked the place but it was time he left; took the money and ran. He looked forward to the cash and the enforced retirement - there was only so long a man could operate at his level without going underground for a time.

He moved quickly and quietly and headed down the stairs, out into the street turned the end and through the dingy street where the parking spaces were filled with abandoned cars and the cats fought with the dogs for the contents of the garbage cans. Goodnight suckers. He did not see the group of men gathering in the shadows that split off in Pairs that, although not following him, were heading in the same general direction.

Horace Revere sweated and felt extremely uncomfortable. The aliens Dart and Drat were much more intelligent than he thought and so well informed that he struggled to hide anything from them. He could handle the Brit PM and did so with ease but with the two aliens he was completely stumped. Whatever he said they had an answer and when they got onto the tricky subject of the nuke strike he was out of his depth. The presenter seemed to have something going with Dart and that annoyed him because she kept on referring to him rather than asking the questions completely herself. He had to admit that the whole program was well thought out and when the Australian Premier and the Prime Minister of New Zealand got on their high horses about the nuke strike he was ready to explode. Miss Aitcheson handled that very well and smoothed over his boiling temper with some timely words.

"You have to remember, mister President, that New Zealand has had a nuclear free policy since nineteen eighty four and Australia conceded to the same thing some ten years ago. Naturally they are touchy."

"If mister Kisogi had come forward with a deal on the arms we needed then perhaps we may not have resorted to a nuclear strike," Horace said.

"Perhaps, but then you were a little slow on the uptake," said Prime Minister Smith interjecting when he realised that Kisogi was not willing to answer.

And it was at this point that Horace Revere made his mistake. Afterwards when his staff were packing his belongings and loading them onto the removal vans as he quitted the White House he recalled the mistake and cringed.

"How could I do that," he was heard to mutter, and all avoided catching his gaze for fear of his anger.

As it was he thought that at that moment the program was cutting to a scene from somewhere else and without thinking about his words he spoke almost as if he were thinking out loud.

"Yeah, and if the cocksucking Nips had rushed across the bloody Pacific a fucking day earlier we might have not have needed the Nukes. I guess the little yellar fuckers are still pissed about Hiro-fucking-shima," he said, and gasped when he realised that what he said was being broadcast to the world. And especially being broadcast to the United States where his words were likely to explode his political career with more personal devastation than Hiroshima, Nagasaki and the Nevada desert combined. His assumption that if the attack in 1941 on Pearl Harbour was launched on the Saturday instead of Sunday the American forces would have been on normal garrison duties.

Up to that point the whole thing had gone well. The Palace had addressed the nation and welcomed the delegates and the leaders of the other nations, praised the prime minister for his efforts and of course had praised all loyal subjects on Zrad for their part in the alien war.

"Heroes come from all walks of life and it is a great honour to know that these subjects of our land, having found themselves embroiled in a deadly conflict have become heroes of the people of a foreign land. It is therefore my great honour to recognise their part, and should we be successful in defeating this scourge, it will be an even greater honour to reward them in the tradition of our nation," HRH said, and added much else that seemed to be encouraging.

Madame President had spoken well on behalf of the French people and Nikolai had done his bit from Russia. A faceless rep from Beijing had explained how the government had curtailed the military Hawks from a nuke strike on the enemy and extolled the virtue of the peace loving Chinese people ecetera, ecetera. The spokesperson for the precarious temporary alliance between the Indians, Pakistanis and the factions from Bangladesh and Sri-Lanka had made her comments. The Israeli premier had declared he was suspending hostilities in the region, as long as the Syrians and Palestinian terrorists suspended theirs, to mop up the Zradian forces.

Mister Kisogi declared that as soon as the Zradian war was over his government was willing to resume normal trading and to trade with the new regime on Dart and Drat's home planet. The discussion had bogged down when the threatened Chinese nuclear strike was discussed. Revere himself had tried to justify the bombing and made his unfortunate remark. Two Aides met him in the ante-room after the program and handed him a message. As he expected it was from his Vice President.

Horace – In the light of your unfortunate remarks on ETV this night it is advisable you offer your resignation – it is with extreme prejudice that impeachment proceedings are being put in place – Senate and Congress are furious. Regards Denise.

"Holy shit," he said, and screwed it up to be handed another that he read immediately. It said more or less the same thing but came from his office informing him that impeachment proceedings were being put in place and that his early reply was imperative.

"Tell them I resign and leave it to that bitch Walker to sort it out," he said to the Aide who hurried off muttering about calling on the Ambassador. Horace Revere felt drained and as the other participants, came back from the studio he stood dejected and tired as he realised what had happened.

"You and your big mouth," said Kisogi.

"Fuck off," he said and sank into a chair.

"So sorry, just trying to help but it seems you cannot forget Pearl Harbour," he said and showed some steel in his eyes.

Horace Revere looked up at the Japanese diplomat and shook his head sadly. If it wasn't for his Southern pride he would have cried but instead he bit back the tears and again shook his head. Surprisingly it was Prime Minister Smith who cheered him up by insisting that he go to the function that evening and forget the troublesome situation until the next morning.

"But I have resigned," he said.

"Good job too," said Smith, "Best to leave it to some other bugger to clean up the shit. You should go back to beef farming. Longhorns isn't it?"

"More or less," said Horace, "But I haven't farmed personally since I first went into politics."

"Never mind old chap, soon pick it up again, one does you know," said Smith and grinned. "I haven't exactly had a clean mouth in my time and I manage."

Horace nodded and as Dart and Drat approached with a tray of drinks he made up his mind to be there. He took a drink and raised it to Dart and Drat and Sally Aitcheson who appeared at Dart's elbow.

"Here's to a damn good program, so help me," he said.

"In spite of the unfortunate remarks," said Sally.

"To hell with them and damn the torpedoes," he said and drank as they all raised their glasses.

Only Ambassador Kisogi failed to drink but then he was teetotal.

"Rear ends elevated is it?" he said and grinned.

Horace Revere spluttered and almost choked at the silly joke.

Julian is my son.

Julia was having a bad hair day. She knew that whatever happened that day was going to be the pits. It started off badly when the Chinese women looking after her refused to give her any drink. They went as far as confining her to a few comfortable rooms and attending her every need, whether she wanted it or not. She needed a drink and badly. She explained that she felt dry and shaky but the women gazed at her kindly and refused, politely, to get her any drink except tea or coffee or water.

"You may have anything to drink you like that has no alcohol in it," the older one said.

Julia sat and stared at her and locked her eyes onto the other woman's and explained again. She spoke quietly but with a sharp cutting edge that her husband and her son recognised as her 'I am about to blow my top' voice and with cold reasoning insisted she go out and get some gin to drink.

"I need it," she said.

"That is correct but you no have it," the woman insisted equally quietly and with a similar edge to her voice.

"You do not understand. I am a free citizen and a responsible adult and I know what I want," she said.

"Ah yes, you may know what you want but do you know what you need?" said the woman giving her an infuriating benign smile.

Julia snapped and with her fists clenched she stamped her feet and yelled at them.

"You fucking slant eyed bitches! I want a fucking drink and I want it now! You rotten slags! Let me out of here! I want a fucking drink!"

Julia tried to dash past them but found herself easily stopped by the small young one who apologised for hurting her and with sharp fingers held her down on the floor. She struggled but try as she might she could neither stop the pain nor get up. The woman apologised again and told her to lie still or, so sorry will hurt.

"Fuck you and your poxy so fucking sorry."

"So sorry must hurt again. You stop bad speaking."

Julia screamed in agony as the fingers delved into her and instead of swearing she said nothing and sighed with relief when the pain stopped.

"Now missy Julia," said the older one, "we no like to hurt you but my Uncle he gave us order that you were not allowed to drink alcohol until he say so. My uncle say you do this a long time and he let you have a drink. Until then you no touch. From today you no go out unless we take you out, okay. You be good and you will get drink okay?"

That was so long ago now she had lost track of time and since then she had modified her language and made her peace with Marjorie. The two women had given their permission for Marjorie to take her to Maurice Bannermann's program where she was going to be named as the mother of a hero of Zrad and talk about Julian to the world. She was thrilled but had to promise to do as Marjorie told her.

"No drink missy Julia."

"Okay, okay, no drink, I promise."

"I will allow you to have soft drinks, tea, coffee and water," said Marjorie, "and you can eat what you like."

"I can get fat but not drunk, is that it?"

"Right on sister."

Julia had to admit that getting dressed and ready with fresh make up, new underwear and being fussed over by the Chinese girls was wonderful. She left the house feeling like a princess and stepped into the car to take her seat beside Marjorie and the escorts and imagined that this was what it was like to be a star.

"This is Gary and the man with the smile is Colin Hicks. Gary will sit and look but Colin, who is in charge will talk. The man beside the driver is another escort and they will look after us." Marjorie explained as the car moved off.

"I'm sorry about your ole man but I unnerstand he's all right. If me and me mates was really on the ball and listened proper to what your ole geezer said we wouldn't a lorst 'im," said Colin.

"Thank you. I was more concerned about my son but it is good to hear that Arthur is safe," Julia said, and smiled at Colin. "I understand that the attack was sudden and you were gassed or something of the sort. Even if you were on the ball as you put it gas is not easy to fight is it?"

Colin grinned broadly and shook his head.

"No excuse really, I should have led him out of the place by the back ways, and then we lorst Mister Byrde and cocked it up all ways. Nuffin seems to go right when you wannit to."

"But you will still get paid because now you work for Dart and Drat," said Marjorie.

"Yeah and I got to thump the prime minister. I hate that bugger," Colin said and rubbed one fist in his hand. "You shoulda seen him hit the deck. Wallop! He went down like a sack of spuds and never got up agin until one of his toffee nosed oppo's came with a sponge and dragged him out. Nice one that."

Julia asked Colin to explain and exploded into laughter when Colin described the incident with all the movements. She was still laughing when the car slid into a parking slot and they were out and heading for the elevator. She caught a movement out of the corner of her eye and glanced in its direction. Something dark slipped into deeper darkness but it was too fleeting to see what it was. She let it go and followed the others to the studio to meet Maurice Bannerman who escorted her to the dressing rooms where girls fussed around her doing lighting tests and politely added more make up to her face.

"What do I say?" she asked, and Maurice who was hovering near her elbow spoke quietly and firmly.

"Just say what you want to and let Sally Aitcheson lead you through. Nobody will ask you any hard ones and if you do not want to answer any questions say so. Sally will not ask anything that will embarrass you. Treat the others in the studio as normal people, they have already had a hard time of it. You are there to talk about Julian and show him off at his best. The world needs a hero or two and you will be one and your son will be another."

Julia felt inspired by his words and entered the studio on cue feeling confident and pleased to be escorted to her seat like the contestant of a game show. The men already seated stood up to greet her and with some confusion she shook their hands in turn and tried to catch the names. It was not until she had sat down that she realised that the man on her left was Prime Minister Smith and the one on the far left was the Japanese Ambassador. There was one empty seat and across from her the two aliens sat looking relaxed. They smiled when Sally announced that they would see a film clip of her Julian and then she could tell everybody about him.

Warming to her subject after the first question about his childhood and his difficult schooling Julia did her best to paint a rosy picture of Julian and with a mother cat ferocity defended his wayward talents with all her verbal claws. She ran out of steam at the exact moment when Sally recalled the president of the USA and when she saw the man enter and take his seat ready to answer more questions she summed him up.

Pompous little prick.

Horace Revere announced that he was resigning the Presidency of the United States and as if he were biting on some bitter weed he apologised for his 'unfortunate lapse' and with as much control as he could manage made an apology to the Japanese Ambassador who smiled and bowed slightly. The lights signalled the end of the program and as the credits were scrolled up past them Sally leaned across the gap and touched her hand.

"Thank you for your input, please join Dart and Drat, Marjorie and myself at our table during the meal."

Julia was pleased and smiled at the younger woman who, when the director gave the call, took Dart's hand as they stood and left the studio. She was pleased when Drat offered his arm and escorted her off the set, the Ambassador walking with them. President Revere had already left.

The small party after the television broadcast was Julia's opportunity to talk about her son, and although Marjorie controlled what drinks she had she enjoyed the experience.

"They are having wine with the food, what about me? Don't I get any?" Julia said.

Marjorie smiled and nodded her head, "Of course you do, the glass on your left is being filled right now, you deserve it. You did all right."

Julia looked at the other woman and saw only warmth and friendliness and realised that she was not being patronised but 'looked after' instead and that was a difference. Somebody cared for her, and that was unusual.

"Oh, I am sorry, if I don't get pissed I can have some more, right?" Julia said.

"That is right," said Marjorie.

"And was I all right about my boy?" Julia asked.

"We got the impression that Julian is an ordinary lad doing an extraordinary job like any other soldier in any other army. I liked the way you showed how proud you were of him but at the same time didn't make him out to be squeaky clean, or even a hero. I think many people would be impressed," Marjorie said.

"I feel sort of humble with all those other buggers on the telly with me; you know, the President of America, Smiffy, the Prime Minister, and all those other foreign buggers," said Julia.

"Oh, don't worry you realise who the star might be?" Marjorie said.

If Julia was about to reply she was to stop short because at that moment Maurice announced that responses to the ETV program were about to be aired. The diners watched the bulletins and although there was much about the program itself the other TV stations were showing their own versions of events, but what dominated the broadcasts was Julian's story. It seemed the world had taken him on as a hero.

Julia watched the screen her face aglow with motherly pride and when the bulletins were finished and there was a silence she said proudly. "That was Julian, he's my son!"

The party was a wow. PM Smith drank far too much and his long suffering wife whose loyalty was tested by his belligerence and owed much to her desire to enjoy her present lifestyle, remained reasonably sober. On his own account Horace Revere hugged a bottle of Jack Daniels and between having to talk with the rest of the guests, his own Ambassador among them, sipped from it without using a glass. He wished he had his wife with him so that he could pour out his troubles to her and get that good old southern comfort. He missed her 'aw gee honey you all know you is the best'; he hadn't reckoned on having to socialise and realised that he had made a pig's ear of the whole thing. He reflected too on his talk with Dart and Drat and the content of the program. He and the world by now were convinced that the aliens were genuine and really did want to help. Drat had told him before dinner that the NMF wanted a new regime and that they were willing to elect the next President and create a two house system.

"We want to have a President but with a lower chamber of Senators linked to the various sectors and an upper chamber of legislators independent of the various factors within our society. The NMF want to avoid the present system which is a dictatorship and also not to embrace one that relies only on the rich. We have decided to create a Senate that will be changed every four four hundreds by half and then half again. No Pair will be able to serve as President for more than one term of four four hundreds. Senators will be chosen by vote and legislators will be chosen from a list. First we have to win the war and set things to rights both here and at home. We want to trade with you and want to offer you some radical new ideas," Drat explained, and smiled warmly.

Horace Revere had agreed that had he still been President of the USA he would be happy to help and suggested that Drat tell the President all about it. He regretted his rudeness almost before he had finished speaking and made an excuse to get away as soon as he could. He sidled up to his Ambassador and waited for the official to acknowledge him feeling awkward wanting to assert his authority but unwilling to suffer the snub that the ex-senator was likely to give him.

"Horace, so nice to see you," the Ambassador said, smiling with his mouth but not his eyes.

"Jeffry, good to see you could make it, er, you have spoke with Denise?"

"The new President has been in touch, yes. She bade me send her regards. I am sorry Horace that you have been, er, deposed. Nevertheless we shall carry on," the Ambassador said and gave the smile again.

Cocksucker.

"Ah yes, I am sure," he said.

He got through the meal by talking with Julia Renfrew who sneaked a few sips at his Jack Daniels which he slipped into her coke. He chatted her up, as the Brits put it, for the main chance of getting her into his bedroom and she let him for the main chance of getting some of his dark liquid. Sex for either of them was not an option. Only the President did not know it.

During the dinner a jazz band gathered and set up their gear. They quietly tuned in and sat around chatting as the diners ate and talked. Horace Revere was glad that there were no after dinner speeches and instead there was to be dancing. Horace Revere liked to dance and he especially liked to dance to Dixieland jazz. He was pleased when Julia said she liked to dance too and when the music started they were first on the floor. Horace Revere was too drunk to notice that Julia was a rotten dancer but not too drunk to notice that the trombone player on the left closest to the stage door looked familiar. The whirling dancers and the bourbon clouded his memory and, like the rest of the guests, he lost himself in the music.

The news that President Horace Revere of the United States had offered his resignation and that it was accepted made headline news for a brief moment and interest for a while centred on Denise Walker the new President of the USA. That she was the first black woman president vied as news with the fact that she was not the first woman and although her sexual preferences were not an issue as yet the gutter news were about to make them so. That she did not care was a bonus the American people were not aware of because from the moment she knew she was to be elected she put her public relations machine into top gear to let the people know all about her. She left the PR people to their task and asked for all updates on the current military and political situation. A file name in the CIA list caught her eye and she made a telephone call to her source in Langley and asked about it.

"You sure of this? No mistakes?" She asked, and watched her screen seeing a picture, data scrolling and pursed her lips. "This is ex-agent McCord, right, so tell me what is he doing?"

The answer came back in a few minutes.

"And a there's a group of unknowns close by?" She listened to the answer and changed telephones. "Damn the man," she said and within moments she was on to her diplomatic staff with an urgent message for Prime Minister Smith. "I don't give a shit if he is at the post program function. Get the Limey bastard and tell him it is urgent!" she said. Two minutes later she was talking to PM Smith who sounded drunk and what she told him was enough to sober him up.

"Fuck me," he said and covered the telephone and muttered to somebody close by.

"Smith, answer me," Denise Walker said but when the PM did answer she heard him say: "Sherry, I have to sort something out." And whatever he was going to say next was lost in a series of loud noises, a clatter followed by Smith swearing profusely and cry out something about a 'bloody idiot woman' and after that the sound of gunfire.

"Smith? Smith? Answer me!" she said but knew there would be none.

We Apologise for the lack of Service

Betty/Anthony/Napoleon subdued the gaggle of personalities trying to upset them and concentrated on the straggling force of Zradian troops that were approaching. Napoleon was tired and it was up to Anthony and Betty to sort out the problem.

"We must respect our father," Anthony.

"He had no time for us," Betty.

"He is coming to see us," Anthony.

"He is coming to destroy us," Betty.

"What does Napoleon say?" Anthony.

"He is unwell." Betty.

"Ah, then we must deal with it ourselves," Anthony.

"Our father approaches and he has a nasty with him, something very nasty and we do not like it." Betty

"He is stopping and we must go and speak with him," Anthony.

"Yes we must go and speak with him," Betty.

"NO!" Napoleon.

"We must,"

"We must!"

The robot lurched forward and climbed the hill that separated it from the column of troops and the lead vehicle filled with the nasty and rose over the top. It aimed its weapon at the lead wagon and waited gathering information from the data streaming out of the wagon's emitters. There was something wrong, something it could not quite understand in the stream of data which needed analysis before there was any reaction.

"Wait! There is something not quite..."

At that moment a query directed at rodent #4 flicked into its memory distracting the robot's Betty and Anthony personalities, confusing the others that were trying to be heard just long enough to allow Napoleon to interfere. Briefly the robot remained static whilst its personalities wrestled for control, and at the moment when Anthony took over something flashed from the nasty in the lead vehicle and its own weapon responded.

Too late! The robot realised it had made a mistake.

"I tried to tell you," Napoleon.

What's happening?" Didi, Gogo, Godot, Pottzo, Lucky, Celia, Murphy and a creature calling itself Gonzo the Great.

The robot had no time to answer and shut down.

An electronic message hung in the air as the robot's entire system failed and left it a smoking wreck.

Normal service will be resumed as soon as possible – please take care of the rodents.

Clard and Dracl squealed when the Leader Pair poked them with his swords. They squealed again when the Pair did the same with their knives. They stopped squealing when the Leader Pair explained that they would be permitted to live if they devised a weapon that would get rid of the robot.

"And if we cannot do that," stammered Dracl.

"Then we will hand you over to the robot."

They set to work and as it happened the weapon did not take so much effort as they thought. It was a simple matter of building a mini bomb that would automatically trigger a negative feed back to the robot's defence system. The only snag was that it needed a response from the robot's own weapon to set it off. They solved the problem by building the device into a wagon and let that lead the column to the robot.

"All we have to do is get there, get in close so the robot sees the threat and will fire. We can sacrifice the wagon and if the driver Pair are nimble enough they will get away before the robot fires," said Clard smugly.

"Then you will drive the lead wagon and if you are lucky you will escape won't you," said the Leader Pair.

Poked into the lead wagon by the swords of the Leader Pair Clard and Dracl led the column and lined the weapon up on the robot. They set the weapon to track and fire and leapt out of it running as fast as they could back to the column and cowered at the door of the Leader Pair's wagon begging to be let in.

"Not until the robot is destroyed."

"Mercy! Have mercy!"

"It hasn't happened yet."

The Leader Pair was right. Nothing had happened and the wagon stood there loaded and ready but so did the robot.

"Go back and sort it."

Clard and Dracl squealed when they saw a small troop of soldiers emerge from the rear of the vehicle with swords ready.

"All right, all right, we are on our way!" they said, together.

With leaden feet they trudged back to the wagon watched by the soldiers who were now aiming laser weapons at them. Half way back there was a flash of light and instinctively they ducked and dropped screaming in fear to the moist ground. There was a rippling explosive noise that vibrated through the ground beneath them and a hot searing wave and moments later pieces of hot metal and plastic plopped down alongside them. They screamed again when pieces hit them burning their tunics and their flesh. They writhed and wriggled and slapped and groaned and moaned until strong hands picked them from the ground and roughly but expertly removed the burning material. As if in a dream they felt themselves carried back to the wagon line, placed on benches and their hurts treated, the dream turned to reality when the Leader Pair faced them grinning.

"You did it you dozy Bulgers," said the Leader Pair.

"What happened?" asked Dracl.

"The robot is a pile of solidified silicon and we can get on our way."

Clard and Dracl saw the screen images and there, as the Leader Pair said, was a pile of silicon where the robot had been and a wide patch of burning bush. The wagon was a twisted mass of smoking metal surrounded by burning vegetation. As they watched the rains began to fall and the scene of destruction was enveloped in clouds of steam.

The idea of the robot being destroyed and that they were the authors of that destruction, they had to agree, was a comforting and pleasant sight.

All they had to do now was to convince their captors to set them free.

Nice one Julia...!

McCord checked his shirt front, adjusted the bow tie and hefting his instrument cases made sure that the one with the trombone was in his left hand and the other with the shotgun was on his right. He grinned at the rest of the musicians as they greeted him and put both cases down by his seat. He laughed with them as they made comments and listened to Con, the leader, as he instructed them on the evening's entertainment. Con's Dixieland Stompers had played jazz at the hotel for years and McCord, who had adopted the name Harry Roy, had played trombone with them for the best part of five years. He always took two cases with him and normally both were filled with instruments. McCord played with the band on Saturdays and Fridays and on all special occasions. Most of the band were part timers; jazz enthusiasts who had homes to go to but loved the music. Con could field a band every night of the week made up of some thirty eight members but usually there were six or eight. Tonight there were eight and McCord was fixed to play second trombone and vocal backing.

He left the gun in its box and took the trombone. He played and sang and watched the partygoers get drunker. He watched Horace Revere smarming up to the English woman who sipped coke and bourbon with him. He was amused by the antics of the pompous prick, Smith and his snooty wife who insisted on dancing more or less formally. The break arrived and the band laid their instruments down to go and get a welcome snack and a drink. McCord slipped away to the bathroom. He grabbed the gun from the dressing room and actually went to the bathroom washing and drying his hands after he had finished. He pulled the shirt front off and threw it and the tie in a trash can and loosened his jacket. With the box in his left hand and the thumb ready on the catch he walked steadily along the corridor to the hall. He halted at the door, slipped the catch on the box and with deft movements lifted the two parts of the gun and snapped them together. He slung it over his shoulder and drew his pistol and with no ceremony stepped into the ballroom. He raised the weapon and took aim.

A wild hysterical shout distracted him only long enough to see who was shouting; it was not long enough to spoil his aim but what happened next was. He was surprised by a number of sudden events. The first was Julia Renfrew's hysterical scream, and the others followed on in such rapid succession that before he realised he had failed his mission he already had. He felt bullets hit him from two different directions and saw the men who fired the guns. He felt the numbing effect of sudden gunshot trauma and tried to stand but his legs and his bowels let go dumping both on the polished floor with a soft squelching thump. He saw the black clad figures rush onto the dance floor and watched as President Horace Revere stood open mouthed as Julia screamed a string of obscenities and threw a bottle at the leader of the black clad men.

"Fuck off you rotten pack of bastards!" she screamed and hurled two more bottles in quick succession. Both missiles found their mark and as McCord slipped into the complete darkness of death he saw Colin and his men take over. Some herded the guests out and others faced the intruders. McCord died realising that he had underestimated the efficiency of Colin Hicks and his crew.

McCord's death, or rather his bloody and twitching corpse, played a minor part in the escape of the intruders giving the Leader Pair and three other Pairs a brief respite from attack. Pressed back to the corridor by a hail of bullets that mowed down three Pairs before they could use their lasers the Leader Pair retired to take cover and tripped over McCord's body. The bullets meant for them passed harmlessly overhead. Other Pairs attempted to fire but at that moment somebody on the control board dimmed the lights in the hall.

Their mission had failed and with a mighty shout from his position on the floor the Leader Pair screamed at his troop to get out of there.

He led the way down the corridor McCord had used, running in the dim light almost blind. Behind them Colin and half his force raced to follow and the Leader Pair was satisfied when they too tripped over McCord's body. Nevertheless the chase was on and the Leader Pair raced through the corridors and down the stairs to the service street at the rear before it occurred to him to shoot back.

"Are we afraid of this pig fodder?" he yelled and crashed into a trash bin he didn't see disturbing two cats scavenging for scraps who dropped to the pavement and turned on them spitting and snarling. The Zradians to a Pair panicked, torn between a desire to chase the animals and to be as far away from them as possible. With their minds filled with images of Carnibeasts they dropped their weapons and ran.

Colin and his men, a little more cautious, ran out after them, scooped up the weapons and pausing only to sling them over their shoulders ran after the Zradians. Such was their fear of the cats the Zradians disappeared and soon outstripped Colin and his men. Colin led his team back to the hotel and watched by frightened staff they returned to the dance hall. Already police and ambulance sirens were wailing and the hall was a confusion of security men, his own people and police including a squad in the lobby from the American Embassy demanding to see Horace Revere and the Ambassador.

In the midst of the confusion Dart and Drat stood calmly with Maurice Bannerman, Marjorie Watts, Sally Aitcheson the jazz band leader, the Prime Minister and his wife surrounding Julia Renfrew who was explaining to them what she had seen.

Colin deployed his men and walked across the hall to speak to Dart.

"We lost them but we got their weapons and hey, Julia baby, you did all right, what happened?" Colin asked.

The group grinned at him and Julia, her eyes squinting a little as she focussed on Colin explained.

"Like I told this lot, the fucking yank stuck his poxy hand up me skirt. I smacked his face, kneed his balls and then I saw them fucking bastards come in. I fair shit myself when I saw them and thought, fuck me, I'm not having this and bunged a bottle at them," she said.

Colin grinned and shook his head.

"So it was you who yelled the warning. We saw the trombone player with his shooter and my blokes got him but we didn't see the others," Colin said.

"Nor did I until that fucking yank tried to stick a finger in me twat. I was yelling at the randy bastard and saw them over his shoulder. As for bloody Smithy, when I yelled for his help all his stuck up missus and he could do was gawp. There was the bloody yank with his eyes watering 'cos I've just kicked him in the bollocks, Smithy on the poxy telephone, his missus standing there looking shocked and a crowd of fucking aliens looking like a second hand SWAT team from the united fucking states of fucking America. What do you expect a girl to do? If they want a fucking shag they can go find a fucking massage parlour!"

Colin stared at Julia and for all the noise that was going on, the fuss that surrounded them as police, ambulance staff, hotel staff, government security staff and the small American group who surrounded Revere he was amazed at how self centred she was, and amazed at her capacity for such bad language, even he would not be so vociferous as that.

"Well Julia it was you who alerted us so all I gotta say is bloody well done! You are a hero like your son! Nice one Julia." Colin said.

"Oh fuck him," she said, "He's just a bloody skinny little wanker."

Colin stared at her open mouthed for a brief moment and then with a roar he leaned against one of his men and laughed. "What a woman!" he cried out shaking his head in disbelief.

Don't try this at home

Dart and Drat took a few minutes to find out where their attackers were gone. The party broke up and at their insistence Dart and Drat were driven back to their hotel taking Julia, Marjorie and Sally with them. Colin and his men kept the Zradian lasers and once back in their rooms Dart ordered coffee, serving it while Drat consulted their Atlas.

"I believe the mob will go to the Bywater Road," said Drat. "It might be an idea to follow them up. Colin? Any ideas?"

"Me and four others might like to do that," said Colin rubbing his hands with anticipation. "I'd like to try out them shooters."

"Okay, choose four and set off like soon. You travel light and grab what you can. Water and weapons, food is no trouble if you can live off what you find."

Colin picked Gary, Trevor, Animal and a wiry shorter man named Reg who favoured anything with a sharp blade.

Colin's eyebrows shot up, knitted into a vee, and spread out wide as Drat explained what he had to do and gave him a series of numbers. Colin repeated them and grinned broadly when Drat gave him another set of figures and asked him to repeat them. "Give it your best and have fun," said Drat.

The five men moved off and outside the hotel watched by jealous security men, Police and curious clean up teams, they and their weapons piled into a large limousine. Colin waved to Dart and Drat as the car moved off leaving the alien Pair to explain what was going on. True to type the press were now howling for a story and some followed the car while the rest, torn between the two stories stayed at the hotel. They were fortunate that within a half hour Dart and Drat opened out and told them all they needed to know.

While Dart and Drat held their press conference and the dead Zradians were cleared away along with unfortunate McCord, Colin and his men rode in luxury to the Bywater Road. Colin gazed at the Thames as they drove along the embankment and then out to the west along Chiswick High Road and caught a glimpse of Kew as they worked around the streets to the Bywater allotments. The allotments were deserted and in the light from the street lamps and the houses Colin and his men walked the pathway to the ruined shed. As they passed the last patch of garden Colin nodded his head in its general direction and remarked to his men that the plot looked neglected.

"Yeah," said Reg who was a keen gardener, "It is a bloody shame to let it go like that. People are crying out for allotments and can't get them."

"Ain't no justice," said Colin. "Right now mate we gotta get going after these foreign ratbags."

He hopped up onto the shed platform and the others followed him. They stood on the dirty wooden floor in a self-conscious group suddenly surprised when media cars roared down the road and stopped by the gate disgorging journalists in rapid succession. Camera's flashed and lights suddenly splashed yellow and white flooding them and highlighting their weapons and the strange background of ruined shed, brick walls and flourishing plots.

Colin fondled the column and before he pressed the buttons he turned to face the media representatives and grinned.

"Don't try this at home," he said and pressed the sequence of buttons.

The cameras flashed and caught a wonderful image of Colin and his men disappearing into thin air. The process took the press by surprise and if it were not for the fact that they saw it happen before their eyes and caught it all on camera they would not have believed it. As it was one journalist from a local paper muttered and then spoke loudly for all of them.

"Now that's just taking the piss!" she said and groaned when from the radio and television reps came a somewhat subdued rendering of A Whiter Shade of Pale.

Late at night in his office at number ten Prime Minister Smith downed another raw whiskey and tried to stop his hand from shaking. His wife was in bed 'suffering' and letting the staff know all about it. His daughter had called first.

"Is mother all right?" she wailed.

"She's in bed, suffering as usual, look we're all right..." he began and winced when his daughter demanded to speak to her mother. He passed her on to his wife and poured another drink.

Typically his son complained about security and what was MI5 doing about it.

"Look, the assassins were after the aliens not us," he said and added. "Apart from stray shots we were not in danger." But his son needed a longer explanation and after that was over Smith refused to answer the telephone.

What rattled him was when Gregory arrived in his inner sanctum to talk about the incident.

"Gregory, what happened?" he said and narrowed his eyes, "The man on the floor? What was it with him?" he asked.

"Er, you need not know sir," Gregory said.

"Assume I do not then shall we?" said the PM, and looked long and hard at Gregory. "That crowd from Maidstone. I want them sorted Gregory, sorted, do you understand? Especially that bastard Hicks."

"And how do you want them sorted sir," Gregory said with a grin. "By type, size, date or name?"

"I don't care how as long as long as you get that bastard Hicks?"

"Do you mean, er, eliminate him sir?" said Gregory brightly.

"Something like that, yes," replied Smith with a cold smile. "Can't have scum like that running around with weapons can we?"

"If it wasn't for that bastard Hicks sir, I would be talking to your successor, sir," said Gregory giving Smith a steady, penetrating look. "I don't like Hicks much but he was on the spot, and it seems rather vindictive to ill treat a family member, sir."

Smith stared at Gregory, his face losing its colour as he realised what the man had intimidated. He hated men like Gregory, upper class and superior with an air about them that excluded people like him.

"Meaning?"

"It might be better decorate him, because according our sources you were a target too, sir," Gregory said, and gave him a thin smile.

Smith shuddered and stood staring blankly first at Gregory and then the space where Gregory was when that worthy made a quiet exit.

"Bloody Harrow snob," he said to the closing door.

The thought of being a target frightened him.

It was all right for the two aliens, they were used to fighting and being hunted, he was used to a public life, revelled in it. The idea that his wife and family were on somebody's hit list was scary. He took another drink and this time his hand did stop shaking or was it because his whole body was shaking? He decided it was probably his whole boshy. Bobby, bothy, sod it, more whiskey and he didn't care. Who wanth a snaky booby anywhay?

The telephone ringing and his night secretary's voice woke him several hours later and he groaned as the light from the ceiling globes hit his eyes.

"There is a call from Australia sir, will you take it or shall I put him off?"

"Who is it?"

"Mister O'Rourke, sir."

"I will speak to him."

He put the receiver to his ear and spoke as carefully and as cheerfully as he could.

"Mike, hello, good to hear from you, how can I help you?"

"Good day John mate, you sound like you got a steaming hangover, er, we got some news for you," O'Rourke said. "D'ye wanna hear it?"

"Of course, of course, fire away," said Smith ignoring the reference to his sobriety.

"Our troops have more or less rolled up the Zradians here. There seems to be something wrong with their communications system. We have found that by targeting the transfer ports they use to bring troops and stuff down we do some damage but they recover pretty quick. We have a foolproof method – quite simple but you have to put up with a bit of interference. Know what it is yet?"

"If you are going to play silly games, I don't want to know," said Smith, annoyed at O'Rourke's ebullience.

"I'll do you a favour and send it to your bloke in Sydney, we moved from Canberra for the duration," O'Rourke said and chuckled before hanging up. "You only had to ask."

O'Rourke hung up and Smith, by now crossing his legs in agony staggered groggily from his chair gasping at the thumping of his throbbing head he groaned as the strains of A Whiter Shade of Pale wafted through the room following him to the bathroom at a level that was far too high for his head to stand. "Oh fucking Jesus Christ," he said and clutched at his ears and then his groin as his need took over.

The Emperor Strikes Back

If there was one thing the Emperor knew how to do well apart from drinking huge quantities of Gin and Tonics it was how to be exceedingly nasty. The nastiness he was plotting at this moment was aimed at his two arch enemies, Angela Breen and Julian Renfrew. He had a plan to bring the pair down to size and a few short periods ago he had set the messengers off to carry out his orders.

The filthy woman and her scumbag army were on the borders of sector red and soon, with the traitors from the rebel army, were threatening to invade Second City and were already attacking Third City. His forces were falling to the new religious force led by Angela and that infuriated him. Not only that but those rotten Bulgers from the New Moral Few had set a Doomsday Bomb on his Star Stations. The picture his Pairs painted looked bleak and for the first time since he took over the rule of the Republic he had refrained from executing the bringers of bad news. Instead he had asked them for their advice and was surprised when they came up with a good sound plan.

He realised that the system of fiefdoms wasn't working and had apologetically rescinded his orders. Instead there were now a system of forces that were directed by the Leader Pairs under the High Leader Pairs and one Twin Vice Consul to pull the forces together. He gave orders that the forces on Earth hold their positions until the war at home was ended. The result was that the rebellious enemy were slowed down, but it was not fast enough so he decided he needed to break the enemy power, and the plan he had in mind was going to do that.

He cackled and took another drink.

Julian was scared. Too scared to run away too frightened stay with the army but unable to run away knowing that if he did he would not live very long. His father and Mister Byrde and all of Tzu's Kung fu people were with them and that made things worse. At least with Glorida and Glorid he could be himself. All they did when he chickened out was to punish him and grab him back, and in their own way encourage him to carry on. That was all right when he was a bomber but now they were waging a full scale war and although he got to bomb things he also had to march and fight with the soldiers.

The army on the move was a frightening thing and although he was with his friends, even Lavia was there, he was like a cat on a hot tin roof, jittery and terrified. The column of wagons was split into four sectors and he was assigned to sector red with Glorida's troop. He was the lead bomber and whenever there was a bomber needed he was given the task. In spite of his desire to be somewhere else he was becoming even more of a hero. With every new task he completed he was praised by the women and his name sent off with his newest exploit by Oliver Braine and Mister Byrde and the women of the propaganda group.

"Please," he begged, "can you just shut up about all the things I done. That bloody President bloke is a loony and he'll be after me. For God's sake don't make it any worse."

Glorida smiled. She was proud of him.

"Crazy bitch," he muttered.

"What did you say my love," said Glorida.

"Nothing."

"You mutter when you don't like things," she said.

"I was thinking about the fighting. I'm scared Glorida, bloody scared and I hate every moment of it. I just said it was a bloody bitch,"

"I hope I can believe that, Julian," she said and stared at him meaningfully.

He said nothing and sat deeper in the seat fingering his weapons as if he were ready to fight. Glorida, he knew, was aware of his ways and with a characteristic slippery gesture he evaded her gaze and let her assume he was being sneaky. He was being sneaky and knew that she knew he was. He knew also that he was going to have to make up to her for his lapse when they made camp.

The wagons slowed and bumped into the camp formation and Julian glanced at Glorida. Her face remained as impassive as it was normally and as they disembarked and started making camp he hoped she had forgotten his remark. As usual he managed to avoid doing any of the work and instead prepared to join the cookhouse queue in his section. Glorida and Glorid gently took one arm each and led him to a quiet spot. They said nothing but forced him to sit on a rock and when he tried to get up Glorid pushed him back down again.

"What you doing?" he said.

"Julian, you are a lazy Bulger. You get no food until you have cleaned your weapons, laid out your kit and checked your bombs," said Glorida at the same time drawing her knife and showing him the blades. "Do it scumbag and when you have done each task Glorid and I will check."

"And if you don't I will cut you too," said Glorid and grinned.

Julian tossed around the idea that answering back would be in order and rejected it. Glorid was more vicious than Glorida. Instead he hung his head and waited.

"So, hero, what is it to be?" said Glorida.

"I'll do it," he said and smiled weakly eyeing the knife as Glorida tapped it in the palm of her hand.

He worked hard too and at each check the two women passed his work as good and when all tasks were done they allowed him to go and get his food. There was precious little left and when he gazed at the portions doled out to him his face fell. The amount was half what he was used to and it was also all the worst bits.

"What's this crap?" he said to the serving Pair.

"It is what is left," she said.

"But it's cold and scummy, I can't eat that!"

"Sorry but that's all there is. Orders, we have our orders. Unless you are on time and have done your work you get the rubbish at the bottom. After the seconds have been dished out," the Pair said, and smirked. "Your Leader Pair's orders."

"Bitches," he said and went off with his dishes to eat. He ate everything and made a point of cleaning his dishes properly in case Glorida punished him for leaving them as he normally did, dirty until somebody else cleaned them. He walked back to their sleeping spot grumbling under his breath and threw himself down. He had hardly stretched out when Glorida approached, stood at his feet and kicked the soles of his boots.

"Come on hero, sentry go. You are on duty with our section until last period. You get to sleep on the second half until dawn. Move it and bring your gun."

"Oh Christ," he said in utter despair, he hated sentry duty. The idea of sitting out on his own watching out for four eyed gits with guns was not his idea of an evening's entertainment. Nevertheless he went, and with his gun and his sword he sat on a bank some distance from the camp with a Pair of Bombers who hardly spoke to him.

He was bored and while the Pair sat in their chosen position he leaned against a rock and dozed. He woke to feel two sharp points against his neck and before he could shriek in terror a hand snaked around from behind him and a voice hissed a warning.

"Quiet or you are dead."

He stayed quiet and watched as the Pair on guard with him were stabbed to death. The hands gripped him stripped him of his weapons and tied his hands tightly together, hooking a loop through the rope to another around his waist. If that restriction wasn't enough they passed another rope around his neck.

"Run with us and do it right or you will throttle yourself, scum. The Emperor wants you alive, pig fodder, so it will hurt but you will not die. So run and keep running," the voice hissed and a tug on the forward rope forced him to move.

Julian ran. He ran and eventually got the hang of not being throttled. In his mind he was screaming and even when his bladder and his bowels gave way he ran. He ran until his captors stopped and unceremoniously threw him onto the floor of a smelly wagon where he lay and sobbed uncontrollably. A foot kicked him and a voice told him to shut up. He wailed louder and a Pair heaved him from the floor and punched him senseless. After that he remained quiet and lay on the floor semi-conscious terrified of what was about to happen. The wagon sped up and soon, or so it seemed, it came to a halt and he was dragged out and frog-marched into a dungeon.

"What are you going to ....arrgh!"

"Shuts ups scumballs!"

He shut up and lay on the floor still bound as the metal door clanged shut behind him.

The Emperor watched the screen and chuckled. Julian Renfrew was within the palace walls. He enjoyed the sight of Julian being dragged in from the wagon and thrown, still bound, into the cell. He liked that because the cell was the same one that had held the Professor. The Emperor raised his glass of pink gin to his lips and sipped, glad he had decided to change to a more suitably upper class drink.

"Now for the next stage," he said.

He clapped his hands and a scribe Pair rushed in to his private chamber where he had chosen to place his war office.

"Send the messenger to the woman," he said and approved as the scribe Pair merely bowed low and rushed off. He watched the screen again and tapped orders into the system and called up his Twin Vice Consul. The Pair appeared on the screen and bowed low before greeting him.

"I want the Imperial forces ready to act when we catch that woman and I want them to storm the centre and kill the religious leaders. That is your prime target," the Emperor said and accepted their obsequious reply.

He returned to the plan screen and sat watching the ebb and flow of the battle and sipped at his drink.

Angela watched the ebb and flow of the battle herself and as the fighting seemed to be bogging down she decided that the best thing to do was to plan a retreat to gather her forces. She called a messenger and gave the Pair an order. The messenger ran off and soon after she watched a flurry of messengers fan out to the various Section Leaders and return to the planning centre. Soon after that the troops began to break off the action and return from the battlefield following her high command to the predetermined positions. The enemy were taken by surprise and instead of following they stayed in their dug in positions. It was time, she thought, to change the plan.

The plans she made had worked so far and now that the army was larger, the rebel army was on the move it was obvious the Emperor was struggling. The only problem now for her forces was that the Emperor was taking them seriously and putting in an effort. The Children were facing crack troops loyal to the despot and desperate to destroy her forces. It meant that she was effective, and now she had to keep modifying her plans and methods to keep ahead. In particular this battle.

With Blard as an advisor she wrote a new plan consulting with the commanders and finally explained. "What we will do is send out two probes left and right and leave the centre looking as if it is the full army. When they are in position to attack we will then put out three forward movements as we have done before and let the enemy expect us to follow our usual tactics. If we time it right we can engage that lot in front of us and get them to commit their forces and swoop on them from behind. And one mobile force to attack the transfer stations when the scouts locate them. The scouts say that the enemy have stretched their lines out only to their transfer stations. Am I right?" Angela asked.

"According to what we know," said Blard, and the other commanders nodded their agreement.

One Half Pair raised his hand and spoke: "We have advance forces engaging with their vanguard and as far as we know the enemy are treating our forces as if we are a pack of frightened citizens. Fortunately they seem to be taking their time, but when they do attack they are vicious."

"We are holding them?" asked Angela.

"Yes but will not be able to for long. Long enough I think to keep them where they are at the moment." The Half Pair showed a rough sketch of the enemy deployment.

"Good, then that is the plan. We start as soon as we can get the two columns off. Now, let us get down to details." She said and for a while there was only quietly muttered discussion as the logistics and the timings were worked out. Later when the planning was over Angela stood on the top of her wagon and gazed across the rough terrain. Blard the Barmy and Sergeant Orange stood on the ground beside the wagon and Holmes stood on the platform beside her.

"What's that?" he said.

"What?"

"There's a wagon moving along the valley. The troops are letting it through," Holmes said and looked worried.

Angela lifted her glasses and adjusted them to suit the distance cursing quietly as the images shifted from her normal to Zradian normal and at times she lost the image. The wagon carried the red banner of the Emperor and under that there was a black banner and a white flag. Angela knew that the wagon came with an emissary from the Emperor and that it was aimed at her. The black banner was always a truce flag and the white one was because the Emperor had studied the methods of Earth and used it to let her know that the message was for her. She called on the open line for the wagon to be let through to the inner ring and halted.

"One Pair escorted and disarmed to be brought to me. I want all weapons trained on them and at any treachery the guards are to immediately slaughter them," she said, and grinned as Sherman Holmes gasped.

The Pair alighted from the wagon and she noted that weapons were trained on it and the Pair as they walked up the slope to where she was waiting. The Pair were dressed in the new livery of the Emperor which Angela thought looked silly but she did not let their appearance bother her, she was curious and cared little for their attire. The Pair came to a halt a few paces from her and spoke formally.

"We, the emissary of his Highness the Emperor of all Zradia and of Earth wish to convey to the Leader of this insurgent force, one Angela Breen from Earth, the wishes of His Imperial Highness. In this instance we bear with us a scroll flimsy bearing the Imperial Seal. What say you?"

"I say don't be so stuffy and show us the scroll," Angela said.

One of the Pair drew the scroll from the long plastic tube and presented it to a Half Pair beside him. The Half Pair carried the scroll to Angela and unrolled it to check there was nothing inside other than the flimsy. She handed it to Angela who spread it in her hands and read the message. It was not a long message but the content was devastating. She handed it to Holmes who read it and handed it to Blard who glared at the emissary angrily until they eventually wilted and clutched each other in fear.

"We need to discuss this," said Angela.

"We are requested to return with you."

"Then you will have to wait," said Angela and glared at them. "Let them wait in the shade with some refreshments and I will confer before I give my answer."

Inside the wagon she waited until Sergeant Orange and Nert had read it and took a deep breath before speaking.

"I shall go with them of course," she said.

"Why. We need you here Angela and there is no need to sacrifice yourself for a person of no account. Particularly when the man is somebody you do not like," said Nert.

Angela stared at him. Sergeant Orange grinned, Holmes' eyebrows shot up and Blard remained impassive. Unlike Holmes, who was again surprised that his eyebrows should react so vigorously, Blard was thinking about how he could exploit the situation.

"Excuse me, I may have ordered the murder of prisoners but when it comes to my friends I am loyal," Angela said and directed her contemptuous gaze at Nert who looked defensive but eventually cringed.

"You will be killed," said Nert.

"Maybe I will but at least I will be trying to save Julian. He says that we will be held hostage until our forces surrender or are defeated and then we will be imprisoned, that is what he promises," Angela said.

"The Emperor never did that when he was a mere President and I think he will not change now," argued Nert.

"I have a plan," said Blard.

"Is it cunning?" asked Sergeant Orange and looked hurt when everybody stared at him blank faced or puzzled. He shrugged his shoulders.

"It's pretty sneaky and the least Angela knows about it the better. If the Polisocs get to work on her she had best know nothing. If she wants to go then she must and it is up to us to use the situation as best we can," Blard said and looked pointedly at Angela.

"Shall I sit outside?"

"Yes but don't leave yet," said Blard.

Angela sat out in the suns watching the enemy Pair who sat on the ground watching the wagon but unable to move any further. She sat contemplating the fate that awaited her knowing that her chances of surviving imprisonment were low. She had a choice, either go and be with Julian or not to go and let him die. Logic told her to leave him to his fate and regret his passing, to treat him as a martyred hero and carry on with the fight. She knew she could not do that and clung to the hope that they would both survive.

"At least we tried," she said and turned her head when Blard called her name.

A few short periods later she faced the enemy emissaries and agreed to their terms. She gave up her arms at the wagon and carried only enough water and food for the journey although she insisted on an escort of her own people on the walk down to the enemy wagon. She forced herself not to touch the raw spot on her neck where Blard had inserted his minute tracer.

"It will send back signals and we can find out where you are whenever we want to. The incision will heal the way an insect bite will," Blard said and smiled at her. "Courage lady."

She turned for one last look at her vacated headquarters and saw Holmes and Sergeant Orange standing gazing at her. She waved to them before she climbed on board the wagon and insisted on standing on the platform with the soldiers. The journey was broken by an overnight camp where it was obvious that she was to be escorted to the Emperor's palace the next morning. As nonchalant as she could she took her food and lay down on the offered bunk to sleep.

Before she dropped off she thought of D.G and held his image in her mind until she drifted off into sleep.

Destiny rears its head

Glorida was inconsolable and no matter what anybody could say or do she wept and continued weeping. Glorid did her best but there was nothing that she could do.

"I wish I had just let him do his own thing and not forced him to, to..." she wailed and fell into Glorid's arms.

Glorid rolled her eyes and looked around at the other Pairs and shook her head. That they had lost a Pair as well didn't seem to bother Glorida and although Glorid realised that Julian was a loss she mourned the loss of her friends much more. For propaganda reasons Julian's capture was a great blow, and since he had gone missing, apart from having to deal with Glorida's grief there was the need to do something to help, and perhaps get him back. D.G suggested that he and his twin go and visit Angela's headquarters and hear what she had to say.

"Listen Glorida, D.G and Glord are off to Angela's army to see what they can do. We know the men will do nothing but at least she will care about him enough to help. Tzu's people and Lugs have volunteered to go on the rescue mission and..." Glorid began and bit her lip, "I will help organise a mission from here."

"He'll be killed! That fucking Bulger will slaughter him!" Glorida wailed and her twin winced at her use of Julian's foul language. This must be serious, she thought, she must love the scrawny ratbag.

"We are doing our best. Even the Leader Pairs are planning a rescue," she said.

"Are they really?" Glorida said through her sobs.

"Backing it to the hilt," Glorid said which was true but not because they wanted to save Julian so much as to penetrate First City. Julian gave them a focus and as they said, if he lived then that was great but if not then at least he died for a good cause. "We should go, so if you can sort of stop your blubbering we can make plans and get underway to go and find him, eh?"

Glorida snuffled to a sniffling halt and gazed at her twin.

"What do you mean, stop blubbering?" she said and sniffed.

"What I say. If you don't stop blubbering you will not be allowed to go on the mission," Glorid said. "We need you dry eyed and clear headed to go get him."

Glorida took a clean cloth from the pile at her elbow and wiped her face, blew her nose and looked at her twin.

"You got it," she said.

"Right, now we had better get our gear together. We start when we hear back from D.G. In the meantime we need you fed and watered and ready to fight," Glorid said.

Glorid managed to keep Glorida occupied and with her troop around her eventually Glorida's demeanour changed from that of grieving lover to, albeit grim faced, fighting fit soldier. Quietly Glorid took control of the troop and let Glorida take a back seat knowing that although she looked good she needed to be watched in case she broke down. Glorida's nerves were as taut as a wire and could snap as easily. If that happened she could either collapse or go berserk. Glorid determined that she would do neither.

By nightfall the troop were ready, and as they camped and set pickets, in the distance they could see the lights of First City. The front was less than three kilometres away and Glorid was aware that this was the first time the rebels had faced the loyalists in strength. She was apprehensive about the coming battle and hoped that what they had planned would work and shorten the war.

She slept on the ground with her twin and held her close when she woke and reached out for comfort. Glorida calmed down and eventually slept deeper, and by the time the call came at dawn she was well rested and went to breakfast looking casual and alert. Glorid watched her twin and knew that she was getting ready for the day, ready to kill whoever was in the way of her and Julian.

"We are in for some fireworks if some Bulger tries to stop her," she muttered.

D.G didn't get back until late that turn and it was all Glorid could do to stop Glorida going off on her own. Glorid was forced to follow Glorida around all that turn and encourage her to remain patient. D.G's arrival was a gift and as his party went directly to Dorid and Dorida's wagon Glorid and Glorida raced along after them. Inside they pushed for a place and sat on a bunk listening to D.G report on what Angela had decided to do.

"You tell me that she has gone with the enemy to try and save Julian?" said Glorida staring hard at D.G.

"Yes and we arrived too late to stop her," D.G said and lowered his head in his hands. "I don't think I can stand it, the thought of her in the hands of the Polisocs makes me want to kill without mercy anybody who even so much as touches her."

"You are fond of her then?" asked Byrde who smiled at him with much compassion, "Seriously fond of her?"

D.G hung his head and twitched his fingers angry but gazed at Byrde with a look that was a mixture of fear and anger and something else that even Glorid recognised.

"I feel as strongly for her as Glorida does for Julian," he said, and fingered his blade.

"Then I suggest that we use Tzu's people to help rescue her and Julian and leave the rest of the army to fight the war as they will. I am going to suggest that we do not merely rescue them but set out as our prime objective to kill the President or Emperor as he now calls himself. Arthur and I will come too. Tzu wants to go with the army and he and the Ferret and Oliver will stay with him. Lugs wants to come with us. Tzu suggests we take about fifty of his people to go with Glorida and D.G." Byrde said and grinned.

"And the rest?"

"Will do as Blard the Barmy suggested," said D.G and turned to speak to Dorid and Dorida. "Your honours, will you inform the men's rebel army of the general situation or of our plans?"

The Leader Pair smiled at D.G and Dorid replied.

"I do not think the trousered ones will listen to our plan and I am convinced that they would in fact reject any suggestion. It is our opinion that it may be better to let them continue with their version of the war and leave them to sort it out afterwards."

"So what is Blard planning to do?" said Glorida.

"Like us he will be sending a rescue team. He says he has a cunning plan that is both simple and effective," said D.G and glanced at Byrde who giggled.

"Where is Glord?"

"He has decided to stay behind with a small guard and help with the task of coordination. Religious leader Nert has asked for his expertise," D.G said, and with a gesture of acceptance he handed over a wad of flimsies for Dorid and Dorida. "It's all written down in there in case I forgot the details."

"Can we adjourn this meeting until after the last meal when we will have a plan sorted out to fit in with Blard's. Glorida, you will get your troop together. You and D.G can work together," Dorida said.

Glorida and Glorid with D.G working closely organised the troop and spoke with Tzu to select his people. They chose the wagons they would need and with Simon and Marion leading the Kung Fu fighters they sorted out who was in charge of who and how the Pairs and the Earth people would fight. Arthur and Byrde were placed with Simon and Marion and Lugs hovered with Byrde declaring that he would protect Byrde at all costs.

"Its me job," he said and added only a knife to his weapons settling for a cudgel as his main tool.

Thus they were more or less ready and when the meeting was recalled after the last meal Glorida, Glorid, D.G and Byrde went eagerly to learn of the plan. Arthur was enthusiastic because as he had said, it was his son in danger and he wanted to help. Besides, he said, getting rid of the Emperor was a task he wanted to be a part of.

"The man is a psychopathic killer as well as a deluded megalomaniac and we can do without him," Arthur declared. "I will do what I can to help."

The meeting was short and to the point and left the participants happy but apprehensive. D.G and Glorida were quietly enthusiastic, and with a flurry of excitement they put aside their misery and reorganised the troop to suit the plan. For the first time in her life Glorida resorted to a drug to get to sleep and at day break when Glorid woke her she was rested but muzzy and ready to go.

Angela stood patiently refusing to look cowed as her captors shackled her arms and legs. She adjusted her step to the shortened pace, and as they led her through the streets to the main square she held her head high and her back straight. She was amused by their caution when they stopped at second square and disembarked from the wagons. The Pairs lined up and with one Pair in front holding a chain that was attached to her waist and another Pair behind with weapons she was made to understand that she should walk apart from the rest. It was obvious they wanted her to be a spectacle but she decided that she was going to remain true to herself and put on a show of superiority. The crowd were silent as she passed and she knew that they were supposed to yell and scream hatred at her, but instead they seemed curious and although there were a few yells and shouts there was no mass hysteria. Angela took the time to look at the rows of faces and when a hand was raised in greeting she nodded back and smiled knowing that somebody was glad to see her, knowing too that the Emperor was not as popular as he thought he was. Her guards urged the crowd to shout and scream at her but instead they remained sullen and if they shouted at anybody it was at the guards.

The march to first square was a sombre affair and as they approached the palace Angela was encouraged by the way the guards led her directly to the door instead of parading her past the crowd on all four sides. It was a small victory and one she knew would have to be played on very carefully. She felt a little like Jesus and immediately blushed at the thought. The Zradian method of execution was as cruel as the Roman and she knew that whatever the Emperor said she was certain to suffer it. She hoped that Blard would not do anything rash to save her and thought of the people instead. Her parting words to them were specific and she hoped they would heed them.

"I want no senseless acts of bravery to try and save me. Think of the people and never give up the fight. The despotic Emperor must be destroyed," she said and made Blard promise to tell D.G what she had said.

"And am I to tell him anything else?"

"You can tell him that I don't want him to do anything stupid," she said, and held Blard's gaze unable to admit to him how she really felt.

She remembered those words now and braced herself for the coming meeting. The escort marched her into the palace through a side door that passed through the traitor's arch and into the main corridor where red and black clad troops lined the sides. She kept her poise as they marched into a large hall and down into an amphitheatre where there was a throne standing on a dais. A middle aged Zradian sat on it dressed in long robes that covered his tunic which was coloured red, yellow, green and blue, as gaudy in their design as his cloak. He looked like somebody who had decided to go to a fancy dress ball and couldn't make up his mind if he wanted to be a wizard or a space cadet. Either way he looked silly and Angela stifled a giggle.

Her escort came to a halt and undid the shackles around her waist leaving the wrist and leg irons on. Angela stood alone on the dirty floor and gazed steadily at the Emperor of Zrad.

"Well?" she said. "Have you got anything to say or has the cat got your tongue?"

Swords slid out of scabbards and Pairs advanced to be stopped by a single hand gesture of the Emperor who gazed down at Angela as he sipped at a foaming pink gin and finally spoke.

"So, this is the great warrior queen is it? Chained and bare of weapons without her army, ready to save her precious compatriot. We are pleased to welcome you to Our humble home," the Emperor said.

"I'm used to slumming," said Angela, "I dare say you will get used to it too in time."

The Emperor straightened in his throne and glared angrily at her.

"We are in command. We have your miserable life in Our hands and also that of the Bulgerbag We have in Our dungeons. Speak carefully or you will regret every wrong word. Our Imperial Polisoc troopers will cause you much suffering. Rape and torture are their favourite type of work. All you have to do is call on your motley army to surrender to Our magnificent forces and your life and Julian's will be safe."

"And if they decide that our lives are not that important and continue to fight?"

"Then you will never know because you will be dead."

"You realise that the end for you and your despotic rule is close. My own army is poised to destroy your forces, the rebel army is descending on you and the Women's Rebel army is about to deal you a blow that will destroy First City itself. The skills Julian brought with him have given their forces a devastating power that is aimed directly at you. They intend to destroy you and free the people from oppression. You are doomed." Angela said, and gazed steadily at the Emperor knowing that her defiance was as disturbing to the Emperor as it was to his Pairs. She could see Pairs shuffling their feet uncomfortably and glancing at each other. She realised that they could be anticipating her sudden death but also knew that her straight back and clear voice was telling on them.

"Silly woman," said the Emperor glaring at her. "Your miserable army and its rag-tag followers will be overwhelmed and destroyed by Our army."

"Then how come we are on the borders of Second City and ready to invade Sector Red and First City? And don't say we have fallen into your trap because we control all the lands we have conquered. The people are of one accord, and that is to rid Zradia of you and all you stand for..." Angela began and grinned broadly when the Emperor rose from the throne and shouted at her.

"Treacherous Bulger!" he yelled. "Take the scum away!"

Guards ran forward and grabbed her and hurried her from the hall into a dark corridor that dived down under the palace to the dungeons. They marched her as quickly as her chains would allow and after many twists and turns they halted before a cage set in the wall and a Pair opened the door. From inside the dark room that it revealed came a frightened whimper and as she was pushed inside there was a scuffle as something or somebody rushed deeper inside the cell and gave a strangled shriek. The door clanged shut behind her and she sprawled on the dirty floor.

"Oh fuck," said a frightened voice.

"Hello Julian," she said. "No need for the bad language."

Ex-fireman Sidney Weddell crawled along the damp corridor. He was lost and hungry. He had tried to kill and eat the Bulger but at the last moment he had remembered his little boy's pet and how he had loved it. Ex-fireman Sidney Weddell couldn't remember what pet his son had, neither could he remember its name. In fact he barely remembered his son's name and sat for a long time crying as he thought about the boy and the boy's mother. He almost had the names but the overriding need to carry out his mission was too much, and all he could imagine was rodents, hundreds of them, millions of lovable bunnies, squirrels, rats and mice, and voles all rushing around happily doing rodent things. He saw a face, an ancient face that leered at him in the darkness of the catacombs and he knew that this was the face that had murdered his family, had demanded all the rodents be destroyed. He shed tears of anger and compassion for the lovely, furry little creatures and his fingers twitched on the axe handle in anticipation of cutting the evil one's neck. He walked on steadily, and as he climbed the gentle slope upwards he felt warmer. It was with some delight he felt the floor level off and there were the occasional set of wide steps. Dim lights set into the walls glowed and lighted his way and soon he found a twisting staircase that led upward. He emerged from the staircase and saw before him a more familiar scene. There were corridors and alcoves and softer footing. The image in his mind led him to see the corridors as the place where the evil one lurked and he knew that soon he would find the creature and destroy him. He saw a welcoming alcove and tired, he entered it gratefully wishing to sleep and recover from his long sojourn below. He sank down on the floor and dozed. Gently he lay the axe beside him and clutched his genitals.

"Ah," he sighed as his hand caressed his penis, "Ah."

Glord the Glorious

Glord's wagon skidded to a stop outside the headquarters wagon of the army of the Children of Glord the Glorious rather too flamboyantly than was necessary. Glord and D.G disembarked and walked smartly to where Blard the Barmy and Nert stood waiting for them in the shade of a canopy erected for the purpose. D.G had called ahead for permission to meet with Angela and was told that she was not there. Glord was surprised that the army had reached so far into the enemy territory and was amazed at the sight of row upon row of troops, some with regular uniforms and others dressed in the peasant garb of workers. Many were women and Glord noticed as the wagon drove past them that they were keeping themselves separate from the rest as if they were an army of their own. His twin was already worrying and his first question when they reached the place where Blard was standing was about Angela.

"Read the message and you will understand," said Blard and indicated that D.G should sit.

D.G read the flimsy and stared at the ground for a long time before he spoke. He looked up sharply at Blard and Glord could see that he was upset.

"She has gone with the emissaries?" he said his face a picture of concern and fear.

"Not long ago. Why have you come?" said Nert in answer to D.G's question. .

"We have come from the women's rebel army to speak with Angela about coordinating our efforts. We have a plan and I believe it will fit in nicely but we would like to get it right. The NMF seem to think that we should go with the main rebel army, but we also think we should work with your forces," said Glord aware that his twin was too overcome to speak.

"Then you should listen to our plan," said Nert.

Glord nodded and looked first at Nert than at Blard.

"I will see it and then we can talk about how we can work together," Glord said and followed Nert and Blard into the command wagon.

The plan, thought Glord, was a good one and as he sat and thought about it sipping at some excellent Outlands brew he saw a way of helping the situation. He listened to Blard explain how they had planned to rescue Angela and at the same time take First City and with a smile Glord's idea became clearer.

"I have an idea," said Glord.

He told them what he thought and apart from a few details they accepted his plan and not long after they finished their talk he extracted a transmitter from his own wagon and set the code so that he and the driver Pair could talk to each other.

"D.G has a problem with a little distraction I think," Glord said and shot a glance at his twin. "So he will go back to be with the Pairs and help me get things together."

What he didn't say was that he wanted D.G to report on Nert and his movement and speak with their NMF contact about how strong it was getting. He knew too that in spite of D.G's infatuation with Angela he was still loyal to the cause. The Children of Glord the Glorious must not gain control of Zrad. That it was Angela herself who had given the movement its start was going to be a problem, and if D.G was there to watch over that then that was fine. He was aware that D.G was as partisan as he was about Angela and Glord would protect her from harm to the point of transporting her and his twin back to Earth if needs be.

Glord watched the wagon with his twin disappear over the nearest hillock accompanied by an escort of his own wagons and some of the new peasant army and he felt a little sad. He kept two wagons and their crews with him more as an escort and rallying point for his own people than a significant battle unit. He noted that the women of Angela's forces gravitated toward him and that they also gathered around Blard and his small party.

It was late the next night that Nert asked his question and Glord answered casually rather than thinking about it. He should have considered the myth and all it meant but he didn't and as a result he was swept up into the madness.

"Are you of the family of Glord?" Nert asked.

"Yes, we are, why do you ask?"

"Pairs are wanting to know. Were you born in the northern sector?"

"Yes, my family came from Third City Yellow," Glord said, and took very little notice of Nert's nodding head and excited glances.

"And are you returning from the wilderness?"

"I have been in the wilderness for many four hundreds planning the return of my own Pairs. Drogl and myself are working humbly toward that end," Glord said, and felt slightly uneasy but was too busy checking the data his transmitter was spitting out. He did not register that Nert had suddenly disappeared, and spent the remainder of the night before sleeping talking over the details with Blard. He knew that before a big battle the Children usually prayed and worshipped their god and had planned to watch rather than take part so it was with a clear conscience he lay down and slept.

At sunsrise he was up and getting ready for the coming fight. He chose his Pairs carefully and was glad to call on some of the women from Angela's converts. He spent part of the turn trying to contact rodent four but all he got was a faint message that told him to beware the Whiter Shade of Rodents and that was it. He spent the mid meal with Blard and listened to the tales Holmes and Sergeant Orange had about life on Earth. The turn was spent in this way until after last meal when the Children began to gather and to sing. Glord was impressed with the music and wished that he too had learned to sing.

"Watch what the people do," said Blard.

Glord stood on the top of his command wagon and watched Nert climb the platform followed by his Acolytes and Priests. He saw Nert stand tall and raise his arms high above his head and listened as he made a speech to the gathered Pairs. Nert spoke quietly but passionately and as he spoke it was obvious he was aware of his power, and as the speech grew to a climax the Acolytes ranged themselves around the porcelain pan and knelt in respect as Nert lowered his arms and with fluid movements dropped to his knees before the pan and vomited into it. The singing began and then with a huge cry of worship the voices of the Pairs raised and chanted a mantra.

"Ralph! Ralph! Ralph! Ralph!"

The chant blended with the singing that began at the rear and spread onward like a wave and finally when it died down a little Nert was once again on his feet with his hands raised for silence. Glord, tired and ready for sleep before the march the next turn, idly listened to what Nert was saying and although he heard the name Glord mentioned he did not connect it with his own. He drew another brew from the barrel and supped at it nibbling a snack at the same time. When Blard dug him in the ribs and pointed he looked up sharply and saw the faces of those nearest in the crowd gazing at him in awe. Somebody called for him to come forward and as casually as he had answered Nert's questions he stepped down from the wagon and walked to the platform. There was a deathly silence as he mounted the steps and stood facing the crowd beside Nert.

"Tell them who you are," said Nert.

Glord shrugged and explained that he was Glord and had come to help Nert and the army of The Children of Glord the Glorious to their final victory. He had come, he said, to help save the people and to help save the great warrior Angela Breen. He told them how long he had lived in the desert waiting for this moment to come forward and help fight the great battle. He thought little of his speech and when he had finished speaking he attempted to leave the platform modestly thanking the crowd for listening to him.

It was not until he heard the crowd chanting and listened to the words did he realise that something was dreadfully wrong.

"Glord, we worship you, Glord we will follow you!

All hail to Glord the Glorious!"

"No!" he cried, "I am not Glord the Glorious!"

But his protest was lost in the cries of acclaim and, pale faced and squirming with embarrassment and anger, Glord turned to Nert his face a picture of adverse emotion.

"Nert! I am not Glord the Glorious! Do you understand?"

"So sorry but they do not think that. It is safer for you to go with the flow. Accept the inevitable and lead the army to its final victory," said Nert, and despite his animosity toward the Half Pair Glord could not help agreeing with him. Until he realised that if he did accept there was no way out.

You will be taken from this place...

Julian huddled in the corner as far from the door of their cell as he could whimpering in terror as he listened to the marching footsteps approaching; coming for him. Angela sat at the cell door quiet and still, her profile in shadow in an attitude of prayer. It was all right for her she was brave, and according to her was about to meet the God she worshipped. She had tried to give him her load of old bollocks about Heaven and the redeemer but that had given him no comfort at all. He wanted to be somewhere else; far away from this stinking rat hole with its stinking food, its stinking president, its stinking, rotten, murderous Polisocs and the dark wet dungeons. Angela had explained that she had come to help save him and had surrendered herself for capture so that the Emperor might spare him.

"He said that we would live and become slaves and put on show as freaks after he wins the war. I half believe him and hope that he will keep his promise," she said, and added a bit about praying to God for His help.

He fell silent when she tried to help him pray and no matter how hard he tried he couldn't utter one prayerful word or even think of God. His thoughts were concentrated on how to escape, and failing that, how to grovel at the Emperor's feet to save his own skin. Bollocks to Angela, all she could do was accept her lot and sing bloody hymns. She even made him turn away when she took a dump. She organized his routine and although he didn't like it life in the cell was less uncomfortable. Unfortunately she could do nothing about the Polisoc soldiers who came each morning and evening to drag him out of the cell and into the corridor where they beat him and pushed him back inside laughing as he snivelled and begged for mercy.

"A beating a day keeps his blues away" said the Leader Pair in harmonic unison.

This time it was different. "The Emperor wants to see you," announced the Leader Pair.

"What the fuck for?" said Julian.

"I expect his Highness wants to tell you when he is going have you executed," the Pair said, and laughed when he collapsed against the electrified gate sobbing and then screaming as the electric shocks convulsed his body.

Angela tried to comfort him with prayer but nothing worked, and as the cell was unlocked Julian pressed himself back against the rear wall. Angela crawled out quietly whilst two pairs rushed inside and grabbed him as he tried to fight them off. "No! No! You rotten four eyed gits, let me go! I don't want to die! Oh fuck! You rotten bastards, oh..." he screamed and yelled as they dragged him across the rough cell floor and hauled him to his feet clamping him between a Pair as they formed up for the march to the Grand Hall.

"On your feet scum!"

"I don't want to go!" wailed Julian and screamed as one of the Half Pairs prodded him with the points of a blade.

"Gets movings scumbag."

Julian got movings and with tears of terror flowing down his cheeks he more or less marched between the Pair behind Angela who strode proudly between her escort Pair as if nothing was wrong. The journey was short and soon they were in the inner chamber clamped between their escort waiting for the summons into the Grand Hall. It came all too soon and despite his struggles Julian found himself in the hall standing before the Emperor.

"Greetings Earth people. We are pleased to see that you are prompt and ready to hear what We have to say to you. We will not be too wordy, so it is without more ado We pronounce sentence on you both. We have decided that We will have you publicly executed in First Square this next turn at sunsset. As this is a messy and painful process We hope you are not looking forward to it. You will be taken from this place and prepared for the slaughter and at the appointed time you will be chained to the executions posts and before Us and Our people you will be torn to pieces by Our High Executioners. We have pronounced judgement. How do you plead?" said the Emperor, and smiled at them.

Julian collapsed and lay at the feet of the guard Pair groaning.

"For myself," said Angela, "I care little because I will be resting in the arms of Jesus, but for my poor friend here I beg clemency. I beg the clemency you promised as the condition of my surrendering myself to your hands."

"Do you plead guilty or not guilty?"

"To what charge?"

"Sedition, raising a riot, rebellion against Our law, uprising and leading an illegal religious movement, murder of citizens and the illegal carrying of arms," said the Emperor, "That will do to start with."

"In that case I am guilty and if I am to be murdered for these charges then so be it. I again call for my friend here to be set free as you promised," Angela replied and gazed unblinking at the Emperor.

By this time Julian had recovered from his swoon and rose shakily to his feet tears streaming down his face, his legs shaking and his whole body trembling with fear. He stared at the Emperor white faced and slack mouthed his eyes showing his fear and he sobbed. He blubbered unashamedly slack bodied and almost falling trying to speak through the sobs, supported by his guards as he sagged to the floor.

"Be brave Julian and speak to the man," Angela said.

"It's all right for you," mumbled Julian, "you're not scared of dying."

"Julian, I am as frightened as you are but I choose not to show it. I will go to my death as Joan of Arc did to hers but first I will plead again for the Emperor to spare your life. You are no hero Julian and deserve to live until the Lord calls you, in peace and love. I have led an army to destroy this man and have failed. You merely fought as any soldier would and deserve to be treated with honour. I ask his Highness again for your release," Angela said and gazed at the Emperor.

"Please, like Angela said, I was only doing my duty, please let me go..." Julian begged.

"Are you willing to stand with Us and watch Angela die?" the Emperor said.

"If that is what you wish. I'll do anything you ask of me, anything but let me live," Julian said, and placed his hands together his whole body shaking.

"Will you help execute her for Us?"

"Show me how but let me...." Julian began but the rest of his speech was cut off by the Emperor's sudden roar of laughter.

"The great hero grovels for his own life! No, my scummy friend, you will die with her this next turn. Take them to the stakes!"

The guards seized them by the upper arms and forced marched them out of the Grand Hall and into the bright sunslight of First Square. Julian struggled all the way and wailed as the guards tightened their grip on him and dragged him inexorably to the stakes in the centre of the square. He wailed even louder when the guards stripped his clothes from his body and clamped steel bands around his ankles and wrists that were then attached by chains to lugs on the stakes. He took no comfort knowing that Angela too was stripped naked and tethered like a sacrificial goat to a stake a further three metres away from where he was staked.

"Now scumbags, you will waits here this turn, and during the night until sunset tomorrow when we wills takes pleasures in watchings you die," said a Half Pair who nodded knowingly at his twin.

"Bollocks, you four eyed Bulger's arsehole," said Julian and spat on the red and black uniform.

"That's my hero," said Angela.

The Half Pair kicked Julian's crotch and laughed when he fell gasping and grovelling on the hot paving.

Their only relief that day was when, later they were forced to complete their bodily functions where they were chained the cleaning crews washed them and the paving down. The water was a balm after the heat of the day and it was a kindness on the part of the cleaners to allow them to drink from the hoses. Late that night other pairs came and gave them some food.

"The Emperor wants you fit and well for the big event," said one Pair.

"How kind of him," said Angela laying on the sarcasm.

"Bollocks," said Julian, laying on the terror.

But in spite of their situation they both ate the food and took the drink offered. It was no surprise to either of them that there was a heavy guard, as they were told, 'for their protection'.

"Afraid we will escape?" asked Angela.

The Guard Leader Pair laughed.

The women on their way

With stolen colours covering their own markings Glorid's wagon line crept through the hot paved circles of First City. Their guides led them through sector yellow until they were close to the Palace. From a distance they looked like the Emperor's troops and if any of the local citizens thought otherwise they kept quiet about it, some hoping that the force was much larger, many not wanting to be a witness to something they did not want to see, and others who cared little for anything but their own problems. There in a minor square they halted and parked up ready to go. Troops were left in strength to guard the wagons and get ready to hover in to support the rescue attempt and create, as Blard put it, a noisy and hopefully messy diversion. Glorida and Glorid, D.G, Tzu, who decided to come at the last moment, and ten Kung Fu artists, six of Glorida's Pairs and three guide Pairs set off to filter through the Palace to the dungeons and find Julian and Angela. The guides led them into a cargo hold and with blades ready and guns over their shoulders the party moved off. Tzu looked back once at the waiting wagons and waved padding quietly across the cool bay into the maw of the palace.

Oliver Braine listened into the news broadcasts scanning the data that filled the air waves, and was amused when he read Bradl's message to the President, although he was unaware that Bates and Fish were involved.

He noted that whoever was on the air were against the Children's movement, or rather the religion of Glord the Glorious, and it was obvious that the rebels were working hard to split the freedom fighters from the fanatics and he had to admit their logic was irresistible. The comments were powerful enough to persuade even the hardiest and most fanatic to separate the myth from the truth. He was amused when one Imperial SpokesPair emphatically denied that the Imperial forces were defeated outside Second City.

"Angela's got the buggers on the run!" he cried out. "Whoopee! Good on her!" And tapped in a request to Rodent#4 and was disappointed when there was no response. But his attention was taken up by a flimsy that emerged from the printer

Read the flimsy – map included.

It was a report from the NMF troops and the Rebel Armed forces who were heading into Sectors Red and Green from positions they had reached in Sector Yellow, and it was reported that there was opposition on both fronts.

"Heavy fighting in all areas of Sector Red and Green and around most major cities," Braine read and looked at the map. He grinned. That meant that whatever Glorida's troop was going to do would be undetected by the enemy until it was too late to stop.

He monitored the broadcasts for the whole of the first shift and when the Ferret came to take over he was still eager to listen. When the Ferret asked to explain something to Lugs Oliver stayed at his post. He tuned into the Imperial station and gasped as he heard the announcer speaking of Angela and Julian.

"Richard! Arthur! Ferret! Blard! Tune into First City News!" he yelled already tapping the record command.

The screens on the monitor picked up the broadcast and the wagon was filled with the dread news of Angela and Julian's execution. There were even pictures of the gathering crowds come to watch the spectacle and a picture of Julian and Angela both stark naked tied to stakes in First Square.

"Code call and fast," said Blard. "Braine, pass the message while I sort out with the guides where they can go."

Braine patched in the code and with the Ferret on the console listening he made contact with the Leader Pair of Glorida's guides. Blard gave him a plain message on a flimsy to transmit and with his most even voice he spoke into the pick up. There was a blip when he spoke the code word for send and with a touch he flicked the system to receive. There was another blip a few short periods later and a voice spoke in his earphones.

"Message understood. Will proceed to main gate cellar. Will mount operation from there. Advise time. Be ready to move prior to sunsset."

And then began the nail biting wait. Braine handed his duty over to Byrde and the Ferret and he joined Arthur and Lugs in the wagon body. Arthur was watching the progress of the team on the rear monitor screen. It was a complex grid of red lines on a dark background and worming its way along them was a yellow spot that marked Glorid and Glorida's progress. Instead of travelling down to the dungeons it had changed to a course that led upwards to the main gate. Arthur calculated progress and estimated that the party would reach First Square just as darkness fell and with concern in his voice he called out to Blard.

"I think we need to do something before the raiders get there. I reckon that they will be too late unless they hurry. Can you let them know they only have two and a half long periods to get to the gate. At their present rate they will arrive after sunset," Arthur said, and showed Blard the figures.

"It will take us half a period to get into place and if we go in too early we may force the Emperor's hand," said Blard. "I will send a message."

Blard wrote on a flimsy and handed it to Byrde who passed the message on to Glorida. At his station Arthur noted the more rapid progress of the yellow spot and as he sat watching he was aware that their own force was getting more tense; weapons were readied and there was a quiet buzz as Pairs and Earth people got ready to move.

The time seemed to race ahead and as Arthur watched the monitor he grew more anxious as the deadline approached. Blard had explained what execution entailed and he realised that he had already seen it on film when he was learning the history of Zrad as a reluctant guest of the former President. It was a messy, nasty process and all they could do now was wait.

Glord was impressed by his compatriot's skill. He had seen the plan that Blard had worked out, modified it a little, passed the information on to the women's army and, ignoring Nert's religious acclimations put the plan in action using Angela's Elite as his core. Blard was happy to do as he was told and now he was making his way to First City with a strike force that travelled light and fast.

The wagons carried the president's colours although as he was now known as an Emperor the colours and the markings were a little fudged to give the impression of hurried change as if the old markings were being changed on the move. The ruse had fooled the troop of Stormtroopers they met who merely saluted them as they arrived greeting them cheerfully until with a viciousness that took them completely by surprise Blard's soldiers attacked them and wiped them out. The Pongos, recognising them as friends immediately surrendered.

"You need us to come with you?" asked the Pongo High Leader Pair.

"If you are against the Emperor, indeed yes, we ride hard and fast."

The Pongos joined with their force and when they met up with another group led by the inevitable Stormtroopers the fight was short, and with the aid of the Pongos their force was now too large for Blard's purposes.

"What I would like you to do is to go with these volunteers," he indicated two wagons with Soldiers of Angela's Elite, "Who will lead you to Glord's army. Gather more Pongos with you and attack the opposing forces from the rear. Glord will know you are coming."

He explained to the High Leader Pair that the plan was to make as much trouble as possible on an all out war against the president's forces drawing the main force out of the First City area.

"If you will meet up with him and create mayhem, let these women guide you because they know the plan, we will be rid of this so-called Emperor, although to me he is still the President. On your way this is what I want you to do, once you have joined with the enemy in your own right," Blard said and explained what he wanted.

He watched the new army of Pongos move off for a few moments and with a chuckle he opened the communications to Glord.

"My friend, I am sending you an army that once they meet up with you will be only too pleased to be part of the main force. The Pongos are turning against his filthiness in droves. I have sent a code for them and leave it up to you. We will be with Glorida's force soon," Blard said and grinned when Glord raised a thumb.

Before they set off on foot to infiltrate the Palace Glorida sat in the wagon knowing that whatever she wanted to do there was nothing to be done except sit and wait. She had asked why they couldn't just storm in cut her Julian free.

"My twin, we have to let Glord draw them off first and Blard has to reach his position to create the diversion. We go in as late as we can to try and catch that despotic bulger gloating, and then kill him, as well as rescue Angela and Julian," Glorid said, patiently knowing that the grim look on her twin's face was her way of holding in the anger and tears. All Glorid wanted to do was to keep her twin calmed down enough to act rationally and not go off berserk, which would inevitably mean both of them would go crazy. She could feel the emotion building up in Glorida and feeling panicky herself she used the empathy and relaxed when Glorida calmed a little and lost her tenseness and became less angry. "Come, let us eat or maybe walk around for a while and then sleep. Okay?"

Glorida gave her twin a warm smile and got out of her seat. "Food, a walk and then sleep, yes, yes, and then I will sharpen my blades ready for that fucking bastard of a prick-faced fuck that's got my boyfriend," she said.

"That's my twin," said Glorid and hugged her close. "But language, my dearest one, language. Most unbecoming."

Glorida chuckled. "Sorry, I will do my best as long as I know we are on our way."

"My twin, we are on our way," said Glorid and the two went off to find some food. Not long afterwards the troop set off on foot to find Julian and Angela. They worked their way into the palace building silently and slowly looking for the cell knowing that it was likely the Emperor would use the same one as before. It came as a shock when Glorid got the message to say Julian and Angela were in First Square waiting execution.

"Bastard!" yelled Glorida, and immediately rushed off to be grabbed by Glorid who was barely quick enough to stop her.

"Listen, we know where they are, all we have to do is get there. The wagons are easing to the square now; we can meet them on the way and when the diversion starts we can be there," Glorid said. "Just calm down and let's meet up with the rest. Okay, we will do it!"

Glorida looked at her twin, gritted her teeth and with her face set grim she replied. "Then let's go. Lead on. I will follow but let's go. We have an Imperial ratbag to slice to bits."

Glorid led the way, and in spite of the need to stay calm she hurried along aware that time was running out. For a reason she could not fathom there were very few enemy Pairs left in the lower regions of the palace and those they did meet were soon cut down. The troop were angry and very, very dangerous.

Cometh the day...

Earth lay quiet; its inhabitants had forgotten local squabbles for a time relieved that the alien invaders were getting a pasting. The fighting continued wherever the fanatical Polisoc Troopers had dug in but it was reduced to hand to hand, mopping up combat that the local troops could do now that O'Rourke had passed on the transfer port jamming method to all and sundry.

The day it was discovered was a momentous one for Brigadier Chin and Colonel Troy. They were directing the last battles outside the original invasion bridgehead when the radio and communications officer called them.

"Sir, we have discovered a simple method of stuffing up the Zradian Transfer Ports system," he said, and Chin saw the un-military smile on the man's face as he explained. "All we have to do is switch on the radio jamming device, you know the gubbins left over from way back I always insist on carrying with me, and that you always..."

"Yes, yes, get on with it Roger," said Chin, grinning as he cut him off.

"Oh, sorry sir, that equipment. We switched it on for a bit of a trial and it seems to have stuffed their system up completely. Er, can we use it?"

"How does it work?" asked Chin.

"It jams the signals from the receivers and simply breaks up the incoming objects. We tried it, as you may be aware it is directional as well as giving out a blanket signal, so we watched the effects on a small group using the satellite link and watched machinery and troops suddenly disintegrate. Messy but effective," Roger said and chuckled. "And in case you think we were buggering around we sent a scout patrol to watch with binocs, and jeez! You should have seen the mess! Nothing arrived in one piece!"

"And what do you want from me?" asked Chin, keeping a straight face.

"Er, sort of approval and pass the method on up top, and a bloody medal, if there's one going, Sir!"

Chin laughed and said: "Give me a report and send it on to Command, okay, and when you've done that let's see if we can equip other groups with it, and well done soldier!"

When O'Rourke saw the report he wasted no time in sending the information on to all other forces and in particular through the

Japanese High Command who were extremely pleased. He sent a recommendation to Chin that Colonel R Walters should be promoted and that he would get his bloody medal. The next message Chin received worried him when he read it and with some apprehension he called Colonel Troy into his temporary office. He handed her the message and asked her to sit whilst she read it waiting quietly until she was ready. Eventually she looked up at him and bit her lip lightly.

"You want me to take it?" she said.

"Of course, it's promotion and all that, you would a bit of galah if you didn't" he said.

"I like being in your command, sir," she said. She gazed at him her face a picture of anxiety and he could see a little moisture gathering in her eyes and as he watched he saw her fist clench and felt his own deep apprehension. They had been together since she had arrived as a subaltern and he would miss her. The High command wanted her to fast track to Higher Command and that meant their working relationship would break up. Bullshit. It meant that they would break up.

Helen, I think ... oh bugger, no I don't. If you want it then take it but before you do I have to tell you what my dear old mother told me," he said, his face glowing pink with embarrassment, committed to what he was about to say.

"And what did your dear old mother say?" she asked giving him a warm smile that took away the tears.

"She said, 'are you going to marry that girl' and although I didn't say anything..."

"Of course, all you have to do is ask," she said interrupting him, grinning and adding, "sir."

"...To her, but what?" he said.

"I said, all you have to do is ask." She laughed and looked at his surprised gaze.

He recovered, as he said afterwards, like all soldiers do, and 'asked for her hand in marriage'. What he actually said was: "Oh, yes, well, if you er put it like that, then I do. Do you really want to marry me?"

"Of course, I thought I would never get a chance to ask you, sir," she said, and when he kissed her they both felt the salty tears run down their faces. The Sergeant Major who entered coughed politely and delivered his message as if nothing was wrong with his two senior officers kissing.

"We are getting married Sergeant," Chin said.

"Yes sir, Congratulations sir, ma'am. Er, about time, if I may say so, sir, ma'am!" he said and saluted.

"Bugger off sergeant, and thank you. Order extra drink rations will you?"

"Sir!" said the sergeant, saluting, boot bashing and exiting with a measured tread.

Chin and Troy hugged each other and laughed.

Execution in the offing

Angela sat with her back against the stake waiting for the suns to drop lower toward the eastern horizon accepting the inevitable. She prayed for Julian and for herself and with her thoughts on staying calm she thought also of Glorida and Glorid and Holmes and all the people she could think of. She thought sadly of her sister and her husband and their small child. She thought of her brother and their parents who would be wondering what was happening to her. She said some prayers for them all and then she said some for the church back home and for the Christian Sisters. She listened to Julian sobbing and ignored the crowd. She sat cross legged most of the time and now and then she spoke words of encouragement softly to Julian. He muttered back in the most vile language but even for that she forgave him and asked Christ to forgive him too.

She tried to sleep but although the Zradian weather was warmer in general than on Earth the night was cold, especially as she was naked, and the paving was hard and uncomfortable. If she sat her buttocks became sore and if she lay after a while the paving became so hard that her joints hurt. Somehow she managed to sleep but the discomfort was too much and she lay or sat awake staring at the stars or trying to comfort Julian.

"Why me?" He wailed.

"Both of us Julian, we are both in the same place Julian. Try and be calm, and before you start yelling again try at least to show the people how much of a hero you are," she said having given up trying to get him to pray and ask for God's forgiveness and love. She winced at the memory of her last attempt and did not want to hear another tirade against Jesus and the Lord.

"Instead of just standing there looking at us why don't they set us free? Bloody four eyed gits," Julian said.

"The guards will shoot them if they try and some would be cut to pieces. Take heart Julian, it will all be over tomorrow," she said, and bit her lip when he began swearing again. Wrong. All over meant death. Maybe, she thought, Blard's plan will work, whatever it was. She had started it off and hoped that it would work. Blard had explained that the President liked to create the maximum agony for his victims and one of his great delights would be to have her and Julian sitting in public waiting execution for as long as possible.

"But remember that both you and Julian are useful propaganda tools and he will want to extract as much as he can from your humiliation. If you can do it, a calm, collected attitude will be in your favour. I assume Julian will fall apart?" said Blard, unaware, as they both were that the newly declared Emperor would execute them both as soon as possible. She sighed. There was no hope.

She was wrong about Blard's estimation. He had assumed that Julian and Angela would be executed so although they used Angela's plan for the main attack that included the Children's Army in force on the west, the Women's Army cutting in from the south, and the Rebel Forces from the east and the south with a force striking north and turning, there were other forces moving as well. Glorida's force was going directly to First City, and D.G's small contingent cutting around even further south and heading for First City to meet up with Glorida, and the NMF forces as a viable distraction cutting into First City. The NMF troops were the elite forces, the people usually sent in to deal with the difficult tasks. Glord and D.G had worked with them regularly before they were attached to the Rebel Army main body. Blard's task was to attack the Loyalist troops on a front between Second City and First City and cut the main road and take the fight to the enemy on their own territory. His twin was supposedly on his way to join the NMF forces. Blard left Glord in charge of the Children's Army to carry out part of Angela's plan and create a diversion, originally devised to draw off the Emperor's City Forces.

"What is the news Pair?" Blard asked the communications officer.

"Glorida is in position and champing at the bit. The execution is set for sunset tomorrow, and we are nearing our diversion point. D.G is in place and in touch with Glorid. Other than that we learn from our contacts that Julian is in a permanent blue funk, and Angela is praying to her God and still as calm as she began," the Pair recited, one speaking the other checking and nodding agreement.

"Julian is a hero right?" said Blard.

"Nah, panics when he sees a sword, or an enemy. Good bomber so they say," said the other half of the Pair.

"Right, so most is in place, but we still have to get there," said Blard.

"Yes, and there will be fighting I suspect. It will be close."

Blard nodded and sat thinking about the situation as the wagons moved slowly onward. It would be a close run thing, he was sure of that. He was diversion and back up but if the diversion got bogged down he might not be back up. He might be clean up instead, and from what he had seen of Angela he considered that would be a dread loss. He wished there was a contingency plan.

Bates and Fish liked working with Bradl. The meeting up with the NMF forces after the brief contact with Julian and the women had been an exciting and bloodthirsty experience. Bradl explained that he was given the task of acting as a virtual spy for Glord and his twin.

"My twin, Blard, is with Angela's Army but as we have sworn allegiance to Dart and Drat we are also part of the NMF watchdog group so I am seconded to this mob. You may as well be part of it. I will lead a Troop. You will enjoy it," Bradl said.

Their job was to attack from the south east from the Wastelands as part of the main Rebel Army thrust.

"We will do what Angela has done and collect sympathisers as we go although it will take us a little longer to arrive at First City," said Bradl.

"Right how do..." Bates

"...we do that," Fish.

"Simple, we accept surrendering Pongos, refugees and send the unarmed civilians back behind the lines. The rest, Polisocs, Stormtroopers and Loyalists we shoot or slice to bits. Should be fun," said Bradl.

As it was when Bates and Fish joined the armoured troop they discovered a skill that was much appreciated by the Pairs. They were good at directing artillery.

Bradl's party grew larger as it moved north and on their third day of travel it met a large column moving south. At the head there was a wagon bearing the red and black pennant of the Emperor's guards and half way along the column another wagon bore the pennant of the Polisocs, a pig on a red and black striped flag. It was obvious that the column was on its way to cut them off from the main force.

Bradl immediately ordered an attack and licked his lips as he set the lead wagon moving with all Pairs fully alert and armed.

"Rockets."

"Rockets ready."

"Plasma cannons"

"Plasma cannons ready,"

"All hand weapons ready."

"All weapons ready."

"Then let's go and kill the Bulgers!"

The wagons surged forward and from the side pods rockets hissed out and snaked toward the enemy column screaming a banshee wail that ended in huge metallic explosions of fire and plasma. The enemy column split into fives and sped side to side but Bradl's troops maintained an arc and fired in a pattern that hit at almost every stroke. Bates and Fish were kept busy with marking the shots and directing the fire of their own wagon while Bradl directed the overall battle. Up to that period in their excursion on Zrad Bates and Fish had an idea that the fighting might be over for them and that all they were likely to see of the battles was their own paperwork and a parade at the end. They soon got the hang of it and took to their part in the fight with enthusiasm and rapidly acquired skill. Their new found expertise, so the driver Pair suggested, was because they worked as a pair.

"Never really noticed..." Bates

"...that meself," Fish.

The driver Pair chuckled and resigned themselves to being directed more accurately than their normal fire spotter Pair.

"Target hard right..." Fish

"...fire pod one," Bates

"Good one Leader..." Fish

"...Pair, now try target..." Bates

"...left fifteen..." Fish

"...and fire pod..." Bates

"...three. Good shot..." Fish

"...but watch for target..." Bates

"...right forty. Nice one coming..." Fish

"...up now...steady...steady..." Bates

"...fire!" Fish.

And so the battle moved until the wagons were close enough to use their plasma weapons effectively. From that moment there was a fierce fire fight which ended with the enemy troops grinding to a halt in a ring of damaged wagons from which they poured a devastating fire. Bradl directed that the plasma weapons be exchanged for the rockets and with a concentration of metal and explosive that poured down on the enemy created a fire storm that destroyed all the remaining wagons and their beleaguered occupants. When the smoke cleared and the fires died down Bradl called for the foot soldiers to mop up any opposition that was left. A few bedraggled troopers staggered out from the burning wagons weaponless and confused lining up where the troops directed and stood dejected and frightened waiting for whatever was about to happen.

Bradl walked along the line and examined each trooper finally selecting one Half Pair and taking him aside walking him to where Bates and Fish stood watching.

Bradl knocked the Zradian to his knees and stood wide legged a little way from him and drew his sword.

"Right you Bulger's excrement, where are you from and where are you going and tell me now or I will let these two Earthmen beat the living shit out of you. They like doing that to people they hate. Talk!"

Bates and Fish cracked their knuckles and with an evil smile produced a set of knuckle dusters from their pockets and slipped them on.

"We've been waiting..." Fish

"...to use these for a long time," Bates.

The Half Pair screamed and started to speak. Bradl let Bates and Fish punch and gouge for a few short periods and then mildly asked them to stop. They reluctantly left off their punching and looked longingly at the rest of the prisoners. The Half Pair started to gabble and Bradl listened carefully while Bates and Fish wandered across to the line of prisoners slapping their weapons against their thighs ready to get to work. The prisoners eyed them nervously as they approached and with their fists full of gleaming brass Bates and Fish stood glaring at the line with a studied look that was meant to be intimidating.

"Which ones of you are Polisocs?" Fish

"And hurry up or we'll..." Bates, hungrily

"...do the lot of you," Fish with glee.

Several of the troopers pointed at several more of the rest and gabbled denunciations as quickly as they could cringing back from the guns of their captors and Bates and Fish's menacing attitude.

"Come forward..." Fish

"...or we will drag..." Bates

"...you out one by one," Fish.

The Stormtroopers pushed the Polisoc troopers forward and shuffled back leaving the trembling Polisocs in a line of their own. Joyfully but grimly and then with a whoop of delight Bates and Fish set to work on the first one in line. When he fell to the ground unconscious they yelled out "Next!" and one of the troopers pushed a Polisoc in their way. They beat six Half Pairs senseless before Bradl strolled over and suggested they stop.

"Why we was just..." Fish

"...getting into a nice..." Bates

"...comfortable rhythm," Fish.

"Maybe so but we know where they come from and I think my people would like to get on with the next bit of the journey. Finish off the one you have and we will sort the rest out with our blades," Bradl said and so saying he drew his sword and slashed a Polisoc trooper across his chest.

Bates and Fish watched as he killed another and grinned as they selected a trooper and started to beat him with their fists humming snatches from A Whiter Shade of Pale as they struck again and again until the Half Pair was dead. They managed two more before the rest were sliced and hacked to bits by Bradl and his soldiers. They left the bodies and the burned out wagons to the Carnibirds after stripping them of useable weaponry and carried on to First City.

"You know," said Fish.

"What?" said Bates.

"Sometimes I worry about you. I think you enjoyed beating up on those poor fellows."

"Didn't you?"

"Yeah, but I did feel a little bit guilty."

"I didn't."

"Nor did I really but I thought you might want to think that I did."

"Why's that?"

"So's you could worry about me."

"What? You thought I might think that you was slipping a bit?"

"Yeah, summat like that."

"You're sick."

"Then I ain't slipping meself then am I?"

Bates grinned. He felt all right.

On their third full turn after the brief fight they met Kord and Krod. The Pair were walking along a track hand in hand smiling happily, smiling idiotically. When Bradl's wagon stopped alongside them they turned and gazed at the machine looking puzzled. Bradl spoke softly and invited them to climb aboard. They hopped in like children at a treat and allowed the Pairs to lead them to a seat where they sat cuddling together and singing a Zradian lullaby. The Pairs brought them cool drinks and with gentle hands took their weapons away from them.

"That is the Pair Kord and Krod. They used to be the best hit Pair in the business short of Dart and Drat and my twin and I. They've gone single and that ain't no good for any Pair or Half Pair to see," Bradl said and shook his head sadly. "Enemy or not we will treat them kindly."

"Why don't we just..." Fish

"...you know..." Bates who drew his finger across his throat whilst Fish nodded.

"No!" said Bradl, "We are not so barbarous as that!"

"But you just let us..." Bates

"...beat some Half Pairs to death..." Fish

"...with our fists?" Bates.

"That was execution. This is different," said Bradl and from the look on his face Bates and Fish knew that it was not a good idea to pursue the subject any further. They said nothing and avoided watching Kord and Krod cuddling happily together on their seat.

Julian makes his mark

The suns rose and slowly lit up the scene in First City's First Square. The light shone on two naked figures chained to the two largest execution stakes before the main door of the palace. One figure groaned and stretched its limbs staggering to an upright position; despite his puffy face, for this was Julian, looked around noting the silent crowd and the grim guards who stood an arm's length apart in a semicircle around him and Angela.

The other figure stood up slowly and faced the rising suns. She put her hands together and prayed; her clear voice cutting across the silence steady and calm as if she were praying in a chapel on her home planet of Earth.

Julian farted.

With a groan he manipulated his chains to hold his penis and stepping forward micturated profusely on the paving between two of the guards who hastily shifted position. The two guards glowered at him.

"Oh shit," he said, and waited for the two men to beat him. Instead they continued to stare at him their faces registering their disgust.

"Bollocks," he said.

"You'll keep, arsehole," said one of the guards.

Julian whimpered.

All day they waited. Julian sank to the paving and slumped. He ate the meal they gave him, took the drink and was glad of the wash down in the late afternoon when the cleaners came and washed the paving around him and Angela. Pairs came and washed them both properly for which he was grateful until he realised they were cleaning him up ready for the slaughter.

He screamed obscenities at them but all they did was laugh.

As the afternoon wore away so the crowd fell even more silent, a troop of Polisocs marched into the square and formed an armed perimeter. The Dog Squad soldiers marched from the palace carrying equipment and lay it on two low tables that normally served as seats for visitors. There were two sets of foot and hand claws and a padded ring adorned with sharp spikes sticking outwards that reminded Angela of the headdress on the Statue of Liberty. Julian squealed and demanded to know what the items were for, and wailed loudly when the guards explained how the claws were fitted to the hands and feet of the executioners and the crowns were placed on their heads. The hand claws were used to grip the victim and the foot claws to rip out the intestines. The crowns were for effect and intended to impale eyes and slice throats when or if the crowd called for it. Mostly, the guard explained, the claws did the trick.

Julian wailed and begged and cried out curses on the Emperor, his nation, the executioners, and anybody else he could find to blame. Angela noted that the crowd was silent and wondered why there was so little noise. It was said that normally the crowd enjoyed executions and as the guards marched up and down keeping watch on their charges it was obvious the crowd were unhappy. As the suns dropped lower so people became quieter and even Julian's whimpering could be heard above the shuffle of feet and the low murmuring of many voices. The First Square clock that had beeped the periods throughout the day beeped the change of period that announced the emergence of the Emperor from his Palace. On either side of him strolled a phalanx of elite guards, and behind them walked two masked executioner Pairs dressed in the ancient tunics modelled on the markings of a Carnibeast. The Emperor stopped and immediately his guards formed an arc with their master as the centre. The executioners strolled slowly forward. Clad in black masks that covered their eyes and noses, tight skins drawn across their bodies striped like the Carnibeast and black tights that clothed their legs down to their light, flexible footwear, they looked evil. The crowd gasped and groaned and Julian shrieked.

Angela rose slowly to her feet and stood gazing at the executioners and at the Emperor. She neither smiled nor let her fear show and although she was naked and pink from the suns she was dignified and calm. Somebody in the crowd sobbed and so too did Julian.

"The prisoners will stand," said the Emperor.

Julian stayed on the paving and sobbed even more deeply.

A guard Pair tried to stand him up but as soon as he was on his feet he dropped to the paving again and tried to back away from the Emperor and the fearsome executioners.

"Stand up my friend," said Angela, "be brave and show this jumped up popinjay that although you are scared spitless you are still a man. Think about what old Tzu would say if you gave in to this piece of Zradian excreta."

Julian stopped his sobbing and shakily got to his feet spurning assistance and stood facing the Emperor.

The crowd cheered.

The guards took their places and slowly the executioners, assisted by two Pairs of young men dressed like their masters, donned their claws and crowns.

"P-pussycats," said Julian.

The Emperor took a few paces forward and smiled to the crowd who answered his gaze with a stony silence.

"Citizens of Our glorious empire," he began, "the prisoners are charged to die on this day and it is Our solemn duty to wish them a painful and unhappy death."

So saying he stepped to where Angela was standing upright and defiant, her hands at her sides and her face raised to the sky. She took no notice of the Emperor and continued to pray for herself and Julian. In fact she looked past him as if he was of no more significance than a dull statue, or a blank wall at a bus stop. She listened to him inform her that she was about to die and nodded disinterestedly.

"Do you not understand Us?"

"Oh yes, perfectly," said Angela.

The crowd cheered and some booed but the ring of troopers silenced their noise with a clash of swords and shouts of anger.

The Emperor walked the three metres to where Julian was standing and stood before him.

"And now hero what have you got to say to Us now that you are about to die?"

Julian mumbled a reply that the Emperor could barely catch and annoyed that Julian had spoken so quietly he moved closer.

"Speak up Earth man scum!"

Julian moved back and muttered again and again the Emperor moved closer.

"What are you saying to Us?"

"Up yours you fucking ratbag!" yelled Julian and with a sudden lashing swing disregarding his chains he hit the Emperor full on his nose with the edge of his hand. The Emperor shot backwards with blood pouring from his face screaming in anger and pain clutching his face with both hands and staggered back into the arms of his guards.

The crowd roared its approval and before the guards could slice Julian to shreds the Emperor shouted out.

"No! I want him killed slowly. Fix by dose fust!"

Medics rushed forward and surrounded the Emperor fussing and cleaning with sprays and healing balms. They fussed around him for a few short periods and then with a congested snarl he rose to his feet and cried aloud.

"Begin the executions!"

The two executioners adjusted their dreadful tools assisted by their acolytes and when the two Pairs were ready one Pair advanced on Angela and the other on Julian.

"Now, kill them!" cried the Emperor.

It was at that moment that a lot of nasty things happened.

The first was that something sharp and painful buried itself in the Emperor's back and the second was that he fell face forward on the paving, and the third was the rough hand that turned him over on his back, and the fourth was the boot that crushed his windpipe. The last thing was the red mist that filled his whole awareness followed by the blackness that snuffed it out.

After that the nasty things happened to other people that did not affect him. His lifeless body was ignored in the general panic as guards fell to the guns and swords of their furious attackers.

Above the noise of the sudden battle and the panic of the crowd Julian's shrill and terrified voice rose in a scream.

"Oh for fuck's sake get the bastard off of me!"

Colin stepped out of the booth and slid sideways. His men followed and with caution they spread out and took up positions behind pillars taking advantage of the shadows. It was daylight but from inside the building lights glowed. They were in a round courtyard divided into four with a seating area in the centre complete with a fountain that was lit by sealed lamps. Plants of strange shape and colour were arranged formally in patterns in four sectors, red, blue, green and yellow each sector itself lined up opposite a different colour in the centre. An arch gaped darkly across the courtyard and despite Reg's whispered desire to stay and look Colin led the group directly to it. Inside there was a lighted corridor that led in a straight line downward. It was empty but Colin urged caution and looked for side doors and places to hide or where people may be hidden. They padded along the corridor on the soft flooring that was neither carpet nor anything they recognised to the bottom of the slope and flattened themselves against the walls one opposite each other and peered cautiously around the ends.

Both ways were clear and Colin decided on turning left. The passage was short and turned into another corridor that was more or less level. A few metres along moving slowly they recognised the Zradians from the hotel attack.

"Shoot the bastards," Colin said and aimed the shotgun he had taken from McCord's body. He loosed off two shots and beside him Reg and Gary used the laser weapons. All the Zradians fell, and running, Colin reached them first with Reg a close second.

There were four wounded Half Pairs and with a look of ecstasy on his face Reg used his skinning knife and slit their throats.

"All same piggy porkers,"[4] he said and chuckled happily.

----

4 *Reg is a qualified slaughter man - he just happens to have a hobby - knife throwing displays in his spare time.*

They marched quickly along a deserted corridor and hid quickly when it gave way to a large hall. They entered from a side door and apart from the smell that reminded Colin of a butcher's shop the place was richly decorated and filled with double seats surrounding a throne set on a dais. A semi-circle of stone tiles glistened with cleaning fluid and from this led a central aisle that disappeared out of a wide door. The place was deserted and Colin led his small group to the doorway. Beyond that there was a smaller hallway entrance that led directly to the outside. Cautiously, keeping to the shadows, Colin led them to the doorway and they peered out. A few metres from them in the open square they saw two figures tied by chains to stakes. Both were Earth people and with an intake of breath Colin recognised them.

"Angela Breen, she's the one with the tits, and Julian Renfrew, he's the one with the dick," said Colin.

"What's 'appening?" asked Reg.

"I think they is going to top them," said Colin. "Look, the geezers with the rakes is getting ready."

"What we gonna do?" said Gary.

"Sort it," said Colin, "We creep up on the bastards and have at 'em. Reg, you top the bloke in the dressing gown, the one with all the mouth, and me and Gary will protect the geezer and Animal and Trevor can look after the bird, right?"

They grunted agreement and keeping to the darkest nooks slipped along the paving close to the walls of the palace. They thought they were too late but when Julian punched the Emperor on the nose they had enough time to get into place.

"Cor, the skinny bloke clobbered the old geezer proper with one of them Karate chops, I like that," said Colin, and as the Emperor gave the order to slaughter Julian and Angela Colin launched his attack.

"Got the bastard," said Reg drawing another blade.

"Nice throw," said Colin. His companions leapt on the two executioners and Colin watched with approval as Gary grabbed his target and slit his throat. Colin threw the body aside and was in time to see Animal tearing at the other executioner with one of the executioner's clawed gloves while Trevor held the screaming Zradian by the arms so that Animal could tear at his flesh slowly and deliberately. And then it was a rush to reach Angela and Julian in time to stop the guards killing them. At that moment there was a sudden noise from outside the square and a small fleet of battle wagons arrived. Before the guards could react a small group of fighters disembarked and leapt at them slashing and cutting their way to stand guard over Julian and Angela. A Zradian leapt over the low chains that marked the edge of the paving and kicked the fallen Emperor's head with a well aimed boot.

Colin watched, amused, as from the Palace behind them a dark haired woman rushed to where Julian was grovelling and crying, kicked the dead body of the executioner aside and fell on him and kissed him passionately. He was also surprised when a Zradian strolled directly to Angela and folded her in his arms and kissed her. He was even more surprised when Angela responded and sank into his embrace like any girl in love.

"Now that is sweet," he said.

"Yeah, bloody cute," said Reg, "'ang on while I get me knife back outer the geezer with the dressing gown and its time we got on with knocking orf some of them black and reds."

Colin watched Reg slip the throwing knife out of the Emperor's back and wipe it clean on the Emperor's clothes and reflected that having Reg around was handy. The man was like a snake, dangerous when disturbed and deadly in action. Reg carried two belts of throwing knives and a short bayonet honed to a razor edge that he used for hand to hand combat, but he was jealous of his small throwing knives and liked to recover them as he worked. He was useful now because as the two would be victims were chained up until they could be freed they had to be protected and the best way to do that was to use blades and hand weapons. Colin saw Tzu and his Kung Fu people take up a defensive circle and the Zradians from the wagons fighting to open a corridor. He cheered when he saw Lugs and the Ferret emerge from a wagon and come out fighting.

"Lugs you old bastard!" Colin yelled, "Good to see you!"

Lugs waved cheerfully and in between smashing heads and breaking limbs he made his way to where Colin was fighting.

"'Ullo Colin me old mate," Lugs said, and dropped a Pair of black and reds with two sudden and massive blows. "Nice ter see yer. Me 'an Ferret 'ave been lookin' after mister Byrde. I bashed a lot of these blokes and they don't arf go down."

A Zradian Pair rushed from the wagons with a pair of bolt cutters and another Pair came carrying cloaks. Lugs bashed two guards that tried to stop them and Colin shot another group with his laser. The crowd had disappeared and all that was left on the square were their own people and the enemy. The enemy force was much larger, but as soon as the crowd had gone, running along the streets to the outer circles, the wagons opened fire and the enemy force collapsed. There was a sudden rush of troops from within the palace but the wagons mowed them down with plasma fire. A few short periods later Angela and Julian were free of their chains and covered in cloaks. Julian was led to the lead wagon by the dark haired woman and Angela by the Zradian. A voice in English called out that they should get in the wagons and with his small group fighting and shooting with the Kung Fu people Colin was swept up into the lead wagon. Shooting from the rear platform Zradian Pairs, mostly women he noticed, mowed down the guards and then they were on their way out of the square.

Colin found himself sitting on a bench with Lugs and as they rolled out along the radial street past the inner city circles he asked Lugs what was going on.

"Oh, we're in the middle of a civil war and we just rescued Julian Renfrew and Angela Breen from the Emperor. He was the old geezer what Reg dropped with his knife. We are part of the women's rebel army," said Lugs proudly, "and we are winning."

"What happens now?"

"We go back to the main army and then we takes over the city. Now the bleedin' Emperor's copped his whack we got it in the bag ain't we?" Lugs said, and lay back exhausted.

Colin grinned.

The pen is mightier

When it came the final collapse of the newly dead Emperor's rule was so complete the NMF was taken by surprise. The chain of events began with the Pongos, who learning of their leader's demise, turned against the Stormtroopers.

The Stormtroopers and Polisocs wanted to continue the fight but with no real leadership they became disorganised. The ordinary soldiers, knowing that their allegiance to the Emperor would be called into question were unsure what they wanted to do. Some groups wanted to surrender; others wanted to continue the fight and some were so confused that they had no idea what to do. The Pongos turned on both Troopers and Soldiers and aligned themselves openly with the Rebels.

The Polisocs panicked.

The result was that wherever the Rebel Army and the Children met their enemy the loyalist troops fought back but lacked resources to fight the renegade Pongos, the anger of the ordinary people and the treachery of their leaders, who seeing their own destruction looming, left them to get on with it. The Polisocs fled in droves trying to escape the vengeance of the people.

Their final collapse was a rout.

The worst humiliation for the Stormtroopers and the Polisocs was that the army that came from the west were peasants with no military bearing at all and whatever tactics they used against them did not work.

The Children's Army swept victorious from the west toward First City but by the time they reached it the Rebel Army and the Women's Rebel Army had occupied Sector Red and First City taking over control of the republic. Nert addressed his Acolytes and Guides.

"My people, we have with us the One, Glord, who will be our inspiration during the coming blessed time. He is here and it is to him we can speak and explain what we need of him. It is this we should do now," he said, and listened to the murmurs of assent. "Go fetch him."

Four Acolytes stood up and moved to where Glord and his small troop were camped. They walked steadily, reverently and humbly as Nert had taught them and stood in the fire light where Glord could see them.

"Er, Glord, would you be so kind and come to talk to Nert, we are worried about him," said the spokespair.

Glord looked at him and his companion and saw anguish and worry. "What is wrong, my friends?"

"Our Leader is in need of advice and direction. He is confused and worried now that the war has been won and needs to consult with you as a Half Pair wise in the ways of the modern Zradian world," said the Pair. "Will you come and speak with him?"

Glord nodded; he was sure that now the war was over he would soon be going to join his twin and, finishing his meal, he said to his Pairs: "I will talk with Nert and then we will be ready to go." He stood up and followed the two Pairs watched by his companions until he was obscured by the darkness and soon he was sitting with Nert and his followers. Nert quietly explained what it was he wanted.

"My friend, we, your Children, need you now more than ever. We need you to lead us in the coming struggle against the forces that have assumed leadership of our land. As the inspiration of our movement we must ask you to lead us to a victory, to carry on what Angela began. We look to you, the great warrior and incarnation of Glord the Glorious to bring us the paradise we seek. You will do this for us?" Nert said.

Glord stared at Nert in disbelief. "I cannot possibly comply with your request. I have a life to live, and things to do that do not include being the titular head of a religion I do not believe in," he said, and got up from his seat to leave.

He felt the points of the blades touch his back and saw the muzzles of two plasma guns pointing directly at him. "Ah, you disagree?"

"I am sorry but we cannot let you go," said Nert.

Hands shifted to his arms and he felt thongs tied around them and more hands linked a chain between his ankles, and others tied another thong around his waist. He was lifted still covered by the guns and shuffled off between two Pairs to a stone hut fitted up as a cell. The Pairs pushed him inside and shut the door mounting a guard on him. He did not ask what would happen to him but he had an idea that martyrdom was on Nert's mind.

Glord's Pairs finished off the preparations for the move the next morning and waited for their leader to return. He was still away when it was time to take to their beds and set watches.

"Pairs," said one. "Something is wrong. We should go look for him."

Quickly and quietly, leaving sentries on the two wagons the group started out and met up with a line of Acolytes who quietly and viciously attacked them. The fighting was intense and it was obvious that they were expected. Of the eleven Pairs only one survived who ran back to the camp to warn the rest of their troop. He reached the wagons and realised he was too late, turned quickly into the darkness and disappeared from where the fires showed their troop lying slaughtered on the ground and Nert's acolytes in control of the wagons.

He managed to evade the searching Acolytes and found a place to hole up where the Pair lay listening to the sounds around them. At first light, tired and angry they slipped from the hiding place and taking advantage of cover managed to reach a unit of Angela's women. If it was not for the day light and the uniform they would have been killed. It appeared that the woman were on the alert.

"What happened to you?" The Half Pair in charge asked, A Hundred Leader.

The bedraggled Pair explained, the dominant Half speaking while his twin sat sipping at a hot drink looking exactly as he felt; exhausted. When they had finished the women took care of them, cleaned and dressed their wounds, escorted them to the latrines where they relieved themselves and washed, and then gave them breakfast.

"Rest awhile before sleeping. We will make plans," the Leader Pair said.

Whilst the Pair rested, guarded from prying eyes in one of the tents, the women sent out scouts and messengers to explain to the women's forces what had happened. One squad was sent off to relay the news of Glord's imprisonment to D.G. At the end of the day when the suns began to set the Hundred Leader gathered the others around her and made a plan.

"We have to snuff this upstart out and save Glord from Nert and his fanatics," she said. "If you agree with what I suggest then we can plan some action. Do I have your approval?"

There was a chorus of assent including Glord's Pair who volunteered to lead the attack but were persuaded to remain in the background. The plan was simple but would need at least one more turn before they could put it into practice. Glord's Pair watched the preparations and saw what others would not see; the movement of the entire women's section as it gathered stores, prepared essential equipment for instant transport and made sure their weapons were ready. They were given a pair of night glasses and told to clean up and stow their equipment after the night meal was finished.

"Are you ready to move Pair?" came the soft request.

They were and took their place in the column.

Glord eventually managed to cut the thongs by rubbing the strong leather up and down against the stone wall, choosing an edge that although rounded was rough. Zradian leather was tough but it finally gave way freeing his hands. There was nothing he could do about the chain until he had a key, and for that he was glad that all locks on leg chains were the same. At a pinch he could use a captured plasma gun to melt the metal. Whatever, he was determined to escape. He heard the guards outside and the chanting of the Acolytes and their stupid worship. If only they knew that Glord the Glorious was not a wholly good man neither was he a bad man, but for all that he was a man and a strong leader, and that was it. These idiots didn't know that.

Night came of the second day and as yet nobody had come to either feed him or take him away; a guard had looked in through the hatch and that was it. He managed to relieve himself without soiling his clothes and that made him feel better, it was one discomfort he didn't have to endure. Outside it seemed the Acolytes were working themselves into a state of ecstasy and he wondered what was happening. Suddenly the door banged open and guards rushed in, but as they were expecting him to be weak and tied up and helpless he took them by surprise when he suddenly attacked the nearest.

"Welcome to my humble home," Glord said, and looked down at the two Pairs who were both decidedly dead. He found a key and unlocked the chain; removed a sword from one of the bodies and armed with a plasma gun and capsules he exited his cell. "Ah, company." He said when Acolytes came hurrying toward him suddenly aware that he was free.

He shot the first ones and ran off before the others could recover.

Plasma flew at him and then suddenly there was the noise of running feet, the clash of weapons, a peculiar crashing noise that came from the worship area followed by a lot of screaming. Somebody called his name, a woman, and he ran toward the sound.

"Glord, over here! Hurry!"

He ran and was surprised to see Angela's women soldiers and one of his Pairs.

"Find Nert!" cried the woman but it was obvious that Nert was already gone.

Glord was taken to a wagon accompanied by his Pair who explained what had happened to the others.

"So, we were ambushed, and I was so naïve as to believe that Nert was not that fanatical, and his religion was a bit silly. I suppose I thought that they followed Angela and added the religion to the battles to persuade the people to follow the army and fight for a just cause and all that, but as I was so tied up with the problems of the NMF I became distracted. I am sorry, because of my distraction Pairs were killed." He said and when the wagons moved off he sighed with relief.

"We didn't see it coming either."

The Hundred Leader told him what had happened. "We destroyed their silly porcelain objects, killed as many of the Acolytes as we could, set light to the bonfire they planned for you, and looked for Nert but that slippery Half Pair has disappeared with some of his followers. We are now on our way to First City and Angela."

"Thank you, so what exactly did you do?" asked Glord.

"We carried out a mini-revolution. Er, we purged the movement," she said and blushed scarlet. "We slaughtered the Acolytes, Guides and any worshipper who opposed us. That was a lot of lives. Such a waste, but they should have let us do what we needed to do, and let us save you from their clutches. Anyway, I suspect we have killed off a lot of the leadership, and that might be useful."

"They wanted me for a living god - dead or alive," said Glord.

"We are sorry, we should have guessed," she said.

Glord laughed at her embarrassment. "I think so!" he said.

"We also have the sacred toilet bowl which we will take to First City and publicly destroy," she said, and pointed to a large, bulging sack.

The people of First City filled the streets waving leaflets and laughing as they dodged the fighting and chanting cheerful phrases about killing the Polisocs they cheered the rebels and the Children's army as they entered the confines of the city.

The Tyrant is dead! The Polisocs are scared!
The People rise up from their sick bed!

At the end of the first turn of freedom the conquering army stood before the palace door where the first Emperor of Zrad lay dead in the centre of a circle comprised of the bodies of his personal guards and the executioners; his sightless eyes stared up at the pinkish sky in which circled Carnibirds hopeful of an Imperial feast.

Dorida and Dorid walked from their wagon and stood beyond the carnage and gazed at the palace doorway. The hover microphones hummed softly as they aligned themselves with the Leader Pair and locked into the communications systems throughout Zrad and connected every source of news media to their busy crystals. The green lights flashed and Dorid and Dorida spoke.

"Citizens of Zradia, citizens of the planet Earth and all citizens on board the Star Stations we declare that as of this moment Zradia is under the care of the former Women's Rebel Army and the former Zradian Rebel Army under the blanket direction of the New Moral Few. Citizens are advised that the former President of Zradia and his forces are now, owing to the death of the President, defunct and illegal. We declare the Second Republic over! All former prisoners will be released. The Polisoc force is no longer a function of the new state and all former officials of the Second Republic are redundant."

The crowd that had gathered joyfully in First Square roared with enthusiastic approval and from every building in First City fireworks exploded and flags and bunting sprouted. Masses of plastic confetti fell like coloured snow on the streets and circles and for the first time for many years even the children rushed out from their homes to sport happily in the sunny squares and parks. Dorida and Dorid's Pairs took up posts at the doors of the palace and with an escort of troops the Pair marched into the Grand Hall to meet their male counterparts from the Rebel army and the NMF. Troops entered the palace at all entrances and mopped up resistance wherever they found it calling on the regular troops to surrender and killing all who resisted. Prisoners in the dungeons were released and handed over to the soldiers, and staff from all departments were ordered to work under the supervision of their conquerors.

The circling Carnibirds flew off in panic looking for other carrion.

Elsewhere in the city and all the major cities of Zradia rebel troops and the forces of the Children's popular army took over and where there was resistance did so forcefully. The Emperor's body was recovered from the square and carried into the palace where it was laid in a cool store. The Polisoc buildings were stormed and with much ferocity all within were either slain or captured. The dreaded Polisoc pigs were rounded up and slaughtered along with their masters and those prisoners who were still sane enough for rational thought yet too weak to walk were taken to the infirmaries and cared for.

In an underground bunker a core group of Pairs took control of the Doomsday bomb and deactivated it. Another group in a room adjacent to the first began the process of laying the transfer beacons that would bring Star Station One back home.

On the morning of the seventh turn since the death of the Emperor a column of wagons and marching fighters appeared on the outskirts of First City. Flying the banner of Angela's Elite Women fighters they marched proudly along the main arterial from the west toward the central square. The news spread rapidly and citizens turned out to watch and cheer as the column marched past to stop and form up in neat ranks before the palace in First Square. A lone figure moved out to greet the Hundred Leader Pairs and stood looking at them for a few moments before speaking. The truth was she was so emotional about seeing them again that it was as much as she could do to hold back the tears. Angela waited for them to speak.

"Angela Breen's Elite Women's Warriors reporting for duty!" said the Leading Pair.

"Welcome, and what have you to report?" Angela said, a smile on her face.

"That we are glad to see you alive and well, and that Nert's followers are scattered into the wilderness. We rescued Glord from Nert and his fanatics and that Half Pair and a follower have gone off to find some enemy to fight. He sends his regards," the Pair turned and waved to one of the wagons. "And that we have also brought with us a symbol of their religion which we wish publicly to destroy."

And as the porcelain bowl was carried from the wagon and unwrapped the Pair looked eagerly at Angela. "Are the cameras on us?"

Angela nodded.

"Good then do we have permission to smash this thing?" she said.

Angela giggled as another Pair handed their leader a large hammer. "Go for it," she said.

"We, the Pairs of Angela's Elite declare the movement of Nert's Children of Glord the Glorious defunct!" And with those words the Leader and another Half Pair took it in turns to smash the toilet bowl to small pieces. Another Pair picked up the broken parts, put them in a sack and unceremoniously carried them to the nearest waste chute, used the code, and emptied the contents. In silence the crowd listened to the grinding as the wheels crunched the pieces to small bits and sucked them down into the waste collectors. When the process was over the crowd cheered. During the cheering the Hundred Leaders and the Leader herself quietly informed Angela that her Elite Warriors were going home. Angela hugged each of them in turn.

On the outskirts of First City Nert and his followers sat around a fire over which they were cooking a Polisoc pig, discussing what they were going to do next.

"I believe we should call in the faithful," said an Acolyte and his fellows nodded in agreement. "I am sure that the following we have will be ready to form a church and rally around the second coming."

Nert sighed and waited for the others to finish speaking before speaking himself. There followed a discussion on the merits of the prophecy, and as it developed into a meaningful argument Nert realised how he could make the idea work. He sat thinking for a while and at last he raised his hand to indicate that he wished to speak. The circle of anxious Pairs and Half Pairs ceased their chatter and waited for him to speak.

"I am aware that we have been shoved aside by the new regime but the people still want us. Glord the Glorious is still a people's hero and we are still the leaders of the Children. We must use the words of our detractors to bring back the faithful. We were wrong to trust to alien help and we were wrong to expect the Messiah to come to redeem us when we asked for him. No, what we must do is let the people know that Glord will come again but that we must prepare the way with his works, and through our teachings we must give the real message to the people. The way we do that is to write down all that we know of him and teach the young to believe in their redeemer!"

The followers nodded sagely and such was Nert's charisma that what he said made sense. Amid a chorus of chatting and speculation each Half Pair put his point of view and came to the same conclusion as Nert.

"We will not be so up front as we were during the holy war of liberation but we will work to convert the people by our words and works. The power of the sword to destroy evil is limited but the pen or its equivalent is mightier," Nert said, and wallowed in the praise of his devout followers.

And so with the perverseness of familiarity Nert and his followers abandoned their previous war-like manner and took to their former lifestyle finding no need for Angela's washing regime nor for any other means of transport than their feet. The feast of Polisoc pig was enjoyed, and with the pork fat still adorning their clothing where they had wiped their fingers they set forth as a band of brothers to spread the good news.

Bates and Fish had their first view of First City from the heights of the very hills Julian himself had first seen it, but unlike Julian, they liked the look of the place. At the foot of the hills below them and heading up the winding road that led south there was a column of wagons and foot soldiers. Behind them and closing was another column and it was certain they were heading for a redoubt they planned to use as a defence against their pursuers. Bradl gazed at the two groups through his quad-ocular glasses for a few short periods his head moving from side to side as he scanned the action.

"The first group are Stormtroopers with foot soldiers and the group below are a small group of rebels and I think my twin is in charge. We will go and help out," Bradl said and grinned. "More fighting lads."

The fugitives reached the redoubt digging in as best they could with rocks and piled earth, arranged their fire patterns and waited for their enemy to try and kick them out. The pursuing troops fanned out and kept a little out of easy range and sat waiting for their quarry to either launch an attack or for nightfall. Bradl guessed that it would be nightfall and ordered his wagons to roll quietly down the slopes.

"When we are in range, it's rockets and a rush forward across the rough, and storm the Bulgers with close weapons. Take prisoners if you feel like it," Bradl ordered.

The lead wagons were in range quickly and waited until the rest were fanned out ready to fire.

"Let them taste our rockets," Bradl said.

Moments later the small force below joined in.

Bates and Fish had very little to do except track the target area and when the strafing was over the wagons raced forward and poured plasma into the redoubt. Caught between the enemy above and the enemy below the trapped Stormtroopers attempted to surrender and for a few periods Bradl was tempted but charged in anyway. There was a massive slaughter and when Bradl and his twin met in the centre of the redoubt there was no enemy left alive.

"We thought you might at least take some prisoners," said Blard.

"Sorry but I think my people forgot," said Bradl. "The good sergeant and Sherman there with you are they?"

"Yes, they came along for the ride. They got a bit bored in the city. You know it has fallen don't you? All we have to do is sort out the Children and we've got it."

"We were on our way. We had a dust up with a group of Pollies and Troopers and then your lot but other than that I think its all over. We'll ride in with you if you like unless you have something else in mind?" Bradl said and looked a little wistful.

"No, there's nothing more to do here that the Carnibirds cannot finish," said Blard.

The twins parted and with much shouting and fussing the two groups marched back to their wagons and formed up on the road to ride back to First City. They drove in via the main arterial spoke that separated sector yellow from sector red and emerged in the open area of second ring where they parked the wagons and disembarked. Two Pairs carried Kord and Krod with them and at last they arrived in First Square. Blard and Bradl marched at the head of their troops with Bates and Fish and Sergeant Orange and Sherman Holmes proudly behind them.

And as they marched into First Square a great cheer went up and the thousands of Pairs, men, women and children, that were gathered there called out their names. On the huge screens that hung from the walls of the palace a series of numbers counted down to zero.

"Bulgers, I forgot about that," said Bradl.

"Yeah, so had I," said Blard as the numbers clicked to zero.

The square filled with the sound, in glorious quadrophonics, of the tune A Whiter Shade of Pale and this time everybody listened.

Within the confines of the Solar system a small satellite moved quickly from its position approximately 0.05 of a light second away from its target planet. Its circuits noted the change with satisfaction, glad to give up the struggle to return to the 0.033 orbit it was programmed to prefer. It moved across the space quickly following the minute beacons placed in a neat path that settled it in a parallel orbit to a friendly satellite spinning around a large gaseous planet. It hummed with electronic pleasure when it detected a welcoming signal, locked on and held steady, and if any sound could have travelled in the emptiness of space an observer close by might have heard the tune A Whiter Shade of Pale emitted in a series of digital clicks. But there was nobody there to listen, so whether the emission of the tune actually happened could only be conjecture. Just moments prior to it leaving Earth's orbit it passed a message to the small source lying dormant in a telephone booth in a sleepy Texas township on a remote back road where, according to Zradian statistics, the incidence and therefore the likelihood of vandalism was as equally remote.

The message was simple: Terminate. Rodent #3 directive. Authorised by Rodent#4.

Neither the residents of the small Texan township nor the representatives of the Bell telephone company were aware that their little used but pristine public call box was the prime target locator for the Doomsday Bomb. The receiver was located in the telephone booth that stood outside the drugstore in the small Texas township. Their priority was to keep their township clean, go about their business and stay out of trouble.

Mervyn Haggard, a youth of that town was using the telephone booth to call his pal to apologise for getting drunk the night before when the operation to cut out the receiver happened.

"Listen Roy, I'm sure sorry for gettin' so damn shit-faced last night, I..." and his end of the conversation was cut off abruptly when the unit suddenly heated up and caught fire, causing him to stagger out coughing and spluttering as black smoke enveloped him. He fell over, giddy and sick from the fumes gasping and feeling faint, but as he passed out he had a confusing image of hundreds of people all vomiting into rows of porcelain toilet bowls.

As he remarked to his pal Roy, afterwards, "Who the heck is this guy Ralph they were yelling for?"

His pal had no idea.

Sadly the explanation eluded him for the rest of his life, and he grew increasingly bitter when nobody could explain the meaning of the images. He developed an irrational fear of porcelain toilet bowls. The experience affected him so much that he was afraid to leave his home and as a consequence he grew extremely obese through lack of exercise and overeating. He changed his WC unit for a plastic model unable to lower his buttocks on to anything porcelain, and ironically, he was found dead of a heart attack sitting on a plastic one that had cracked underneath him. The Doctor who was treating him for his gross Obesity said that a porcelain bowl would have stood the strain better and recommended that stronger materials be used for such amenities used by Obese patients.

A Close Shave

Pour and Roup stared at the screens and gibbered. The Doomsday Bomb was aimed directly at them and there was nothing they could do to stop it. They had tried ordering their staff and the troops they commanded to remain on board but no matter how much they ordered, cajoled, threatened or begged none would stay.

The small but vicious looking guard that went everywhere with them stopped them from getting anywhere near a transfer port stood watching the screens and grinning.

The information on the screens, accompanied by squeaks and chitterings from the cute cartoon rodents that bounced around from one screen to another each announcing the defeat of the Regime and the victory of the rebels in its own revoltingly cute fashion.

"Until all loyal troops and personnel have safely evacuated, you two are going nowhere," the lead Half Pair said.

There was only one transfer port open and the Pongos were not going to let them use it. What they saw on screen One scared them witless.

"Some screaming Bulger's excrement has realigned the bomb and that treacherous Pair Blard the Barmy has dumped receivers on the star stations. We don't stand a chance!" exclaimed Pour.

They watched the news as it happened delighting at first in the prospect of seeing enemies of the state executed, happy that they now served an Emperor despite the feeling that this was a wrong move on their Glorious Leader's part. They were unhappy that the two alien dissidents were not used as bargaining hostages which they thought, was a mistake. It seemed that the Emperor was forgetting that people like to rescue their heroes.

What they saw on their screens was the last gasp of the Second Zradian Republic, and although they found Julian's death defying, but eminently foolish act of Karate chopping the Emperor across the bridge of his nose, amusing, the resulting assassination of the Emperor was terrifying.

It was not long after that when, as troops were being pulled out of the invasion, the Pongos revolted and attacked the Stormtroopers and Polisocs on board. Pour and Roup were captured by Stormtroopers who tried to bargain with the Pongos threatening to take the Pair with them thus on exit destroying the Star Station and all who were in it.

Pour and Roup were relieved when the Pongos attacked the Stormtroopers, killed them all and took charge. They were less impressed when the Pongos put a guard on them whilst the evacuation took place.

One turn before the countdown zero the Pongo guard gassed them and left through the last transfer port. They woke groggy and sick on the floor of the central control room.

"Nong's teeth! I feel awful," moaned Pour and struggled to stand up only to fall again as if somebody had grabbed his ankle. "Nong! The swines have handcuffed our ankles!"

Roup groaned, struggled to rise, succeeded in getting partway and fell over. "My twin, we have to try," he said.

That they managed to reach the transfer port, to stand clutching each other tightly trying to pre-program the exit was a feat of determination. It was also an heroic effort to carry their packs with them to the port in the hope that somehow they would free the handcuffs and walk normally. Sobbing they heard the countdown move steadily toward zero and prepared for the inevitable.

In the dark recesses of its torn mind Clard and Dracl's robot dredged up enough power to send a feeble message out to its numerous sources. It touched Star Station One and discovered that the source there was as strong as ever but the friendly contact was silent. It whispered a last message to the Doomsday Bomb and was pleased when one of the sources flickered out. It tried to contact rodent three on Star Station Two but there was no reply and as the energy it had was suddenly absorbed by the dominant personality attempting to revive the contacts disappeared there was a mumbling electronic hum that in computer terms lasted an aeon and then silence.

We are lonely, Betty

Mother, Anthony,

Shut up! Napoleon.

And so with an electronic sigh the robot slid into shut down and a much modified stand-by.

The NMF High Leader Pair smiled as the technicians deactivated the doomsday bomb receivers in Star Stations Two and Three. He watched the countdown and as it approached zero he waited for the automatic contact through the transfer system to tell him that all was well. The figures clicked over to zero and exactly one third of a second later a red LED lit up on all of the monitors covering Star Station Three.

"Safe. Stand by to occupy." He said and smiled at the staff happily, both Half Pairs speaking one after the other with the right fraction of time between them to make the other Pairs in the room feel comfortable.

The monitors watching Star Station Two registered red for safe and immediately prior to the action there was a blip that showed up on the system. Before the High Leader Pair could make any congratulatory remarks the red LED went out and shifted back to green and then sat at yellow. All signals from Star Station Two ceased and instead there was a continuous roar of static.

"Silence the monitors and investigate!"

"Star Station Two has exploded your honour!" cried one Pair.

"How?"

"An on board bomb your honour. It was placed there to prevent Pour and Roup from escaping."

"Then can we assume that they did not survive?"

"It is possible."

"Good, good."

"But we have lost a Star Station your honour."

"A small price to pay for winning a war."

"Yes your honour."

"For Nong's sake move it!" panicked Pour as his twin carefully opened the transfer port door and pushed their packs in first and deftly set the coordinates on 'delay'

"Together, we must enter together," said Roup and took his twin's hand gently, easing him closer to the door. "When I say go we must jump into the portal and touch the activate button."

"Yes my twin, I am sorry but I am frightened."

"So am I but we must try."

Roup waited and then as the 'delay' light flickered to ready he took a deep breath.

"Go!"

The Pair hopped into the port and Roup pressed the activate button at the instant the red ready light came on. He watched the door bulge for a brief instant and felt the split second rumbling as the bomb hit, but their timing was perfect, and with only minor burns from the remnants of a captured part of the explosion they arrived at their destination. In a cloud of smoke and dust accompanied by a small shower of debris they crashed through a row of prickly bushes and landed at the feet of a group of surprised workers.

"Bulger's teeth! That was a close shave," said Roup, "we only just made it."

"But what about that lot?" said Pour pointing at the group of men.

"Oh cripes," said Roup.

They sat up clutching their packs and gazed at the workers who carried sharp slashers or grubbers and hooks. Beyond them a pile of cut bushes was burning and more workers were feeding the piles with cut branches.

"Its Pour and Roup!" one of the workers cried out, and turned to another for confirmation.

With no chance of standing up or attempting to run away they were surrounded by workers who menaced them with slashers, removed their packs and weapons and casually tied twine around their bodies and dumped them on the ground clear of the work area.

"We got a swag of work to do before we finish today, so you best sit where we put you and shut up. If you're lucky we might give youse some tucker. The joker that took us in will know what to do with you mate," said the worker, and grinned.

"Where are we?" asked Pour his voice tinged with fear.

"Sitting on the grass in a paddock on the edge of the forest in New Zealand watching us cut gorse for Trevor Thompson, he's the joker who took us in when we was lost after one of your teams cocked up the invasion landing. If you're lucky we might turn you over to the locals. If you're unlucky we might just slit your throats and bury you. If we are lucky we might get some money for your live bodies if we can turn you over to the rebel army. We all owe you bastards a kick up the arse so just pull yer heads in and sit quiet," the Half Pair said, and threatened them with his slasher.

Pour and Roup cringed.

"We..." began Roup.

"Say nothing, scumbag!"

Pour and Roup cringed even further and lowered their gaze.

They were going to be very quiet and stay very still.

The journey back from the paddock was uncomfortable. The farmer turned up with a wheeled vehicle into which the Pairs and Half Pairs clambered with familiarity and settled down on the rough wooden benches that made up the seating. Pour and Roup were thrown onto the floorboards along with the tools, and as the truck bounced along the rough track they were hit by blades and handles and trodden on as the seated workers juggled their feet to balance themselves against the violent movement of the truck. The journey took at least a half period, and by the time the vehicle had stopped in the farmer's yard Pour and Roup were battered and frightened. They squealed when they were dragged out of the truck and thrown onto the gravelled surface and lifted roughly to their feet.

"Who are these jokers then?" said Trev.

"Pour and Roup. They are the bastards that sent us here."

Trev looked at them with contempt taking in their fine clothes and their soft hands. He grinned at the livid scratches made on their skins by the gorse and was amused at their cowering manner as they gazed back at him. Their clothes were torn and it was obvious to him that the Pair had never done a day in the bush in their lives. Under their cowardly demeanour there lurked a haughtiness that if it were allowed to surface would become a problem, so Trev decided to stomp on it directly.

"Remove the shackle, wash the buggers and give 'em clean clobber and give the buggers some tucker. I'll see what we can do with 'em tomorrer. Make sure the buggers don't do a runner. They oughter know there ain't nowhere ter go. Lock them in the spare store room," Trev said, and grinned.

"What do we do if they try to scarper?"

"Shoot the buggers," replied Trev with an even bigger grin. "They might make good dog tucker?"

The Pairs and Half Pairs laughed and took great pleasure in following the farmer's instructions. There was nothing like a carefully worded bit of intimidation to control a rebellious nature in a Pair so used to intimidating others. Pour and Roup didn't like it but they had no choice in the matter.

"Okay you jokers," said Trev as the Zradian Pairs and Half Pairs he had employed for so long sat at the long table and drank from their glasses some of the Waikato four X ale he had saved for the end of the scrub cutting. "I got news for you. Your President, who calls hisself an Emperor has been knocked off by yer rebel soldiers and you got a new governmint. I reckon that calls for a celebration. Er, I gotta ask yer what you blokes wanna do?"

The outspoken Half Pair who was named Coln and now took the anglicised name of Colin, answered for them all.

"Er, we're quite happy here Trev, the blokes like working fer you and we reckon that if you want you could run an agency and hire us out. Now that our land is in different hands we reckon we want to stay here. We like it. Isn't that right mates?" he said turning to ask the rest of the Zradians.

There was a chorus of assent and one offered a comment on Pour and Roup. "You can tell the authorities that if they want Pour and Roup back they kin have them, we kin do without the bludgers?"

Trevor laughed when he realised that the Half Pair had spoken like a true Kiwi.

And so Pour and Roup's fate was decided.

The process was a little bit more complicated than that, but when Trevor contacted the local police office and a Sergeant drove out to see them he was made welcome with some of the four X, and had the situation explained to him. He arrested Pour and Roup promising to do what he could to help the remaining Zradians.

"There's a mob of youse blokes up north that might wanna help ya. As far as I can see if Trev here wants yer ter stay and if youse blokes want to then I ain't goin' to do nothing, eh?"

The Sergeant handcuffed Pour and Roup to the rear of the passenger seat of his four wheel drive and headed back to town. Nestling in the trunk of his wagon was a case of four X protected on either side by Pour and Roup's survival packs. Their weapons were encased in tough plastic bags on the floor of the passenger compartment, and as they travelled toward the small township Pour and Roup slumped in the seat as much as the handcuffs would allow them and wept. The Sergeant switched on his radio and from it came the tune A Whiter Shade of Pale. The Sergeant hummed along with it as he turned out onto the main road.

It was exactly twenty minutes to three.

Zrat and Traz blinked in unison as the Sergeant explained what had happened.

"You mean that as far as you are concerned we are no longer prisoners of war but we are troops ready for repatriation?" they said, and looked around at the township and gazed out across the flat land to the east and the hills in the south and west. From the north there was the sea and the endless sands and the welcome smell of sun drenched flax and scrub. "You mean we will have to leave all this?"

The Sergeant shrugged and looked sad. Zrat and Traz were dressed in shorts and black singlets, their feet in boots, and socks that drooped at the ankles. On their heads they wore wide brimmed hats and if they were different from the citizens it was only in their accents and their looks. Their skin was darker than the Maori residents and there was a peculiar cast in their eyes that showed their four pupils but, like their New Zealand hosts they squinted in the bright light, and it was only when they blinked or looked indirectly away from the bright reflections of the sun that the twin pupils showed.

"Sorry but unless we can git you in as residents you gotta go home," the Sergeant said.

"Well we did apply and you reckoned that because we have a lot to offer we should stay. I mean it's not as if we can't pay our way. I mean technology for Aotearoa and especially for Kaitaia. We did help with the fishing contest and our Pairs are settling in all right. And then there's the ideas we gave to your locals that seem to help them a bit?" the Pair said, and scuffed their feet as the sergeant gazed at them.

"Yeah, well, the Minister's still talking about it eh?" the Sergeant said. "I reckon that if you was to get together with the council and the Elders I reckon you might have a case for staying."

"We talk to Mani again eh?"

"Yeah and let him know that I can get all the forms sorted out for him, okay?" the Sergeant said, and grinned. "We want you to stay, you guys are neat and our young jokers take notice of youse eh?"

Zrat and Traz were getting used to the question at the end of the sentences and no longer tried to answer them. After surrendering to the locals and discovering that most of the armed forces who were sent to guard them were Maori and many came from the north they had explained how they felt to a huge muscular Captain. This man had listened patiently, and then suggested that if they explained the workings of the wagons to them and helped find what they needed to get them going again the Zradians could stay. Traz and Zrat agreed and later when the wagons were once again mobile the Pair volunteered to transport the fishing competitors to and from the beach if the township wanted to re-run the competition. It was then that they met the council and the elders of the Iwi and made some tentative proposals. The elders promised to take them away and discuss them, and the councillors decided to wait until the elders had reached a decision. The mayor explained that the decision would not be final but as long as they had something to work with there would be a good reason for them to stay. The army Captain was happy to let them stay as long as his government would allow it, and with a feeling of belonging Traz and Zrat and his troops settled down to wait. In the meantime the Zradians were encouraged to work for the locals, unpaid but well fed, and within a few weeks became a part of the town scenery. The television crews and the newspaper journalists eventually disappeared, and toward the end of the winter and at the onset of summer the Zradians were more or less left to their own devices.

The day after the Sergeant told them that the President was dead the media arrived again, and when they were asked about Pour and Roup they smiled and rubbed their hands together.

"I wish we could get our hands on that Pair. We would show them what torture and pain can really be like," said Traz and grinned at his twin.

"You can tell them we are glad they are in the cactus, I can think of no better Pair to be in captivity from the ex-president's forces than that Pair, hooray," said Zrat.

Their comments were spread across the television screens of the Earth, and if Pour and Roup had any intentions of evading retribution they were sadly mistaken. The luckless Pair were paraded first in the local police station and then later in Wellington where they were placed before a barrage of journalists' microphones and asked to explain themselves. Part way through their media interrogation a small force of New Zealand Customs Officers cut short the proceedings and escorted the pair to a waiting dark van. Inside they were handcuffed to a rail and driven to Wellington International Airport. With no explanation they were whisked into a small aircraft and carried first to Auckland, and then after a series of rapid and confusing transfers from aircraft to a plain detention room and then onto yet more aircraft the Pair were taken to a room in London Airport and held by silent uniformed officers in yet another plain room. Confused and tired but well fed and given plenty of drink, none of which contained any alcohol, they waited for whatever would happen next.

Sitting side by side and clutching each other they started with fear and surprise when at last the door opened and a body of officers walked in. Behind them were the Pair, other than Blard the Barmy, they had never hoped to meet.

"Good morning Pair as they would say here," said Dart while his twin grinned from one pace behind him.

"Before you go home to Zrad to face execution the government of our host country have requested that you appear on ETV and apologise for your misdemeanours. We advise you to confess all and be very contrite because the people of the planet you thought to conquer on behalf of our ex-president and emperor are extremely annoyed. They want to string you up from a couple of lamp-posts," said Drat.

"Other than that it is so nice to see you," said Dart.

And from the speakers in the room came wafting the tune A Whiter Shade of Pale, and as it played Dart and Drat hummed along with it and smiled. Pour and Roup groaned, and with a sob they cocked their legs against the wall and urinated.

As a reward for their efforts and their donation of the hover wagons to the New Zealand government Zrat and Traz and their men were allowed to stay. Some Pairs elected to stay in Kaitaia and others made applications to join the New Zealand Army, and some applied for the Navy. Of those that stayed a few sent for their wives and others, not yet wed, let it be known that they were available, especially for twins.

Zrat and Traz stood on the beach looking across the ocean, their eyes shaded by the rims of their floppy towelling hats and for a few minutes they were content to look at the action of the sea.

"My twin, I am happy that we have solved our problems and although I am confident that our home planet will be a peaceful place to live, I am happy here," said Traz.

Behind them there was a cheerful call and the pair turned to see two women walking across the sand towards them. "Our wives," said Zrat, and led his twin back across the sand to meet them.

It was one of those intimate moments made even more intensely exciting knowing that the couple had found peace.

The Axe Man is coming

Deep in the dark and damp dungeons below the palace a lone figure crept through the gloom dragging with it an axe and the rotting carcass of a dead Bulger. It stopped and stroked the filthy object and occasionally cuddled it close to him. His naked body was scuffed and streaked with grime, ex-Fireman Sidney Weddell was searching for a way out to the surface. The twists and turns of the fetid dungeons were too many for him to remember where he had been or to sense any direction as to where he might be going. The damp walls and floors reminded him of the sewers under west London where he was once sent to fight a fire and that confused him too. Noises echoed from the levels above and with his unerring ability to get anything wrong he headed down and away instead of up and toward. Now he was lost in the dark and starving. The body of the Bulger was too fetid now for even his insensitive nose to ignore and he had given up trying to nibble bits of poor creature for nourishment. He had found some dried sausage in a niche close to a cell where lights were still burning and he had eaten that but that was a long time ago.

For how long he had gone without he did not know but it was a long time and even though he was tempted to eat the Bulger he refrained. It was like eating his little boy's Teddy Bear. He cuddled the Bulger close to him and kissed it gagging at the foul taste and almost but not quite throwing up. He stumbled against some steps and was pleased when they took him up one pace at a time through the profound darkness of the extreme lower reaches rising slug like from one step to another. He tried counting the steps but the numbers wouldn't stay in line. He reached five more times than he could remember and gave in confused by the need to count the steps and the compulsion to embrace all of them at once or lose them. He cried real tears when the steps gave way to flat flagstones and for a moment he was tempted to go back down and feel the steps again; they were good company, reassuring with their nice angular shapes and flat stones that seemed to caress his toes.

"Must move on, must keep going," he said, and struggled to his feet walking haltingly upright instinctively avoiding the walls as if the darkness was no barrier to sight, and when after many turns and upward movement he met more steps he embraced them with loving gurgles not even realising that somewhere along the way he had dropped the axe. The Bulger was a stinking mess that was now wrapped around his neck which at some time, maybe as he climbed the last set of steps, he had tied the Bulger by its tail and feet the way a fox fur was tied around a Dowager Lady's neck. At the top of the steps the corridor took a turn and for the first time since he had entered the palace dungeons he felt a smooth and even surface under his feet. Ahead there was dim light from small wall mounted lamps and doors opening out onto the corridor but there was nobody in any of the small rooms and only occasionally signs of recent occupation. There was a set of steps at the end made of metal that led to a platform which in turn opened out to a well lit corridor. On either side of the corridor there were rooms that held equipment puzzling in kind to him, and as they were all empty he ignored them passing by without bothering to enter. More stairs and then he was out onto the lower levels where although the rooms were deserted he recognised their use and with a gnawing hunger sought out a place to find food and a place to sleep. He wandered into a small chamber that was clean and lit with dim lights containing a bed on which he could stretch out and sleep. With some food and proper drink inside his aching belly he lay on the inviting bed and slept. The lights dimmed and with a static crackle the portal closed and warm air wafted into the room creating a comfortable soporific atmosphere that helped him close his eyes and slumber the sleep of the truly mad and innocent.

Through the speakers hidden in the wall the soft notes of the tune A Whiter Shade of Pale soothed him and as he snoozed into sleep he smiled gently.

He liked music.

The music that announced the major news of the day was the usual introduction relating to the republic's communications system, but before more than a few bars had played it was interrupted by a strange voice.

The voice was that of Dorida and Dorid which, being a woman's voice took the elderly Leader Pair by surprise.

"Eh, what?" they began when the newscast started. "Women?"

The Aide Pairs and senior Leader Pairs listened as Dorida and Dorid explained how they were going to form an interim government and conduct a general election.

"And so, we ask all parties to register their interest as soon as possible. Later, as soon as we have put in place the means by which all eligible citizens can be registered, and a structure for the new democratic government is finalised, we will hold elections. In the meantime we call on all troops loyal to the now dead Emperor to surrender to the forces of the Zradian People's Democratic Republic..."

And at that point the Leader Pairs of the Rebel Army called for clarification from their staff .

"That Pair mean us, do they not?" said the Elderly Pair.

It came as a disappointment when the braver members of the senior staff explained the situation. They were shocked when they discovered that at least half of their forces rallied around D.G and Glord and not their own leadership. The remainder of their forces were split between loyalty to their leaders and to the leadership of the NMF. It appeared that Glord and D.G's reputation was a greater influence than the rebel leaders had bargained for.

They were even more disappointed and puzzled when the Pairs in charge of the NMF arrived and explained to them that their services would no longer be required.

"Do you mean you are taking over the fighting and mopping up?"

"No, your services in any capacity are no longer required. You are outdated and your attitude towards the citizens of Zrad leaves much to be desired. You are fired."

"But we have served so well..."

The Pair were not allowed to finish.

"Your services are no longer required, please go before we, er, purge you," came the reply.

The Pair and their staff did as they were bidden.

In spite of the fall of their leader many loyalist troops fought on and the victorious Rebel armies were forced to engage them wherever resistance flared up. One such force gathered north of First City and, taking advantage of the holiday mood, attempted to wrest the government seat from Dorida and Dorid's forces. The mopping up had stopped in First City and many units of the former Rebel Army were sent to locate the Polisoc work camps and free the inmates. It was at that point the Pair Torz and Zort, who was a fanatical President's Pair led an equally fanatical force of Stormtroopers bent on a counter-revolution.

It was unfortunate for them that the Pongos were already in the process of mopping up the residual troops left in First City. Torz and Zort's assessment of the situation left out the feelings of the ordinary citizen against them, and the equally fanatical hatred of them on the part of the Pongos; and also the fact that Tzu and his people along with the Women's Rebel Army were ready to swing into action.

"There's a large force on its way through Sector Green," announced Glorida, "Stormtroopers it seems and the Pongos are having a go but they need our support. My twin, get that Oliver Braine to order all citizens to stay indoors and we will go and help the Pongos."

Glorid grinned and before he could disappear she grabbed Julian and pushed him into the wagon: "You fight with us mister, right?"

"Okay, okay, gimme a gun," he said looking terrified.

"Good boy," Glorid said.

The wagons moved off along the empty streets to meet the would be insurgents head on. Julian alighted from the wagon with the rest of the soldiers using his gun the way Glorida had shown him, and doing what Angela had said to do, shoot Half Pairs.

"Look, the four eyed gits are getting their bloody beans. The bastards!" Julian said, shooting a stream of plasma into the mob and ducking for cover. He was cool even when it was time to draw swords and, instead of running back to the wagon line he followed Glorida and Glorid into the fight. He saw Tzu's people diving and ducking, kicking, cutting, striking, slicing and punching seemingly dodging the swords and knives aimed at them. He was getting used to seeing his opponents falling over wounded and bleeding, or dead, and instead of panicking he felt confident, heroic, and thought that at last he had got the hang of sword fighting.

"I wish Angela was here to see me," he yelled, and screamed as suddenly his blade was knocked out of his hands and a Pair of Troopers were getting ready to cut him down. He jumped back terrified as two swords flicked down either side of him and watched, horrified as two heads bounced away like bloodied footballs "Oh shit," he groaned and slipped on the blood that spilled from the falling bodies and fell into a faint.

He woke just before sunsset and wandered from the wagon where he discovered somebody had dumped him and was surprised to see they were back in First Square. He was in time to see a bedraggled delegation of Pongos with a Stormtrooper High Leader Pair force marched between them arriving under a four coloured flag of truce asking to see the High Leader Pair in charge of the rebels.

Glorid and Glorida wandered out of the palace flanked by Tzu and Julian with Dorid and Dorida standing in the background. Behind them and surrounding the delegation at low plasma range was a semi-circle of rebels and a mobile pack of Tzu's Kung Fu artists.

"What, if anything, can we do for you?" Glorid asked almost casually.

"We want to surrender and this High Leader Pair wish to surrender the Imperial forces," said a weary Pongo Half Pair. "We insisted on it."

"Okay, that's fine," said Glorid. "Tell your people to shoulder their weapons, halt all wagons where they are and vacate them and march the prisoners with their hands on their heads to the nearest square where they will be sorted each according to his kind."

"You are the High Leader Pair? We expected to, er,..." began the dejected looking Stormtrooper Pair.

"Be dealt with by men?" Glorid said, and casually examined her nails.

"Well yes, we did."

"Bit of a shock is it?" she said, and didn't let the Half Pair continue. "We will take your surrender and if you wish to you can come with us and let your troops know over the citizen's media bands. Pity really but we were enjoying beating the Bulger shit out of your soldiers, Pongos excepted."

The High Leader Pair paled and glanced at their escort saying nothing but giving the impression that they were in charge and failing to realise that as far as any observer was concerned they were prisoners. Glorid glanced at Glorida who in turn glanced at Julian.

"Why don't we let the Pongos surrender and shoot the shit out of the rest?" said Julian, and glowered at the High Leader Pair.

"That's my hero," said Glorid and gave him a look that could have meant anything.

Tzu chuckled, and with a glance at Dorid and Dorida he turned and bowed to the Pongo Half Pair, and with a hand gesture that meant follow me in this direction he straightened and smiled.

"Walk this way," he said and twisted his body into an awkward stance and limped along the pathway to the palace door.

Julian watched in amazement as the delegation of Pongos copied Tzu's gait and forcing the High Leader Pair to do the same followed the old man toward the Palace. Dorid and Dorida and Glorid and Glorida shrugged and joined in the farce to create a long line of limping Pairs. For the first time since he had landed on Zrad Julian laughed with a real belly laugh that made his body ache with the effort. The watching citizens seeing the delegation humiliated by a silly joke laughed with him and it was amid an uproar of distant gunfire and laughter that the final surrender was taken.

Oliver Braine cobbled a message that placed the victory firmly in the hands of the rebels and soon the firing in the city died down and the partying began.

He broadcast the message on all channels.

"We, the new Leadership Committee of the Government of Zradia, announce that we accept the unconditional surrender of the former imperial forces. The High Leader Pair, Hordl and Hlord have surrendered their command to the former Women's Rebel Army and the Leaders of the New Moral Few and to the military arm of the NMF, the former Rebel army. We will call on Angela's forces, Glord's army and all other forces who have helped bring about our well earned and hard fought victory and ask you to be kind to our allies and firm with our enemies. Soon, after we have repatriated the troops from the former President's abortive invasion of an innocent planet, we will hold proper elections in which every citizen of whatever loyalty or persuasion will take an equal part. We call on all opposing forces, Stormtroopers, Polisocs, Pongos and Guards to immediately cease hostilities. March to the nearest square and lay down your weapons, vacate your war wagons and surrender to our forces. Long Live the New Democratic Republic!"

In the squares and on the radials and circles that made up the streets of First City, and on the battlefields the fighting came to a confused halt. When the Pongos tried to surrender the Stormtroopers and the Polisocs, incensed at their seeming treachery ordered them to keep on fighting.

"Bulgers! Stupid Bulgers!" Replied the Pongos and turned on their oppressors discovering after all that training as efficient foot soldiers was superior to the Stormtroopers and Polisocs who relied too much on their battle wagons and their reputation.

In the last battle in First City two circles from First Square Lugs was enjoying himself. With Colin and his men and some of the women he was cut off from the rest of the mopping up force leading Colin and his small group bashing and hammering with their fists, boots, heads and forearms, and in Reg's case with his sharp knives, to create devastation among the enemy troops.

Lugs bashed one trooper and yelled with pleasure when another one leapt at him with a double blade.

"Cor, look at this git!" he cried out and evaded the blade so smoothly that the trooper was not even aware he had missed. With a carefully placed blow of his left hand and a touch of his right hand on the wrist of the swordsman he threw the unconscious warrior into the path of his twin and felled him with a well placed kick.

"Nice one Lugs," said Colin and bashed two of his attackers heads together grunting with satisfaction when Reg slid a blade into each body and giggled. Animal delighted in grabbing his enemies by their faces and literally tearing into their eyes and mouths with his strong fingers. Trevor and his mate were using cudgels they had taken from two Polisocs and were using them with consummate skill mainly for the task they were intended, smashing skulls.

When the enemy eventually gave in to line up with their weapons at their feet Lugs and his happy company were taken by surprise. It took a few short periods for Colin to realise that the fighting had to stop. The men with guns were Pongos and were actually taking their masters prisoner. A woman Pair gently explained to Lugs that he should stop bashing the red and blacks and help march them to First Square.

"Sorry mister Lugs but the war is over now, er we have to stop hitting them and make them walk. You can hit them if they misbehave," she said, adding the last phrase brightly as Lug's face showed his disappointment. The Pair had enjoyed Lug's enthusiasm for the fighting and had watched his methods with great interest. His fluid movements opposed to his lumbering gait and actions when he was at peace were so disparate it was like watching two different men.

"The Pongos are helping us," she said.

Lugs got to bash a few more red and blacks as they marched but all too soon they were handing over their charges at First Square and he was reunited with the Ferret.

"I had a whale of a time bashing blokes," he said, his face beaming with pleasure, "Like you said Ferret, there's enough fer everybody. I could do with a beer?"

The Ferret grinned and handed him a sack that clinked happily.

"There's a half dozen of Outlands Brew in there to keep you going mate. Enjoy, you've earned them," the Ferret said. "We gonna do a lot of political stuff now so when the city settles down you can have a trip out and go and see it while I gets on with me work. I might even come with yer."

"I'd like that," said Lugs and dragged a bottle from the sack and expertly flipped the lid off and sucked the liquid into his throat.

The Ferret grinned.

He didn't even mind when the tune A Whiter Shade of Pale wafted across the square and as he watched Lugs gurgle the beer down his throat he hummed along with the song.

Time and Tide

Julian gazed out at the sky-scape at the dark line that was heading toward the city from the hills. Below in First Square the people were filing past the former President's body; some to gawp and others to stand and give the peculiar Zradian insult of thumb and forefinger clasped to the nose. He was pleased that the president was dead and that the war was now finally over; it meant that at last he could live without being terrified of everything happening around him and he and Glorida could get on with being normal people.

But he was puzzled by the dark line heading their way and wondered what it was. Glorida was sleeping and with a question on his lips he turned to look at their bed. She lay on her side curled up under the sheet with her thumb in her mouth and her dark hair spread on the pad. She lay in the bed like a cat, relaxed and yet alert, soft and supple and utterly desirable. Julian loved her and loved the way she came to him and demanded his body. He liked watching her sleep and loved to watch her as she did things around the place; he loved everything about her including the snarl of anger she made when he annoyed her, and the way she held the knife she threatened to cut him with.

But he was puzzled about the dark line.

She stirred and gave a sigh and with a yawn she woke and looked at him dreamily.

"Oh hello, what are you looking at?" she said and sat up.

"I'm er looking out at the city," he said, "there's something odd."

He gazed hungrily at her body as she eased herself from the bed, stretched, yawned and walked to where he stood dressed in his robe by the window. He opened his robe as she approached and enfolded her in it feeling his hard body against her soft warm sleepy flesh and for a few moments he was lost in her woman smell.

"Give it to me," she said and slid herself onto him and for a while as they tangled with each other in his robe. He forgot about the approaching dark line.

He prolonged the pleasure the way she had taught him and cried out when after she had reached her climax he reached his. She bit him and dug her nails in as she reached a second climax and they both fell to the floor gasping, clutching each other as the shudders took over.

"Christ Glorida I thought I was going to fall apart then," he said and kissed her mouth.

She giggled and crushed herself against him.

"What was odd?"

"Oh, out the window," he said.

They stood together naked gazing out of the window and looked across the city circles looking directly along a radial and out to a desert stretch to the south and the hills from which they had launched the rebel attack. Closer now the dark line was larger and beneath it was a shadow and above that the sunslight glittered pink and purple.

"What is it?" asked Julian.

"It's rain my silly," she said, "the rainy season has started. This is seventh tenth so it will rain. You should remember that from last orbit when we all bogged down and trained instead," she said.

He remembered. That was when she and her twin had forced him to learn the sword and knife techniques. He was glad of that in the last battle. "Yes, I do, you made me work hard. I hated it," he said.

"Yes, but you have to admit it was worth it in the end, in the last fight," she said and giggled. "Until you fainted."

As she spoke the rain crashed against the sloping window rattling like hail. They stood watching it as it drenched the city. Pairs filled the streets or rushed out onto balconies and stood out in it rejoicing as the raindrops battered at them soaking their clothes and creating temporary rivers along the radials and circles and filling any open space with life giving water. He and Glorida stood watching water gushing until the mid day meal was called, and reluctantly they dressed to join the diners on the first floor.

Angela watched the rain clouds sweep across the city. The harsh difference between clear and dry and deluge was so marked it quite took her breath away.

"What are you looking at?" said D.G.

"Rain clouds and rain but they are so odd. There is sunsshine and right behind it there is rain, no shadow or drizzle but simply a deluge," she said.

"Rainy season, come back into bed," he said.

She stood by the window and for a few moments she watched the rain envelop the city and smiled to herself. That's the way D.G is to me, she thought, and I am completely overwhelmed. The first time they made love in this room, a room on an alien planet, she cried out with joy calling on her God not for forgiveness but in thankfulness. The pleasure was so intense that she was unable to stop her body responding, feeling wanton but not caring whether or not she did. All she knew was that not being a virgin, being wanted and wanting felt right. The moment that D.G enclosed her in his arms on the day of the Emperor's death she was, according to her church, a lost woman, a sinner. She gave herself to D.G with enthusiasm and loved his rough hands on her body and she found herself doing all the things that the fallen women she had worked with did to their men.

The thing she was surprised about was that it all seemed so natural and giggled at the thought. Sex was natural, she thought, even if she was acting like a tart. She left the window and walked to the bed dropping her robe on the floor before climbing in beside him. She nuzzled against his warm hairy body with her lips kissing hungrily and with no inhibitions she did whatever he asked. Afterwards she lay on her back close to him listening to him breath and wallowing in the wantonness; loving the smell of their bodies and feeling the power of her responses, the blood coursing through her veins, her nipples still erect and the wet between her legs ready again to receive him.

"D.G?"

"Mmm?"

"I love you."

"I know."

"Arrogant Half Pair."

"I know that too. I love you also wanton woman."

She turned onto her side and snuggled up to him her warm belly touching his body and her whole being aching for him loving every touch, every small move he made and loving the way she felt totally his.

"My husband, I may be wanton to you but I am totally under your spell. I would melt myself into you if it would give you pleasure," she murmured, and gasped softly when he drew her closer. She felt him respond and again he entered her and she shuddered with pleasure knowing that although this was physical and so satisfying she was in love with this man who so commanded her. This time they both lay on their backs fingers twined together with the sheet on top of them marking the shape of their bodies.

"My God D.G why on Earth and Zrad did I ever think I hated you?"

"Because we did not know each other well enough. Because I never realised how lovely you are and because at the time you were bent on looking out for Julian," said D.G.

"I wonder how he is," she said.

"If he feels the way I do then he is totally besotted and so wrapped up with Glorida that he will think of nothing else," said D.G and although he was about to say more the mid meal bell was rung and, like her, he felt ravenously hungry.

At the mid meal table the Ferret greeted the four lovers with a knowing smile. He looked across at Richard Byrde who sat with

Arthur and Dorida and Dorid and inclined his head toward each couple as they entered.

"The will of Theseus prevails," said the Ferret stumbling briefly over the word prevail.

"What's he talking about?" said Julian, suspiciously.

"Shakespeare, A Midsummer Night's Dream," said Byrde and grinned as Julian made a wry face.

"That old git," he said and took a seat at the table ignoring Glorida as she dodged around him to sit next to his place.

D.G showed Angela to her seat and sat with her after she was comfortable and raised his eyebrows as he glanced at Glorida. Glorid sat beside her twin and she too raised her eyebrows. D.G thought of saying something to Julian but declined, preferring him to find out for himself. It was up to Arthur to make a comment.

"That's my boy," he said.

"What you on about?" said Julian not noticing Glorida's furious look.

"Should you not show the lady to her seat?" said Arthur.

"Oh, yeah, sorry I jest forgot. Sorry Glorida, I'll try and remember next time," he said and eyed her knife hand nervously.

"I'm sure you will be my love," she said and turned her head from him to sweep her gaze across the others at table. "I think he's a bit over excited."

She pretended to ignore their smirks but couldn't help blushing angrily as she and Julian settled uncomfortably at the table to eat. Tzu was with his own people eating the meal on another set of tables in the dining hall but even he had heard the exchange and with a grin and a wagging finger he looked at Julian. Glorida glared at him but the old man's smile disarmed her and she blushed even deeper and stood up flushed and angry.

"Julian Renfrew!" she said aware that the company were staring in her direction, some puzzled and others amused.

"What?" he said cringing.

"You have got to be the most ignorant, stupid, backsliding, rude Half Pair I have ever met!"

She kept her knife in her belt but with a movement that began from her feet, rippled up though her hips and rolled through her shoulders with a smooth well placed blow she hit him with her fist and knocked him backwards from his chair where he landed on the hard floor and lay still. Pairs struggled out of their chairs but Glorida's voice cut through the sudden rush and stopped them.

"Leave the bastard, let the shithead suffer," she said and glowered around at the company who mostly avoided her gaze.

"Right on sister," said Angela.

"Get stuffed fat tits," Glorida said.

Somebody giggled and Glorida looked around flustered trying to locate the giggler and discovered it was her twin. She looked at Glorid and started to giggle herself realising how funny the whole situation was. She had just belted the Half Pair she loved and laid him out because she was embarrassed by his rudeness. Women didn't do that did they? This one did and she realised that her twin thought it funny; realised too that she had neglected Glorid and her support since Julian had gone missing from sentry duty. Nong, he was useless! The sex was good but as for the rest, well he left a lot to be desired. She sat down at the table.

"All right," she said giggling, "drag the Bulger out, give him some smelling salts or something and send him back for his meal

The company, including, she noted, Arthur Renfrew, laughed loud as she and Glorid giggled together trying hard to apologise to Angela and trying hard to control their mirth as the meal was served by the catering Pairs. Julian came back to his seat, sat down and behaved himself at the table, and when the meal was at the stage where those who had eaten enough were easing their tunics, and those who had not yet eaten enough were merely munching, Dorida and Dorid made an announcement.

"The NMF wish us to run an election. They suggest that we leave the organisation of the voting to them and allow us to use their resources to conduct a campaign. Now that the rains are here we will get on with campaigning. The NMF will announce the call to register parties and political groups and nobody will be refused a party but let it be known that all parties will be given Tokens according to their numbers. We will be running on the Rebel ticket," Dorida paused, and looked benevolently at Angela, "and inspired by Angela and the Pairs who fought with us our party will be a women's party although any votes for us will be welcome. A list of our candidates will be published late this turn and this will be added to the candidate data-base. It will be an electronic poll."

The Pairs and most of the Earth people clapped and cheered and for a few short periods there was much chatter until Angela stood to speak.

In the subdued noise that burbled to silence Angela faced Dorida and Dorid and addressed them mostly but made certain she included everybody.

"I wish to ask what will happen to the Children of Glord, will they be permitted to run a party and campaign?"

"Yes," answered Dorida, "we expect all interested parties to make their presence felt."

Angela looked at them with a gaze that meant more than she showed and with a thin smile she kept her gaze on them before speaking again as if she were thinking over what she was about to say.

"So what you are saying is that the Children may contest the election but I suppose you are aware that recent developments more or less destroy the credibility of the movement?" she said, and waited for an answer. The room was tense as the Pairs and some of the Earthmen involved in the propaganda war guessed what she was referring to.

"And to what do you refer?" asked Dorid.

"I am talking of the telescreen campaign in the newscasts that tell of the finding of the so-called Glordian Bible and the massive circulation of the texts along with the suppression by the rebel authorities, whom I notice are the women's section, that more or less ensures the text is read by all. I notice too that when a preacher of Nert's movement rises in the squares to speak there are plenty to heckle and refute his teachings. I note also that the election campaign is to be conducted on the screens which means that in effect a good orator will be wasted because crowds cannot form to work on the people's emotions. I warn you that you will regret the subterfuge and regret the involvement of the women's movement in the whole affair. I warn you, let the NMF and the men's section do the dirty work or you may as well kiss goodbye to the women's section and your chances of having a female Pair as President." Angela paused, and saw that she had their attention. "I tell you that I have lived and fought with Nert's people and I know Nert well enough to know that he is a great orator; he can move an audience with his presence and I am sure that he will find a way of changing the movement to suit. I am sure that the NMF knows this and have given you the task of dissemination so that when it all blows up in their faces you will take the blame and the men will dominate. The LandPairs of the old regime do not trust the new Zradians as they call them, that is yourselves, and if Nert does his work properly they will find a way of following him. It is a time bomb waiting to go off and like all things of change time and tide will wait for no Pair, least of all you. I warn you, do not be fooled by Nert and his people and do not be fooled by your leaders."

Angela sat down again and was grateful when D.G took her hand in his and squeezed it.

"And by what authority do you make these pronouncements a Pair asked from the end of the table.

"Because I have the biggest tits in the room," she said.

Glorida exploded with laughter.

The rains fell continuously for ten complete turns and on the eleventh the suns shone through the clouds giving way to sudden heavy showers. The following turn the dead president was removed from First Square and taken to a place outside Sector Red where the remains were laid on a platform, covered in flammable liquid and burned.

From their window Angela looked at the rain falling; fascinated by the way the water ran off the paving and in the distance when the suns shone the amazing growth of the plants that sprung up from the harsh desert soil. Far in the distance the sand and rocks were covered with bright points of colour that spattered the land in between the less colourful plants that grew taller each day. She watched an instant forest grow around the city and marvelled at the change.

"D.G, the change outside is as great as the change we face here."

"Sorry Angela but I don't think I understand."

She turned from the window to face him where he sat working on a flimsy sent from the central administration. They needed a report and D.G was trying to work out what it was he was supposed to write. She had offered to help but he had insisted on doing it himself and, remembering his obsession with trying to learn how to use a can opener she let him. He was on his third attempt and getting grumpy.

"Are you sure you can do that?" she said pointing to the flimsy.

"I can manage," he said angrily.

She turned away from him and stared out of the window trying to ignore his exasperated sighs and the quiet stream of curses as he attempted to tap out the script. Eventually she got fed up with it and started to clear her stuff from the table then dressed in her clean tunic ready to go out.

"I'll leave you to it," she said and punched the portal button. "I'm going to start a campaign of my own."

She was out of the room before he could follow, and with a smug look on her face she set the portal to a different code knowing it would take him an age to find it. She saw him behind it trying the buttons as she headed for the stairs and waved to him as she disappeared down to the lower floor.

She determined that while D.G sorted himself out on the computer she would help the women who had supported her during the war. Whatever, she loved the man but he was difficult and during the rains she knew there was no way she was going to mould him to her own use. She tromped down the stairs and found the campaign office where there was a list of contacts. She logged on to a workstation and began to write a short piece that should let the women know she was on board. She finished writing it and then with a secretive smile she called D.G.

He looked ruffled and as he was still in the room she realised he had not managed to open the portal.

"The code is four, five, six four X," she said and giggled.

D.G grinned and stuck his tongue out at her.

"I knew that, I knew that," he said and looked silly. "Sorry but I got a bit preoccupied. You will be back?"

"Of course but just be aware that I can help you and will help you but you have to let me help you. Remember that I am a computer whiz and I have a diploma that is useful, if somewhat boring and I do have some writing skills and that means in your language as well as mine, dummy."

She mouthed a kiss at him and with a flourish clicked him off knowing that however much he tried he would not reach her workstation until she was ready to let him. There were many replies on the screen and she touched the analyse and check key and the screen came up with a screed of data that registered support for her item. She tapped in the word 'respond' and waited for more data to appear. In the corner of the screen there was a small icon that slowly and deliberately turned and tumbled as if it were tired. She tapped on to it and the screen filled with a gradually forming picture. As usual with Zradian screens the picture not only had depth and movement but it was in real time and not a recording; that was if the small indicator at the bottom replacing the icon was correct. The picture resolved itself into an image of a burnt out robot that had collapsed in the centre of a clearing. The plant life around it looked as if it was regenerating, and on the edges of the clearing the trees were shrivelled and black. Beyond the blackened trees jungle marched on into verdant valleys watered by rainstorms and surrounded by misty mountains that she recognised as possibly from the Amazon rainforest. The robot was still except for a slow and pathetic movement of one shattered arm. A small glow from the centre of what was probably once a head flickered and spread a pulse of weak energy out to where the remote camera was hovering. The small indicator expanded, held for a few short periods and then flashed back to its corner.

"Rodent four?" she said, and was surprised when a weak disembodied voice spoke in her ear.

Friend, are you helpings me?

"Who are you?"

We are our mother and our son

Okay, she thought, a split personality, so what next.

"What can I do for you?"

Help us find a transfer port.

"And what will you do then?"

Gets backs to our place of makings and be repairs.

"How can I do that?"

We am showings you. Watches your screen and do as you is askings.

"Are you failing?"

We is nearlings go-ink so sorry.

"I will do my best."

We am thanks.

Figures appeared on the screen interspersed with instructions and as the screen scrolled slowly so a flimsy printed out and Angela took it from the slot. The instructions were easy to follow and with concentration she made certain she did everything right and waited once she had completed the task for the expected confirmation of results. The small icon tumbled in the corner faster and larger and with some surprise she saw that it was an exceptionally cute cartoon rabbit. It bounced, looked cute, bounced again, turned a somersault and stopped and grinned toothily at her.

Thank you. Rodent four is happy. Do not be afraid of the rodents!

The message puzzled Angela, and as she attempted to remake contact with the mysterious rodent four the workstation's speakers changed tone, clicked and from their depths a tune played. At first Angela didn't recognise it but after a few bars she found herself humming to the strains of A Whiter Shade of Pale.

While the revolutionaries settled in to their new role as leaders, Julian and Angela were enjoying their virtual honeymoons, Fireman Sidney Weddell was trying to get out of the suite of rooms he had wandered into. True there was food and drink and a pleasant place to sleep and a wonderful television screen that showed him many interesting things. That he could not understand the language hardly mattered, there was so much of interest in the material that in spite of not being able to understand a word of the dialogue he watched as often as he could. The last few weeks had weakened him and although he couldn't leave the rooms he was happy to sleep and eat, and steadily he become stronger.

"All the better for my task," he said and giggled.

He found a weapon in the rooms to replace his axe and with his eyes glowing he caressed its sharp blades and trembled at the idea of slicing and cutting, slicing and cutting, cutting and slicing and cutting.

The remains of the Bulger were a small dehydrating pile of bones and fur with strands of leathery flesh attached that no longer stank as fetidly as it had done. Fireman Weddell himself was smellier. Washing did not occur to him and with the irrationality of the truly crazy he was not too worried about where he relieved himself.

He laid the twin blade sword on the low shelf he used as a dinner table and gazed at it happily. It was beautiful, so beautiful and so vibrant. He loved it. He had watched the screen stories and seen how the swords were supposed to be used and knew that when the time came he would be able to use it. He sat cross legged on a futon watching the sword blades glisten in the light and he felt content.

If there was one thing he knew and that was as long as he could find a way out of his pleasant prison he would be equipped now to carry out his mission.

"Renfrew," he said and saliva dribbled down his chin.

"We are coming President Renfrew," he whispered.

Election time

Despite the rains the election campaign was not confined to the screens and as Angela had predicted there were plenty of people willing to stand in support of the Children and Nert's movement although of Nert and his little band of followers there was no sign. In effect the election was conducted in a party atmosphere as Zradians anticipated the coming celebration between their land and its new government and the new found friends on the planet Earth. Dorida and Dorid had relented and enabled candidates to arrange speaking venues. The Pair also declared that it was illegal to prevent speakers from addressing their listeners which allowed all candidates to campaign properly. When the campaign was over and the voting began the Zradians anticipated a party.

The rain beat down on the buildings, watered the lakes, filled the gullies and channels and sudden rivers poured their liquid music out into the shallow seas. Plants grew to the rhythm of the season and the music adopted the sound of thundering water, tinkling streams and laughing rivers. During the last rain filled turns of the middle tenth the people got ready and on the first sunshine day they poured out of the buildings to rejoice in the sunshine, goggle and wonder at the myriad plants, the steaming heat that drew mist into the sky to fall again as light rain that for the next two tenths would bring on the food plants to ripeness and harvest. The people were ready for a celebration and ready to meet the Pair they had elected as their new leader. Bunting flapped in the cool breezes and banners flew to show who was supporting who. The election was an electronic triumph. Organized so that all citizens of considered adult age, twenty four hundreds worked back from the first turn of the middle tenth, were entitled to vote, the register was automatically counted, divided, preferences allocated and parties given their seats on the Senate and the Upper Chamber. Those who had no access to the electronic media were taken to the nearest station and shown how to vote, or had their vote faithfully recorded by a scribe. The Presidential count was taken from the votes cast in the second ballot plus the proportional votes from the first ballot. First the party of power was chosen and then the individual Pairs were elected.

The result was a resounding win for the Moral Democrats and for Dart and Drat as their President. Dorida and Dorid were elected Leader Pair of the Senate and Blard and Bradl became the Legislative Leader Pair of the Upper Chamber. Angela's party took twelve percent of the votes and Angela was elected to the Upper Chamber although she had to take out Zradian citizenship before the campaign began. Her party was a popular movement although there was a large number of male Zradians totally opposed to females being allowed in government.

Nert and his Children gained two senate seats and none in the upper chamber. Their party came a lowly last but in all fairness they did have some sympathisers in the western sectors who campaigned on the Second Peasant ticket and gained eight senate seats and two in the upper chamber.

Of course after the election there had to be a party. It was difficult to decide who was to be the guest of honour so in true Zradian fashion they decided not to have one. Instead Dart and Drat posted a list of celebrities who would be honoured and a list of guests who would be invited.

"We will speak for all," said Drat

Among the celebrities attending the party in the palace as a guest was Arthur Renfrew who consented to staying on Zrad for two reasons; one was to see Julian honoured and the other was for Angela who had asked him to act as a father at her wedding.

"I would like you to give me away when D.G and I get married. My local Vicar is coming to preside over the marriage and make it legal on Earth, although D.G and I are already joined according to Zradian custom," she said.

"Er, how is that carried out?" Arthur asked.

"Oh, we just sort declare we are Half Pairs together and register it in the records. Er Glord has to agree, oh it is sort of complex," she said, her face red. "It's not like living in sin."

Arthur smiled. He understood.

Surprisingly Julian and Glorida was granted a formal joining Zradian style.

Glord worked on behalf of Dart and Drat who would arrive on Zrad with the guests from Earth. It was notable that President Revere was not invited and as yet, with the US elections being called there would be no American representative.

Glord missed his twin and as a result he threw himself into the work organising the structure of the new administration, and on the side taking control of the party and its arrangements. It was during one of these frenetic working sessions that he spoke to Drat.

"I have everything under control here but I am beginning to flag a bit. Drogl is always with Angela and I feel left out – I know he is the passive half, but I feel his absence – know what I mean?"

Drat took a while to answer and Glord could see him looking a little uncomfortable. He and D.G were great friends with Dart and Drat, cousins actually, and had shared much together as rebels. Dart and Drat were also past organisers of their own Fourball campaign and had managed them as agents when they were young.

"Fine, listen, I feel disturbed by Dart's attraction to Sally – an Earth woman journalist here – and like you I feel isolated. Maybe we can get together and give a pairing a try out when we get back? We are cousins. We might make it work, maybe look for a wife pair together. What do you think?"

"If our other halves agree, yeah, I'll go with that, it's better than going half," said Glord.

"We can take a gene swap"

Glord looked grim. A gene swap was a drastic step and meant a total break from his birth twin, but it was better than going half. He knew the signs, and knew too that if D.G and Angela were to make it as a married couple then it would have to be done.

"I'll think about it."

Drat smiled warmly. "Please do. We can work something out. Better tell Glorida and Glorid, eh?"

And that was something Glord had forgotten about.

The news was broadcast to the Zradian people and to the people of Earth alike. In London Maurice Bannerman kissed the contract he had made with Dart and Drat and danced with Sally Aitcheson as she tried to tell him that she too was going to Zrad with Dart to live with him as his wife.

"My lovely girl," he cried, "I will be there to watch you tie the knot."

"And watch the profits mounting," she said laughing breathlessly as he whirled her around the studio.

Julian at bay

The party was a huge national celebration. The party promised dancing, plenty of drink, plenty of good food and a very good time to be had. Julian's idea of a good time was to get as drunk as he could with his mates and leer at the women and make lewd comments with the intention of getting one into his bed. He usually failed to persuade a woman to share a bed with him but he often succeeded in getting grossly drunk. Sometimes he was punched silly by irate boyfriends having made one lewd remark too many. Sometimes it was the woman who punched him. He hated parties like that.

The one the Zradians were organising had all the earmarks of being a humdinger. The Zradians brewed good ale and beer, especially the Rebels, and Julian had watched tankers of it being shipped into the Palace stores. All over First City squares were festooned with flags and bunting, bars were set up in the green quadrant, food stalls in blue quadrant and bandstands in yellow with red left free for dancing and performers. First Square had a huge stage set up before the Palace doors with access to the main hall left open and everywhere on all circle and radial corners there were huge drop screens to let the people watch the proceedings. With one day to go the lesser radials and circles were cleared of traffic and in every lobby tables and chairs were stacked ready to be rushed out and set for diners and drinkers to be seated for the nation-wide feast.

The main radials and two outer circles were left open for traffic and all but essential vehicles were banned from the rest of the city. Children played in the clear streets and made noises of happiness that hadn't been heard in First City for many four-hundreds.

Julian hated it.

There were kids everywhere.

They threw balls.

Laughed at silly jokes and pointed him out to each other.

When he tried to tell them a story of his exploits they laughed at him and said they had seen it on the 'telly', a word they had adopted from the Earth people.

He hated that,

It was all Glorida's fault. She insisted that the correct and official stories be broadcast, and although they did show him as a hero they didn't tell the story properly.

"It's a history of the war not a story book," she said, and glowered at him when he complained. "You embellish too much and tell lies. I just want you to be a proper hero and not a figure of fun, so can it Julian."

He hated that too.

And now that the party was being organised and Glorida and Glorid were involved in the arrangements he was left to his own devices. The rains were over and he had to admit that when Glorida took him on a tour he was impressed. The surrounding lands looked wonderful. There were none of those stinking Carnibirds or Carnibeasts wandering around so when they got out to walk in the bush for the first time he enjoyed being on Zrad.

Apart from the fantastic sight of a wild mixture of reds, oranges, purples, yellows and myriad browns with the odd dash of green and white there was a scent in the air that filled his senses with its sweetness. In a clear patch of ground covered with a soft moss-like fungus Glorida grinned at him and pulled him to the ground.

"Shall we?" she said.

Afterwards half naked and replete they lay on their backs looking up at the pink sky and sighed.

"That was different," he said.

Glorida leaned over him and smiled.

"Yes, it was, now we should get back to the wagon before it rains again."

They ran hand in hand through the rain to the small wagon and once inside Julian felt as if he had lost something.

"I feel as if summink good has just happened and I don't know nuffink to say what it was," he said.

"Remember it well then, my love, because it is a magic moment that will haunt you with pleasure for the rest of your life," Glorida said.

As he walked the streets of First City and wandered around the palace feeling out of place he thought of that moment.

"Oh fuck it," he said "I'm bored."

He found a bar and demanded drinks.

Two periods later when D.G came for him he was belligerently drunk.

The serving Pair was trying to explain to him that he was too drunk to stand straight and too drunk to take anymore beer without making a mess all over the carpet, and that he, the serving Pair, was no longer willing to give him any credit. Julian spotted D.G and waved him over.

"Tell this four eyed pair of gits I want more beer," he said and leered drunkenly at D.G supporting his body by his hands against the bar.

D.G grinned.

"Too pissed to stand are you?"

Julian staggered more or less upright and gestured with one hand wide and high, expansive. "Of course I'm not too..." He began and promptly fell over backwards and lay looking surprised with one arm stretched behind him on the floor and the rest of his limbs and body totally awry without any apparent form.

He was, as his mother would have described, absholutely shit-pissed legless.

"Oops," he said and passed out.

With impassive faces the serving Pair looked at D.G and then at Julian and back to D.G.

"Shall I call the clean up squad?"

"May as well. I'll go with them."

"Hangover treatment with that Sir?"

D.G regarded Julian with a disgusted look on his face.

"No let him suffer. He's used to it," he said, and grinned.

"He is your friend?"

"In a manner of speaking, yes," said D.G and when the two pairs came with the drunk stretcher to cart Julian off to detox he marched happily alongside them whistling A Whiter Shade of Pale.

On the day of the party Julian was suffering from the shakes and a rotten headache. He had woken up in a strange room in a strange bed, naked. Somebody had obviously taken him there. He woke to subdued lighting and cool air that circulated carrying wafts of a beautiful scent.

"Christ, what a stink!" he said, and groaned as the sound of his voice hit his ears. Beside the bed was a large bucket and into that he threw up. A Pair came into the room quietly and with no fuss but plenty of forceful determination they made him drink water.

"Sleep, you will feel better soon."

They were right. After a short sleep he felt better but he was tired and still had a headache. He managed to eat a meal and wandered from the detox unit in search of Glorida. He found her in the main hall with the other Pairs adding the finishing touches to the list she was carrying "Hi," he said.

"Julian! Where have you been?"

"I was er, somewhere else," he said and jumped back suddenly.

"Don't mess around. Tell me where you have been," she said and drew her knife.

"I was in detox," he said. "put that away, please!"

She looked at him keeping the knife steady and her eyes on his face looking for the tell tale twitch and drop of the head that meant he was lying. It didn't happen.

"Okay, I believe you. Now go and get washed up and ready to start. I will be finished here soon and the reception will begin in just over two periods. Shave, do your hair properly and look smart and lay off the drink, take it easy, remember we have to put on a good show for the visitors before the dancing and general entertainment. Okay?" she said and looked at him sternly.

"Okay, okay, I understand. Clean up, don't get pissed and behave properly until after the presentation tomorrow?" he said hoping he was right.

"Right."

At least she put the knife away.

Julian walked away ignoring the amused looks of the other Pairs and ignoring also Glorida's angry looks as she saw Pairs giggling. He hated being treated as a joke.

Prime Minister Smith and his long suffering but elegant wife stood apprehensively outside the transfer port. Assured that it was working properly they were still a little apprehensive.

"And you say that we will be arriving at a pleasant location on your planet and from there we will all be taken to your First City in vehicles?"

"That is correct Sir. The Minister of Trade and his wife are already there and the rest of the dignitaries including the Japanese Prime Minister. The Premiers from Australia and New Zealand, China, India and Europe will be arriving at the same place within a few minutes of you both. It's an adventure as great as any you have ever experienced," explained Dart.

"What do we do?" asked Smith.

"Well sir, it is quite straightforward, we all get into the Port and I tap in the code and off we go. In less than a second of your time you will be in Zrad," said Dart.

"Won't we get mixed up?" asked Mrs Smith.

"No madam, the system recognises each Half Pair or person, or object or group of objects as an integral unit," he replied but didn't explain that if you did get it wrong then the said persons, Half Pairs and objects tended to occupy space that was already occupied by something else. Nasty.

"Okay, if you say it is safe then I will do it,' said Smith.

And to show he meant what he said he led the way into the port with his wife beside him. Dart and Drat and Sally Aitcheson and the aide, Rodney, followed and with no hesitation Dart pressed the buttons, closed the door and stabbed the send button. There was the usual feeling of being taken apart and then of being put together again and they were in a different and slightly larger port.

The door opened and Dart stepped out.

"Welcome to Zradia Prime Minister," he said and bowed.

Prime Minister Smith had to agree that the sight they were greeted with was fantastic. His wife gasped and exclaimed with awe and pleasure her appreciation of the scenery before them. "Oh John, what a beautiful place!" she said, and clutched his arm in excitement.

They were travelling in an open wagon, one of six that carried the dignitaries from a resort hotel recently refurbished on the newly opened track that led to First City. He too was impressed by the colours and the harsh beauty of the landscape that was made up of sharp rocks and pointed cactus-like plants. The vegetation was more complex than his idea of a desert and reminded him of a garden filled with succulent plants some of which, he saw were growing in fields as crops. The wagons were travelling as Dart had informed him at a slow pace to allow them to enjoy the view. Even so, he noted, they were travelling as fast as the latest railcars his own government had so thankfully been able to add to their rail network. The wagons hurtled, that was the only way to describe their progress, over the brow of a line of low hills and there gleaming in the light of the twin suns was First City. The track ran dead straight to the outskirts and although it was clear either side of it there was a myriad small plants that clumped like grass but were so varicoloured that the ground looked as if it were covered by thousands upon thousands of quilts.

Prime Minister Smith thought it was the most beautiful sight he had ever seen.

"Where the hell are we in relation to the solar system?" he asked.

"Eight and a half light years away," replied Dart.

"And we got here in less than a second?"

"Yes, it is a standard measure, one small period which in your terms is nought point seven two of a second," Dart said and smiled, "makes calculating your time and coordination with your media extremely tricky."

"That's a helluva distance to travel in such a short time, how come?"

"We haven't a clue. All we know is that it works," Dart said, and grinned broadly at the Prime Minister's appalled expression.

Smith and the rest of the party were distracted by the sudden arrival of the column at First City. The wagons slowed to a speed more to his liking, and as they travelled along the highway that was a radial cutting a series of concentric circles heading toward a huge square in the distance with a large palatial building in the centre he was aware of people waving and cheering. Every now and then he glanced along the circles and saw more people partying and everywhere he looked on all the buildings there were huge screens and on all of them he could see their column of vehicles as it progressed to the centre of the city.

This was definitely an official welcome.

The column slowed to a crawl as it entered the square and formed into an arc in front of a huge platform beside an ornate doorway much like a church doorway back on Earth.

"Please wait for a few moments," said Dart. "The protocol here is that the President of Zradia should go last and as a matter of honour to my host you and Sherry should be with us now as our guest. You will also be meeting our Leaders. Prime minister Smith did as he was asked and as he was led to his seat he was amazed to see a large number of people dressed in martial arts uniforms, mostly Asian looking and another smaller group of Earth people other than those he had arrived with sitting close by.

He was even more surprised when Dart and Drat moved to the front of the platform and began to speak in their own language to the huge crowds gathered in the city square.

He was also aware of a skinny lad with a dark scowl on his face sitting uncomfortably next to a dark-haired Zradian who glowered at him and put her hand on the hilt of her knife every-time he tried to speak to her.

Julian was pissed off.

It wasn't his fault.

She didn't understand.

He had a raging thirst and all he wanted was one drink to help him come right. Glorida came into their apartment and caught him drinking the last of the four bottles of Outlands he had grabbed from the fridge.

"I told you to remain sober. There will be enough drink at the reception after the speeches. I know you, you get stupidly drunk and insult people. Your Prime Minister is coming and all the others who helped fight the war and our new President Dart and Drat. There will be the media of both worlds reporting everything that is going on and you are about to stuff it up by getting drunk. You stupid, no good Bulger's arsehole," she said, and glared angrily at him.

He belched and wiped his mouth.

"Oops, sorry," he said. "I'm only having a little drink to celebrate and get me head clear."

The problem was it hadn't cleared and when he stood up to get ready to evade the blade he thought would follow he staggered.

"Have you washed yet?"

"Er no," he said and belched again.

Glorida glowered at him.

"Get in there and clean up and when you have done that get your clothes on and sit down and do nothing."

He did as he was told and came out.

Glorida glowered at him again and with her own washing gear she went into the shower room. She came out almost straightway, grabbed him by his ear between her finger and thumb and pushed him inside.

"Clean it scumbag."

He did.

He sat in the lounge bored and scared. If there was a time for a man to have a drink then this was it. With furtive movements he undid the drinks cabinet and found the Zradian equivalent of whiskey. It was in a screw-top bottle close to the front and with hurried movements he took it out, unscrewed the top and took a long drink. Scared by a sudden sound from the shower room he hurriedly put it back and cursed as the top flipped off. His fumbling attempt to pick it up and put it back failed, and with a cry of anger and frustration he let the bottle slip. It fell on the hard floor and smashed spilling the contents across the tiles to the edge of the carpet.

It was at that moment Glorid came in and saw him desperately trying to clean it up.

"Don't tell her," he said. "Please."

But it was too late.

Glorida came out of the shower with her towel wrapped around her and saw him on the floor trying to swab the drink up with a cloth.

"It dropped out of the cabinet," he said.

"He was having a snort," Glorid said.

"Bloody bitch!" Julian yelled.

Glorid waved her hand in front of her face and screwed her eyes up.

"Yuk, he smells like a brewery," she said.

Glorida walked across the room and glared at him.

"Stand up!"

He stood and fell down again.

"Oh fuck," he said and watched the room twist and turn,

"Right Julian Renfrew. As of now I have finished with you. You have no manners, you embarrass me in front of everybody. You cannot do as you are told. I have had enough. You haven't even thanked me properly for saving you from execution and you treat me like a tart. Do your duty today at the reception or I will personally slice you until your bits fall off," she said and in spite of the fact that she was unarmed and covered only in a towel Julian was scared.

And that was why he sat, silently, feeling miserable with Glorida and Glorid at the speechmaking and was so polite and formal when later at the reception they were introduced to Prime Minister Smith who knew who Julian was, but Julian, in his turn had no idea who he was talking to.

The reception, to all but Julian, was a diplomatic success. Julian tried to talk to Glorida but she didn't respond.

"I told you. Behave or else," she said.

He knew what the 'or else' meant and did as he was told. He shook hands with the leader creeps and was stiffly polite with everybody he met. Towards the end of the reception when all the meetings and hand-shakings were over Glorida allowed him a drink. He had eaten enough food, drunk more hot drinks than he wanted and longed for a beer.

His drink was spoiled by the appearance of detectives Bates and Fish alongside him.

"Young Julian ratbag..." Began Fish

"...Renfrew, late of..." Bates

"...Brentford, my young felon..."Fish

"...we want to have words with you..." Bates

"...after all this is over about..." Fish

"...a certain arson and the murder of..." Bates

"...one of our more clodhopping but..." Fish

"...nevertheless, diligent officers..." Bates

"...namely Constable Rice," finished Fish.

"Bog off rozzers, I ain't done nuthin' and you blokes know it. I'm a hero I am and I ain't going nowhere. I'm staying here on Zrad I am," Julian said.

"...Don't you be too sure of that..." Bates

"...sonny," said Fish.

Julian didn't answer.

"...We also heard that your old mate..." Bates

"...the axeman, Ex-Fireman Sidney Weddell..." Fish

"...is on the loose," Bates ,who grinned.

"Oh shit," said Julian.

Bates and Fish left him alone to think it over.

And it was with this disturbing piece of information to mull over Julian went in search of something stronger than beer.

For somebody who was at the bottom end of the criminal world Donald best was well connected. He and Denny were watching the television news when, in all the other related items, there was a short article on Julian Renfrew's exploits.

"'Ere boss, there's that Renfrew kid what owes us a lot of money," said Denny, "do you reckon we oughter go and get him?"

"What?"

"You know, he owes us a lot. I oughter go and bash him," said Denny who had not bashed anybody for a long time and was getting restless.

"We'd have to go there," said Donald Best.

"Where is he then?"

"On that planet called Zrad where those two aliens what was on the telly come from," said Donald Best.

Denny sat watching the television with his brows knitted and his eyes tightened to slits and worked his lips together. He was obviously trying to absorb the information and trying, Best supposed, to remember recent events. Denny wasn't too bright when it came to the big issues.

"Oh," said Denny.

But going there was not a bad idea. Donald Best was about to call in a couple of favours.

A Duty to be done.

Ex-Fireman Sidney Weddell woke to the sound of a sudden click. "What was that?" he said, and looked across the room, realised the door was now open and with no hesitation he grabbed his sword and rushed for the exit. The surprised Pairs who had responded to a delayed query about an unscheduled portal operation had arrived to inspect the room. That they were in a holiday mood made them less alert and when the naked figure carrying a sword raced out of the doorway and into the corridor to disappear cackling they stood and watched in mute surprise.

"We should report that," said one Pair.

"Yes, but after we have sorted out the room, and when we get back up top," said the other.

"Good idea Pair, the place stinks," came the reply.

Pour and Roup sat side by side in a comfortable room in the palace residential section attended to by a mixed group of Pairs. Their mental and physical health was checked and they were fed well and treated fairly. At one stage, they were allowed a visit by their wife. That visit was unsatisfactory because the Pair turned out to be in sympathy with the women's movement and explained that unless Pour and Roup recanted and confessed to their crimes against the people it was all up for their marriage.

"I have no intention of confessing or recanting," said Pour and Roup.

"In that case I revoke my part of this marriage," she replied.

The women left with no further comment and with their passing Pour and Roup felt lost and alone.

"This is all that Clard and Dracl's' doing," said Pour.

"We should let our captors, know where they are," said Roup.

The Pair sat silently for a while letting the thought play in their minds.

"Do you think it would be worth bargaining with these people my twin?" said Roup.

"I think so."

Three periods later the Pair sat at a table talking to D.G and Glord.

"And you say that if you tell us the location of Clard and Dracl you want us to be lenient, why?" asked Glord.

"Because it was they who blew up Star Station Two and before that made it difficult for us to properly carry out our duty ..."

"Which was to expedite the defeat of an innocent people and advance the cause of a despotic President, right?" Glord replied interrupting Pour.

"You could say that," said Pour.

"But you know that Clard and Dracl murdered many people by their avarice and indifference to Zradian lives in pursuit of their own fortune. Is that what you mean?" said D.G.

"Yes, yes, we know where they are. All we want to do is help," said Roup.

"To put right what went wrong," added Pour.

"We will have to consult with Dart and Drat," said Glord. "If he agrees then we will make a bargain with you but I do not guarantee anything until I see him," said Glord. "It may be that we don't care about Clard and Dracl."

"But they are war criminals!" said the Pair.

"So are you," said D.G.

D.G and Glord spoke with Dart and Drat that evening as the party was in full swing and explained what the Pair Pour and Roup proposed.

"Ah, good, then this is what we will do," said Dart and explained.

Glord looked pleased and soon he and D.G were back with Pour and Roup listening to their story. They promised them what they had asked for and promised also that Dart and Drat would announce the sentence in their favour the next morning at petition time.

"We are on the list?" asked Pour anxiously.

"You most certainly are," said D.G.

It was Roup who gave them the exact last known location for Clard and Dracl and with that knowledge Glord and D.G made preparations.

It was this minor interruption to their enjoyment of the party that created more problems for Julian.

The moment the formal reception was over Glorida dropped him. She was quite straight about it. "Find somewhere else to stay tonight scumbag," she said and turned away before he could answer.

"And fuck you too," he said to her retreating back.

He was glad when D.G came over to talk to him and took him to the bar where he filled him up with a couple of beers and listened to him rant and rave about how unfair the world was, and that he wished he had never come to this shitty place where everybody was a rotten, stinking, murderous four eyed git."

"And me?" D.G said.

Julian was stumped.

"Oh fuck it, find me a shag D.G so's I can forget bloody loony knickers."

But before D.G could do anything to help he was summoned by his twin to talk to Pour and Roup.

"Oh bollocks," said Julian, "I knew you didn't give a shit."

"Who doesn't give a shit?" said his father who had come to find him.

"D.G," Julian said, and for the first time in his life he confided in his father and did so over beers drunk in a bar.

"What you need to do is apologise and grovel to her. Admit everything and above all tell her you love her and show that you do. Son, women need treating with kid gloves," Arthur said, and smiled.

"And you know all about it do you?" said Julian.

"No, I don't otherwise I would have long ago sorted out your mother," he said.

"It's crap isn't," said Julian.

"Here's to crap," said Arthur and raised his glass and sipped.

"Yeah, to crap," said Julian.

"Let's go dancing," said Arthur. "Loosen up and find a partner, eh?"

And that is what they did except that when Glorida and Glorid came by dancing with a Zradian Pair Julian pushed his partner aside and flew at the Half Pair clutching Glorida in his arms.

"That's my girl you bloody bastard!" he shouted and swung a punch at him.

It was a lucky blow taking the Half Pair by surprise knocking him to the floor but, yelling in anger he was instantly on his feet and fighting. If it was not for Tzu and a small group of his Kung Fu artists Julian would no doubt have been beaten to a pulp. As it was Tzu gripped him and pulled him away to the edge of the dance floor whilst his men restrained the Pair. The band stopped playing and the dancers all halted in mid step to stand and watch as Julian screamed obscenities at Tzu and made a foolish attempt to take a swipe at him.

"The four eyed git's got no right...Argh!"

The partygoers were treated to the sight of an old Chinese man forcefully taking a skinny Earthman to the nearest chair, putting him over his knee like a naughty child and spanking him. Accompanied by screams and further obscenities Tzu paddled Julian's rear end with a fighting stick and when he had finished he stood up with him and pressed a nerve behind his ear. Julian fell like a loose sack and Tzu turned to the silent company and bowed.

"So sorry," he said, "I think the young man is quite overcome with emotion."

The laughter followed him as he and two of his men carried Julian from the dance floor.

Colin and his mates enjoyed themselves.

"Remember yer wives pals," he said, "this party like all the rest is on the telly back home so Gawd help yer if yer steps over the line, all right?"

Sherman Holmes remembered in time and confined his activities to dancing.

"Can I have a drink now?" he asked Blard.

"Yes but not too many, we may be needed. There are still some fanatics around. Besides, you have to kick the habit," Blard said and grinned.

Holmes believed him and with a feeling of anticipation he sipped at the first glass and discovered he could take it or leave it. The first one lasted long enough for him to enjoy it and after the second one he was dancing with a Half Pair who had invited him to take the floor providing 'the gorgeous' Sergeant Orange came too. Holmes thought that if there was one thing other than fighting that the Zradians were good at it was entertaining. On the whole, Holmes reckoned, including the unfortunate incident with that skinny no-hoper Julian Renfrew, the party was a wow. Not only were they entertained by good music and dancing there were also juggling acts, a weird conjuring act where one Pair did the trick between them that totally mystified Holmes. Tzu and his people provided a demonstration of Kung Fu that wowed the Zradians so much they demanded a repeat.

All of it was recorded by little flying cameras that made the cameras of the Earth media redundant. And so it was that apart from Sally Aitcheson the entire media contingent from Earth suffered the following day from hangovers.

The medics on the morning of the presentation ceremony were busy handing out the standard Zradian cure.

And Holmes was pleased to discover that he did not need one.

Below the hall a small but fully armed group of dark clad Pairs moved cautiously through the lesser known service passages to a small room not far from where once their former President had his living quarters. These passage were built to allow the incumbent to receive secret messengers or to dispatch his spies. The Leader Pair knew that the traitor Dart and Drat were assuming the Presidency but that was no bar to their purpose. The last orders of their President were to kill Dart and Drat and that was what they were going to do. The passages were narrow so it was Half Pair in line with weapons ready following the dominant half of their Leader

Pair. They took time to check each turn moving as quietly as they could aware that the slightest sighting of them could trigger an alarm. At a junction where the circular passage was crossed by the radial they needed to take there was the sound of padding feet.

"Halt and be silent," said the Leader Pair. They flattened themselves against the wall and listened as the owner of the feet approached and went past running. When the apparition was past, for so they thought it was, the Leader Pair whispered.

"A naked Earthman?"

"That's what I saw," said his second in command.

"Strange."

"Extremely strange," agreed the 2IC.

Presentation

Julian sat with the women's rebel army. He was grumpy, hung-over and wishing he was sitting next to Glorida. She had told him to get lost so instead he sat with Lavia feeling miserable. He had tried to apologise to Glorida but she snubbed him and again told him to get lost. "Go sit as far away from me as possible," she said and glowered angrily at him.

Disconsolately he found a place next to Lavia who did their best to make him welcome but even with them he was grumpy.

"She's a bitch," he said.

"I think not but that you are upset with her, right?" Lavia said and smiled. "we still like you."

He fell silent knowing that he was likely to lose even their support if he complained anymore. Instead he sat in his seat and endured the ceremony. He listened to the speeches and grew bored. All the old farts had to have their say and the so-called bloody heroes of the revolution wanted their bit of the political cake, and made a meal of it. Even D.G and Glord had spoken for too long. All he wanted to do was get this over with and bugger off back home to his mother. He groaned. Bates and Fish were after him and then there was Denny Block, the scummy Landlord of the crummy flat who wants his money, the telephone bill and the power bill, as well as the chance that that crazy axeman was still after him.

He was glad when Dorida and Dorid took their honours followed by the heroes of the women's army. Glorida and Glorid went up for theirs to great cheers and returned to their seats after a short speech. It meant that at last they were getting near the end of the boring bloody useless process. He watched resentfully as Old Tzu was presented to that old git Smith and despite his misery a little smile creased his face when Tzu spoke to the PM.

Tzu moved along the platform to where Prime Minister Smith was waiting and with a toothy grin shook the big man's hand.

"Well done mister Wu," said Smith.

"Oh yes, thank you verra much," Tzu answered and laughed. "Old Chinese joke."

Smith looked puzzled.

"Nevah mind, you I tell later," Tzu said.

The hall erupted with cheers and hand clapping and Tzu turned and bowed to the audience before tripping lightly down the steps.

Next up on the platform were the leaders of the Rebel Army who were applauded loudly but not so enthusiastically. They were followed by Blard and Bradl the Barmy who were hooted, cheered and stomped at as they mounted the platform. Byrde, Lugs and the Ferret had already got their gongs and along with Blard and Bradl, Holmes, Sergeant Orange and Bates and Fish also got a mention. Oliver Braine characteristically kept out of the way red faced with embarrassment when his name was mentioned. They left the stage and then Angela was called up. The audience went crazy with cheers and cat-calls, whistles and clapping and a great rolling chant calling out her name.

"Crazy cow," said Julian as she stood on the platform.

Dart and Drat made a speech praising her and before she was allowed to leave the stage called upon her to say a few words.

"Like being in bloody church," said Julian but nobody was listening. He had to admit that her speech was excellent, especially the last part.

"...and although I commanded the popular army which has now been disbanded to go back to their homes and families, I owe my success to the women of the women's rebel army and the women of the Children's army. But, if I had not followed Julian Renfrew to your planet in the first place I would have not been able to do what I did. So, indirectly your Bomber, Julian Renfrew, is responsible for the success of the revolution," she said and bowed.

During the cheers and the clapping and the stomping that followed Angela she shook hands with the Prime Minister and spoke briefly with him. Julian thought little of her speech about women's rights and the way the men of Zrad should be prepared to share equally the benefits of Zradian society; that women should not be treated as second class citizens. And her call on the women of Zrad to create a women's rights movement all went over his head as so much do-gooder speak. It was her speaking of him that made him feel better.

"Up yours Glorida," he said and was suddenly aware that the crowd were calling for him.

Julian! Julian! We want Julian! Where's our Bomber?!

"You are on," said Lavia and dug him in the ribs. "Go on, go get your award."

He stood up and walked down the outer aisle to the platform and to wild applause he walked cockily up the steps to where Dart and Drat were waiting for him. Their smiles of welcome were real and the old farts sitting on the benches behind them were clapping and smiling. Cameras, both the familiar TV cameras of Earth and the little floating ones of Zrad were trained on him. He shook hands with Dart and Drat and together they waited for the applause to die down.

"Thank you for your efforts Julian. Although we were on your home planet working with your people we followed your progress and were glad to know that one so young could give his skills and energy to fight our cause. You may not have wished to fight a war or to become a soldier but when you were put into the situation you rose to the occasion and became a hero of Zrad," said Drat and Dart together.

Julian looked over his shoulder when a sudden gasp and giggle came from the audience. It came from Glorida who, knowing the truth, could not prevent herself from laughing.

"Hero! Coward on the run more like it. In a Bulger's bum is he a hero," she said, and leaned against her twin wiping her eyes and giggling. Her twin quieted her and looked up at Dart and Drat.

"Er, she's overcome with emotion," she said and gave them a weak smile.

The women's army members burst into laughter.

"Nevertheless it is my humble duty to present Julian with his award," said Dart and Drat.

Julian took the package gratefully.

"Keep the speech short and light Julian, no bullshit please," said Dart quietly.

Julian turned to face the audience.

"I bloody deserve this," he began, "I bloody near got killed because of all you four-eyed gits. I admit I ain't no hero. I admit I ain't no good at being polite and pleasant, and that I can be a right Bulger's arsehole at times but I got better. I jest got bored hanging around this crummy city with nothing to do when all you lot was doing the election bit. I don't understand politics and Presidents and Prime Ministers and all that crap. All I want is to get me girlfriend back, see me Mum and not have me Dad being nasty to me, and all the other ratbags what want a piece of me for the things I done orf me back. I ain't innocent and I done a bit of time back home and," he paused, "with that ratbag what we knocked off."

He waited for the laughter to die down and continued.

"All I want to say is that I am sorry I am a rotten arsehole and that I love Glorida and I wanna learn to love me Dad. That's it." He said.

Whether the audience understood all that he said or not they gave him a standing ovation. He stood gazing at where Glorida and Glorid were standing with the rest applauding him and tried to catch her eye. She didn't look at him. As the applause died down he turned to face Prime Minister Smith. Trying to hold back the tears of disappointment he forced himself to listen to what Smith had to say to him.

But whatever it was Smith was going to say to him he had no chance because it was then that the remnants of the Zradian Dog squad launched their attack. They raced out of the dark alcove where they had hidden during most of the presentation and made a sword wielding beeline for Dart and Drat. Julian jumped off the stage screaming for his mother and ran. He cared little for where he went as long as it was as far away as possible from the men with the swords.

Behind him he heard angry, warlike yells and whimpered with fear as he raced up the aisle. He heard screaming and the noise of blades on flesh and that added impetus to his flight. He did not see Angela leap at the enemy with her sword slashing nor did he see Colin and his mates and Lugs rush across the floor to join the fight. What he did see was even more terrifying.

The naked form of ex-fireman Sidney Weddell wielding a sword racing across the hall to head him off.

"Renfrew you bastard child molester! I am going to kill you!

"Oh Christ! Where the fuck did he come from?" Julian cried, and changed direction turning in mid stride to race back the way he came.

Ex-fireman Sidney Weddell was quicker, and almost a repeat of the chase in the hospital grounds began to gain on Julian. He felt the blade swishing close and screamed.

"Help me!"

He was aware of a couple of figures racing toward him and felt the blade slice through his clothes and cut his flesh slicing into his buttocks and with a scream of terror he leapt forward redoubling his speed. Somebody grabbed him and pulled him aside and he heard the sound of blades swishing around and fainted.

Prime Minister Smith was not idle, or slow and reacted quickly when one Half Pair leapt up on the stage screaming in fury as he attacked Dart and Drat. Smith stepped across the stage and thumped the warrior with a curving blow of his right fist and knocked him off the stage. When Colin saw the Prime Minister hit the Half Pair he grinned. A brownie point for a neat blow, he thought.

"Cor the old fart can't half pack a wallop," he said, and reacted immediately he saw the black clad Zradians. "Them bleedin' buggers are after my client!"

He yelled out for the others to join him, and with Lugs in tow they pounded down the aisle and dived onto the enemy. Dodging blades and cudgels they waded through the black clads to protect

Dart and Drat. Prime Minister Smith thumped the other Half Pair who had already reached them and Colin gave him another brownie point for quick thinking. Along with some of the women's rebel army Pairs including Glorida and Glorid and Angela, Colin and his group made short work of the remaining Pairs. Angela used her short blade so effectively that the sound of the swish and slice of the twin blades followed by the yells of pain from her victims was a satisfying rhythm to Colin's ears. The survivors were pinioned by their arms, disarmed and held whilst soldiers went to fetch fetters.

"Nice one Angela," said Colin as she wiped the blood from her blades on the uniform of a live and awake prisoner. "A bit over the top for a good Christian girl?"

"We fight the good fight," she said and grinned.

Bates and Fish saw Julian run and lumbered after him.

"Why are we..." Fish

"...chasing this bugger," Bates.

"Dunno," said Fish.

And then they spotted ex fireman Sidney Weddell.

"Cripes its that..." Bates

"...loony, with a sword!" Fish.

They ran faster with one intent. Stopping him. They caught ex-Fireman Weddell at the moment his sword made contact with Julian and before he could cut again they grabbed him. With one arm each they lifted him off his feet and dumped him head first on the floor and whilst Fish thumped him hard with his fists Bates removed the sword and gave it to Lavia who happened to be nearest.

"Hold that whilst we..." Bates

"..........................." Fish.

"Deal with the problem?" said Lavia and grinned.

"Yeah, right," said Bates, puzzled and slightly annoyed.

Fish finished thumping the naked fireman and together they lifted him from the floor and carried him to the platform where the rest of the prisoners were already being manacled.

Unconscious and bleeding Julian was gently lifted from where he had fallen and carried on a stretcher to an ante-room by medics who immediately set about cleaning his wounds and stitching them up. Knowing his fear of pain and the needle they gave him a local anaesthetic. Luckily the sword cut was not deep but as a precaution they gave him antibiotics in case it was infected. One Pair worked on him whilst the other spoke softly to reassure him he was safe and not going to die. In a state of shock he remained quiet and let them work on him. A period later when the mess in the hall was cleared up and Dart and Drat had agreed to listen to the petitioners he was wheeled back into the hall to be greeted by cheers.

He grinned and waved his arms at the joyful audience. This wasn't bravado but merely the effect of the mild tranquilliser he was given to calm his nerves and his relief at having survived another attack.

He felt like a hero.

Judgement Day

The Petitioners occupied very little time, and by the time Julian was back in the hall there were only the prisoners to be judged. Julian was wheeled to the end of the first row and although he was happy to be nearer Glorida he was still unhappy because she had yet to acknowledge him. He saw the captives brought in Pair by Pair and vaguely remembered who was who, but took little notice of names. Most were sentenced to isolation in a labour camp and some were sentenced to a similar fate in their absence. Even the surviving Dog Squad members were sentenced to hard labour. One Pair who babbled insanely as they were led onto the platform were sentenced to a life-time in what Julian understood to be the equivalent of their own asylums. Ex-fireman Sidney Weddell was to be sent back to Earth and held there for assessment.

"Shoot the mad bugger," said Julian, and shuddered, glad that the madman wasn't there.

The last Pair up were Pour and Roup who walked onto the platform with a certain amount of confidence certain they were about to get better treatment than the other Pairs. D.G and Glord had said so. Special case they said and Pour and Roup were pleased with that. They had only done their duty.

Dart and Drat looked down at them from their high seat.

"Pour and Roup, you have been charged with conducting an illegal invasion on the orders of the former President. That this was against the will of the people is not an issue, but that you knowingly carried out a war against an innocent people is. According to Vice Consul Vreed you were willing to carry out your appointment to the benefit of the former president and did so with all your most capable abilities. What have you to say for yourself?"

"We were doing our duty according to the law of the President," they said.

"Against the will of the people," said Dart.

Drat grinned and waited for his turn to speak.

"The President's will was the will of the people," said Pour and Roup nodding vigorously.

"Of course, we understand that but we have a sentence to read, which my twin will read to you," said Dart.

Drat ignored their eager nods and began to read.

"It is decided that the Pair Pour and Roup in the light of their confession and their assistance in locating the criminals Clard and

Dracl former directors and owners of C&D Enterprises, will not be sent to a labour camp," he paused and looked at the Pair.

Pour and Roup looked anxiously back at him. He gave them a wicked smile.

"Instead we pronounce a sentence much to their liking we hope..."

Pour and Roup nodded.

"and decree that they be transported to a separate location," he paused again, and watched the Pair waiting in anticipation. He smiled again and enjoyed the return smile they gave him and finished the terms of the sentence. "Where they will be reunited with Clard and Dracl and the ex-Polisoc prisoners who were transported to the same location. I am sure that they will have something to talk about. Oh, and as a companion on your journey you will have the right honourable Vice Consul Vreed."

Pour and Roup visibly blanched and as the guards were dragging them away their legs cocked and with a wail of terror they urinated on the floor.

Cheers and catcalls from the watching Pairs and the bemused Earth people accompanied their exit.

"I declare the first judicial session of the new Democratic republic of Zradia closed," announced Dart and Drat. "Let us go and have a drink to celebrate!"

It was the matter of a little money, the promise of considerations for services rendered and a little coercion that got Donald Best and Denny a visitor's pass to Zrad. They joined the stream of media personnel at a transfer port and arrived on Zrad where their passes allowed them access to the media section of the party in First Square where the new President of Zrad was about to meet the people. He and Denny edged up to the group that had emerged from the huge central building.

"Bloody ugly building," said Denny.

"Yeah, the whole place is a dump," agreed Donald Best.

They moved through the crowds until they were close to the main party. Donald Best was surprised to see Prime Minister Smith and his wife there and ex-detective Inspector Sherman Holmes who was quietly chatting with one of the Aliens. The bloke looked sober and that was a shock to Donald Best who hadn't seen him sober for years.

"I fink I know that big bloke in the whistle," said Denny.

"That's the Prime Minister yer pillock," said Best.

"Oh," said Denny.

And there in a wheelchair following along behind the Prime Minister and the other world leaders including the new president of the USA, who had managed to arrive at the last moment, was Julian Renfrew.

"Got the bugger," said Donald Best. "Denny me old mate, there's our punter."

Denny grunted, and together they pushed through the crowd and headed directly for Julian. "Gotcha," said Denny and snatched at Julian.

But Julian was quick and with a shriek slipped from the wheelchair and all Denny grabbed was his tunic and that meant he had to haul him in like a fish before he could bash him.

"You owe me a lotta dosh," said Donald best, " so where is it scumbag?"

"Yeah…" Began Denny but that was as far as he got. A sword swished down whistling through the air as it descended on his wrist and the hand that grabbed Julian's tunic suddenly parted company with its arm. Denny screamed in agony and anger and turned, confused and hurt to confront his attacker.

A dark-haired girl faced him and if it was not for Lugs who punched him so hard that he toppled sideways the next blow would have sliced him neatly across his body from his shoulder to his hip. Instead the sword swung and rested with the twin points a millimetre from Donald Best's neck.

"You leave my boyfriend alone arsehole," screamed Glorida, or so help me Nong I'll kill you!" Donald Best noted that the sword remained rock steady; as steady as the girl's gaze on his face. "And if that piece of shit on the deck moves so much as a testicle I'll cut them off at the belly after I've sliced your neck," Glorida said, and called out. "My twin, draw your blade and guard this arsehole whilst I go and tell my boyfriend I love him."

Glorid glided to her side grinning, and touched the point of her blade to Donald Best's neck.

"Like my Twin said. Move, either of you and you are dead."

Glorida sheathed her sword and rushed to where Julian was standing supported by his father and the Ferret and wrapped her arms around him.

"I'm sorry Julian, I'm truly sorry, please forgive me," she said and kissed him until he came out of the clinch gasping for air.

"No," he said, "please, you forgive me."

"Julian Renfrew if you don't let me forgive you I will…" She trailed off embarrassed having reached for her knife.

"Attagirl," said Angela and laughed.

"Yes, I forgive you," Glorida said. "I love you."

"And I love you," Julian said. "You don't need the knife my love. Try teaching me instead."

"Until I need it again," she said and kissed him again.

The watching crowd cheered enthusiastically.

Glorid accidentally raised her sword in her enthusiasm for the event.

"Oops," she said as Donald Best's head slipped sideways from his shoulders and bounced on the pavement. His body followed spurting blood onto the paving.

"Good job too," said Julian.

"Oh well, said Glorid, " may as well go for the double."

And before anybody could stop her she sliced her blade into Denny's body. Denny yelled with pain and died with a flat gasp and a spurt of blood."

"Sorry," Glorid said, "I think I was overcome by emotion."

Nobody except Richard Byrde laughed.

Oliver Braine who had kept a low profile during the celebrations looked at Byrde white-faced.

"How can you laugh? Two men have just been killed," Oliver said.

"It has a lot to do with my sense of irony," said Byrde. "I'll explain over a pint when this is over."

And so, with the bodies cleared away Dart and Drat and the dignitaries continued their walk about.

"You approve of the, ah, execution of the two Englishmen?" asked the Japanese Prime Minister.

"Two have to take expedient measures," said Dart and Drat, "some sacrifice is expected and unfortunately in the heat of the moment, especially in wartime, mistakes are often made, If you get my drift?"

"Ah yes, a regrettable mistake," the Japanese Premier agreed.

Julia Renfrew sat in Marjorie Watts' flat watching the events as they unfolded on Zrad. With Marjorie's help Julia began to appreciate what her son and her husband were involved in.

"Is this really happening?"

"Every bit," said Marjorie.

"Holy shit. My boy a hero, wow!"

"And Arthur," said Marjorie.

"Julian getting an award, wow!"

"And Arthur."

"My Julian being made an honary thingy of that whatsit place."

"And Arthur."

"He must have been very brave."

"Who?"

"My Julian of course."

"What about Arthur?"

"Oh yes, Arthur, him too. But I'm proud of my Julian," Julia said and smirked. "Will we see him soon?"

"I expect so," Marjorie said.

Julia reached for a glass and sipped from it.

"Ugh, lemonade," she said.

"All you are going to get sister."

"Fucking bastards," said Julia and finished the drink.

Colin's men, who had watched their leader collect an award for himself, laughed. They knew how Julia felt. Without their beer they too would be upset and although they were ordered to prevent Julia drinking any alcohol they were downing as much as they could. They knew about alcoholics.

Julian did his best to please his new wife. Married under Zradian law he was happy to agree to live there as long as he could visit his mother. He did as Glorida told him and found the experience acceptable. True he made mistakes but at least he tried. On this day a few divisions after the war was over and all the dignitaries had gone he knew there was something different. Glorida was acting strange, moody and odd, biting her lip and looking at him with glances that were both curious and fearful. The signs were not good and he wondered what he had done wrong.

"What's wrong?" he asked.

"Nothing," she said.

"But you're acting odd. What have I done?"

"Nothing."

"Something wrong with you is there?"

"Nong, you're so stupid," she said and hurried out into the kitchen space where she rattled around in the ice-box looking for something.

"Tell me, for Christ sake. How can I guess?"

"Nothing's wrong."

"Then if nothing's wrong why were you acting so strange or is it some women's thing that I don't bloody know about," he said, and stormed out of the room to sit in front of the screen to watch some dumb chat show. A few moments later she came into the room with a tall glass of best Outlands brew and handed it to him.

"Sorry hero," she said, and sat beside him. She took his hand in hers and waited until he had finished drinking.

"Put the glass on the table," she said and gave him a look that scared him and melted him at the same time. It was the twin pupils that did it. They seemed to switch her gaze as if she was scanning him from four different angles. Which she was.

"I've got something important to tell you," she said.

"What?" he said and braced himself for bad news.

"I'm pregnant," she said.

"Oh fuck," he said, "you mean we're going to have kids?"

"Yes, the pattering of tiny pairs of feet," she said.

"Oh fucking Christ! Do we have to?"

She put her arms around his neck and smiled at him and pouted her lips making a delicious mew of her mouth and giggled.

"You just don't have a bloody clue do you?" she said. "You are going to be a father. You had better get used to it."

She let go with one hand and touched the hilt of her knife.

"Or else."

"Right," he said. "I will."

"D G, I have some good news for you," Angela said, and wisely moved the glasses and cups from the low table and put them on a side bench.

"Oh, what is it?"

"We are going to have children. I am pregnant," she said, and giggled waiting for him to stop staring at her with his mouth wide open with a stunned mullet look on his face and come to life. He did and she braced herself. He leapt from the chair, grabbed her around the waist kissed her and danced her around the room. In the short breaks between the dancing, kissing and waist grabbing he shouted with joy.

"I've go to tell Glord!"

Dance and kiss.

"I'll buy a round of drinks!"

Kiss and dance.

"Wow!"

More kissing and less dancing as he came to a stop and gazed into her face. The four separate pupils did as they always did, disturb her with their mobility. Split horizontally they could change independently and when DG was excited his eye reaction was most exciting.

"I've got to tell Glord!" he said and dashed off to the portal leaving her standing breathless for a moment.

She waited and listened.

"Damn door. Bulgers! Why don't they work when I want them too?" he said sounding peeved.

"Why don't you call Glord on the screen first and perhaps we, I say we meaning us, go and visit him?"

He came rushing back.

"Ah yes, how practical," he said "but why doesn't the portal open?"

"You were tapping the close button sweetheart," she said and giggled.

"Right but I'm going to be a father right?"

"Correct and I am going to be a mother. Now call Glord and let us go out together and on the way we might as well work out how to get him married off, what do you say to that?"

"And Drat, er, you don't think Sally has any spare friends do you?" he said and watched her face cloud over.

This time it was his turn to giggle.

The good news was that, none too soon, the gene swapping therapy that Glord, Drat and Glorid undertook had worked. Glorid herself was happy to become more dominant, and Drat and Glord became like brothers. The arrangement meant that when the group were ever together D.G, Glord, Dart and Drat and Glorid were able to share empathy waves. The result was an odd combination of emotions that eventually spilled over to Angela and Julian. The effect on Julian was that he became friends with Glorid, not because she had gotten rid of Denny Block and Donald Best, but that he began to appreciate the concept of Twinship. He saw Glorid as the other half of Glorida.

He felt slightly jealous when she talked of finding a fellow of her own.

"My lovely girl. My dear wife will be so pleased that you have married a nice, upright boy," said Maurice Bannermann to Sally as he said goodbye to her a few moments before transferring back to Earth and his beloved television studios. He was doubly pleased that Sally had consented to be his chief Zradian Correspondent and that he had secured a nice, fat contract from the Zradian media system. "You should come and visit. Meet my good lady."

"I will do so mister..." she began but he waved her to silence.

"Maurice, please, we are friends. Why, I was at your wedding, giving you away already, we may even be related," he said, and uncharacteristically he took her in his brawny arms and hugged her giving her a warm and friendly kiss.

"Thank you Maurice," she said when they had parted and squeezed his hand warmly before standing beside Dart and watching happily as Maurice stepped into the transfer port with the others of the ETV crew. The door closed; the lights changed and she and Dart turned and walked back to their quarters hand in hand content to be with each other.

Back Home

The Drunken Clown was full. Most of the drinkers and diners belonged to Richard Byrde's party, and those who didn't were somehow included. The centre of attention and quite embarrassed by the compliments of the crowd was Professor Arthur Renfrew. The reason for his embarrassment was the large cake that stood on a table in the centre of the lounge. What added to his embarrassment was the effort he and Marjorie were making to cut through it.

"The knife is blunt," said Arthur.

"Extend Ki and cut the thing," said Marjorie, "that's what you are always telling me."

Arthur relaxed and together they cut into the icing and through to the cake to the platform. A great cheer went up as the caterer's came forward to remove the cake for cutting and dishing out. For the first time in his recent life Arthur was dressed neatly and his hair was tidy. He was, as Byrde put it, spruced up. The Drunken Clown was filled with Arthur's guests including Colin and his mates and their wives and girlfriends, Lugs and the ferret, the Ferret's younger brother, Oliver Braine and Hermoine Braine with Sherman Holmes in tow. Tzu stood by grinning toothily trying to hold a conversation with Bates and Fish.

"So the skinny bugger..."Fish

"...declined to come to his..." Bates

"...Old man's wedding," Tzu.

"Uh?" Bates and Fish.

"So sorry but the trick of anticipation had so far eluded me. I learned from our Zradian friends, to whit, Blard and Bradl the Barmy," Tzu said.

The two officers whose promotion to plainclothes was confirmed by their senior officer upon their return were for once lost for words.

"Julia is noticeable by her absence," Tzu said.

"I expect it is because..." Fish

"...she might get the needle..." Bates

"...because her ex has found ..." Fish,

Bates hesitated unsure whether to speak waiting for Tzu,

"...somebody else," Bates.

"Spoil your rhythm do I?" said Tzu.

"A bit," Bates and Fish.

Oliver Braine looked on and sighed. Since he had been away with Byrde he had discovered an inner confidence that allowed him to tell his mother that he was going to jolly well do what he wanted. As a result he had sold the General Assistance Service business to Sergeant Orange and taken a position with a public relations office. A year later he was happy to announce that he was doing all right. He had even watched the Ferret's younger brother racing cars at the re-vamped Brand's hatch race track and enjoyed it. He sighed now because he was jealous of Arthur Renfrew's happiness, and the fact that the girl he recently met could not be there with him.

Lovelier than Penny and a thousand times smarter, Cassia was working this weekend and he wished she wasn't. His phone rang and with some embarrassment he answered it. Cassia's face appeared on the screen and grinned at him.

"How do I get into this joint?" she said.

"Where are you?"

"Outside the Drunken Clown. I quit the job. Come and escort me in."

"On my way," he said.

Service With a Snarl

Pour and Roup and Clard and Dracl stood nervously one either side of the service table alert for any small request from their captors. They were servants to the Leader Pairs stranded in South America.

"More wine Pairs!"

Pour and Roup gathered their trays and almost ran with the bottles to the top table. Clard and Dracl were not so quick off the mark but caught up within seconds. Each Pair carried four opened bottles of wine on their trays ready to pour into as many glasses as they could in the shortest time and then rush back for some more. Four bottles each was all they were allowed.

Pour and Roup reached the table first but made the mistake of stopping without looking to see where Clard and Dracl were.

The two Pairs collided and wine, bottles and trays flew in all directions. Both Pairs tumbled to the floor and lay sobbing in terror. Hands reached down and pulled them roughly to their feet.

"Clean it up."

No compromise.

"Clean it yourself," said Dracl.

The year and a half of grovelling and trying to survive the vagaries of their captor's whims had worn him down and now he became a rebellious Half Pair. His twin panicked and looked at Dracl as if he were an alien.

"No! Don't do that! Don't say that!" he screamed.

Dracl jumped back away from his twin and screamed at the Leader Pair, his face red and angry and his hands twitching in that typical Zradian state of going Half.

"You want it cleaned, you Bulger's arsehole, you clean it yourself!" Dracl screamed and dived for the sword at the waist of the nearest Half Pair. He didn't reach it.

The Leader Pair cut him down and turned to face Clard.

"Pig fodder!" yelled Clard and lurched toward the body of his twin.

A sword cut him in two before he could reach his dead twin.

Pour and Roup clutched at each other and whimpered. And no matter how they tried none of the renegade Pairs could separate them until they were taken to their room. Once there they sat on their chair and stared at the wall rocking to and fro.

Rocking to and fro.

Rocking to and fro.

Vice Consul Vreed stood staring at the catatonic Pair. The bowl of warm water he held in his hands shook as he approached them and carefully he placed it on the rough table beside them. He took a cloth from his arm and dipping it into the water timing his actions so that he could bathe their foreheads as they reached the lower point in their movement. There was no reaction; the herbal remedy that was normally effective enough to stop them moving long enough to take some nourishment this time did not work. Already traumatised by the state of the Pair, Vreed recoiled and turned to look at the Leader Pair his face showing his distress.

"I cannot do this," he whimpered.

"Then they will starve to death, scumbag." The Leader Pair looked at Vreed intently. "You have plenty of food and water?" Vreed nodded knowing that whatever he said the outcome would be the same.

"Then, goodbye to you for the time being," said the Leader Pair, and pulled the door to and locked it.

Vice Consul Vreed stood continuing to stare at the rocking Pair and wept.

The pile of electronic parts rested on the bench, some in boxes and some still in their plastic film packets. Underneath the bench lay a long box sealed and labelled and on top of that was a square box also sealed and labelled.

The Zradian Pair who owned the workshop had a hobby. Normally their trade was in refurbishing electronic components for city wagons but what they liked to do was to build robots.

The Pair lifted the boxes from under the bench and opened them up. From inside they removed the charred parts resting there and placed them on the bench. First the head that held the major portion of the processor followed by the torso that held the power system and the remainder of the processor. The four limbs were in a bad shape but the skeleton was there and the Pair looked pleased.

One Half Pair hooked up the power unit and made a temporary connection to the head and pushed a charge through the completed circuits. A faint sound came from the face speakers and the Pair leaned closer to listen.

Do not be afraid of the rodents.

"Strange," said the Pair together.

And so concludes the Zradian Chronicles leaving a future that in the tradition of all such tales should include the well worn cliché 'they lived happily ever after'. Which, of course, begs the question, 'did they?'